THE BEEKEEPER

S.M. SHADE

D1519667

Copyright © 2024

All rights reserved. No part of this publication may be reproduced, distributed, or transmitted in any form or by any means, including photocopying, recording, or other electronic or mechanical methods, without the prior written permission of the publisher, except in the case of brief quotations embodied in critical reviews and certain other noncommercial uses permitted by copyright law.

This is a work of fiction. Names, characters, businesses, places, events and incidents are either the products of the author's imagination or used in a fictitious manner. Any resemblance to actual persons, living or dead, or actual events is purely coincidental.

Cover created by Qamber Designs

Formatting by CPR Publishing Services

❀ Created with Vellum

To all the other women who would follow a strange, reclusive man into a graveyard at night despite the danger because he's tall with big hands and a deep voice.

This one's for you.

"Do I dare to eat a peach?"
-T. S. Eliot, *The Love Song of J. Alfred Prufrock*

PROLOGUE
CALLIOPE

Everything is blue. Pale moonlight casts a glow on our bare skin and turns our surroundings into an ethereal dreamscape, decorating the mound of earth and the weathered headstones, but this is no dream. It's all real. It all happened.

Maybe it's the adrenaline surging through my blood that's making me hyperaware of every little sensation. The faint scent of damp leaves, the sting of my blistered hands, the cold ground under my back, and his warm body on top of mine. It's exhilarating.

Soil clings to our bodies as he pounds into me, helping me forget the smell of blood and how it painted the shower floor in crimson streams. Helping me forget everything. The years of fear and loneliness fade to nothing, wiped into irrelevance by his touch.

There's no more worry about the future or what may happen. No remorse for what we've done. I'd do it again, and I know he would too. Everything we've been through until now was worth it. He's worth it.

Getting railed on a freshly filled grave in the dead of night is just a bonus.

CHAPTER 1

CALLIOPE

NINE MONTHS EARLIER

THIS IS THE PERFECT WAY TO END UP ON A CRIME DOCUMENTARY, MEETING a stranger at a cabin in the woods. It's not the first time the thought has occurred to me on the long drive down here.

Sunwood, Kentucky—population eighteen thousand—looks similar to the other small towns I've driven through. Bigger than some but not large enough to be a city. If there's more than one high school in town, I'd be surprised. It's not what I'm used to or how I grew up, but if there's one thing I am, it's adaptable.

A few restaurants and stores give way to rows of houses. Lawns stretch out between them, pushing them farther apart until the fields take over. Not being accustomed to rural areas, I'm worried I may miss my turn, but Old Church Road is clearly marked. Two signs stand at the corner, one bright green that bears the street name, and one hardly legible under rust which reads *Dead End*.

About a half mile down the road, the forest creeps up to the shoulders, broken only by an occasional driveway. With no street-lights in sight, I'm glad I showed up in the daylight. The road is

3

paved, but barely wide enough for two vehicles to pass each other, and it has more twists than a crazy straw.

Two small mailboxes mark the edge of a gravel driveway, one bearing my new address. The trees thin out on either side as I drive down it, then open to a clearing. A moment later, the cabin comes into view on my left, and it looks exactly like the pictures. It fits right in among the forest with its dark green roof and wooden siding. To my right, a bit farther along and across the gravel drive sits a modern farmhouse.

A blue pickup truck is parked in front of the cabin, and a woman leans against it, giving me a wave as I step out of my car. "Hi, glad you found the place okay. I'm Silver."

"Calli, nice to meet you."

"It's a shared driveway with the neighbor," Silver announces when she notices me staring that direction.

It's not the house or driveway I'm looking at but the area behind it. "Are those tombstones?" I ask, squinting against the sun.

"Ah, yeah. There used to be a church here that burned down years ago. The graveyard was part of it." She flashes a sheepish smile in my direction. This is probably why I had no competition to rent this place.

The ground is soft under my feet as I follow her to the door. The scent of fresh cut grass hangs in the thick air, with only the slightest breeze to accompany it. The inside of the cabin is cozy and I'm happy to see a fireplace. The generous living room tapers down to a dining area that's more of an alcove. A doorway to the left leads to a small kitchen with dark wooden cabinets and black appliances.

"The last tenants left some furniture. If you want the place, you can keep it, or I can have it removed. Up to you," Silver explains while I explore.

Considering I'm moving with almost nothing, it's definitely a bonus. The grayish green couch and loveseat look and smell clean. They also left a small dining table with chairs, and a coffee table. The only furniture I'll need to get right away is a bed.

"What do you think?" she asks, leaning against the kitchen doorway.

A cabin in the woods, not visible from the road which dead ends at a graveyard. With only one neighbor in sight but still a good distance away.

I wanted a peaceful place to start over and get away from everything. "It's perfect."

Once I've signed the lease and paid the rent, we walk back outside. "If you have any problems or questions, you have my number. You can also find me at Lucky's Diner and Donuts most days. My mom owns the place."

My mom is in a white cardboard cylinder tucked between a couple of boxes in my backseat.

Our heads turn when a black pickup truck pulls into the shared driveway. The driver raises a hand to wave when they pass my cabin, and we both reciprocate, but the passenger doesn't look our direction.

"Do you know the neighbors?"

"Neighbor," she corrects. "His name is Arlow—the one getting out of the passenger side." She nods across the driveway. "He lives alone as far as I know."

I can't make out any of his features, but I'm struck by his height as he closes the door and starts toward his house. He must stand over six and a half feet tall.

"I don't know him personally. The last tenants said he keeps to himself. They lived here for two years and never met him. He comes to the diner occasionally to pick up an order, but he isn't the type to sit and chat, I suppose. Maybe because he draws some stares."

"Because he's so tall?"

"And he appears to have some kind of skin condition on his face. People can be such assholes," she says, shaking her head. "Anyway, he owns a good chunk of the land behind his place along with everything west of the driveway to the end of the street."

"He owns the graveyard, then?"

5

"Yeah, and past it, actually. I know because Mom was looking at buying that property too since it was adjacent to this one, but he beat her to it."

"How far back does this property go?" I ask.

She nods towards the forest behind the cabin. "If you follow the path into the woods, you'll find a creek, then a field that was previously used for crops. Mom hires a guy to mow back there a few times per summer so if you hear a motor, it may be him. Keep going and there's a tiny patch of woods that runs along the edge of a cliff. You don't want to be out there at night. It's a sheer drop to a rocky ravine that's hard to see, even in the moonlight." She raises her arm to point in the opposite direction of the farmhouse. "If you go to the east through the forest, you'll hit a wire fence that separates it from the adjacent property owned by the Daltons. No one lives on it anymore."

We chat for another few minutes before the truck descends the driveway from Arlow's place, minus the passenger. After he passes and turns back out onto the road, Silver heads for her truck. "Welcome to Sunwood. Stop in the diner sometime. We serve breakfast and dinner all day."

"I'll do that. Thank you."

Once the sound of her motor has faded away, I take a deep breath and just stand there for a moment. It's so peaceful, if not exactly quiet. The wind makes a soft whooshing sound through the trees, rattling the leaves. Birds sing back and forth. A big bug buzzes past me. After living my life in cities, this is going to be an adjustment, but I think I'm going to enjoy it.

Most small town businesses close early and there's shopping to be done, so I waste no time unloading my car. It doesn't take long. Boxes and bags are all I have. And the container of my mother's ashes. During the drive, I couldn't resist peeking back at it a few times. It's such a comfort to see.

One thing I'm going to like about living here is how efficiently errands can be accomplished. I manage to shop for furniture, get my internet turned on, buy groceries, and stop at a fast food restaurant to pick up dinner before dark.

When I return to the cabin, the sun is starting its descent, stretching the trees' shadows across the ground. It's so quiet. A few bats swoop and dive overhead, feasting on bugs. As I turn to go inside for the night, movement catches my eye from the neighbor's place.

A tall figure walks away from the house. He pauses for a moment, looking up at the sky, then continues without hesitation, winding his way between the headstones. Why is he going into the graveyard at night?

It's eerie. Unnerving. Goosebumps rise on my arms.

Time to go inside. It's my first night in a new place. Of course, I'm a little spooked. It'll be fine.

After dinner, I get my internet working, put on the TV for company, and unpack some bedding, clothes, and bathroom stuff. My last move was much more chaotic, and I got rid of a lot of my possessions. Once the couch is made up with my pillows and a blanket, and I'm freshly showered, I can't resist stepping outside before bed despite my earlier nervousness.

My breath catches at the sight of the sky. A solid inky expanse, painted with so many stars, it seems impossible it could hold them all. It's gorgeous.

From this distance, the lighted windows of the farmhouse are visible, but the graveyard has faded into the night. The forest draws a dark boundary around our homes, where the pale moonlight can't penetrate the canopy.

It's not scary as I feared.

It's peaceful. It's perfect.

———

One of my first priorities is to find some things to do that will get me out of the house and make me socialize. I'm not going to spend any more time closing myself away like I did for the last two years. It was a nice break after years of working multiple jobs and being surrounded by people—a needed break—but it gets too comfortable. Anxiety I can manage. I don't want to end up agoraphobic.

Instead of making the pasta I had planned, I decide to have dinner at Lucky's Diner and Donuts. Silver spots me when I enter the diner and take a seat at the counter. "Hey! Is everything alright?"

"It's great. I really like the place."

She beams and slides a menu to me. "Nina will get your order when you're ready."

"Thank you." Someone calls for her and she disappears back into the kitchen.

The dinner rush is dying down, but a few tables are full. Others are being cleared and cleaned. The waitress, Nina, puts in my order then goes to sit at one of the tables, talking and laughing with the customers. It's odd to be in a place where it seems like everyone knows each other. Like being the new kid at school.

It doesn't feel unfriendly. Lots of looks, smiles, and nods are tossed my way as people leave, and others come in and out to pick up their orders.

The cook shouts to Nina to pick up my food, but Silver walks out and waves her away. "I've got her." She places my plate of chicken fried steak and mashed potatoes down, along with her plate of food, then pulls up a stool to sit across the counter. "Tell me to get lost if you'd rather be left alone, but I thought you could use some company."

"I'd love some. So, your family owns this place?"

"My mom does. She's run it for twenty-five years. I grew up in this dining room. She had me waiting tables in kindergarten." Silver grins, looking behind me.

"Oh, quit your exaggerating!" The faint smell of cigarette smoke reaches me as an older version of Silver takes a seat beside me. "It was second grade." She turns to scrutinize me. "You're the new tenant."

"I am. Calli Barnes."

"Mona Mills. It's good to meet you. I know you have Silver's number, but if you have any issues, you're welcome to come find me too."

"Thank you. The cabin is adorable."

"Isn't it? I thought so too." Mona leans her elbow on the counter, propping her chin on it. "When I bought it, I planned to live there."

"You changed your mind?"

"Yeah, it wasn't for me."

Silver snorts and takes a bite of her sandwich. "You bitched about bugs, then spent two nights afraid to walk to your car after dark because you heard coyotes."

"I am not the damn roadrunner. Living in the woods sounds good, but it turns out I'm a town girl at heart."

"I've never lived in the woods or a small town. Indianapolis isn't a huge city but it's a big difference from here," I explain, digging into my food.

"Culture shock for sure," Mona agrees. "What brings you here? Do you have friends or family in town?"

"No, I just wanted a change. When I looked at the online ads for rentals, I saw your cabin and decided to go for it."

Mona nods at Silver. "It's like I told you when you were talking about moving to Nashville. People always think they want the opposite of where they grow up. City folks want to live in nature, country folks want to try the city." She lightly slaps the counter as she gets up. "Anyway, I hope you enjoy it. Welcome to town."

"Thank you."

She disappears through the swinging kitchen door. "Your mom is nice."

The words are barely out of my mouth when Mona's shout echoes through the diner. "Gary, what the hell did I tell you about leaving this stepstool out? I almost tripped over it! Are you trying to send me headfirst into the fryer, you asshole?"

Silver looks over the counter at me as I force down my sip of iced tea, so it doesn't get sprayed everywhere. "Yeah, she's a sweetheart."

While I'm here, Silver would probably be a good person to ask. "Do you know of anywhere that's hiring for part time work? Or a place to volunteer in town?" A job or a volunteer opportunity will be a good place to start if I'm going to build a new life here.

After pondering it for a moment, she nods. "The community center has a volunteer program. I think it's mostly roadside clean up and yard work. Gray care is usually looking for people to hang out and spend time with their clients."

"Gray Care?"

Silver grins, sipping her drink. "It's actually called Golden Hours Day Center for Seniors. But it's like a daycare for old folks so it's gained that nickname."

"Got to drop the kids off at daycare and dad off at gray care?"

"Exactly. What kind of work are you looking for?"

"Nothing specific. Something to get me out of the house a few days a week that's not too demanding."

"Well, the factories are full time only, but the grocery store and fast food restaurants hire part time. Actually." She pauses and waves to her mother. "Mom, are you still looking for someone to help with the donuts?"

Mona is busy with a customer, but she nods.

"How do you feel about overnight work? We need someone to come in and help make the donuts. We had one employee quit, and another just had a baby so she can't work as many hours. It'd be from about nine at night until four in the morning. I'm not sure what wage Mom's offering, but I'll check if you're interested."

"That sounds perfect. I like to bake but I've never made donuts."

Silver flaps her hand, dismissing my concern. "It's easy. I can teach you in a couple of shifts."

We talk for a few more minutes and finish eating. Silver is easy to talk to, funny and a bit of a smartass. I like her immediately. Once the place clears out a little, Mona joins us again.

"You're interested in the night job?"

"I am. For part time."

"Can you follow directions?"

"Yes."

"Can you fill in occasionally if our other girl calls in?"

"Sure. Any night, really."

"Fifteen dollars an hour work for you?"

It's more than I expected her to offer, to be honest, and the money isn't important. "That sounds fine."

"Great, we'll try you out for a couple of weeks and see if it works out. I'll have your tax paperwork for you when you start." She regards Silver. "What night do you want to start training her?"

"Tomorrow?" Silver suggests, looking at me.

This has to be the easiest, fastest job search of my life. "I'll be here."

It's nearly dark when I leave Lucky's. With a stomach full of delicious food and a new job, I'm feeling good. I've accomplished a lot in the last couple of days.

The heat of the day fades into a muggy night, and I pull my hair up into a ponytail to get it off my sticky neck, then sit out on my porch to watch the light recede. Cicadas scream from the trees, overpowering the crickets that try their best to outdo them.

It's strange how such a cacophony can somehow seem peaceful. The last of the glow has dissipated from the sky when a light draws my attention to the neighbor's barn as the door opens. A moment later, the light goes out and Arlow walks between the barn and his house, disappearing into the graveyard.

Again? Silver said he keeps to himself and that the last tenants never even met him, so I doubt I have to worry, but why does he hang out in a graveyard at night? It's so creepy.

My second night in the cabin is better than the first, mainly because I have a nice new bed to crawl into thanks to today's delivery. With one of my favorite albums playing, I sink into my pillows.

11

In a blink, night turns into day, and I'm squinting at the beam of sunlight sneaking in between my curtains.

Despite my good night's sleep, I wake with a familiar rattly feeling, like electricity is coursing through me. It puts me on edge, but I'm not going to let it ruin my plans for today. I'm too eager to explore. Silver mentioned a creek. Undeterred by the heat, I fill my water bottle with ice water and set out to find it.

The trail through the woods isn't hard to locate, but it clearly hasn't seen many feet recently, judging by the overgrowth along the edges. Grass has started to crawl over the narrow dirt path. I take out my phone and check what direction my cabin is in on the compass just in case I lose the path or get turned around.

Stepping into the forest feels like entering another world. The temperature drops in the shade of the fragrant trees, cooling the sweat on my skin. The soft rustling of leaves is accompanied by the musical rise and fall of bird songs. My earbuds sit in my pocket, but there's no desire to put them in as I'd planned. Instead, I soak in the murmur of the forest. My steps are languorous, allowing me time to take in my beautiful surroundings.

Not too far in, another trail splits off to the right. Pausing, I look around, ultimately deciding to keep heading straight. I'll see where that branch leads another time. The forest is getting a little dimmer, taking on a hazy look. By the time I reach the creek that pushes the trees back from its borders, the sun has disappeared behind rolling clouds.

The creek is bigger than I expected, maybe twelve feet across. The water is unbelievably clear, and the sound it makes as it flows downstream is wonderful. After dipping my fingers in to feel how cool it is, I walk alongside it, just listening to its gurgly song.

It meanders, growing wide and shallow in some spots and more narrow and deeper in others. I'm not sure how long I've been walking, lost in my thoughts when I look up to see a small wooden footbridge.

What did Silver say was on the other side of the creek? An empty crop field, I think, and some more forest before the drop off she warned me about. The soft thunk of my footsteps on the thick wooden planks frightens off a few birds from a nearby bush, startling me for a second and making me laugh at myself.

My fear that I'd be afraid in the woods is unfounded. From the second I walked onto the trail, my anxiety began to dissipate. I'm more relaxed than I've been in a long time.

It's not an empty field that I find on the other side, but an overgrown copse of trees. A sweet smell wafts over, and I realize what it is before I get close enough to see the branches hanging low with fruit. A peach orchard. Or maybe it's considered a grove with so few trees.

Long wild grass grows underfoot, and I'm careful to watch for snakes while approaching one of the trees. A few peaches decorate the ground as well, most being devoured by ants. What a waste. Peaches are delicious and they don't get any fresher than this. A ripe peach comes easily off the branch when I pluck it.

My plan to walk back to the cliff can wait until my next walk. It's so warm and muggy. Suddenly, sticking my feet in that cool creek and enjoying the peach sounds like the best thing in the world.

CHAPTER 2

ARLOW

THE EARTH IS SOFT AND WORKABLE, THANKS TO THE RECENT RAIN. IT makes my job much easier, but leaves my hands coated with damp soil when I'm finished. I wipe them off as much as possible on the grass before picking up my tools and weaving my way through the weathered gravestones.

Clouds lazily push the blue out of the sky. Shade crawls across the ground closing in on me as I wash my hands at the outdoor spigot. The fading light promises the perfect condition for capturing what I saw yesterday in the woods and my afternoon plans have suddenly changed. Instead of spending it indoors, I step inside only long enough to gather my supplies into a bag and sling it over my shoulder.

I know the forest surrounding my house well. My footprints must lie buried on every inch of ground as many times as I've wandered and hiked through it. It doesn't take me long to retrace the steps I took yesterday, and the fallen tree waits right where I remembered.

The reason that certain things grab my attention and insist their way into my art eludes me. It can be a simple object like a dirty shovel or rain-streaked window. More often, it's nature. The forest, the fields, the animals. It sometimes feels like they're demanding to be drawn, immortalized somehow. That was how it felt when I found the dead tree that lies in front of me now.

It's rotted almost completely through but had kept its shape until a large branch from a neighboring tree fell on it, splitting it almost in half. The end of the offending branch rests in the crater it caused, spilling crumbles of wood onto the ground. A layer of moss has grown over the scar as if the softness might bring some comfort to such violence.

When I came across it yesterday, it was too sunny. I needed to see it like this to fully capture the gloomy feel it portrays. At least that was the excuse I told myself.

I'm full of excuses lately. Something is off. The desire is there but once I get the first few lines, it fades to nothing. What used to come naturally now feels forced. Even if I expend the effort to push through, what results is trash, empty of any emotion.

"Damn it."

My head whips around at the sound of the soft curse. No one ever comes out here. Other than one time that some teenagers got lost and ended up back here with their four wheelers. I've never had to bother with no trespassing signs or anything like that.

The voice came from the direction of the creek nearby, and when I spot the source, any thoughts of drawing the fallen tree vanish.

A woman stands at the edge of the creek, sipping from a water bottle. She walks back to set it on the grassy bank. A quick perusal of the area convinces me she's alone.

It's the new neighbor who rented the cabin. I don't know her name, but I got a glimpse of her with the owner before, and I've seen her coming and going from a distance.

She returns to the creek and reaches down. Her fingers scrabble at the mud until she digs out a small rock. Leaning over, she swishes it back and forth through the water then holds it up to inspect it. It's just a river rock, grown smooth from the current, but the smile that blooms on her face is radiant. As if she's discovered some precious gem tucked away in the back woods.

I'm frozen in place, watching and fascinated by her every move.

The stone gets tucked into her pocket, and she rinses her hands again, then picks up a peach that sits beside her water bottle. Her teeth pierce the soft skin of the fruit, and she closes her eyes, savoring it. No doubt she picked it from one of my trees, but she can have the whole orchard.

She sits at the very edge of the bank, stretching out her legs over the water to submerge her feet. Something about her, some indescribable quality holds me in thrall. Every movement from her exudes joy. Like the quiet grin she wears at the simple pleasure of eating a peach in the forest. In that moment, she's nothing less than peace and contentment personified.

Without taking my eyes off her, I sit on the ground at the base of a tree and pull out my sketchpad. From this angle, she likely won't see me, considering I have to tilt my head to see her between the trees. My pencil seemingly works on its own while I race to record the way her mouth curved when she found the river rock. The way she closes her eyes after each bite of peach.

A cloud moves overhead, but the gauzy light can't dim whatever shines in her. Time slips by as I sketch, switch pencils, and sketch some more. She lies back on the bank, throwing an arm across her eyes and for a few minutes, I wonder if she's sleeping. Until the sun comes back out and hot, heavy air presses in, warning of late afternoon storms to come.

It drives her to her feet, and she steps into the water. Hesitating, she looks around, then tugs her shirt off over her head.

My mouth seems to have lost all moisture as I pull in a sharp, dry breath. I fumble to grab the pencil and start drawing again while my eyes drink her in.

I should leave, but I can't do it. She's so beautiful, wading out to the center of the creek that's about three feet deep, and dropping down until her bare breasts are covered. Leaning her head back, she

17

dips beneath the surface, emerging with a euphoric expression, water dripping from her lips as they part slightly.

Mine. The word slips out under my breath with no forethought.

With her shoulder length brown locks slicked back and darkened, she returns to the bank, taking her time retrieving her shirt.

When she picks it up, a branch snaps nearby, and she frantically covers her chest, looking around. It's followed by the familiar sound of a deer crashing through the woods. It's a common occurrence, but not one she's familiar with judging by her reaction.

With wide eyes, she jerks the shirt over her head and scans the forest. "Is someone there?"

Her gaze skips over me each time while I hold my breath.

Gathering her things, she tosses them in her pocket and starts toward the trail, casting glances back until she's out of sight.

What the hell just happened? I stare down at the frantic sketch that tried so desperately to capture the unique beauty of the scene I witnessed. What anyone else might see was a woman bathing topless in a creek, but it wasn't as simple as that. It wasn't sexual or lewd.

What I sketched and will draw in more detail later isn't about her body, but the beguiling adoration that washed over me without explanation. While objects and nature often cry out, demanding to be drawn, this is the first time I've felt that from a person. The only portraits I've ever drawn have been commissioned, and those are few.

With my previous project of the fallen tree forgotten, I start back toward home, excited to work for the first time in a long time.

CHAPTER 3

CALLIOPE

M̲y̲ s̲u̲d̲d̲e̲n̲ p̲a̲n̲i̲c̲ i̲n̲ t̲h̲e̲ w̲o̲o̲d̲s̲ d̲o̲e̲s̲n̲'̲t̲ k̲e̲e̲p̲ m̲e̲ f̲r̲o̲m̲ g̲o̲i̲n̲g̲ b̲a̲c̲k̲ out there. At the time, my skin prickled with the sensation of being watched, but by the time I made it back to the safety of my cabin, my thoughts were more rational. It was probably just an animal. The forest isn't quiet, I know that. My anxiety got the best of me again, that's all. The memory of calling out like my imagined serial killer in the woods might reply makes me roll my eyes at myself.

Other than that one moment, it's been a great week. Making so many types of donuts for Lucky's Diner turns out to be more compli-cated than I expected but after my third shift ends on Saturday morn-ing, I think I have the hang of everything. The recipes are always there if I need them, but I've learned sticking to the schedule that Silver showed me is most important. That way a lot of other work can be done while certain doughs are proofing, and no time is wasted.

The diner closes at nine—the same time my shift starts—so there are no customers, but the grill cook, Gary, stays until eleven to help close up. They have a young guy, Ethan, who comes in when he leaves. He's responsible for prepping all the produce, making sandwiches for premade box lunches, refilling, restocking, and some nighttime cleaning.

Working alongside Silver and sometimes Misty—who I'll be filling in for occasionally since she's juggling a job and being a single mom to a newborn—is enjoyable. A speaker sits on one of the shelves and we take turns choosing the music. With the restaurant empty, it's a very laidback atmosphere no matter who else is working at the time. Mona and Silver are both happy to have me stay on, and I'm added to the schedule for the next week.

I may still look for a volunteer opportunity since the job is only three nights a week, but for now, I'm happy to spend my time exploring the woods, catching up on books I've been meaning to read, and discovering some new hobbies.

Being in the woods has made me eager to learn more about the nature around me. I want to know the names of the trees and which birds are singing so beautifully every day.

Sunday turns out to be rainy, and rather than stay indoors, I drive to a big home improvement store in the next town to buy some bird feeders. It took a little research for me to learn exactly what kind of bird seed to get and which feeders work with the different types, but they had a huge selection to choose from. I'm lured in by a pretty birdbath made of sea glass that must go home with me, along with a couple of lawn chairs, and a small portable firepit.

It's pouring down and lightning streaks across the sky when I get home so everything gets left in the car while I make a mad dash for the house. I roll a joint, grab myself a glass of iced tea, and sit out on the porch.

I'm surprised to find a voicemail on my phone from the private investigator I hired a few weeks ago. I didn't expect to hear from him on a weekend, but maybe PI's don't keep business hours. It's not a field I'm very familiar with. I wish I didn't have to be now.

Dread fills my chest while I stare at the screen. Less than a minute duration. It must not be big news. Probably just a request to call back.

If I don't check it now, I'll think about it all night. My finger trembles a little as I press play.

"Ms. Barnes, I just wanted to let you know that I received your payment, and my partner has started looking into your missing person's case. It may take a few weeks for us to have an update, but you're welcome to check in with us any time or contact me if you remember any further information that may help. Thank you."

No news but not bad news is a relief. With a sigh, I light the joint and sit back in my chair.

The storm has passed, leaving a steady rain in its wake. It's a lovely sound. Drawing the smoke into my lungs, I relax, letting the feeling wash over me while darkness paints the landscape. A vague memory surfaces of how my dad used to refer to the pitch dark as country dark. At the time, I didn't think anything about it, but it makes sense now. Especially with the cloud cover and no moon.

The rain lets up about an hour later, and mosquitos start to recognize me as an all you can eat buffet. As I get up to go inside, a light catches my eye across the driveway. Arlow stands in the open doorway of his barn, the backlight displaying him as a long shadow. He leans against one side, and I wonder what he's doing.

That familiar eerie feeling of being watched creeps in again. Is he watching me while I look at him? Surely not. It's too dark over here for him to even make out that a person is on the porch, isn't it? I couldn't see him if it weren't for the light coming from inside the barn.

A snorting laugh leaps out of me when I realize if anyone should feel watched right now, it's him. It's time to take my high ass to bed.

———

I fall into a satisfying routine over the next week. My bird feeders are all set up and filled. It only takes a day for the birds to locate it, and my mornings—or afternoons if I worked the night before—are spent watching them while I have coffee on my back deck. After running any errands that need to be done, I hike down the trail again.

My time in the woods has become my favorite part of the day. Sometimes I take a book or a notebook to journal. Sometimes I sit and watch the water flow past, or hunt for pretty rocks while I listen to the birds. I'm sure my routine would bore the hell out of some people, but I'm loving every second of the peaceful lazy days.

In the evenings, I read, listen to music, and sometimes take a walk along the road while it's still light out. From the road, the graveyard doesn't seem as scary during the daylight, but the charred remains of the church that's visible through the tree line has an ominous feel. Only a few feet of two walls stand, intersecting, a black scar against the blue background of the sky.

I'm not interested in walking down the road today. I've had the urge to bake lately and with all those fresh peaches available, a cobbler sounds like just the thing. I have to work tonight, so there isn't time to bake right now, but I can go get the peaches and make it tomorrow.

Usually, my walks in the woods are leisurely, but this time my strides are quick and purposeful. It doesn't take me long to follow the trail back to the bridge and over into the orchard. The edginess I've been feeling fades. The calming influence of the woods is in full effect. Wandering through the trees, I pause here and there to pick the healthiest looking fruit, humming a song that's been stuck in my head.

My hand is halfway to plucking another when I catch a slight movement out of the corner of my eye. Expecting to see a branch bobbing in the wind or maybe a bird, I glance over. It takes me half a second to register the tall looming figure, and my entire body jerks like I stepped on a live wire.

A man steps out from under the tree.

Instead of the scream that almost made it up my throat, his name escapes in a whisper. "Arlow." It must've been audible because his eyes widen on a blink. "Silver told me your name," I explain quickly.

22

"She's the owner of the cabin. I'm living there. Renting it. Just for a year." I'm rambling while he stares at me like I'm an unfamiliar bug. It would be intimidating even if he wasn't towering over me like a skyscraper. "I'm Calliope Barnes...um...Calli."

"I didn't mean to scare you." His voice is soft and deep, almost rattly, but I'm so struck by his appearance when he steps into the sunlight, I barely register the sound of it.

Silver said he had a unique look, and he does look different. He has the most interesting face with an angular quality that sharpens his jaw and chin. His dark scruff and moustache are segmented by a pure white stripe that dyes a streak through both.

"You didn't scare me." Hardly believable considering my shaky voice. "I was just...getting some peaches."

Another step toward him lets me study his face, despite my fear. It's not the first time I've seen vitiligo, but on his tanned skin, it's stunning. His right eye is ringed with white, and ivory lashes flutter together like delicate feathers when he blinks. Another patch of pale skin arcs over his left eye. It continues down to draw a white line in the hair of his eyebrow, cutting through it diagonally. His dark lashes on that side are interspersed with a few snowy hairs as well. His impressive height, broad shoulders, lean build, and long limbs add to his unconventional combination of characteristics.

Gorgeous. That's the word that whispers in my head at the sight of him. "What are you doing out here?" I ask. It comes out sounding accusatory, but he startled me and attractive or not, this is the same man who spends his nights in a graveyard.

"Catching a fruit poacher, apparently." His tone isn't cold, but his words drop ice into my stomach.

Didn't Silver say a fence marked the boundaries? Or was that only on one side? "This is your orchard?" I put a few more feet of space between us until something soft underfoot makes me stumble. A sickly sweet smell fills the air, and scraps stick to my shoe when I lift my foot off a rotting peach.

He nods and the corner of his mouth twitches up into an almost grin.

"Shit! I'm sorry. Silver didn't mention an orchard and I should've known to ask before I assumed...I didn't know I crossed onto your property." The sun is setting fast, and my anxiety ramps up. I'm alone in the woods with a man who just caught me trespassing and stealing.

"It's all right," he begins, in the same soft tone, but I'm already dumping my bag of peaches out and backing away. "You don't have to do that."

"Sorry," I repeat. "It won't happen again." Whatever he says is lost in the wind over my ears as I turn and run back to the path. With legs as long as his, I have no chance of outrunning him if he pursues me. I'm back across the footbridge and onto what I hope is my side of the property before I look back. Nothing waits behind me but the darkening forest.

There's no sign of him when I come out of the trail behind my cabin. Of course there isn't. Because he wasn't some psycho chasing me through the woods, to what? Murder me for taking his peaches? The surprise on his face when I dumped them out, he must think I'm an idiot. Whatever, I won't be going back onto his property.

I'm lost in my thoughts as I cross my yard, but the sight of my cabin jerks me back to reality and stops me in my tracks.

The front door stands open. Wide open.

From my vantage point in my front yard, I can see it move slightly, opening wider. I'm frozen in place, my blood racing through my veins. Someone is in my cabin. Fumbling my phone from my pocket, I grip it tightly, ready to call the police. There's no one visible in the doorway and as I watch, the wind picks up, and the door swings all the way back, bumping the wall.

Did I forget to lock the door and the wind blew it open? It's hard to think back to whether I turned the lock when my heart is beating in my ears. If that's what happened, I don't want to call for help. I haven't had to deal with police here but my experience with cops in the past tells me they're likely to be annoyed and not take any future calls from me seriously if it's a false alarm. I couldn't get them to believe me when I really was in danger before.

A slow scan of my surroundings doesn't reveal anything. No strange cars or anyone in sight. In any other situation, I'd probably ask a neighbor to investigate with me, or to at least keep an eye and make sure nothing happens. Somehow, grabbing creepy graveyard guy minutes after getting caught stealing his peaches doesn't sound like a good idea. Either I go in by myself or call for help.

Evening shadows begin to flow across the ground. If I'm going to do this, it needs to be now, before dark. There's a knife and pepper spray in my car. Keeping an eye on the cabin door, I retrieve them from the glove box. I'm not going in totally alone if I can help it. I send a quick text to Silver.

ME

Are you busy? Can I call for a second?

Silver and I are becoming friends, but I haven't had a reason to call her in the two weeks I've been living here. Instead of texting back, she calls within a few seconds.

"Hey, is everything okay?"

"Yeah, I mean...I think so. This is going to sound weird, but I was out in the woods and when I came back my front door was open. It doesn't look like anyone is around. I think I may have left it unlocked and the wind blew it open. But would you mind staying on the phone with me while I go in and look around, just in case?"

A moment of silence greets me before she replies. "Are you sure you should do that? You can call the cops and have them check it out. Or I can ask Gary or one of the guys to come."

"No, don't bother anyone. It's probably fine. I just thought I'd be extra safe."

"All right, yeah, but put me on speaker and if I hear anything, I'm calling for help, you crazy ass. Do you have a gun on you?"

"You're on speaker, and I don't own a gun. I have a knife and pepper spray."

"Well if anyone is there, cut and season their ass before asking any questions, you hear me?"

"Absolutely. Okay, I'm going inside." My demeanor might be confident, but my entire body trembles. Small hesitant steps carry me across the yard.

"Do you see anyone inside?" Silver asks in a hushed voice.

"I just made it to the porch."

"Well, come on, the suspense is awful."

Giggles seize me despite my fear. "I'm going." The door is still open as far as possible, and I pull it toward me a tiny bit so I can peek through the crack between the hinges. Nobody is waiting behind it to grab me.

My living room is empty, and I can see into the kitchen as well. "So far so good. My TV is here, and my laptop is sitting on the coffee table. I don't think I've been robbed. I'm going to check the other rooms."

"Stay ready just in case," she warns.

I'm grateful I left my shower curtain open and don't have to suffer that terrifying moment of whipping it aside hoping not to see an axe murderer. It only takes a peek into my little bathroom to see it's not occupied.

One more room to go. My bedroom door is open. Everything appears to be how I left it and I start to relax a little.

"Nobody in the bathroom or bedroom, but I'm going to check under the bed and the closet." My closet door is ajar. Keeping a clear path between me and the bedroom door, I reach, yank it open, and jump back like a lion might be waiting to pounce on me. Nothing but my clothes and boxes.

Retreating back, I bend down on one knee to look under the bed. "Oh shit."

"What? What happened?" Silver cries.

"There's a huge spider under my bed."

"Bitch, are you trying to give me a heart attack?"

"I'm sorry." Relieved laughter pours out of me. "There's no one here. And it doesn't look like anything is missing."

"Thank goodness. I can't believe you went in. I'm over here about to pee myself on your behalf."

"Everything's fine. Sorry I had to drag you into it, but I didn't know who else to call."

"Don't be silly. You can call me anytime. We're friends. Just don't tell my mom I let you go in alone or we'll never hear the end of it. And get yourself a gun, for fuck's sake." Someone calls her name in the background, and she adds, "I have to go."

"See you at work. Thanks girl."

Once we hang up, the silence around me feels thick, probably because my adrenaline is still high. An inspection of the front door shows me the latch doesn't catch well. If it's unlocked, you barely have to press on it to swing it open.

Finally, I relax. I'm confident it was only the wind because who breaks into a place, doesn't take anything or touch anything? I'm glad I didn't call the police and I'm grateful for Silver because today would've been far more terrifying without her. It's good to know I have a friend here.

I'm not due at work for another hour, but I'm too keyed up to sit here. The urge to look over at Arlow's is too strong to resist as I get into my car, but there's no one in sight.

A stop at the grocery store for some fruit and other cobbler ingredients kills some time before work. The peaches don't look nearly as appetizing as the fresh ones so apples will have to do.

Silver is filling in for Misty who was supposed to work tonight and I'm glad to have her company. "Everything still cool?" she asks, dropping her voice a little too late as her mother walks by. It takes me a second to realize she's asking about my cabin door being open. The second time I had the life scared out of me in the last few hours.

Mona glances over at us in time to see me nod. Before she can question what we're talking about, I ask her, "Do you know where the property line runs between the cabin and the neighbor beside the graveyard? Like once you get back to the creek?"

"There aren't any markers out there as far as I know, but the little bridge is his and everything to the west of it." She looks at me over her glasses. "Has he been behind your place? If he's giving you trouble..." Her expression finishes the implied threat and brings a smile to my face. This woman takes no shit.

"No, if anyone has a complaint, it's him. I wandered into his peach orchard and sort of helped myself."

"I definitely don't own an orchard," Mona says with a chuckle, pulling out her phone.

"In my defense, the trees were nearly bursting with fruit, some of it rotting, and the grass was long. I thought it was abandoned to grow wild."

"He probably won't notice any missing then," Silver says, emptying a mixer.

"Catching me in his orchard with a bag full to make a cobbler may have given me away."

Both of them stop what they're doing to stare at me. "Was he angry?" Silver asks.

"No. He said it was all right."

"So, you met him?"

"If throwing the peaches at his feet and running off counts as meeting, then yes." Laughter fills the fragrant kitchen. "I panicked! It was getting dark, and he stepped out of the woods like Slenderman. I almost peed myself."

"Sounds like something you'd do," Mona says, glancing at her daughter.

"You wouldn't catch me out in the forest alone anywhere near dark."

It worries me that my words sounded mean. "I'm not insulting him. He's not bad looking or scary, really, but it was like he appeared out of the trees."

Silver passes me the shaker of sugar and cinnamon when I gesture toward it. "I wonder if that's why he keeps to himself. Because he freaks people out. The skin condition that affects his face probably doesn't help."

"Vitiligo. It's just an absence of pigmentation in areas. One of my childhood friends had spots on her hands and a beautiful white streak through her hair."

"One of my cousins was born with a white patch in the front of her dark hair. Her kids were born with it too, right in the same spot," Mona says. "I was jealous of it as a kid. I wanted to bleach mine to match."

"I know Mamaw was not having that," Silver snorts, and the conversation steers away from my mysterious, graveyard dwelling neighbor.

The night of hanging out and laughing with Silver helps me shake off all the remaining uneasiness of the past day. By the time I clock out, I'm looking forward to getting some sleep then doing some baking.

Driving the winding road to my cabin at night is still something I'm getting used to. At four a.m. the darkness swallows my car, narrowing the world to a few feet of pavement. The trees cast distorted shadows in the thin moonlight, as if they're bending over to watch the road beneath them. It's not frightening, but it feels a little claustrophobic, like going through a tunnel.

My headlights illuminate something sitting on the porch when I park in front of my cabin. Is that a cooler? I learned quickly not to leave the porch light on unless I want to fight through bugs so big they could carry me off, not to mention a thousand moths.

Instead, I use my phone's flashlight to investigate. Why is there a cooler on my porch?

A glance around reveals nothing but the distant light in one of Arlow's windows. Did he leave this here? Oh god, what if it's grave robbed body parts? Or some kind of serial killer offering? The thought raises the hair on my nape. My instinct is to leave it and get my ass in the house until it's light out, but my curiosity won't let me.

My hand trembles a tiny bit as I unlatch the lid and throw it open. It's full of peaches.

The giggle I let out sounds loud in the pre-dawn silence. I'm so ridiculous. I really need to cut down on watching crime documentaries. A note sits on top of the peaches, and after dragging the cooler inside, I unfold it.

I apologize if I scared you. You're welcome to explore and loot my peach trees.
-Arlow

Well, now I feel like an asshole.

Stripping off my clothes to shower, I consider making him a pie or cobbler in return while I'm baking today. It'd be a nice thing to do. To say thank you and I'm sorry for running away like you intended to use my skin to make a lampshade.

I typically enjoy the sunrise with a cup of tea on my porch after work, but today my eyes are struggling to stay open so it's time to go to bed. The sky is beginning to lighten in the east by the time I'm curled up under my covers.

The last thing that flashes through my mind is Arlow's face. Those feathery white lashes.

CHAPTER 4

ARLOW

IT'S TOO HOT TO BE IN THE BARN TODAY. NO MORE THAN HALF AN HOUR after entering, I close it all up, stopping to double check that the locks are secure. There's other work waiting for me.

I pause to wet my head with the hose, chug some water, then grab my tools and start through the tombstones. Along the north side where the thin woods separate the graveyard from the road, some of the dirt has already been tilled up—as far as I got yesterday before my intended break for dinner was interrupted by the sight of her entering the forest.

Calli.

With an empty bag in hand, it was an easy assumption she was heading to the orchard. The argument with myself was brief, and despite knowing I should leave her alone, I took a more direct route to the peach trees. My intention was only to watch her like the times before. To capture her in memory and later in my work.

Once she was so close, I couldn't resist. I needed to meet her. The first time I saw her by that creek, she exuded peace and a calm sort of joy, but I've come to realize that may be rare for her. She often wears a pinched frown that doesn't always fade once she's seated by the creek or on the bridge.

I didn't mean to scare her or expect her to run away like she did. If I talk to her again, it won't be in the middle of the woods where she doesn't feel safe. Hopefully, the peaches and note will reassure her that I'm not angry about her being on my property. There's a ton of land around me and I'm not selfish.

Why am I thinking about her again? It shouldn't matter to me what she's doing or how she feels. She's just a neighbor. A temporary person nearby, the same as the two women who stayed there before. The renters don't bother me, and I don't bother them. I'm not a social person by nature, but her...I can't seem to look away.

Focus. Holes don't dig themselves.

Grabbing my shovel, I get started on the job that was interrupted by my fascination with her yesterday. My wet hair and sweaty skin become a dirt magnet as I dig and shift the heavy soil around. By the time the ground is prepared, I'm coated in grass and dust. The sky has clouded up, blocking the fierce sun but making the air thick enough to scoop with a spoon. The only thing I'm thinking about is a cold drink as I gather my tools and turn to start back toward the barn. My forehead slaps into a low hanging branch, halting me. It wasn't hard but the sting tells me the rough bark probably took a little skin off. At my height, it's not an uncommon occurrence. I've hit my head on more things than I can list.

As I walk to where my ATV is parked behind the barn, I pull my shirt up by the bottom to drag it across my forehead, not surprised to see it comes away with a little smear of blood. The ATV starts up easily and it only takes a minute to get the steel trailer attached.

My phone buzzes in my pocket while I'm pulling the large burlap wrapped bundles out to the trailer.

"Yeah," I answer, winded.

My friend, Lee, snorts on the other end of the line. "Don't answer the phone if you're beating off."

"I'm doing yard work, asshole."

"Yard work not inch work, got it. Lacey is here and I'm grilling steaks if you want to come over for dinner and some beers tonight."

As he's talking, I look up to see Calli walking up my driveway. She spots me between the barn and the house, veering in my direction.

"Thanks, but I can't today," I reply, my gaze glued to her.

"You have something better to do?" Lee taunts.

I do now.

Calli approaches with a tentative little smile and a cake pan in her hands. Her hair is tied up, displaying her long neck. My fingertips itch to trace down it. To plot out the perfect line of it where it softens and curves into her shoulders.

"I have to go. Next time," I tell Lee, hanging up.

"Hey, Peach Bandit," I tease, happy to see her grin in response.

"That's Ms. Peach Bandit to you. I didn't mean to interrupt but I brought you a cobbler. It's half peach and half apple. I bought some apples after I…you know…left the peaches and then once you gave them to me, I had too much fruit so I made both."

Her nervous babbling is fucking adorable. "Thank you. You're welcome to help yourself anytime. Most of them went to waste this year." There have been times I've taken them to the farmers market, and once I tried to give them to the food bank, but they wouldn't take anything fresh, only shelf stable.

I'm not sure if she heard me. Her eyes widen as she looks at me, at the nearby bundles, then back to me again. Thrusting the pan into my hands, she stammers, "I'll let you…um…get back to…whatever. Thanks again for the peaches."

It strikes me what she's seeing. Blood on my forehead and my shirt. A shovel nearby, between two bulky wrapped bundles, both big enough to be a person. And me standing in the middle, covered in dirt, getting ready to load them onto a trailer.

She takes a couple of steps back as I try unsuccessfully to choke back a laugh. "Wait. You don't—don't take off. Look." How many times am I going to terrify her by accident?

Her teeth sink into her lower lip, and she keeps increasing the distance between us while I set the pan on the seat of the ATV, untie the string around the bundle, and jerk back the cloth.

"Trees?" she mumbles, taking a closer look.

"Forsythia bushes. I'm planting them in the graveyard to help with the soil erosion." Tying it closed, I glance at her and see the indecision in her expression. "Do you want to see the other one?"

She shakes her head, and her shoulders drop a little. "No, I see them." Eyes the pale blue color of the cloudy sky travel up to my face. "You're bleeding."

"Yeah, I scraped my head on a tree branch."

A slow grin curls her lips. She glances down, running her hand over her forehead before peeking back up at me. "In my defense, you know what this looked like, right?"

"Like I killed someone, wrapped them in burlap, and you caught me mid burial?"

"Two someones."

"In this heat? That'd be crazy."

Amusement widens her smile and creases her eyes as she shrugs. "Murder's definitely more of a fall or winter activity." Both of us turn when a car pulls into our shared driveway and parks at her place. "I have to go. It was nice meeting you again, Arlow." She walks toward the driveway, glancing back with a grin when I call after her.

"See you later, Peach."

I call Lee back and he answers his phone right away. "What time?"

"Food will be done in two hours," he replies, not bothering to give me shit about hanging up.

"I'll be there."

———

"Arlow!" Lacey calls, rushing up to give me a hug as soon as I step into Lee's backyard. "Lee didn't say you were coming!" With the pan of cobbler in one hand and the six pack of beer in the other, I'm trapped until she lets go. "What did you bring?" Before I can answer, she peels back the cover on the pan. "Ooh, cobbler. Did you make it?"

"Let him get to the deck for hell's sake," Lee calls out to her, earning him a quick middle finger in return.

"No, I didn't make it."

Unbothered by her brother's admonishment, Lacey takes the pan and falls in step beside me as we cross the yard. At twenty-two, she's fifteen years younger than Lee, with all the optimism of that age and enough energy for four people. No matter how annoyed he may get, it's hard to be mad at someone who is so incessantly happy.

The reason Lee invited me at the last minute becomes clear when a short redhead steps through his back door as I climb the stairs to the deck. To his frustration, Lacey is always trying to play matchmaker to her brother. With me here, she can't keep leaving them alone with the hope they'll suddenly realize they're perfect for each other.

"This is my friend, Madison," Lacey says.

"Arlow." I nod at Madison as she steps back and stares at me for a moment.

"Good god, you're tall."

It's amazing how often people feel the need to tell me that, like my six foot seven inch height might have escaped my notice. She spends another few seconds studying my face. I've never minded if people ask about the vitiligo. If it were someone else, I'd be curious too, but they rarely do at the risk of sounding rude.

"It's nice to meet you," I tell her, then glance at Lee and hold up the beer. "Kitchen or bar fridge?"

"There should be room in the bar."

Lee has a great outdoor setup. His large wooden deck overlooks the lake, with a bar running along one end and patio furniture on the other. A firepit sits in his backyard, surrounded by chairs. On the other side of it, the ground slopes down to the water and a small dock where his boat is tethered.

"I'll take this inside," Lacey volunteers, carrying the pan of cobbler into the kitchen with her friend behind her.

I tuck the beer into the fridge under the bar, grab two and hand one to Lee. "Sneak attack?"

"I should really see it coming by now," he scoffs.

"She's pretty," I offer, leaning back against the railing.

"So was the last one. Do you think if I start fucking them then not calling, she'll give up?"

"You're not that much of an asshole."

"I can learn." The sound of the sliding door silences our conversation as they return.

Despite Lee's annoyance, the evening isn't a bad one. After a few beers, we sit around his kitchen table to eat. Lee tells me about some of the repairs that need to be done and accepts my offer to help him with a few projects that require an extra set of hands. His job as a caretaker for the surrounding cabins and lake houses isn't usually a very demanding one, but his busy season is coming up. Lacey talks excitedly about her promotion to manager at the formal clothing store where she works, along with Madison.

All evening, Madison keeps sneaking looks at me. Every time I glance in her direction, her gaze veers away. I'm not sure if she's staring because she finds me odd looking or if she's trying to flirt but it doesn't matter. At this point, I prefer the former. What people think stopped affecting me a long time ago. If you have body differences, it just comes with the territory. I'd rather be left alone than explain that I don't date. Though our reasons are different, it's one thing Lee and I have in common.

"This is delicious!" Lacey exclaims, when we get to dessert. "Who did you say made it?"

It is good. So good I almost regret bringing it and not hoarding it for myself. "My neighbor."

Lee shovels in another mouthful. "The woman who rented the cabin?"

My only response is a silent nod, but Lacey is not one to give up

36

before she knows every detail. "You have a neighbor baking for you?" she teases. "What does she look like?"

My mind flashes to the sight of her by the creek, her hair slicked back, water dripping from her breasts.

"Oh wow, the look on your face," Lacey says before I can manage a reply. "She must be hot. Are you seeing her?"

It's been pointed out to me multiple times that I could never be a good poker player. My expression displays far too much no matter how hard I try to suppress it. "No. I caught her in my orchard, picking peaches. She didn't realize she was on private property and brought the cobbler as an apology. That's all."

"She's pretty though, isn't she?" Lacey pursues.

She's fucking beautiful. "I suppose."

Lee grabs my empty dessert plate and his, getting to his feet to put them in the sink. "Help me grab some logs and we'll get a fire started."

"Sure."

Lee offers me a shot of whiskey, which gets declined. The food has soaked up the few beers, but I'm not staying much longer, and I don't drive buzzed. He leads the way down to the firepit while Lacey and Madison finish eating. By the time we have a fire going, they've moved out to sit on the patio again with a pitcher of margarita between them. Maybe it's the effects of the alcohol making them unaware that they aren't dropping their voices as low as they think, or maybe they don't care, but we can hear their conversation clearly when Madison leans over to Lacey.

"No offense, your brother is hot and everything with that stern, grumpy thing he has going on, but tell me about Daddy Long Legs over there."

Christ. Lee's chest shakes with stifled laughter while he forces down his shot of whiskey.

"Arlow's a good guy. Quiet, but he's always been kind to me," Lacey replies.

"I love the broody ones. How old is he?"

"I don't know." She raises her voice and calls out. "Arlow! How old are you?"

She rolls her eyes when I shake my head at her.

Lee makes a show of holding his hands to his mouth to amplify his voice. "Thirty-three!"

Bastard.

Lacey slaps her arm and stands up, grabbing the pitcher. "I'm getting eaten alive by mosquitos. Let's go back inside."

"Dick," I mumble, after they've gone.

Lee chuckles and takes another shot. "Broody Daddy Long Legs." We're quiet for a few minutes until he looks over at me. "Do you still call her?"

There's no need for him to explain who. He knows my past just as I know too well what he's been through.

"I try not to." Silence ticks away long seconds. "Not as often, but yeah, I still call." His nod holds no judgement, only understanding. "Are you still going to therapy?"

He gestures to the water. "No, this is all the therapy I need."

I get it. Nature helps me more than talking ever has. "Did you get the shingles you need to patch the Nolan's place?"

Happy for the change to a lighter subject, Lee nods. "I did. Just waiting on the downspout that I had to order. Might as well get that replaced while I'm on the roof."

We hang out and talk for another half hour or so before I thank him for dinner and go inside to grab Calli's pan. Lacey is loading the dishwasher in the kitchen, and I spot the empty cobbler pan sitting at the edge of the sink, already washed.

"Hey, thanks."

"No problem." Her little side eyed grin is teasing. "I thought you'd want to get it back to her quickly."

"I'm heading out. Stay out of trouble, you little instigator."

I'm about three steps away from the door when Madison catches up with me. "Arlow, would you want to go out sometime? I can give you my number."

Damn, so close to escape. She was straight and to the point, at least, instead of flirting and hinting. "I'm flattered, thank you. But I don't date."

"Well, if you change your mind, Lacey has my number."

It's not often I get asked out, mainly because I don't go anywhere to meet new people, but it doesn't matter. Dating isn't a possibility for me. It's just not right. That's something I accepted years ago.

It's late when I climb into my truck to go home, but I know I won't be going to bed. During the entire drive, all I can see is Calli's smile as she joked about murder being a cold weather activity. Her cabin is dark, and her car is gone when I return.

I head straight to my studio. Calliope's eyes are on me from a handful of different directions as she smiles back from the sketches taped to the walls. Different poses and expressions, none of which quite capture her luminant beauty.

I'm certainly not done trying.

CHAPTER 5

CALLIOPE

I'M RESTLESS THIS EVENING. IT WAS TOO HOT FOR MY USUAL WALK IN THE woods, and I've spent the day inside, trying to get interested in something. After flitting from trying to read about birds, to watching ten minutes of a show, to cleaning my cabin, I end up rolling a joint and sitting out on my porch. I'm having what I always refer to as an edgy day—where unsettled seems to be my default even if I'm not worried about anything specific.

Before I can smoke, Arlow steps out of his front door. I'm surprised to see him walk in my direction instead of disappearing into the graveyard like he usually does. He slouches a little, one hand in his pocket as he crosses the driveway. His long limbs make routine movements more pronounced, giving him an awkward, gangly appearance despite his broad shoulders and wide chest.

Yesterday, Silver and I went to a local flea market where I got a cute glider that will be perfect to replace the lawn chairs on the front porch once I repaint it. Right now, it sits in my yard, covered by a tarp. He eyes it curiously as he approaches.

"Don't worry. That's not a body either." I get to my feet to meet him.

"Of course not. What are the chances two killers move in next door to each other?" His dark humor matches mine, lightened by his soft tone. "The cobbler was delicious."

"I guess so if you ate it all in a night," I chuckle, accepting my pan from him.

"I shared it with some friends. Terrible mistake. I should've tasted it first and kept it for myself."

He seems so kind when I talk to him that it's easy to forget that he's also the guy who creeps around a graveyard at all hours. The question spills out of me without forethought. "Why do you hang out in the graveyard at night?"

His lips twitch, and he raises an eyebrow. "What's your going theory? Seances? Graverobbing?"

"I haven't completely discounted those but I'm also entertaining the possibility that you're building a Frankenstein."

"That sounds like way too much work. Plus, I can't sew." He runs a hand through his dark hair, and it flops back down, a few waves reaching his earlobes. "I'm not hanging out there, just cutting through to get to my bonfire pit or to watch the sunset."

It never occurred to me what might be on the other side of the graveyard. Before I can reply, he adds, "Do you want to come with me, and I'll show you? It's a beautiful view."

His invitation catches me off guard. "Now?"

"Unless you're busy. I'm pretty sure there's another sunset scheduled for tomorrow night if this isn't a good time."

My decision is impulsive and maybe not the smartest. "Sure. One second while I lock up." He waits outside while I grab my phone and keys, then lock the cabin door behind me. My jitteriness fades as I join him.

This is what's fundamentally wrong with me as a person. I'm a ball of anxiety at a crowded restaurant or when the self-checkout yells at me about unexpected items, or for no reason whatsoever like today, but following a mysterious guy into a graveyard at dusk? Perfectly fine.

Maybe it's his demeanor or the calming sound of his voice. I feel bad about the way I reacted to him, first in the forest and again yesterday. After all, I'm the one who was trespassing, and he's been nothing but nice about it. Sure, the nightly walk among tombstones is weird but it looks like there's a simple explanation for that too.

A major part of my personality that I've worked most of my life to overcome are the cynical snap judgements about people that pop into my head. My first thoughts are never kind and I hate it. Because it's like her. Conditioned into me by growing up with the woman who is now ashes on my mantel. It's not who I am or want to be.

It'd be nice to be on good terms with my only neighbor. I should give Arlow the benefit of the doubt and stop letting my imagination run away from me just because he's a little different. I'm sure I appear mysterious to some too. A woman who moved into a small town she had no connection to and spends most of her time in the woods. That didn't stop Silver from becoming my friend or Mona from hiring me.

Still, being alone in the boonies with any guy I don't know isn't risk free and I want to make sure he knows I'm not easy prey. "I texted my friend that I'm with you so if I'm being lured as a human sacrifice or dinner for zombies, you'll be the main suspect. I'm just saying."

He glances down at me with a flash of a smile. "Don't worry. The corpses don't reanimate until midnight. We have plenty of time."

One of his long strides is easily two of mine but he takes his time so I'm not rushing to keep up as we cross the driveway and walk through his yard to enter the cemetery. The upright gravestones cast long shadows in the setting sun. Most of the names carved into them are barely legible, and a few can't be seen at all. Lying toppled and broken, or crumbling to dust, some are losing the fight against time and weather.

Despite the state of the markers, the grounds are well tended, mowed and weeded. "Are you responsible for maintaining the graves?" It's never occurred to me that a person could own a grave-yard or what that might entail. "Letting families visit and stuff?"

"No one comes to visit. The last date of death I've seen is over eighty years ago. I'm not permitted to remove the graves or stones but other than that, there are no regulations. It was abandoned and buried in honeysuckle when I bought the property."

A few honeysuckle bushes still sit at the far edge, lush and bloom-ing. "You keep it up well," I remark, letting my fingertips trail over the top of a stone as we pass.

"Thank you. Just staying on the good side of the undead so they'll spare me when they rise."

"I'm going to need you to stop with the undead talk once it's dark."

He glances down at me, a small smile inching across his face. "Are you superstitious?"

"No, but I'm not typically hanging out with dead folks at night."

"They aren't bad company if you don't mind doing all the talking."

There's no fence around the graveyard but a hill on the far side forms a natural boundary. My legs burn a little as we climb but it's worth it when we crest the top, and the sky stretches out before us in brilliant shades of purple and pink.

"Oh wow."

He nods, his gaze on the horizon. "Best spot to watch the sunset. Or just sit by the fire."

I tear my attention away from the sky to take in the stone ringed bonfire pit that's surrounded by chairs on three sides. On the fourth, a large log provides more seating. A pile of firewood waits a few yards away.

"Why not put your firepit closer to your house?"

"Stay until the stars come out and you'll see," he says, gesturing to the sitting area.

I perch on the edge of the log while he pulls a couple of split chunks of firewood from the pile and arranges them inside the stone circle. Tucking some kindling around them, he lights it, and sits a couple of feet away from me.

No words are spoken as we watch the pastel sky deepen to burgundy. It's not an awkward silence, just the opposite. I'm content to sit here and take in the view, smell the thick scent of wood smoke, and enjoy the tranquility. It feels like we're so far away from everything. From everyone and every problem I've ever had.

The clouds begin to clear as the last of the color fades to black, letting the stars burst across the sky like a handful of thrown glitter. Arlow was right. He chose the perfect spot. With the edge of the forest far away on all sides, we have an unobstructed view. It's stunning, giving me an urge to lie in the grass and stare up for hours.

When I glance over at him, he's looking at me. "Okay, I get it. It's definitely worth a nighttime journey through a graveyard." The flames light up his modest smile and it hits me again how distinctly gorgeous the man is.

"You should explore the graves in the daytime. It'll feel less alien and scary. Get familiar with the place when it doesn't seem so ominous."

His voice is like honey dragged through ground glass. Deep and soothing but coated with grit. He uses it so softly. It's calming.

"I'm still getting accustomed to being surrounded by a forest and bugs that look like they've come into contact with nuclear waste."

"Where are you from?"

"Indianapolis. What about you?" His lack of a southern accent makes it clear he isn't from here either.

He picks up a thick stick that's propped nearby to shift the logs in the fire. "Northern Illinois. A small town not far from Chicago. Are you here to attend the AG college or do you have family here?"

"Neither. I'm not here for school or a job or anything. I just wanted a change. I've always lived in cities. Indy, then Cincinnati for a bit. I found an online ad for the cabin, and it looked like a nice place. Peaceful."

His eyebrows rise, his head tilting a tiny bit as he regards me.

"You picked up and relocated to a random town where you didn't know anyone?"

"It's crazy, right? I promise I'm not a wanted fugitive. My crime spree in your orchard was a first offense."

His chuckle matches his voice. Soft and deep. "More adventurous or brave than crazy, I'd say."

"That sounds better than restless and impulsive so let's go with that. How did you end up here?"

"I was living in Paducah for a while and looking to move somewhere more rural. My friend Lee lives nearby, and he told me the property was up for sale. Do you like it here so far?"

"I do. It's beautiful and quiet. There's been some culture shock but the people I've met have been kind."

We fall into a comfortable silence again. It's funny. I usually feel the need to make small talk or keep a conversation going when I'm around someone new. Then later I worry that I talked too much just to avoid that awkward gap. Overthinking is my default mode. Tonight, none of that applies and I'm happy to sit here, admire the sky and watch the dancing flames.

The buzz of my cell phone breaks the spell. "You'd better not be calling me in to work," I joke, answering Silver's call.

"Why, are you stoned?"

Arlow runs his fingers over his mouth, not quite concealing a smirk. She's not on speaker, but my call volume was definitely loud enough for him to overhear in the stillness, and I tap the button to lower it.

"No. What's up?"

"I'm actually calling to see if you can swap shifts with Misty. Work tomorrow night and take the night after off instead. She doesn't have your number, so I told her I'd ask."

"Sure, no problem. And you're welcome to give her my number for next time."

"Great, I'll let her know."

Arlow glances over at me once I hang up. "Okay, so maybe the peaches weren't my first time breaking the law." I'm not actually concerned. We may be in a non-legal state but other than cops, no one really cares about weed anymore.

"You're clearly an outlaw. Do you know there's a dispensary about forty miles away, right across the Illinois border?" He gets up and sets another log on the fire, circling the pit to poke at it with the stick until it's behaving the way he wants.

"That's good to know." My fingers fiddle with the joint tucked in my pocket. "Do you smoke?"

"Sometimes. I'm more partial to edibles."

I hold up the joint, raising my eyebrows at him. He nods at the invitation and sits beside me on the log as I light it. "What do you do for a living?" I'm curious since he doesn't seem to leave very often.

"I don't work a conventional job anymore."

It's the only information he offers, but I don't pursue it. He could work online or maybe he came into some money like I did. It's really none of my business. "I make donuts at Lucky's Diner and Donuts a few nights a week."

"That sounds fun," he replies. "Do you get to take some freebies home?"

"Absolutely. That's the best part." His hands catch my attention. Unusually large, with long fingers, they make the joint look tiny in comparison as we hand it back and forth.

Our small talk dies out as the weed works its magic. Arlow moves to sit in one of the chairs across from me. It must be uncomfortable to sit on a log so close to the ground at his height. He practically has to fold himself in half like a lawn chair.

The fire roars, pushing back the night and making the darkness feel like a solid wall around us. It's strangely cozy. I shift to straddle the log then lie back, planting my feet on the ground. With my hands tucked behind my head, it isn't uncomfortable. Though the wood feels rough under my spine, I enjoy it, along with all the other sensations that suddenly seem heightened. The heat of the fire makes the night feel chilly on the half of my body that isn't facing the flames.

The stars look close enough to reach out and grab a handful. The distant scream of cicadas provides a backup choir to the crickets singing around us.

A lightning bug hovers over me, and I reach out to let it land on my hand. It obliges, crawling over my palm to my wrist, its glow pulsing on and off. "It's nice to see a lightning bug again. They've really died off in the cities. I remember them being everywhere when I was a kid."

Arlow watches the little bug crawl up to my fingertip then fly away. "I see fewer of them here too."

"I was obsessed with lightning bugs as a kid. I'm sure my teachers were sick of reading my reports on them. They light up to attract mates, but each species has a distinct flashing pattern that suitable mates will recognize."

"It'd be nice if people had something like that." He pokes at the fire, sending a shower of glowing ash into the air as the logs begin to burn down. "A signal to recognize a soul mate."

"You believe in soul mates?"

A half smile raises his lips as he regards me. "No, but it's a nice thought."

"Lightning bugs are also cannibals. If things get bad, they'll eat each other. There's even one species of females that have learned to mimic other lightning bug's flashes to lure in the males of a competing species so they can devour them."

"That is not a nice thought."

Turning my head, our eyes meet, and his sudden laughter triggers mine. "Sorry, high thoughts."

He shrugs, gesturing to the surrounding forest. "What if humans signaled like birds? Imagine if people climbed trees to yell about being horny."

Giggles overtake me. "Talk about high thoughts. Maybe we're better off that the human mating call is just 'Can I buy you a drink?' or 'Hey baby, want to go to my place?'"

I sit up, brushing the scraps of bark from my back, and he teases, "Is it getting past your bedtime?"

"Nah, I'm practically nocturnal. My sleep schedule is a mess, especially since I started working at the diner. Do you want to finish this?"

He nods at the half a joint we have left and joins me on the log again. "We have that in common. I've seen more sunrises at the end of my day than the beginning."

I assumed as much, since his lights are often on late, and I've noticed him coming and going from his barn in the middle of the night.

We're quiet as we finish smoking and watch the fire burn down to embers. He breaks the silence with a sudden announcement. "I've got cotton mouth like a motherfucker. Do you want a Coke or something?"

"I'd love one, but you aren't leaving me up here by myself," I snort, getting to my feet when he does.

"Would you rather go back through the graveyard alone?" He chuckles at my horrified look. "I'm teasing you. Come on."

"Very funny. And to think, I was going to offer you some of those leftover donuts." We trek back down the hill and enter the graveyard. The high humidity has spread a light fog over the ground.

"I humbly apologize. Especially if you have an apple fritter. They're my favorite."

"It's your lucky night." I move to walk closer to him. "You have me out here stoned in a cemetery at night. I knew you were trouble."

"You're the one who brought the weed."

Fair point. "I could've done without the added creep factor of the fog."

"Do you want a piggyback ride, so they don't grab your feet?"

"You're an awful person for putting that image in my head."

His laughter fills the air, bringing a smile to my face. Once we make it to his front yard, I pause. "I want to clarify this isn't a 'Hey baby, want to come back to my place?' mating call."

He looks me in the eye, the moonlight shining over his features, making the white patches on his face seem to glow. "That wasn't my intention at all. You're welcome to come in but if you aren't comfortable with that, I'll bring you a Coke and we can sit out here." His soft expression is reassuring.

"I'll come in with you. Just making sure there wasn't any misunderstanding. Let's go grab the donuts first."

He accompanies me to my cabin, ducking a little to get through the doorway. The healing scrape on his forehead shows how often the poor guy must hit his head on things. My ceilings give him a few inches of clearance, thank goodness, but he appears almost comically large in my tiny kitchen.

"You have a nice place," he remarks as I retrieve the box of donuts from the table.

"Thank you. Most of the furniture was left by the last tenants."

"My house was furnished when I bought it. I kept a lot and replaced what I didn't like. You knit?" he asks, noting the yarn and hooks lying on one end of my couch as we walk back through my living room.

"Ah, no. I'm trying to learn to crochet but I've just started."

He picks up the blue lumpy misshapen blob and looks over at me with amusement. "It's not a bad unicorn for a first try."

"Thanks for that, but it's a bunny. Or supposed to be. Look, the ears are hard, okay?" I defend with a giggle. He returns the monstrosity to the end table then follows me out to the porch. "Will you hold these for a sec?" I ask, handing him the donuts so I can lock the door. "The latch is fiddly and has to be lined up just right." He carries the box as we walk back to his place.

Judging by the exterior, Arlow's house is a bit smaller than most traditional farmhouses. It's more modern with two stories, a new stone chimney, and a wraparound porch. A porch swing rocks slowly in the breeze on one end, past a sitting area with a table and chairs.

He opens the door and escorts me inside, turning on some lights as we go. The air is lightly scented, a pleasant mix of cedar and a

50

spicier earthy smell. "Your place is beautiful," I remark, admiring the hardwood floors, exposed beams, and impressive stone fireplace.

"Thank you. I had a lot of renovations done before moving in."

We get to the end of a hallway that opens into his kitchen, and he places the donuts on the table, then opens his fridge to pull out two bottles of Coke. Five small jars of honey sit on his counter, labeled in marker.

"Are you a honey addict?" I tease as he hands me a drink.

"It's from my apiary."

"You're a beekeeper?" We sit across from one another at his table.

"I have a few hives on the far northwest side of the property."

"I didn't trespass far enough to see them, I guess." I open the box of donuts and slide it toward him as he sets a few napkins between us.

"You aren't allergic to bees, are you?" he asks with concern.

"No, not at all."

His smile is hesitant, almost shy. "I'd be happy to introduce you if you'd like to meet the bees sometime."

Meet his bees? How can a man as physically intimidating as him be so adorable at the same time? It's the only description that fits him at this moment. "I'd love to meet your bees. Do you have one of those suits?"

He swallows a bite of the apple fritter and nods. "I have an extra one."

It strikes me how strange things work out sometimes, how much has changed for me in such a short time. Not three years ago, I was working two terrible jobs and was absolutely miserable. Six months ago, I was a total recluse, hiding from two crazy psychopaths. Now I'm free, sitting at a table with an intriguing new friend, stoned, and eating donuts at midnight.

We devour two donuts each, still talking and getting to know each other. By the time I head home with the jar of honey he insisted I take, most of my reservations and suspicions about him have been alleviated. He isn't creepy or dangerous. I've known dangerous men.

He's different, soft spoken and funny, but his smiles seem so hesitant and fade quickly. Shyness or sadness? I don't know, but there's something about him that's attractive in a way I can't place. The quiet way he conducts himself, his easygoing demeanor. It's as calming as his voice, and as I drift off to sleep, I realize that my edgy day was turned around the moment he showed up.

CHAPTER 6

ARLOW

CALLIOPE—SHE WAS APTLY NAMED, ALTHOUGH MUSE DOESN'T FEEL LIKE A strong enough word. If witnessing her from afar is inspiring, spending time with her impels me straight to the barn as soon as I see her front door shut behind her.

Inspiration or obsession? Is there even a difference? If there is, I can't measure the distance between them.

It's dawn when I come out of the barn, covered in sweat, spent, but satisfied for now. I couldn't get her out of my head, and I knew there would be no sleeping until the early hours regardless. I'm not complaining. This is the most alive I've felt in a long time. Exhaustion takes over once I lie down and the next thing I know, the afternoon sun is beaming across my room.

My hand aches from last night but I know I'll be back at it later tonight. I've just showered and turned my coffee pot on when my phone rings with a video call from Mom. We usually talk a few times a month, but typically on the weekend.

"Hey," I answer.

"Hi! Are you busy?" Her smiling face fills the phone screen.

"No, not at all. Is everything okay? Dad alright?"

"We're fine." She hesitates before getting to the point of her call. "Listen, I saw Chris Handleman's mother post on social media that he'll be getting released from prison soon."

A weight instantly settles on my chest at the sound of his last name. Guilt is a heavy vest to wear.

Mom continues, "It didn't say when, but if I see—"

"Mom, it's fine. There's nothing to worry about. You don't need to stalk them online." I'm one to talk, watching as Calli comes out of her cabin to get into her car.

"I'm not stalking! I'm sure he won't give you any more trouble after all this time, but she mentioned he'd be staying with her."

"Did you get the honey?" I ask, changing the subject and pouring myself a cup of coffee.

"I did, and it's absolutely delicious. I put it on our pancakes this morning. Oh, you'll never guess what your father brought home!"

"Is it another roadkill horror?" Shit-faced drunk at a local flea market, Dad once bought a taxidermy possum that bears very little resemblance to an actual possum. It's a cross-eyed monstrosity that he still won't admit he hates. Mom set it on the fireplace mantel in his office and it's lived there for years now, haunting the room.

"No, these are alive! Let me show you." It's good to hear her enthusiastic voice. Mom has always been the cheerful family optimist, desperately dragging me up to see the bright side with her. It's impossible to hear her excitement and not smile. Two little calico fuzzballs appear on the screen, mewing as she holds them up. "A little girl was trying to rehome them outside the hardware store, and he surprised me with them."

"Have you named them yet?" I ask, once she sets them loose and comes back to the camera.

"No, your dad has been calling them Thing One and Thing Two but I'm not going to let that stick."

"Uh-huh," I chuckle. "I'm happy for you. You're going to have your hands full."

"I am, and I'll have to ask Teresa to pet sit over the winter holidays. That's what else I was calling you about."

"It's July."

"I know that! But your aunt Gina is planning ahead and inviting the whole family out to stay from Thanksgiving to New Years. You know she just moved into a huge new house? Your dad and I plan to go. She wanted me to extend an invitation to you too." She grins at me and raises her eyebrows. "She's right on the beach."

"I'll think about it."

We talk for a few more minutes before a loud crash sounds in the background. "Oh hell, the kittens got in the cabinet. I have to go. Love you."

"Love you, Mom. Good luck." Her concern over Handleman's release is understandable but I'm not worried.

My phone shows me an alert reminding me of my Thursday night standing appointment. I've slept half the day away and I need to get moving if I'm going to get anything done beforehand. After having a quick meal, I head out to my ATV, gas it up, and switch the trailer to the log hauler. There are five fallen trees that need to be moved.

Once I get them laid behind my barn, it's too late to chop them up. That can wait until a cooler evening anyway. My ATV is almost out of gas, and my cans are empty, so I toss them into the back of my truck then go inside to wash the sap and dirt off my hands. After putting in an online food order, I return to my truck and head to the gas station to fill up the cans.

My next stop is Hatty's Seafood Shack. It's crowded, likely with people traveling to and from the lakes. By the end of October, more than half of the traffic and people will be gone until spring. Since I'm here for a carryout and most of the crowd are waiting for a table or to place an order, it doesn't take long for me to get our food.

It's getting dark when I drive the winding road back to Earl's place. Someone has cut his grass. No need for me to come back for that this week. His mutt, Harvey, trots alongside my truck as I pull into the driveway and get out, escorting me to the door.

"I don't want no girl scout cookies!" Earl calls when I knock. Every week, it's something similar. Last week he said he wasn't interested in buying encyclopedias. I don't think encyclopedias have been sold door to door in about fifty years.

"Let me in before I eat your hush puppies, you old bastard."

With a grin that's missing multiple teeth, Earl opens the door. "Did they have tea this time?"

I hold up the gallon jug. Harvey darts around my legs to enter before me, then follows us both to the kitchen.

Earl digs the cartons of food out of the bag while I pull two glasses out of his cabinet, fill them with sweet tea, and store the rest in the fridge. After three years of weekly dinners, I know my way around his kitchen.

He peeks inside the containers to see which is his, trades me mine for the glass of tea, and we take our food to his living room as usual.

"Who cut your grass?" I ask, sitting on the couch while he settles into his chair.

"A boy down the road was going door to door trying to make some money from yardwork to buy a four wheeler. One of the Billing's kids. Rider or Striker or something like that, I can't remember. They name them anything these days. Sweet kid, though. I'm going to pay him to keep it cut the rest of the summer."

"Good for him." I know Earl hates the fact he can't keep up with his property anymore, but at seventy-five, it's too much.

"Works for both of us. He needs money, and the last time I got on that riding mower, it nearly shook my bones to powder. Did you get those trees cut up this week?"

"Got them moved but not chopped yet. I took your advice and got the Forsythia bushes planted."

Crunching into a piece of deep fried catfish, he nods and swallows. "They should help with the erosion, but they won't spread like the honeysuckle."

We spend a few minutes discussing landscaping and my plans to have a well dug near my bee hives. Once we're finished eating, he grabs a deck of cards for a few hands of Rummy. It's the most boring card game ever invented in my opinion, but Earl loves it. He hosts a weekly game at the Golden Hours Senior Day Center.

After he catches me accidentally discarding a playable card twice, he looks up at me with one scruffy eyebrow cocked. "Did you rent out your brain today? If so, they paid too much."

My brain is stuck on a certain neighbor while my fingers itch to get back to work. "Maybe I felt sorry for beating you last time."

He scoffs and takes his turn. It's quiet for a few minutes as we finish the hand. "You're in your own world. Something on your mind?"

Earl is a gruff guy with some sharp opinions, but he also possesses plenty of wisdom and isn't shy about sharing it. He's become something of a second father figure.

"I've been working a lot. Not sleeping enough, probably." With a shrug, I finish the last of my drink. "A new neighbor moved into the cabin."

The offhand way I offer that information doesn't fool him.

"Oh, now we're getting to it. What's she like?"

"I didn't say it was a woman."

"You didn't have to."

"She's…distracting." That's an understatement and untrue at the same time. She distracts me from everything else but sharpens my focus on my work.

"Seems to me you could use some distraction. Especially the pretty kind."

"You know I don't date."

With a sigh, he sits back in his recliner. "I said the same thing when I was young. I didn't want a girlfriend holding me back. Lord knows I had my fun. Fucked my way through my town and the surrounding ones but look at me now." He tilts his glass at me and looks me in the eye. "Bachelor life ain't fun forever."

It's not fun now, but it is necessary. "I'll keep that in mind."

His warning is warranted even if it's unhelpful. I might not be out here banging every woman in sight like he claims he did, but his future is waiting for me and likely at a much younger age. I've always been fine alone but the thought of so many years ahead of the same long nights and empty days is hard to face.

My mood is low when I leave. I've been riding that high of inspiration and as it fades under my dark thoughts, all I want to do is spend time with Calli again to reignite it.

CHAPTER 7
CALLIOPE

"Let me get this straight," Silver says, filling the end of the glazing table. "When I called you last night, you were sitting in a graveyard with your freaky neighbor."

"I wasn't in a graveyard. We just had to walk through it to get to the bonfire, and he isn't freaky. He was really easy to talk to. We ended up hanging out for hours."

"What did you talk about?"

I think back, a smile growing on my face as I pick up the donut sticks to flip over the batch in the fryer. "The mating calls of birds and lightning bugs. And whether soul mates exist."

Silver looks over at me and blinks a few times. "That's…nice?"

"It was, actually. We have some things in common. We're both night owls, and we both relocated from the Midwest."

"Well, be careful. If you had your eye on any other guy in town, I could likely give you a full criminal and family history. You chose one nobody knows."

"I don't have my eye on him. Not like that. I'm not interested in getting involved with a neighbor, but it was a relief to meet him and see he isn't the sinister graveyard creeper that I had built up in my head."

"That is a relief." She steps back so I can slide the fresh donuts onto the glazing table.

"How was your anniversary date?" I ask, changing the subject.

"It was good. Kyle took me dancing and out to dinner." She drops her voice to avoid her mother overhearing from the nearby office. "I'm thinking about asking him if he wants to move in together."

"Wow. Ready for that next step?"

She leans against the table. "I think so. I love him. We get along great and spend like four nights a week together anyway. His lease ends in a few months. If I'm going to ask, it should be soon."

"He told you when his lease ends?"

"Yes, kind of out of nowhere, too. He may have been hinting."

"That's what I was thinking."

"I was talking to Sandra about it, and she thinks I should wait."

I've only met Silver's best friend, Sandra, once, but she seemed to be pretty level headed. "Does she have an issue with Kyle?"

Silver shakes her head, trading places with me so she can fry the donut holes while I ice the cake rings. "I think she's just more cautious about guys in general. She always has been. She thinks a year is too early to move in together." She sighs, glancing over at me. "Do you think so?"

Considering Silver and I are new friends, I'm flattered she wants my opinion. "Would you be on his lease, or would you get a different place together?"

"I own my house. He'd move in with me."

"I don't know that there's any amount of time you should date before living together. A year, or two years doesn't guarantee anything. If you want to be with each other more, that's what matters."

"I do and I'm sure he does too."

"Then my opinion is go for it." I bump her arm with mine as I pass by with a tray. "Besides, it's your house. If he gets on your nerves, you can chuck him out. No harm no foul."

"True," she says, beaming at me.

"Just drop kick him now and I'll move in," Ethan calls out from the far side of the room where he's clearly been eavesdropping.

Silver rolls her eyes. "Boy, prep your tomatoes and let the adults talk."

The indignancy in his voice makes both of us laugh. "I am nineteen!"

"Exactly. I could be your mom. Well, if I had you at fourteen."

Ethan turns around to lean against the counter, crosses his arms, and grins at her. "I'll call you mommy if that's what you're into."

"Hard pass. Don't forget to ring the onions." Unfazed, she turns back to her work.

Ethan teasing Silver is nothing new. He likes to flirt with me and Misty too. We're always joking around, and I love how fun and relaxed our workplace is, unlike others I've endured.

"I'm wearing you down, Sil, I can feel it!" he says, disappearing into the walk-in cooler.

"Those Yeager boys. He has three older brothers just like him. They're trouble, the whole family," Silver says, shaking her head in his direction. The little fond smile on her face argues with the sentiment, and I'm glad she isn't serious.

Not that I have any interest in any of them, but I don't like the idea of judging someone by the rest of their family. I've spent too much of my life being blamed for half my blood and hating the other half.

Silver puts some music on, and we all work silently for a while. Ethan finishes what he's working on and goes out to the dining area to restock while Silver and I braid dough for the donut twists.

An unfortunate habit of mine is getting lost in my thoughts then blurting out random stuff as if everyone knows what I was thinking. Silver is a victim of it tonight. "Did I tell you he's a beekeeper?"

Her eyebrows rise. "Arlow?"

"Yes, he asked if I wanted to meet his bees."

"Okay, that's cute."

"I thought so too."

She peeks up at me, biting back a grin. "But you aren't interested in him."

Maybe there's a little fascination. He's so different. There's a softness to him despite his rugged masculine demeanor. "I'm just innocently trying to make friends in a new town."

She holds up her oil coated hands. "I'm not judging. If midnight graveyards and swarms of bees are appealing to you, I'll tell you the same thing you told me. Go for it."

———

I'm excited to visit the hives when Arlow invites me, but I'm surprised when he leads me to an ATV with a trailer attached. "Oh," I pause. "We aren't walking?"

"We can but I need to take some supplies up there. Do you mind riding with me? There's an access road on the other side of the church. It isn't far."

I've passed the edge of that road—which is scarcely more than a dirt path barely wide enough to accommodate a car—on my walks down the street. Guess I'm going to see where it leads. "Okay, do we wait to put the bee suits on when we get up there?"

Slinging his foot over, he plants his ass in the seat, moving forward to give me room to get on behind him. "Yes, they're stifling hot on days like this." His long legs don't let him sit too far forward which leaves little space for me. Straddling the seat, I'm so close to him my thighs press against his hips. "Put your feet behind mine on the footrest and hang onto me."

I adjust my feet and bring my hands to his sides, gripping him lightly. "Are you ready?" he asks, tossing a shy smile over his shoulder.

"As I'll ever be."

Chuckling, he starts the engine and cruises down the driveway. The wind feels good once we turn onto the street, cooling the sweat on my skin despite our limited speed. The metal trailer rattles behind us. He navigates the corner onto the dirt road, bringing the church ruins into sight from a different perspective. I wonder if he'd mind if I explored them, too?

Thick forest marches past us on my right but it's the clearing on the other side once we get past the church that makes me sit up straight and crane for a better look. An emerald field of clover appears vibrant against the duller grassy hill behind it. Gorgeous wildflowers spring up alongside the road and overtake the clover until all I can see is an exuberant mix of color. Wow, this was hiding just out of view?

Arlow slows down as the flowers turn back to a mix of clover and grass that's been recently mowed. He steers us off the road toward three light colored wooden boxes standing in a line. The ATV stops before we get too close, and he kills the engine.

"You didn't tell me it was a damn fairytale land up here!" I exclaim, climbing off.

"You like the flowers?"

"And the clover, it's beautiful."

The biggest smile I've seen from him bursts across his face, displaying his teeth. "Clover and wildflowers are beneficial for the hives. The bees don't have to go far to find plenty of food." He pulls two white suits out of the trailer and hands one to me. "Slip your shoes off first. There's a strap that goes under your foot and the elastic should be tight against your ankle."

The material doesn't feel as thick as I expected, but it's crinkly. We both step into the suits and get them zipped up. Before I can reach for it, Arlow pulls the hooded mask up over my head and reaches on either side of my neck, tugging two zippers forward to secure it.

"Are you okay? Not going to get claustrophobic on me?" he asks, his fingers still on the zippers as he looks through the netting. The way the sun highlights his eyes, turning them a light caramel color is distracting. They're so pretty.

"I'm good."

"Okay, hold your hands out." He holds up a long glove and waits for me to slide my hand inside. It almost goes as high as my elbow, where the elastic holds it tight. After doing the same on the other hand, he puts his own hood on and slings a bag over his shoulder.

"Are you collecting honey?" I ask.

"No, it's hard for bees to survive in this type of heat, so we're going to help them keep the hives cool." He picks up a smoker canister and a flat stick. "But first, let's go have a peek at them."

The buzzing is louder than I expected when we approach. Arlow stops to light the smoker and nods toward the first hive. "Do you see how they're congregated around the entrance? That's what they do when they're too hot. They gather and use their wings to fan the hive, drawing out the hot air."

"They're smart."

His nod is enthusiastic. "They are. In the winter, they all go inside and beat their wings to generate heat when it's too cold." He leads me toward one of the boxes. "Slow movements. The heat makes them grouchy."

"Got it. I do not want to be on the wrong side of a grouchy bee." We approach the hive and I catch his arm. "Wait! You forgot your gloves."

"I don't wear them unless I'm dealing with an aggressive hive, and these are pretty docile."

"Don't you get stung?"

"Occasionally, but the gloves are bulky and make it easier to accidentally smash some of them when I'm removing the cover or frames. When they're hurt, they give off a warning pheromone that riles up the others to attack." Smoke rises out of the can, and he aims it for an area around the top, dispersing a small group gathered there. "Bees don't want to hurt you or attack for no reason. We just have to be easy with them." He holds out the smoker. "Do you want to help?"

"Sure. What do I do?"

"Just follow along with the smoke while I get the top off."

It's easy enough to keep the smoke where he needs it as he takes the flat tool and gently pries around the top of the hive. I can't help but wince at the sight of them crawling over his bare hands, but it doesn't seem to faze him. "Okay, step back a little," he warns. Slowly, he removes the top. It's a little unnerving once the bees start landing on us and crawling over my face mask, but I'm also fascinated.

"Give them some smoke," he directs, reaching into the box.

"Sorry for the lung damage, guys," I tease, and he chuckles.

"Don't worry. Bees don't have lungs. The smoke interferes with their sense of smell, so they won't react to the warning scent." He brushes a few bees aside with his fingertips and holds up the frame.

"There's no honey," I point out.

"They haven't started filling this one yet." He pulls out the other frames one by one until he finds one that's half covered in little sealed cells. "See, they've just begun on this one."

"What are you checking for?"

"To see if the frames are full enough to need to be replaced. This top box is called the honey super. It's the excess that I can take from them. First, they fill the brood box below this. They won't start working on the top one until they have enough to support the colony."

He replaces all but the last frame, offering it to me. "Do you want to put it back in?"

Of course I do. He takes the smoker while I carefully grasp the edges of the frame. I line it up and slowly slide it down, glancing at Arlow when a bee climbs in between the side of the box and the frame.

"It's okay. Keep going."

"I don't want to hurt them," I murmur, pressing the frame down the rest of the way. He's right, gloves do make it hard to be precise.

"I know," he says, his voice soothing. "It can't be helped some-times." He puts the lid back on, but leaves it propped open on one side. "Okay, let's get them some water and shade. Are you burning up in that suit yet?"

"Sweating like crazy, but I'm good."

"This won't take long." He leads me back to the trailer where we grab some white cloth cut from bedsheets. "We're going to drape these over the top to give them some shade and reflect the sunlight. Just be careful not to cover the entrances."

Once that's done, we return to the ATV where he pulls out a large plastic jug with a tray attached. "Are you giving them water?" I ask.

"Usually, the creek and another water station that's in the clover field is enough, but they need a closer source right now." He holds the jug up. "This is made for chickens, but it'll work. It'll go on one side of the hives and that container will go on the other." He nods toward a wide tray filled with clay marbles.

Unfurling a length of hose with a siphon on the end, he sticks the other end into one of the water tanks and fills the jug, then the tray. "Where do you want it?" I ask, picking up the jug.

"On the ground on the far side of that hive." As I'm doing that, he fills the tray and places it on the opposite end. We meet back at the ATV, and he circles me, sweeping his eyes over the suit and brushing a couple of bees off me. They head lazily back toward the hive, too hot to bother with us.

"Okay, you can take the suit off." Without bothering to see if he had any bees on his, he strips it off. His hair is damp at his temples, sticking to his head. "Thanks for the help."

The relief of the breeze on my skin is immediate. "It was fun."

We both grab our water bottles and take a long drink. "I need to stop to fill the other water station, but if you're ready to get out of the heat, I'll run you home first."

"I'm fine. I'd like to go." Arlow returns the smoker and hive tool to the trailer, and we climb back on the ATV.

The watering station is a round container about the size of a kiddie pool. It's about two feet deep, and one side is filled with rocks. Earth has been piled up against the outside rim to make a ramp on the same side. When I first put the birdbath in, I read about how you're supposed to add a couple of rocks for the smaller birds to stand on. I assume the clay marbles in the water tray serve the same purpose for the bees. It's not hard to see he's arranged this so smaller animals can reach the water without getting stuck inside the pool.

"Tell me you have a camera out here to see which animals visit," I remark, as he hooks the siphon up to the water tank again.

"That's a good idea. I've never really thought about it. I put it here as another source for the bees and because there are a few wild rabbit dens close by. They love the clover." He points to the trailer. "Actually, there's a bag back there filled with vegetables for them. Do you want to spread them out near that rock?"

The bag is stuffed with peppers, lettuce, cabbage, and tiny misshapen carrots. "Did you grow these?" I ask. They're from someone's garden judging by the state of them.

"Mm hmm," he replies absently, pumping water into the pool.

The more I learn about him the funnier it is that I was afraid of him before. A man who tends bees, grows a vegetable garden, and feeds bunnies. "Do you feed any of the other wildlife?" I ask, after laying out the food.

"I have a couple of squirrel feeders behind my barn."

"So, you aren't out here at night feeding coyotes or anything, right?" I tease.

He grins at me, turning off the flow of water. "I tried but they won't come to me."

"I'm almost convinced you're joking." He's so at home out here, so comfortable. If I stayed, I think I could be too. It's more than the quiet that makes it peaceful. The more I'm out in nature, the more it feels like I belong here. Pretty funny considering I was what the people here like to call *raised on concrete*.

Patches of wildflowers grow nearby, as if they've trickled away from the lake of them at the far end of the field. A beautiful mix of purples, blues, and yellows. "You can go and pick some," Arlow offers, noting the direction of my gaze.

"Yeah?"

"Just watch for snakes in the tall stuff."

The heat is forgotten as I jog over to them, breathing in the sweet scent. After I pluck out enough to fill the vase in my bedroom, I look up to see Arlow returning the hose to the trailer, his back toward me. He turns to see me watching him, and a shy smile blooms on his face, making me realize Silver might be right.

Neighbor or not, maybe I am interested.

CHAPTER 8

ARLOW

THE HEAT AND HUMIDITY HAVE TAKEN A FEW DAYS OFF AND IT'S A GOOD opportunity to get some outdoor work finished, no matter how much I want to be in the barn. That can wait until the overnight hours. Right now, the grass needs to be cut.

Calli's driveway is empty, or I'd offer to mow hers as well. I'm not sure if she plans to do it or if that's her landlord's responsibility. I wouldn't mind doing it. It's an easy, enjoyable job with my riding mower. My shirt gets stripped off and hung over the back of the seat before I tuck my noise canceling earbuds into my ears, turn on some music and get started.

It's easy to get lost in my head while the mower rumbles beneath me. I'm not sure what I expected when I invited Calli to go with me to the hives, but her reaction gave me a peek at who she is. She's cautious, but not afraid to try new things. Hell, even with a suit, I couldn't get Lee out there for weeks. What I loved seeing the most was her compassion. She was so worried about harming one of them accidentally. Some creatures are easy to love. The songbirds and fluffy rabbits of the world get the bulk of consideration, and to see her sympathy for an insect most would run away from says a lot about her. She's as sweet as her face.

There's something about her that affects me in the best way possible. From the first moment I saw her in that creek, there was a shift inside me, and whatever was blocking my creativity broke free. She's inspiring.

After cutting my yard, I cross the gravel to mow hers, then finish up with the weed eater and head inside to shower the sweaty grass off me. My only remaining plan for the evening is to draw, but a tap on my door right after dark changes that.

"Hi," Calli says, fidgeting with her hands. "I just wanted to say thanks for cutting my grass. I know it was getting too high. Um...I was going to hire someone or buy a mower. Anyway, can I give you some money?"

"No, it was no problem."

She blinks, her tongue wetting her lips. "Did you used to cut it for the last residents? Because Silver said it was my responsibility."

It never even occurred to me to do it before. That cabin and whoever lived in it may as well have been invisible before she moved in. "I didn't. I think they had a service come out or hired a high school kid."

"Oh, you have to let me pay you then."

Leaning against the doorway, I stare down at her. "Well, I have been known to do yardwork for cobbler."

Her lips tilt up. "That's a pretty strange thing to be known for."

"It could be worse. You don't want to know what I'd do for pie."

"Now I kind of do want to know." She pauses and holds up a joint. "Are you busy?"

Not anymore. "Not at all. Do you want to come in? Or we can go to the firepit."

"It's nice tonight. I'm up for stoned stargazing if you are."

I grab us both a drink and we start across the yard. Her eyes scan the darkened graveyard as we wind our way through the graves.

"Just run in a zigzag if they come back to life. It's well known that zombies can only shuffle in a straight line."

She rolls her eyes, glancing up at me. "Have I told you that you're hilarious?"

"I don't think so."

"Good." Flicking her lighter, she fires up the joint and hands it to me. "What about ghosts? Do you think your zigzag theory holds up for them?"

Amusement rings in her voice and I'm glad to see she isn't nervous to be here like she was before. "Probably not."

"We'd need one of those little handheld vacuum cleaners to suck them up. That'd be my chosen weapon."

"You've clearly thought this through. Do you believe in ghosts?"

"No, I don't believe in anything supernatural, really. What makes it eerie to me isn't the bodies or supernatural myths, it's the fear of seeing a person. A graveyard at night isn't scary. What someone might be doing in one is scary." She grins over at me. "I watch too many true crime shows." We climb the hill, passing the joint back and forth. "Do you believe in ghosts?"

"No, I'm not superstitious either."

The night sky stretches out in a brilliant display of stars, drawing both of our gazes upward for a moment when we get to the top. It's a sight that never gets old and she seems as captivated by it as I am.

Extinguishing the joint, she takes a seat on the log while I build a fire. Comfortable silence wraps around us. She lies back like she did last time, and it takes a conscious effort to resist staring at her. My fingers itch to draw her as she is, under the deepening sky, reclined on a log, hair spilling over the side like a waterfall.

After a few minutes, she turns her head to look at me. "Have you ever used a metal detector out here?"

"No, never thought about it. Do you have a metal detector?"

"I just bought one. I thought it might be fun to see what I could find. Imagine the old coins and stuff that could be hiding out here. I promised Silver if I discover some buried treasure, I'll split it with her. You know, since it's her land and all."

"Of course. That's only fair. If you unearth some stolen bags of money on my property, do I get the same deal?"

Her eyebrow rises. "Stolen bag of money is very specific. Is there something you're trying to tell me?"

"There are rumors that Jesse James held up banks and stage-coaches in this area."

She sits up, her eyes lighting up. "Really?"

"Among others."

"Now I can't wait to get started."

Considering that a lot of this was pasture, she's probably doomed to find mostly barbed wire or fencing pieces, but one spot would be a better choice. "The church that burned was there for nearly two hundred years and was also used as a schoolhouse at some point. It isn't safe inside, but you could search the perimeter."

"You don't mind me digging on your land? I'll refill the holes, of course."

"Anywhere but the graveyard," I tease.

"Graverobbing was not part of the plan." The flames illuminate her pensive face as she pauses, then adds, "That reminds me. I still need to return your cooler that you brought the peaches in." I'm baffled by how those two things are related and my silent contem-plating stare makes her look up from the fire and ask, "What?"

"I'm trying to figure out why graverobbing would remind you of my cooler."

Her eyes land on mine and she starts to speak, falters, then drags her teeth over her bottom lip. "I don't know…I'm high."

"You're also full of shit."

She looks me in the eye and her little embarrassed grin is fucking adorable. "Okay, fine. I kept seeing you go into the graveyard and then you left a cooler on my porch. I may have had a moment that I worried it could be, you know, an arm or something."

Nothing can prevent the laughter from pouring out of me. Her lips twitch, fighting back a smile as she crosses her arms and stares at me. Her confession is so unexpected and unhinged, but it's not only that. "Let me get this straight. You suspected that I may have left you a cooler full of scavenged body parts, and then you made me a cobbler."

"Well, it wasn't body parts!"

"And followed me into the graveyard days later."

Her shoulders shake when she can't fight her laughter anymore. "I'm a weirdo, Arlow. It's better you find out now if we're going to be friends."

I want to find out everything about her. I want to know every angle and edge of her. What she thinks and how she feels, why she's so fascinating to me, and most of all, why a few minutes near her fixed the worst artistic block of my life.

"That's okay, I'll be the normal one in the friendship."

She snorts and takes the stick from me to poke at the fire. "Somehow, I doubt that. What do you like to do when you aren't beekeeping or tending to the boneyard? Do you have other hobbies?"

"Sure, let's see, there's taxidermy, funeral photography, and my amateur tooth collecting group meets monthly."

"Great, you can stuff the squirrel that won't stay out of my bird feeders," she chuckles.

"I fish and hike. I'm just getting the hang of gardening after a few years of trying." Shrugging, I rest my foot on my knee and lean back. "I like to draw."

"That's cool. I have zero artistic talent. What do you draw?"

"Nature mostly, just sketches and scribbles. What do you do for fun?"

She sighs and props the stick against the firepit. "I've recently been looking for new hobbies. You saw my beginner crochet abomination, but I haven't given up on that yet. I'd like to learn an instrument, but I can't decide which one. I like to read, and I go to a lot of concerts." Her expression fills with joy. "That's my favorite thing. I have a group of friends that I met online years ago. We meet up at different music festivals and concerts. I saw Blue Orbit a couple of months ago."

Blue Orbit is one of my favorites, though I haven't seen them in concert. I haven't been to a live show since I was in my early twenties. "Have you heard their latest album? They went in a different direction."

"I have! I love it. I can't wait to hear it live," she says, beaming at me.

"Is that the genre you prefer? Rock?"

"Indie rock, some folk rock and blues. Some of the hard stuff is good, but I'm not really into metal. How about you?"

"I listen to a little bit of everything except country."

We spend a good hour discussing our favorite bands and songs before the conversation switches to books we've read and shows we've watched. By the time we've relit and smoked the remainder of the joint she brought, it's almost midnight. The evening hours that can often torture with the way they drag have moved by effortlessly. Too quickly.

I could spend forever here, listening to her laugh light up the night.

————

My day starts with a call I've been waiting for but always dread. "Mr. Shaw?"

"This is him."

"I'm calling from Doctor McAllister's office with your test results."

I want to believe her peppy voice means good news, but I've been fooled before. She can give devastating news in that same tone. "I'm ready," I sigh, and the seconds seem to stretch out as the sound of papers shuffling fills the brief silence.

"The ultrasound results look good. There's some minimal regurgitation that the doctor said he talked to you about before, but it hasn't progressed. We'll continue to monitor but he isn't concerned at this point. Everything looks the same as it did on your last visit."

"That's good," I breathe, relieved.

"Yes, it is. I've called in your prescription refill. Continue it as usual. You know the routine by now. Moderate exercise is fine but nothing too strenuous, and if you have any symptoms or anything changes, let us know. Otherwise, we'll see you in six months."

After thanking her, I call my mom to set her mind at ease as well, then head outside into the bright afternoon sun. There's nothing that needs to be done today that can't be put off until tomorrow. I'm just going to enjoy the day.

My intention was to take a walk through the woods, but the sight of Calli turns my steps in her direction. She leans against the huge trunk of a tulip poplar tree behind her cabin, holding her metal detector. Shadows shift and dance across her face, courtesy of the sunlight filtering through the foliage as she holds a hand over her mouth. The sound of laughter leaks through her fingers and cloaks the soft crunch of my footsteps, allowing me to remain unnoticed.

The sight of her joy is as beautiful as she is. My opportunity to admire her discreetly is cut short by my laugh when I see what has her so amused. A few yards away, at one of her bird feeders, a squirrel desperately tries to climb the pole. Its tiny paws scrabble at the slick surface, but only halfway up, it begins to slide back down. Her head whips around, and she beams at me.

Christ, look at her. Tendrils of sun-streaked hair float on the slight breeze as pale blue eyes meet mine, gleaming the gray of burnished metal in the light. The way she makes me feel is almost indescribable. I'm so drawn to every inch of her. Her laugh lightens something inside of me, loosens my chest and brings a smile to my lips every time I hear it. She makes me long for things I've long ago given up.

"I greased the pole," she snickers. "Watch."

The squirrel tries again and after hitting that halfway mark, starts to slip again. Instead of scrabbling for purchase this time, it simply holds tight and makes a steady descent.

"I didn't know a squirrel could look defeated," I remark as it gives its bushy tail a swish and ambles away. "But that one looks devastated. I'm a little embarrassed for him."

"He has a whole forest he can forage without terrorizing my birds." She glances over at me. "What are you up to today?"

"I was going to take a walk. Have you found any treasure?"

"I don't know who lived here before, but they must've thought planting bottle caps would grow more beer because those bastards are everywhere. I was heading back to the creek. Want to try it out?" she asks, holding the detector up.

"Let's go."

A smile bursts across her face, and she hands it over, then picks up the small shovel. We head down the trail, in silence for a bit until she asks, "What do you do in the barn all night?" She responds to the look of surprise on my face with a sheepish shrug. "I'm not spying on you. I see the light still on when I get off work sometimes."

"Sweat mostly. I should get the air conditioner fixed."

Her flash of a smile is half-hearted, but she doesn't pursue it. I don't like how her expression changes, her posture tensing up as we walk. In her silence, I can almost feel the anxious thoughts running scenarios in her head. She once suspected my cooler contained body parts so who knows what horror she's dreaming up.

"Hey." Her steps halt when I do. "It's nothing nefarious. I told you I like to draw. I work on art projects in the barn. It's just something I prefer to keep private."

"I understand. I didn't mean to be intrusive."

"You weren't. I didn't mean to creep you out."

"You don't creep me out." Squinting as a thin ray of sun sneaks through the canopy to hit her face, she looks up at me. "You have a really calming presence. Has anyone ever told you that?"

It might be the best compliment I've ever received. "I can't say they have."

"You do. My anxiety always seems to disappear when I'm around you."

She has no idea the effect she's had on me in the short month since she moved next door. It wasn't just the creative block. She cured a loneliness I wasn't even aware of.

The way she's gazing up at me—her face so full of sincerity and vulnerability, a more beautiful muse has never existed. She's my inspiration and my friend, but the urge to taste her parted lips is almost irresistible.

Almost. "I enjoy being with you too."

A sweet, shy smile is her reply before we continue down the trail.

CHAPTER 9

CALLIOPE

I'VE BEEN WAITING FOR A CLEAR DAY TO PAINT THE GLIDER I BOUGHT AT the flea market and the opportunity finally comes. The base coat of cloudy gray is finished and dry, but the next part may not be as easy as I thought.

When Arlow approaches, I'm happy to set the stencils aside to get the pie he's coming after. For a little over two months, we've been spending time together. On most of the nights that I'm not working, midnight finds me with him, either at the firepit on the hill or lounging on one of our porches. Occasionally, we get high or have a drink. Sometimes we talk until the sky begins to lighten, and sometimes we just relax in silence, enjoying the stars.

"How's it going?" he asks.

"I think I've been too overconfident in my abilities." I get to my feet, brushing off the seat of my jeans. "I was going to paint some simple vines and use these stencils to add flowers."

"What's the problem?"

"I have no talent."

He snorts out a laugh. "You just need some practice."

"You didn't see the part I painted over already. I'm done for today anyway. Silver is supposed to be coming by with someone to snake out my clogged bathtub." Thunder rumbles in the distance despite the sunny sky. So much for the clear weather forecast. "Will you help me move this to the porch?"

"Of course." Arlow grabs the opposite end of the glider. Between the two of us, it isn't heavy, just cumbersome.

"Your pie is on the kitchen table. Blueberry this time."

"Thank you," he says, ducking inside to retrieve it. When he returns there's a tinge of blue on his lips.

"You already took a bite," I chuckle, sitting down on the top step.

"You have no proof of that." He takes a seat beside me, scooting the plastic pie carrier away when I reach for it.

Ugh that grin. He's adorable. All ruggedly scruffy, pretty eyes and white lashes shining in the sun. His hair has grown to just past his ears, giving it that sexy messy look.

A sudden wind strips a few leaves from the tree, and one lands on his head. It sits there like a bird perched in his hair. With a silent chuckle, I pluck it off him, my leg pressing against his. The cute smile that usually appears when he's amused is nowhere in sight. His lips are slightly parted, and he studies my mouth for a long moment before gradually lifting his eyes to meet mine.

Tiny wings beat inside my chest and my cheeks grow warm under his gaze. Those eyes, my god. So soft but flickering with heat. I can only imagine the passion that lives behind them. He reaches up to tuck a lock of hair behind my ear, letting his fingertip trail over the back of my lobe and down my jaw.

Neither of us have the ability to tear our eyes away. My heart is beating a crazy rhythm as I reach up to run my fingers through his scruff, brushing over the white patch. His chest rises with a deep breath at my touch. We're both caught up in something out of our control, this visceral reaction that separates us from the world and leaves only a desperate desire. His restraint is visible as his throat contracts on a hard swallow. It vanishes the moment I lean in and catch his bottom lip in a tentative kiss.

It's quick, soft, and so sweet, sending an ache through my chest. Before I can put an inch of space between our mouths, he slides his hand behind my neck and pulls me back in. A tiny hum escapes me when his tongue slips in to brush mine, tasting faintly of blueberries. My entire body lights up as he deepens the kiss, and I wrap my arm around him.

Our surroundings fade and time slows, stretching the seconds of pleasure. Oh, he can kiss. I'd be happy to live in this moment forever, consumed by him. We break apart and intense eyes look into mine. As my heartbeat calms, all I see is the same desire he must be witnessing in my gaze.

For a second, I think he's going to kiss me again. Instead, he takes a deep breath and scrubs his palms over his face, leaving behind an expression that drains any hope that this is going to go well.

"Calliope." My name comes out with a sigh, dripping with regret. He gets to his feet and steps off the porch into the yard as if he needs to put as much space between us as possible.

My face heats with embarrassment. Did I imagine the way he looked at me or read too much into it? "I'm sorry, I thought you—"

"Don't apologize...I got caught up in you—in the moment," he stutters, correcting himself. "But I can't."

This is so awkward and uncomfortable, something I've never felt with him. "I understand." It's hard to keep the disappointment out of my voice but I do my best. "It's okay."

At the sound of a motor, we both turn to see Silver's truck coming up the driveway, a white van right behind her.

Arlow forces an uneasy smile. "I should go." He takes a few slow steps. "I'll see you later."

"Sure."

By the time Silver and the plumber's van park in front of the cabin, he's almost back to his house. An older guy with wild, curly gray hair approaches with Silver.

"Hey Calli, this is my uncle Lou, the plumber I told you about."

"Nice to meet you."

"You too. It's the tub that's backed up?" he asks, getting right down to business.

"Yes, I've tried one of those plastic zip tools and got some hair out, but it still takes hours to drain."

He nods and holds up a tool. "Let's give the drum auger a shot at it. Have you used any caustic liquids? Drain cleaner?"

"No."

"Good, good," he mumbles, and follows us inside. Once he's working, Silver pulls me back out onto my porch.

"Okay, what did we interrupt? You look upset. Are you alright?"

"I'm an idiot," I sigh, flopping into one of my chairs.

Silver sits across from me. "I'm going to need more information than that."

"I kissed Arlow."

Her eyebrows bounce, and she sits up straight. "Oh."

"He's so sweet, and the way he looked at me, I thought..." I shake my head. "I was wrong."

"He didn't kiss you back?" she suggests softly.

"He did, and it was so good. But it was followed by instant regret, like he suddenly realized what he was doing. We've been spending all this time together and I read too much into it, I guess. He was being kind and I thought it was something more."

"Did he say anything?"

"He said he got caught up in the moment with me. Then he just said he can't."

"That's it?"

"Well, you guys showed up. Good timing, by the way because things were awkward as hell."

"I'm sorry. Him kissing you back like that, it sounds like he's into you too. Maybe there's something else going on with him."

"Maybe. It doesn't matter. It isn't what he wants and that's okay, but I really hope I haven't ruined our friendship."

"I'm sure you can smooth things over if you talk to him and let him know you're happy staying friends."

Arlow is reasonable, along with his kind nature. Silver's right. "I will. I just need a little time for the rejection and embarrassment to fade."

"You had to try to know," she points out, then tilts her head, thinking. "Maybe he's gay."

"He doesn't have to be gay to not be interested in me," I laugh, and she beams.

"Well, you're hot! Plus, you're fun and crazy enough to follow the guy into a graveyard, for fuck's sake. He should be beating down your door for a chance."

Giggles spill out of me. "At least I know I have one friend."

"Absolutely. Don't kiss me, though. I've been known to hop over to the other side of the fence, if you know what I mean, but the grass isn't always greener there either."

"Don't worry. I am regrettably only attracted to men. It's a terrible affliction to be born with."

She looks across the driveway as if she might be able to see him through his walls. "Good kisser, huh?"

"I guarantee that man is good with his tongue everywhere."

Talking and laughing with Silver makes me feel better. It's going to be fine. Stuff like this happens. It was just a kiss.

Silver and I hang out for a little while after her uncle unclogs the drain and leaves. It's nearing sunset when she takes off to meet her boyfriend. Arlow comes out of his front door when I'm heading inside. It's the time of night that he'd usually go to the firepit and gesture for me to accompany him, but he doesn't even glance my way. Instead, he starts through his yard toward the graveyard.

Maybe he wants some solitude tonight. After all, he doesn't always ask me to go with him. Should I wait? No, I need to get this over with or I'll procrastinate and make it harder. I'm going to clear the air and then I'll leave him alone.

He's out of sight by the time I have my door locked. My steps are hurried along by a rumble of thunder and the increasing wind. If he's at the firepit, he won't be there long. I'm in such a rush that I almost don't see him and pass him by. He's sitting on his little back porch, his phone to his ear.

With his back to me, I'm not in his field of view but his voice reaches me clearly.

"I'm sorry," he exclaims, to whoever is on the other end of the call. "I know that doesn't mean shit, but I am. Every fucking day, Melody, I'm so sorry. I wish I could talk to you, tell you in person. Instead of talking to this fucking machine every time I call." His angry tone is shocking to hear.

I shouldn't be listening to this. I need to go, but my legs won't seem to cooperate. It never occurred to me there was someone else. He's never mentioned anyone. His tone is sharper and louder than I've ever heard it, but it rattles with despair as he hangs his head. "I wish you could forgive me. I'd give anything to go back and change things. Anything to have you back."

I can't. His simple declaration makes sense now. He's heartbroken over an ex, one that won't speak to him by the sound of it. If I'd known, I wouldn't have kissed him. Being a rebound is never fun.

"Fuck!" he shouts, tossing his phone aside. It clatters across the porch and topples over the edge into the grass as he lays his head in his hands. His pain is so palpable, it puts a knot in my throat. My first impulse is to go to him, comfort him, but I doubt he wants to see me right now or know what I overheard. Instead, I quietly retreat. Tomorrow, I'll talk to him. He doesn't need me propositioning him or pursuing any kind of romance. What he needs is a friend.

———

Arlow wouldn't leave my mind last night. The way he kissed me. The agony in his voice later. Both haunted me into my dreams. He's become important to me, and I need to know things are going to be okay between us.

His truck was gone when I finally dragged myself out of bed and he hasn't been home all day. To add to my growing anxiety, my phone rings with a call from the private investigator.

"Calli, how are you?" he greets.

"I'm doing fine. Yourself?"

"Can't complain. I'm calling to ask if your father was known to use any aliases?"

He still hasn't located him then. My body relaxes with equal parts disappointment and relief. At least it's not the call I'm dreading. "Not that I know of."

"Do you recognize the name Harold Raines?"

"That was his brother's name. He died when I was a kid."

"Okay. Since you advised us that he usually lives in hotels, we've worked our way through them. There are records of him in a few in the city, but nothing for the last two years. The Express Inn on the east side of the city evicted him. A lot of these hotels share a blacklist of those who owe them, and that may have prevented him from getting another room under his real name. There's a record of a Harold Raines at more than one hotel. The same name could be a coincidence, or he could be using his brother's name to get a room somewhere."

"That makes sense."

"It's the best lead we have at the moment, but I wanted to check in with you before we pursue it."

"I appreciate it. Yeah, keep looking. Whatever it takes."

Not dead, I tell myself after we hang up. My gaze settles on the cardboard urn sitting on the edge of the fireplace mantel. I'm going to find him. I want to tell him Mom's dead and give him the gift of the same relief I felt when I got that email to pick up her ashes.

The same ashes I can't seem to get rid of. The urge to snatch it up and go flush them down the toilet hits me, but that's not something I want to explain if it clogs. Hey, sorry, dumped a bitch in the toilet.

Arlow doesn't return by the time I leave for work and it's the longest night ever. Misty was due to work with me, but she calls in sick. Silver is out of town with her boyfriend, and it's clear Mona is exhausted after working all day.

She's grateful when I assure her that I can get everything done and I don't mind doing it alone. Tonight, I prefer it. Ethan is working on prep but once Mona leaves, we both tuck earbuds into our ears and do our own thing. Without the second set of hands, it's nearly six in the morning by the time I put the last of the donuts in the display case. It feels weird to leave in the daylight.

Arlow's truck sits in his driveway. There's no sign of him but I'm not surprised. These are the hours we're both usually asleep. Talking to him will have to wait. The scent of fresh paint reaches me when I step onto the porch, and I stop in my tracks.

The glider is where I left it, but now green vines climb around the wooden slats. Bright yellow flowers grow along them, and every-thing is so detailed it looks like you could tug on the vines or pluck one of the flowers. This wasn't done with any stencil. He said he likes to draw. Scribbles, he called it, but this is beyond talented.

It's absolutely beautiful.

Tears fill my eyes. I could blame it on the lack of sleep and the long night, but that's not it. While I was worried that he may not want to be around me anymore, he was spending the night painting this for me. It's the sweetest thing.

Wiping my eyes, I head inside and crawl into bed, confident that things will be okay. After such a restless night before and a long night at work, I'm asleep as soon as my head touches the pillow.

The grating motor of a chainsaw wakes me, and it takes a few blinks to clear my bleary eyes enough to see the clock. Two in the afternoon. That's late even for me, but I needed it.

After dragging myself to the kitchen for a coffee, I check my phone to see a text from Mona, thanking me for staying late and telling me that Misty will be in tonight, so I won't be needed on my scheduled night off.

I need to shower and eat, but instead, I throw on some clothes and follow the sound of the chainsaw. Arlow doesn't see me at first. He sets the chainsaw aside and loads a chunk of wood into the log splitter. Sweat stains the sides of his shirt and beads on his forehead. No one could blame me for kissing a man who looks this sexy in the heat. I'm only a foot away by the time he notices me.

"Hey," he says. That deep soft voice seems to reach out and remind me that everything is alright.

"Hi, can you take a break?" He shuts off the splitter and turns to face me. "Someone left a masterpiece on my porch. Any idea who that might've been?"

His lips crease into an impish smile. "I didn't see anyone, but I'll keep my eye out."

"Seriously, Arlow, it's stunning. I love it. Thank you so much."

"You're welcome."

Wetting my lips, I spit out what needs to be said. "Listen, the other night, I misinterpreted things."

Before I can continue, his eyes land on mine and he shakes his head. "You didn't misinterpret anything, Calliope." God, the way my name rolls off his tongue. "I wanted to kiss you, but I shouldn't have." His hand travels up to rub the back of his neck and he sighs, looking away. "I'm not in a good place for anything romantic right now."

"I understand. You don't owe me any further explanations. It's not what you want."

"It's not what I can have." Sincerity shines in his eyes when he regards me. "I didn't want to hurt your feelings."

"You didn't. It was just a kiss. It's no big deal. I don't want things to be awkward between us." There's no way I'm going to forget a kiss that good, but he doesn't need to know that.

"I don't want that either."

"Still friends, then?"

"Of course. You can't get rid of me that easily."

"Okay, I'll let you get back to work." As I turn to leave, he calls after me.

"Bonfire tonight?"

"Absolutely. I'll even bring you an apple fritter."

CHAPTER 10

ARLOW

THE AWKWARDNESS CALLI FEARED WOULD COME BETWEEN US NEVER materializes. It took everything in me to walk away after that kiss. I'm not capable of staying away from her. This week, we've spent an evening at the bonfire, talking the late hours away, and she made me dinner a few nights ago—a thank you for the glider.

It's just past dark when she taps on my door. "Okay," she says, without the preamble of a hello. "I'm completely embarrassed about this but there's some kind of mutant hopping bug in my bathroom."

"Do you want to borrow the bee suit?" I tease.

"Very funny. It jumps like a coked up kangaroo and is almost as big. It could tackle me." A sheepish smile is accompanied by a shrug. "Will you please kill it?"

That smile could convince me to do anything. "Come on."

"Thank you," she says, as I pull my front door closed and accompany her back across the driveway. "You might want to bring some bug spray or a hammer, maybe a flamethrower."

"What's it look like?" I'm trying to figure out what kind of bug she could be talking about.

"Like a spider fucked a cricket in a pool of radioactive material."

I'm pretty sure what she's dealing with is a harmless cave cricket and my suspicions are confirmed when I step into her bathroom. Calli is right behind me. Until it leaps from one end of her tub up to the sink.

"Nope," she announces and darts back out.

To be fair, it is one of the largest ones I've seen. Before it can jump again, I scoop it up and carry it into the living room. "Will you get the door?" I hold up my cupped hands. "Unless you want to pet him first."

Calli looks at me in horror. "You didn't kill it?"

"There's no reason to. I'll let it go outside."

She opens the door and steps back. "Far, far away. Maybe take it for a ride on your ATV."

Distant lightning flashes, outlining the edges of approaching clouds as I take it out to the tree line and let it go.

"What was it?" Calli asks, standing on her bottom step as I return.

"A cave cricket. Some people call them sprickets. They can't hurt you. They like damp places and find their way inside when we have prolonged dry periods like we have lately."

"It's supposed to storm all night. The bastard could've waited instead of interrupting my margarita night." She grins at me. "Thanks."

"Anytime. Margarita night, huh?"

"Silver was supposed to be bringing her best friend over. I was two drinks in when they cancelled. I thought I'd sit out here, have another and watch the storm. Do you want to join me? I also have some bourbon."

My plans to spend the night working disintegrate. "What kind of friend would I be if I let you drink alone?"

"A boring sober one." She leads the way back inside. I'm not a big fan of sweet drinks so I take her up on the offer of bourbon. Frowning, she holds up the nearly empty bottle. "There are only a few shots left. I thought I had more."

"I have a bottle at home we can grab later."

I've been in her cabin plenty of times, but we never usually hang out here. While she's making her margarita, I wander around her living room. She has a nice vinyl collection, and her bookshelf shows she prefers fiction. Thrillers, mysteries, and horror novels are joined by a few romances and some poetry.

A cardboard urn sits on the far side of the fireplace mantel, but it isn't really displayed, just shoved behind a picture of a man leaning against the hood of his car. The resemblance in the picture is hard to miss. I'm very familiar with that smile.

"Is this your dad?" I ask, as she joins me.

"Yes About twenty years ago."

"You smile the same as him." The remark seems to please her. "Is he…"

She shakes her head when I gesture toward the urn. "No, he's not gone. Those are my mother's."

"I'm sorry."

"Don't be. She despised me." The words are tossed carelessly but the weight they hold is evident. "It's raining. Let's sit on the porch." We settle onto the glider, and she changes the subject. "Did you get Lee's truck fixed?"

"We did. It was the alternator. He could've done it alone. I think he just wanted an audience."

"Your company is in such demand. You poor guy," she teases.

The sky opens up and torrential rain pulls a thick curtain around the porch. Both of us fall silent, sipping our drinks.

Calli glances over at me. "I love this." Her eyes shine with the glaze of alcohol, but it's not the drink she's talking about or the rain. It's the moment, and I know exactly how she feels. Closed off from the world, just the two of us, buzzed and surrounded by the storm and the smell of wet forest. The scent is always so much stronger after a dry period.

"Me too. It's perfect."

Silence resumes but something shifts in her expression after a few minutes. Both of us have a tendency to get lost in our own thoughts, but this is different.

"Hey." My tone is soft, not jarring, but she regards me with vague surprise, as if she forgot I was there. "Are you okay?"

A forced smile dies quickly. "I'm fine. Just thinking."

"You can talk to me, you know. If there's something on your mind."

Her hesitation only confirms that something is bothering her. "You asked about my dad before. I told you that I hadn't heard from him in a while." My nod encourages her to go on. "It's been nearly two and a half years."

While I don't see my parents often, I can't imagine having no contact with them for so long. "Did you have a falling out?"

"No, it wasn't like that. There's never been any animosity between us. We were close when I was younger, but he has a lot of substance issues and while he was a safe person to be around, a lot of the people he surrounded himself with weren't. I haven't seen him in person in ten years. He moves constantly. We always kept in touch by phone every few months. Sometimes it would be longer because he goes through phone numbers like underwear, but mine stayed the same so he'd always end up calling me. But I had to change my number, and his was already disconnected. I figured I could still find him through his sister, but by the time I tried, she was in a nursing home with severe dementia."

The little waver in her voice breaks my heart. Her fingers wrap around mine when I take her hand, and she looks me in the eye for a second with a reticent smile. "I even reached out to my brother, Mark, that I hadn't had contact with in about ten years to see if he'd heard from him." Her gaze skips away as she adds, "Mark's in prison. Dad used to call him monthly and send him stuff, but it's been two years since he's had any contact from him. I've hired a private investigator and so far, no news is good news, but the longer it takes..." She shakes her head with a sigh.

This is the most she's told me about her family and there are about a thousand questions I want ask, but I'm not trying to upset her by prying too deep. We've spent hours talking about everything from music to whether the universe is really infinite, but any time her family came up, she shied away. Just tonight I've learned her mother hated her, her brother is an inmate, and her father is an addict. It's clear why she chose to avoid the subject.

"Have they traced his last phone number?"

She nods and finishes her drink. "It went dormant and then was recycled. He often lived in hotels so that's where the investigator is searching now. It doesn't help that I'm the most impatient person in the world," she says with a chuckle, leaning back. "And once I get stuck on something, it's hard for me to let it go. I had a dream that brought back a childhood memory of him. I need to know he's okay but also, I want to ask him about it."

"It's got to be hard not knowing."

She glances at my hand in hers with a tiny embarrassed smile. The alcohol put holes in the wall she's built around herself and she's just realized what's leaking out. She gives my hand a squeeze and releases it. "I didn't mean to bring the mood down."

"Don't be silly. Do you want to tell me about the memory?"

A sudden earsplitting crack of thunder interrupts me, making us both jump and grab each other. My arm is wrapped around her, and her face is hidden against my shoulder. She peeks up at me and bursts out laughing. "I almost pissed myself."

"That might've scared me sober," I agree with a chuckle.

She shifts so she's not facing me anymore, leaning against me while my arm remains around her. With the spell broken, I expect her to change the subject and I'm surprised when she continues.

"When I was five, we moved to a new neighborhood. My new school was a few streets away. Usually, Mom walked me to school and Dad picked me up afterward in his car. One day a snowstorm hit while I was at school. They released us early and called all the parents to come pick us up." A soft smile stretches her lips as she reminisces. "He probably figured walking would be faster than getting the car out because the ground was already covered, and snow was coming down fast. I was so excited to walk home in it.

"The wind was blowing hard, and he kept hold of my hand, our gloves smashed together. We were meant to stay on the road that runs beside the school and pass three streets before making a left onto ours, then our house was another block down. On a good day, it was a ten or fifteen minute walk. Except he got confused in the whiteout and we turned on the street before ours. It wasn't until we got about halfway down it that he stopped and realized the mistake.

"I was learning that a snowstorm wasn't always as fun as it looked. I can't remember if I complained or if he just knew my legs were exhausted from trudging through the snow, but he put me on his back. I held on while he walked us all the way to the end of the street, around the block and up the next street to our house. His sister was there with my mom, and I remember them laughing so hard when he announced we got lost.

"I don't know why I dreamed about it, but I'd forgotten it until a few months ago. It was one day that probably wasn't a big deal to him, but it must've imprinted on my young brain." With a sigh, she leans her head on my shoulder. "I want to ask him if he remembers carrying me home in the snow."

I tighten my arm around her in a half hug. "I hope you find him soon. If there's anything I can do…"

"You're sweet," she murmurs. "Thank you."

It's funny how you never know what's going to make a vivid impression and become a nostalgic memory. It just happens. There's no doubt in my mind that this will be a sweet moment I look back on, sitting with Calliope tucked against my side, wrapped in the darkness and music of the storm.

"What are your parents like?" she asks after a few quiet minutes.

"They're great. Mom was a nurse and Dad was an illustrator. They're both retired now and living in the same house I grew up in. My younger sister lives next to them with her husband and kids. They help her a lot with the babies—my sister had twins not quite a year ago. I don't see them often, but I talk to them every week. There's usually at least one baby screaming in the background."

Calli grins up at me. "Not a fan of kids?"

"Kids are fun. As long as they can go home."

She chuckles and drains the rest of her drink. "It's safe to say there are no little broody beekeepers running around out there then?"

"Broody beekeeper?" It beats Daddy Long Legs, I guess. "First of all, I do not brood."

"Whatever you say." I'm glad to hear her tone has lightened again.

"And secondly, I've had a vasectomy so no accidental babies for me."

"I don't want kids either. I'm enjoying my freedom. Did your dad teach you to draw?"

"He did when I was a kid, but we have pretty different styles."

Calli tilts her head, peeking over at me. "Will you show me one of your drawings sometime?"

"Will you take back that broody remark?" I tease.

Her lips press together as she pretends to think about it. "Mm, quiet introspective beekeeper doesn't have quite the same ring to it, but I'll think about it. It's an upgrade from where you started at Graveyard Creeper."

"Okay, Peach Bandit."

A smile leaps to her lips. "That could be a children's book. The Adventures of Graveyard Creeper and Peach Bandit."

"Peach Bandit looking for severed limbs in a cooler is probably a little intense for a kid's book."

"Everyone's a critic," she giggles, getting to her feet. "I need a refill. How about you?"

"You're out of bourbon. Make your drink and we can go to my place. I'll let you see a sketchbook while you're drunk so you'll be scathingly honest."

I follow her inside and wait while she blends the ingredients for her margarita. "Whoops, made way too much," she mumbles. "Oh well." She grabs a big glass and pours the drink in, filling it to the top. "Future Calli is going to hate me tomorrow."

When she excuses herself to go to the bathroom, I sneak back to her living room, pull out my phone and take a picture of the photo of her father.

"Ready," she announces, returning a moment later, and we start toward my place.

The rain has let up but not for long judging by the ring of dark, lightning filled clouds around us. The temperature is dropping quickly, so we forgo the porch for my living room.

She sits beside me on the couch, scooting closer when she sees I have the sketchbook in my hand. It's an older one that contains mostly preliminary sketches of landscapes. Some trees and flowers. The drawings of her are tucked safely away in another room. I'm not sure how she'd feel about them.

"Arlow!" Her sudden exclamation makes me blink and raise my eyebrows. "These are fantastic!" She takes her time flipping through the pages. "Scribbles," she grumbles. "You're ridiculous."

The warmth that grows in my chest as she admires my work should be concerning. I've never cared much what anyone thought of my art. It's an outlet for me and an income, not something I do to impress, but the way she looks up at me with her mouth slightly open in awe affects me more than any praise or criticism I've ever received.

"You're an artist." After a moment of thought, she adds, "Your unconventional job?"

"I sell some prints and originals." All my work is under a pseudonym. She won't be able to find anything online if she tries to look.

It's not the sketches of trees or flowers that catch her eye. The drawing she stops on is one of my favorites, one I never tried to sell. I couldn't imagine anyone else would see what I did, but as she gazes at it, something about it grabs her.

"Will you tell me about this one?"

With a nod, I take another drink of bourbon, letting the buzz loosen my tongue. Talking about my thought process for drawings always makes me sound crazy. "It's the storm drain in the curb at the end of my parents' street." She scoots closer to me and rests the sketchbook on one of her knees and one of mine. "Whenever it would rain too much too fast, one end of our street would fill up with water. All the dirt, tree limbs, leaves, and litter would get caught on the grates."

When I hesitate to think about my next words, she waits patiently, silently. "There was nothing wrong with the drain. It was doing its best, what it was designed to do, but the burden of the trash being thrown into it was too much." She nods as I run my fingertip over the empty Coke can, a plastic bag, a clump of leaves. "When I was a teenager, I saw something...relatable in it. In being overwhelmed, I guess. After every hard rain, I'd sit on the curb and watch the water struggle its way through until I cleared away the trash."

"You drew this as a teenager?"

"No, I drew it from memory. It kept coming back to me."

"Like the snowstorm with my dad?" she says softly.

"That's a sweet memory, a significant one. This was literally watching water pour through trash. I know it sounds crazy. It's not the easiest thing to explain, but objects or moments can stand out, shine in some way that sets them apart, no matter how mundane they might be. That's what I like to draw." Like to draw might be a bit of an understatement. It feels more like a compulsion.

Her lips tilt up. "The things that shine?"

"I know it sounds like bullshit," I chuckle.

"No." She shakes her head and looks me in the eye without a hint of amusement. "I understand. I have one of those moments too. I just don't have the talent or skill to draw it."

Now I'm intrigued. "Will you tell me what it is?"

"A broken orange juice bottle on a balcony." It's her turn to look a little chagrined. The alcohol has both of us opening up tonight. "You can't tell me that's not just as odd as your storm drain. I've thought about it, remembered it, since I was seven years old and have never really understood why." Her tongue wets her lips. "We were at Dad's apartment, a little two room hole in the wall with a sagging balcony. I couldn't sleep. There was no TV or cell phone or anything to occupy myself with. My brother was asleep and so was Dad—or passed out, maybe, because he wouldn't wake up when I tried.

"I was afraid and experiencing loneliness in a way I hadn't before. Things were awful at Mom's house, the divorce was recent and the loss of having Dad in our daily lives was still a fresh wound. It was the longest night ever. Alone with bad thoughts. Finally, the sun came up and I was so happy to see it. I grabbed my little bottle of orange juice from the fridge and went out on the balcony to watch the day come. When I set it on the ledge, it tipped off and shattered by my feet. I wasn't upset but I just stared at it for so long. It's a moment that's always stuck with me."

She sips her drink, thinking for a second, then continues, "I think it was the dichotomy of it. The crushing despair of thoughts with no distraction, a dark feeling like it was soaking into me, then the relief that the sun brought. The new experience of being up outside alone at the crack of dawn." Shrugging, she sits back. "But mostly I remember the moment staring at a broken bottle on the balcony. The thin sun catching in the jagged edges of the glass, how dew dampened everything, the smell of the air. Almost like I could step back into my second grade self for a few seconds." She tilts her head to look at me. "I've never told anyone that because it sounds so odd, to repeatedly picture a broken bottle for over twenty years."

"Like watching litter in a storm drain," I reply, nodding. My chest is tight with two realizations.

She sees the world like I do, like an artist, and I could fall in love with her too goddamned easily.

CHAPTER 11

ARLOW

It was nearly three a.m. when I walked Calli back to her cabin last night. After our talk about our families and memories, things lightened up. We ended up talking and laughing in my kitchen, eating French toast in the middle of the night. It doesn't matter if we're hiking in the woods, at a bonfire, or just sitting on one of our porches, I always have a good time with her. I need to keep things at a friendship level but it's getting difficult. Ever since she kissed me, I can't stop thinking about it, her fingers playing through my whiskers, the little moan she let out when my tongue brushed hers.

Fuck. Drinking around her isn't a good idea. My self-control is too tested by her when I'm sober, much less when I'm buzzed. It's not only because she's gorgeous. When we were sitting on her porch glider with her cuddled up to me, my arm around her, it felt so comfortable, so natural. She's a private person, like I am. Neither of us talk much about ourselves but the more she's opened up, the more I want to know everything about her.

For the first time, it feels like someone genuinely gets me. It's so gratifying but also heartbreaking because it makes me want things I can't have. As friends, we can keep some distance between us. I can't stand the thought of hurting her by letting things go any further. She's so sweet.

She's also the first thought in my head when I drag my eyes open just past noon. I need to work. I need to get focused on that and spend a little less time with her so these feelings will lessen. Scrubbing my face with my palms, I climb out of bed to shower and get ready for the day. My mouth is a desert, but at least I'm not hungover. After a quick meal, my intention is to spend the day in the barn, but that plan is halted when I step outside.

My truck sits parked in the driveway where it usually waits, but the driver's side window is shattered. Glass clings around the edges, outlining the gaping hole in the center. Déjà vu washes over me as I open the door to survey for other damage.

Handleman. Mom warned me that he was being released from prison.

No. There's no need to jump to that conclusion. Maybe this isn't even vandalism. The column doesn't look tampered with so stealing the truck wasn't the goal. The console and glovebox are closed, and a quick inspection shows nothing is missing. Not that a thief would want an aux cord, tire gauge, or some proof of insurance paperwork. The window has had a tiny chip in it for over a year. The temperature changes recently combined with the repeated opening and closing of the door may have weakened it. It's possible it broke from the storms last night.

My phone rattles in my pocket with a text from Lee.

LEE

I'm right down the road. Need to borrow your ladder so wake the hell up.

ME

I'm up.

He pulls into my driveway a couple of minutes later while I'm bringing out my shop vac. My truck is a mess. Everything is soaking wet inside and covered in crumbling fragments of glass.

"What the hell did you do?" Lee asks.

"I found it this way. From the storm last night, maybe, I don't know."

He does the same thing I did, scanning around for an obvious tree limb or something that could've bounced off it. "Was it hailing?"

"No." By the time I walked Calli home, the storms had passed leaving only rain. It's possible the window was already broken, and we didn't notice it in the dark. We were both drunk. "I can fix it, but can you run me to the auto parts store?" It's not my first time replacing a window. Handleman saw to that before.

"No problem. I'll help you get the new one in." Lee rubs his chin, studying the truck. "You don't think this was intentional?"

"I don't want to," I sigh.

"It's been a long time. Surely not."

"He got out of prison recently, but this could be a coincidence. The storm or some random asshole." I'd be a little more confident of that if something was stolen. "The ladder is behind the shed if you want to go ahead and grab it while I vacuum up the glass and water."

The shop vac works well for the glass, but it'll still need some time to dry out. Hopefully the auto parts store or junkyard will have the correct replacement window.

"You have company coming," Lee says as I'm wrangling in the extension cord.

Calli crosses the driveway, grabbing her hair in one hand when the wind whips it around her face. "Oh no, you too?"

"Was your car broken into?" Lee asks before I get the chance.

She nods and presses her lips together. "They busted out my window too. I had to call the police to get a report for my insurance company. That's what I was coming up to tell you so you wouldn't be alarmed to see a squad car at my house. They're supposed to be on their way."

"Did they take anything?" I ask.

"The knife out of my glovebox, the two twenty dollar bills I keep in the console for emergencies, and like five bucks in change, probably. Nothing worth breaking the damn window for. I should've just left the car unlocked." Frowning, she slides a hair tie off her wrist and pulls back her hair. "I'm too hungover for this shit."

I hate that she has to deal with it too, but it is a little bit of a relief. This was likely some assholes out robbing cars. "I'm sorry. We're going to go see if the auto parts store has a replacement. Come with us and I'll fix yours if you want."

"Thanks, but it's a new car with full coverage insurance. I pay them too much so they can deal with it. The cops might want to talk to you since it was both of us though." As if her words summoned him, a squad car pulls into the driveway, and she starts back down to her place.

A few minutes later, she returns with the officer, who gives my truck a cursory look. "We've had a rash of vehicle break-ins lately in town. She tells me you aren't missing anything?"

"No, there wasn't anything of value to take."

Nodding, he jots something down in his little notebook. "Give it forty-eight hours and you can pick up a report for your insurance company."

"That's not necessary."

"Suit yourself."

He nods at Calli, then walks back down the driveway to his car. As soon as he's gone, Calli looks at Lee. "I'm sorry to ask under the circumstances but could you please do me a favor? I need a ride to the county jail."

"You can't get the report for two days," Lee points out.

"Ah, yeah, not for that. I need to bail out my friend." She glances at me. "Silver got arrested last night. I'm not sure what exactly is going on, but she asked me to get her."

Lee looks over at me, biting back a smile. "Let's go. We'll swing by there first."

The county jail is right downtown. Lee and I wait in his truck while she goes inside. A few minutes later, she emerges with Silver right behind her.

Silver stops in her tracks when I climb out of the truck and hold the door open. "Did you have to bring your entourage to witness this?"

Calli chuckles and shrugs. "Someone vandalized our vehicles overnight. Luckily, Lee said he'd bring me to get you." Lee dips his head to look at her. "Lee, this is Silver, Silver, this is Lee, Arlow's bestie."

"I am a grown ass man, not a bestie," Lee growls as Silver climbs in and sits beside him.

"Well, thanks for the ride, not a bestie. I really appreciate it."

Calli gets in next, scooting as close to her as possible to give me room. "Where's your car?"

"At my house." She addresses Lee. "Over on Webb Avenue beside the park."

Lee smirks down at Silver. "What did you do?"

Silver grins at him and chirps, "Rearranged the balls and teeth of a cheating asshole."

"Kyle cheated on you?" Calli exclaims, outraged, and Silver nods. "Do you want to tell me what happened or wait until we can talk privately?"

"No worries. I'm sure the whole town will know soon. You know how things spread. I'm not the lying, cheating bastard or whore in this situation so people can say what they want." Rage and pain battle for dominance in her voice and Calli reaches over to take her hand.

Silver takes a deep breath. "Remember how Sandra didn't want Kyle to move in with me? She failed to mention it was because it would be harder for her to keep fucking him. She was supposed to meet me at my house when I got off work yesterday so we could head to your place for margaritas. Business was slow at the diner, and I was able to leave a bit early. Sandra was already at my house even though I hadn't told her to come yet, but I didn't think much of it. We've been friends for almost ten years for fuck's sake. I figured she was excited to have a night out since she rarely has a babysitter, so she showed up early."

She points out her house to Lee and he parks in the driveway beside her huge fenced yard.

"Did you catch them, like…in the act?" Calli asks as we exit the truck.

Silver scoffs, "It was a fucking act all right. That bitch was moaning and hollering while she rode him on my couch. Sounded like a fake ass porno."

"I'm so sorry," Calli tells her and grabs her in a hug. "What can I do?"

She hugs her back and wipes her eyes quickly. "Help me throw his shit in the yard?"

"Hell yes, let's do it." Calli turns to me and Lee. "Thanks for bringing us. I'm going to stay with Silver. I'll deal with my car later."

Lee shakes his head in unison with me as I argue, "You don't know if he'll come back here. It might not be safe." I'm not leaving her here in the middle of some domestic fight that could get out of hand.

"Both of my brothers are on their way to spend the night with me. They'll be here any minute," Silver assures us.

"We'll stay until they arrive." I glance over at Lee who nods his agreement. It's not that these two couldn't take care of themselves but you never know how situations like this might go. Especially after a fight and a night in jail.

Silver thanks us and invites us inside but we hang around by Lee's truck instead to keep an eye on things while Calli goes in with her.

Lee leans against his bumper, then grins over at me. "Your neighbor has made your life much more interesting. Vandalism, a jail pickup and bodyguard duty in only a few hours."

"None of that is her doing."

"I didn't say it was a bad thing. You need some excitement."

"Your most exciting day is fishing," I point out. Before he can reply, the upstairs window screeches open and random items begin to fly out. A gaming system topples end over end before hitting the ground and bursting like an egg. Clothes, personal items and electronics pile up.

"That is not a woman to cross," Lee remarks with a tinge of admiration in his voice.

"Fucking her best friend in her living room. Can't blame her."

A car parks on the street in front of the house and a woman gets out. "What the fuck do you think you're doing here?" Silver shouts, charging out the door as she approaches. Calli is right behind her and catches up to them in the yard.

"I'm sorry. It just happened."

Lee glances over at me as we both realize this must be Sandra.

"Really? It just happened? That's the best you've got? Oops, sorry, I accidentally got my pussy out and it jumped on his dick."

"I wasn't trying to hurt you—"

"How long?" Silver demands. "Don't even try to lie and tell me it was only the one time. How long have you been fucking him?"

She shakes her head. "I'm sorry. You don't understand. I love him." Silver glares at her until she answers her question. "Six months."

"You're a sorry piece of shit and so is he. Get the fuck out of my face. Tell him his shit is in the yard and whatever is still here by tomorrow will be ashes."

Sandra's tearful attitude shifts and she glares back. "You knocked out his front tooth!"

"Good," she snorts, while Calli covers a smile.

"Maybe if you'd paid more attention to him instead of spending all your time at the diner, he wouldn't have needed to look somewhere else."

Oh, this is about to get ugly. Calli's glare is as fiery as Silver's.

Silver puts a little space between them, her restraint clear in her action. "You're lucky I can't afford to pay bail again."

"I can," Calli declares and abruptly punches Sandra in the eye.

The shock on Sandra's face rips a laugh from me as I rush to get between them because I sure didn't see that coming either. Calli calmly watches from my side as blood wells from a split in Sandra's eyebrow. She doesn't try to go after her again, and Sandra doesn't retaliate. She's too busy holding her eye and backing away.

"Don't you even *think* about calling the police again," Silver warns her. "I have screenshots of all the dirty sexts you sent him. If you press charges on Calli, I'll print flyers and pass them out at church. You fucking *know* I will."

Bursting into tears, Sandra turns and rushes to her car while Silver shouts after her. "I hope he whistles through that gap in his teeth every time he bends your skanky ass over!"

Lee glances over at me. "This was definitely more entertaining than fishing."

CHAPTER 12

CALLIOPE

Arlow taps on my door shortly after Silver drops me off. He and Lee left after Silver's brothers showed up, but I didn't want to leave her when she was so upset. It's been a long day and it's not nearly over since I'm supposed to work tonight. I see a lot of coffee in my future.

"I'm sorry you guys got dragged into that earlier," I tell him, as soon as he's inside.

"No need to apologize. I'm glad to see you aren't locked up."

He follows me to my kitchen while I retrieve an ice pack from my freezer. I've ignored my aching hand until now since no skin was broken but my swollen fingers have developed their own heartbeat. "I think she knew Silver was serious about her threat."

"Did you hurt your hand?" he asks with concern.

"It turns out that eye sockets are not soft."

He takes a seat beside me at my little kitchen table, turning the chair to face mine and pulls the ice pack away from my hand. "Is anything broken? Can you move your fingers?"

"I'm okay. Nothing's broken. I think I jammed them."

The ice pack is set aside, and he slides his hand beneath mine, letting my fingers extend over his large palm. He takes hold of my pinky and gently bends, then straightens it. His hands are warm, and his touch is tender as he repeats the action for each of my fingers. It feels so intimate. I'm caught up in his gaze, those gorgeous brown eyes the rich color of autumn leaves. It takes me a moment to realize he asked me a question.

"Hmm?"

"Can you bend them all?"

Slowly, I make a fist then open it with a wince. His lips press together, and he takes my hand again, running his thumb softly over my knuckles. "You bruised it good."

The deep timbre of his soft words and the simple touch shoves everything else away. Someone could hammer my other hand right now and I'd barely notice. My mouth dries out and when our gazes meet again, I can see I'm not the only one affected.

His eyes darken as his pupils grow, and my attention falls to the way his tongue slips out to wet his lips. The memory of our kiss is still fresh in my mind and there's nothing I want more than to lean over and feel those lips on mine again.

The air thickens around us. He's so close to me. I'm suddenly aware of his knee touching my outer thigh as I breathe in the clean scent of him combined with the faint undertone of wood smoke from his jacket.

Seconds tick away.

He closes his eyes for a moment, then pulls in a deep breath and retrieves the ice pack, resting it on my knuckles. "I'll get you an Ibuprofen." The chair scrapes against the floor as he gets up.

"I took one already. But if you don't mind, you can grab the pitcher of cold brew from the fridge for me. I need a boost before work." My smile is as forced as my light tone.

"You're working tonight? With a sore hand and busted window, it might be a good time to take a night off."

"I'll be fine. Misty is picking me up. If I don't go, Silver will have to cover for me, and you saw what kind of day she's having."

Arlow sets a glass in front of me and fills it with ice and coffee. "She needs a good friend like you."

Yeah, that's me, a good friend.

The bitter sarcasm in that thought is unfair, born from frustration at not getting what I want, and it's the kind of gut reaction that I don't let myself ruminate on anymore. "That's sweet of you to say."

Arlow might not be ready to move on from his ex but there's something between us. Maybe in the future, things will be different. For now, I need to accept that we're only friends and let that be enough.

I spend a lot more time with Silver over the next two weeks. She takes me to get my window repaired, and we stay at her place some nights when I'm not working. The betrayal of her friend hits her harder than the break-up and cheating. Maybe because we've come to expect that from men. With everything women go through, there should be a lot more loyalty between us.

I'm rolling out a batch of dough for cinnamon rolls and Misty is filling a tray of jelly donuts while Silver hangs out, chatting to us when someone knocks on the locked front door.

"Anyone else scheduled tonight?" Misty asks.

Silver frowns, shaking her head, and peeks out through the kitchen door. "It's Charlotte."

"Who's Charlotte?" I ask Misty once Silver has gone out to talk to her.

"She worked the overnight donut shift until about six months ago."

"Oh." I glance in the direction of the door, straining to hear the conversation but it only reaches us as mumbles. "You don't think this is like a disgruntled employee situation, do you?" It's past eleven at night, not the time you expect someone to show up.

Misty laughs, handing me the cinnamon. "No, Charlotte is nice as can be. And she wasn't fired or anything. She quit to take care of her grandmother who had cancer."

Silver spends fifteen minutes or so with Charlotte before returning. "How's she doing?" Misty asks.

Silver snatches a fresh donut hole and pops it into her mouth. "She's alright. Just got back in town. Her grandma passed a couple of weeks ago so she's looking for a job again. I told her to check with Secondhand Thrift and More. They had a sign up recently."

The conversation drifts to other things but I'm not paying much attention. I've requested a week off work to meet up with my concert friends for a music festival, and though Mona was fine with it, I know it leaves them short-handed. My friends tried to convince me to hit a few more concerts with them, travel with them for a few weeks as I've done before, but I didn't consider it since I have a responsibility here. I like working here, but I also hate the thought that I may be taking the job from someone who actually needs it.

"How long did Charlotte work here?" I ask Silver, a few hours later when we sit at the counter to take a break.

"Three years. We waited as long as possible to replace her, but with Misty needing more time off and everything, it was too much for me to handle alone."

"Was she a good employee?"

"She was. I told her if we get an opening, she'll be my first call. Eva on morning shift swears she's going to be a stay-at-home mom as soon as her husband gets out of jail next month, so that's a possibility."

We get back to work but I use the hours to think it over. My impulsive nature often gets the best of me. But I knew when I moved that I'd be trying different things. Jobs, hobbies, whatever. That was the point, to figure out what I want. I'm not sure what that will be, but I know I love living in the country. I'd love to learn to garden or maybe keep bees like Arlow does. This job was never a permanent plan and maybe I can help someone by letting it go.

Misty leaves about a half an hour before us. Silver locks up and as we're heading out to our vehicles, I pause and grab her arm. "So, um, would you want to hire Charlotte back if I quit?"

She blinks at me. "You don't want to work here anymore?"

"Don't get me wrong. It's been great and I love working with you, with everyone, really, but I don't need the job. I took it to meet people, make some friends and keep myself occupied. I've done that. She needs the income."

"Are you planning to leave town?"

"No! I love it here. I'll find a volunteer opportunity. Plus, I've been thinking of taking some classes at the community center. I don't want you to think I'm not grateful for the job but if Charlotte is capable, I think it'd be the right thing to do."

She leans against my car. "I wasn't telling you about her to make you feel guilty. We would've replaced her with someone regardless."

"I know that. It's not the only reason. I have other stuff I'd like to do too."

With a sigh, she nods. "She wants full time which means I'd get more of a break, and Misty can stay at part time. It would work, but are you sure? You do a great job too, and I'll miss scaring the shit out of you by tossing ice in the fryer when your back is turned."

"And I'll miss tilting the sink sprayer just right, so it blasts you when you turn it on, but if you think you're getting rid of me, you're crazy."

"I knew that was you!"

"Then why did you blame Ethan?"

Both of us burst into giggles. "Poor Ethan," she says. "Alright. I'll call Charlotte today."

I give her a quick hug and we promise to hang out soon.

It's still dark when I get home, but there's a strip of light coming from Arlow's barn. I haven't seen much of him the past couple of weeks. On the nights I've been home, he's been in his barn and hasn't invited me to hang out at the firepit like we used to. I'm beginning to wonder if he's purposefully avoiding me because I hit Sandra. He's such a laid back person, and he learned that's not always who I am.

Or is it because of the moment we had afterward in my kitchen? Whichever it is, I miss him. Since Silver is doing better, and I no longer have to work, I plan to catch up with him soon.

My eyes slam shut the second I crawl into bed, and I wake up in a good mood. I'm on my way out of my cabin to go shopping when I nearly trip over a package on my front porch. *Happy Birthday* is stamped all over it in bright colors. What the hell? It's nowhere near my birthday. A closer look at the label reveals the mailman made a mistake. It's Arlow's birthday?

I grab the box and cross the driveway to his house.

Arlow answers the door and the genuine smile he gives me loosens something in my chest. He isn't unhappy to see me. "This came to my house by mistake," I explain, as he steps out onto his porch. "Is it your birthday?"

"Not until Sunday. My parents always send me a box of my favorite cookies."

"The way to your heart is truly through baked goods."

"Guilty."

"Listen, um…about me punching Sandra. I don't want you to think I'm, you know…violent or a troublemaker or something. I didn't mean for you or Lee to get dragged into the drama that day. Nobody filed any charges or anything. Even the charges against Silver were dropped."

His grin grows the entire time I'm talking. He tilts his head, studying me. "Do you think I was bothered by that?"

I can feel my cheeks start to heat up. "I feel like you might be avoiding me a little and if that's why, I want you to know it's not a common occurrence. I don't go around hitting people."

His lips press together, and his expression softens as he sets the box on the ledge of the porch. "I didn't think anything like that. You didn't upset me in the least, Calli. I love that you stuck up for your friend. I can get caught up in my art sometimes and obsessed with a project. The time and days get away from me. I'm not trying to avoid you. I'm sorry if I made you think that."

"Don't apologize. I overthink. It's what I'm best at," I chuckle. "We're good, then?"

"Absolutely."

"Okay." It sucks to need such reassurance but it's a part of anxiety that never seems to give me a break. The conclusion I usually jump to is that I'm annoying people or pestering them. I'm still not convinced he didn't need a little break from me, but that's alright.

"Are you busy this evening?" he asks, picking the box back up, and I shake my head. "Would you like to have dinner with me and a friend?"

I'm a little surprised at the invitation. Lee is the only friend of his I've met. "Sure, sounds fun."

"Great. I'll text you later."

On my walk back down to my car, I consider how many times I've convinced myself that someone is sick of me only to find out it was in my head. In the past, I'd let people go or start avoiding them. A couple years of therapy taught me a lot, including that the simplest thing to do is to be direct and ask. It's humiliating if the answer is *yes, please leave me alone*, but it saves me a lot of stress.

As I'm pulling out of the driveway to head to the mall, Lee turns in, and I wave for him to stop, then roll down my window. I have an idea, but I'll need his help.

"Everything okay?" he asks.

"Yes, everything's fine." He listens to me explain with a growing smile, then gives me his phone number. If Arlow thinks I'm going to let his birthday pass without celebrating, he's crazy.

The mall is in a town nearly an hour away, but it's worth the drive. Along with some new clothes for myself, I find the perfect gift for Arlow in a tiny music store, and another hilarious one from a novelty shop. Most of my day is spent shopping, and I've only been home for a few minutes when Arlow texts me.

ARLOW

Do you like catfish?

113

ME

Love it.

ARLOW

Good, would you mind driving?

ME

Not at all. I'm ready when you are.

He shows up a minute later, and we head to my car. He catches me grinning as I watch him slide the passenger seat as far back as it will go, so he can fit comfortably. "Are you laughing at me?"

"I'd never."

"Uh-huh. Let's go shorty."

"Excuse me. Five foot seven is almost tall for a woman. Just because you have to duck when a plane flies over doesn't mean I'm short."

Laughing, he looks over at me. "Have you been saving that one?"

"Maybe." I've missed us teasing each other. "Where am I going?"

"Do you know Hatty's Seafood Shack?"

I turn out onto our road. "I know where it is, but I've never been there. Is your friend meeting us?"

"Earl is seventy-five and doesn't leave his house much. We'll pick up dinner and take it to his place."

His friend is a seventy-five-year-old man? "How did you meet him?"

"He sold me my hives a few years ago and taught me how to care for them. When I went to pick them up, his property was overgrown, and it was obvious he couldn't keep up with it anymore, so I cut it for him. He doesn't have much family or many visitors. I bring him dinner once a week to check in on him. Just a heads up, he's absolutely going to ask you all about yourself and try to get you to play cards."

How in the hell am I supposed to stop myself from falling for this man?

After we pick up the food, Arlow leads me through a winding

back road to a small house tucked into the woods. "That's Harvey," he says, as a dog circles the car, tail wagging. "He's friendly."

"He's adorable!" I exclaim, kneeling down to scratch the mutt behind the ears while Arlow carries our food.

His knock on the door is instantly met with a gruff voice calling out. "I already found Jesus! It ain't my fault if you keep losing him!"

"I brought company, old man. Behave yourself."

"Now you know that ain't happening," Earl says, opening the door and grinning at me as we enter. "Where did you find this pretty thing? Did you come with him voluntarily? Blink twice if you need help."

"No worries, I could take him down if I needed to."

Earl cackles, throwing back his head, and Arlow snorts while we walk to the kitchen. "As long as I'm not carrying a cave cricket?"

"Well, that's just cheating."

Arlow sets the bags down and gestures to me. "Calli, meet Earl, Earl, this is Calli."

"You're the one who moved into the cabin next door to him," Earl says, as Arlow retrieves plates and glasses from the man's cabinet.

"I am. It's nice to meet you."

"About time he brought you over. He talks about you all the time."

My heart leaps in my chest at the thought of that, and I do my best not to react. Instead, I turn to raise my eyebrows at Arlow with a little smirk.

"He's a dirty liar. Can't believe a word out of his mouth," Arlow says, handing me a plate of food.

"Too late. You're busted. You like me."

We eat in Earl's living room, and Arlow was right, the food is delicious. Greasy as all hell, but heaven just the same. Earl is one of those people who is unintentionally hilarious. Just the way he talks about the other seniors at the day center has me wiping tears away. As he and Arlow discuss everything from the honey harvest to the new bushes he's been planting, it's clear to see how fond Earl is of him.

After dinner, Earl leans over and asks, "Do you know how to play Rummy?"

"Are you going to get mad when I wipe the floor with you?"

His gravelly laughter fills the room, and he waves to Arlow. "Move the coffee table so we can all reach. Let me teach your girl some humility."

Arlow and I exchange a glance at the "your girl" remark but let it go. We spend another hour playing cards and he does indeed teach us both some humility. We never had a chance. Before we leave, Arlow excuses himself to use the bathroom.

Earl drops his voice, looking me in the eye. "That boy is crazy about you."

I'm not sure what to say to that. "We're just friends."

"Save that bullshit to fertilize your garden, my dear. You look at him like he's made of stars, and I see how he is since you've been around. Happier, less uptight. I know he's more closed up than a liquor store on a Sunday, but he'll get out of his own way eventually. Don't give up on him."

Arlow reappears before I can digest that, much less respond. "What are you whispering about?"

Earl is quick. "I asked her to stop wasting her baking skills on you when I would appreciate a pie so much more."

"Apple or cherry?" I ask, getting to my feet.

"Sweetie, I never met a pie I didn't like. Whatever you feel like making."

We talk for another minute before leaving, but Earl's words stay with me long after we're home and Arlow has gone to his barn. *Don't give up on him.*

I'm not giving up, but I'm respecting what he wants, which is friendship. Not someone lusting after him and hanging onto hope while pretending to be his friend. Despite what feels like some mixed signals when we're together, he said no when I kissed him. If it ever becomes more, the next move will have to come from him.

Arlow shows up at my place right on time. My little plan would've been a struggle if he hadn't accepted my invitation to go to the fall festival in town with me and Silver. I was pleasantly surprised that he agreed since he isn't the most social person.

I send a quick text to Silver and Lee, who are parked out of sight down the road, then excuse myself to finish getting ready while Arlow waits in my living room.

"Will you get the door?" I call, heading for the small pantry in the kitchen to retrieve the cake.

Arlow opens the door to see Silver, Lee, and another younger blond girl that must be Lee's sister, Lacey. "Happy Birthday!" Lacey cries.

Arlow spins around to see me holding the cake.

His lips twitch as he restrains a smile. "This is a birthday ambush."

"I think the word you're looking for is surprise. It's a birthday *surprise*." I hold up my finger. "And I didn't lie. We're going to the festival. After presents."

His attempt at a disapproving look fails, taken over by a smile as he shakes his head. "I'm going to kick your ass." His words are lightly spoken and the warmth in his eyes is mirrored in his face.

"Save it for after cake."

Lacey bounds over to me. "It's nice to meet you! This was such a great idea. So sweet! Arlow never lets us do anything for his birthday."

"I didn't really give him a choice. You might have to hide me later." It's true, but I wasn't going to let him spend his birthday in the barn. I asked Lee to bring anyone else who may want to help surprise him. He was happy to show up with his little sister.

Giggles burst out of her, and she turns to grab Arlow in a hug, then steps back to thrust a gift bag toward him. "Happy birthday, old man. Open mine first."

There isn't room for everyone in my kitchen, so the cake gets left on the table while everybody gets comfortable in my living room as Arlow pulls a bottle of whiskey out of the gift bag. "I didn't know what to get and Lee said that's your favorite one," Lacey explains.

Arlow grins at her. "It is. Thank you."

Silver hands him a white gift box, and he cracks up laughing when he removes the lid to find half a dozen huge apple fritters. "Calli told me you tear through these like a badger so they're twice the normal size."

"Fuck yeah," he exclaims, taking a bite of one. "Thank you."

Retrieving my gift for him from beside the coffee table, I hand it over. He grins at me from his seat on the couch while I stand nearby, suddenly a little self-conscious. "Is it peaches?" he teases.

"Very funny."

He pulls out a vinyl record I found at a little music store near the mall. It's a copy of one of mine that he admired. "Hey, this is great!" He beams at me. "I've been looking for this forever."

"I lucked into it in a little vintage record store in Owensboro." When he starts to set the bag aside, I add. "There's something else in there. In my defense, I'd already got the record but once I saw it, I couldn't pass it up." It hung on the end of a rack of shirts at the entrance to a novelty shop and it was too perfect.

He bursts out laughing, then holds up the tee shirt for everyone to see. It's the brightest shade of godawful yellow and dotted with tiny bees that surround the words, WARNING, SEXY BEEKEEPER, scrawled across the front.

"You don't actually have to wear it," I assure him as he gets up and catches me in a hug.

"Are you kidding?" He shrugs off his hoodie, turns his back to us, and pulls his shirt off. It's only a few seconds before his broad back is covered again by the beekeeper shirt, but my eyes stay glued to his skin the entire time. I have to stop lusting after this man because getting turned on over a glimpse of a back is absurd. I feel like some man getting a peek at a Victorian woman's ankle. So ridiculous.

"You are not wearing that to the festival," Lacey exclaims with a giggle.

"The hell I'm not."

We all decide to wait for cake until we return and get ready to go. "Anyone want a shot before we go?" I offer.

"I'm designated driver," Lacey says, regretfully, glancing at her brother.

"Oh, are we getting fucked up?" Silver looks over at me.

"You know you're welcome to crash here if you do."

"There's supposed to be a beer garden. I'm not going to this thing to browse the pumpkin patch," Lee replies.

Arlow pulls out a package of edibles and offers them to everyone. Silver and Lee accept one, but I hesitate over the bright, sugar-coated candy being held out to me.

"Are you not an edible girl?" Arlow teases.

My gaze skips up to his. "I mean, I've never had any complaints." Jesus Calli, stop flirting with him. "But they usually hit me hard and make me tired."

Lee, Silver and Lacey have checked out of the conversation and are heading out my front door.

"These are sativa, energizing. If you want to try one, I'll keep an eye on you," he offers.

"It's your birthday. You're not supposed to be babysitting."

"Can't think of a better way to spend it." His soft words reach inside of me, driving up hope that doesn't belong there.

Friends, friends, friends.

I pluck the gummy from his palm, tear it, and chew half. "If I freak out in the haunted house, it's all your fault."

"I'll smash those costumed teenagers out of your way."

The edible hits me about thirty minutes later, and he was right. Instead of feeling near comatose, a wonderful light euphoric sensation washes over me. We start at the beer garden where Arlow, Lee, and Silver grab drinks. I learned long ago that I can't mix alcohol and weed in any form. It causes instant puking. It doesn't matter. I feel great as we listen to a local band play for a while, then laugh our way through the haunted house, and walk around to play some little carnival games.

Lacey pauses by a bobbing for apples game. "Anyone want a turn?"

Silver snorts, backing away like someone might force her to participate. "Do I want to open my mouth in a barrel of water that every scroungy, sticky kid in town has dunked their sweaty heads in? Hard pass."

"Ew. Good point," Lacey says. "How about the corn maze? Look, you can race!" She's right. The sign outside the massive field of corn displays an arrow to two different entrances and a challenge in red paint. *Race your friends to solve the maze!*

"I'm on Arlow's team!" Silver announces.

"That's not fair. He can probably see over the top," Lacey exclaims.

Silver points at her. "Exactly."

The exasperation in his voice sends me into giggles, helped by the edible, no doubt. "I'm not ten feet tall!"

"What exactly keeps me from just walking through the corn to get out?" Lee asks. Lacey grabs his arm and my wrist, tugging us toward the left entrance. "We aren't cheaters."

The teams are decided then. Arlow glances over at me. "Calli gets turned around in our patch of woods. Good luck."

His taunting smile is adorable, but it doesn't keep my competitive side from roaring to the forefront. "Oh, is that how it is? We'll be waiting on the other side for you. Text if you need a rescue."

"Keep dreaming, sweetheart."

Trying not to let my heart fly out of my chest at the sound of the endearment, I cross my arms. "How about a bet?" His eyebrows rise as he waits on me to continue. "Whoever loses has to get their face painted and the winners pick the design."

Lee jerks to look at me. "Wait a minute, I never agreed—"

"You're on!" Silver calls, and they disappear into the maze, getting a head start.

It's dim in the narrow paths carved between the stalks, but the full moon helps light the way. Lee is heading the charge, and Lacey huffs. "We aren't running!"

"If you think I'm getting a damn puppy dog nose or something painted on my face, you're crazy."

"But you'd make a cute puppy," I tease.

Lacey rubs her chin pretending to think. "I don't know. Maybe a bunny rabbit."

"Move your asses or I'll carry you one under each arm."

Laughing, we fall behind him and let him lead. "So, your friend, Silver, is she single?" Lacey asks me.

Lee stops, turns around, and points a finger at her. "No."

It's the only thing he says before continuing on. She bats the word away with a roll of her eyes, slows her steps, and looks over at me for an answer.

"She is, but the breakup was recent and brutal. She isn't dating yet."

Sympathy presses her lips together. "That's too bad."

"Lee doesn't like you playing matchmaker, huh?"

"No, but if he had his way, he'd never leave the lake house. He and Arlow compete over who can be the biggest recluse, I swear." She pauses for a moment, tilting her head. "Arlow is different tonight. He's always seemed so quiet and serious…sad. It's good to see him having fun and acting silly. Maybe he'll rub off on my brother."

"Lacey!" Lee calls from somewhere ahead of us.

She turns to beam at me. "Come on, we'd better win, or Lee will never let me hear the end of it."

CHAPTER 13

ARLOW

SILVER'S REASON FOR CLAIMING ME AS HER TEAMMATE FOR THE MAZE becomes clear as we make our way through the stalks of corn. "Tell me about Lee. Is he single and does he now or has he ever had felony charges against him?"

"I see why you and Calli are friends. Did she ever tell you she suspected me of grave robbery?"

My attempt to change the subject doesn't work. "To be fair, you live in a graveyard. I'm not trying to end up chained in a basement of a stranger so answer the question."

"Lee isn't dangerous, but he also isn't interested in dating."

"I'm not looking for a date, just a night." Silver grabs my wrist, stopping us with the exit in sight. "Wait, are you two into each other?"

"What? No, why would you think that?"

She shrugs and starts walking again. "Neither of you date, and you spend a lot of time together. It wouldn't have been a big deal."

Calli, Lee, and Lacey wait on the other side, sitting in the grass. "It's about time. We were getting bored," Calli calls. "Hurry before the face painting booth closes!"

Joy shines on her face and it reminds me of how she looked that first day I saw her by the creek. So relaxed, without a trace of worry in her features. I love to see her happy. "Fine, but then we hit the food trucks because the smell of barbecue is torture."

At the face painting tent, there's a brief huddle between the three of them while Silver and I wait. Once a consensus is reached, Calli mumbles to one of the artists while Lee talks to the other. We aren't allowed to know what we're getting until it's done.

Calli sits beside me to watch with a growing smile as the guy paints on my forehead. "How's the edible treating you?" I ask her.

"Like I might want the other half after we eat."

"I take green tips, you know," the artist says at the mention of edibles.

"Tell me what you're drawing, and we'll talk."

Calli shakes her head at him, and he chuckles. "Sorry, dude."

He finishes quickly and Calli snaps a picture with her phone. I expect it to be something completely goofy, but when she holds up her phone to show me my reflection in the camera, my glare goes straight to Lee. Because I know damn well whose idea turning me into a giraffe was.

"If you're jealous of my height, just say so, asshole!"

There's laughter from both artists and the few people gathered around to watch or wait their turn. I slip the guy an edible. Calli is the only one who notices. Everyone else is too busy looking at Silver as her artist finishes. "Tattoo artist?" I guess, and he nods, thanking me under his breath then nodding toward the other artist. "He is too. Easy extra money."

Silver gets a first glance at mine and cracks up which is hilarious because hers is so much bigger. My artist only painted my forehead and nose. It's very good and detailed. He's put an ear above each of my eyes and the little giraffe horns between them. Yellow paint covers a thin strip of my forehead, spotted with brown splotches, and leads down my nose, turning black at the tip. It's unmistakably a giraffe but done minimally compared to Silver's.

"Who are you laughing at?" I ask, spinning the little mirror on the table near her around so she can see.

Her jaw falls open at the sight of the shark that's tail takes up most of her forehead. The body bends around her cheek, and her mouth has been turned into the shark's mouth. Her lips are even painted. So much dark blue. She grins up at the artist. "That's fantastic." She opens and closes her mouth, making the shark do the same and everyone laughs.

"It suits you," Lee tells her as we all leave the tent. "You look like you bite." She leans to say something directly in his ear that I'm glad I don't hear, judging by the reaction on his face.

We grab dinner from the food trucks and have a few more drinks before piling into Lacey's SUV to go back to the cabin. I accompany Calli into her little kitchen to help cut up the cake while the others wait in the living room, and she asks me for the other half of the gummy.

"These hit you better, huh?"

Her glazed eyes and instant smile say it all as she chews the other half, then uncovers the cake. "They're great. No anxiety and I'm not tired at all. I could eat this whole cake though, even after those corndogs."

"Calli." She pauses and her eyes widen slightly when I put a hand under her chin to keep her gaze on mine. "Thank you for tonight. No one has surprised me like this on my birthday since I was a little kid. It was so sweet."

Her cheeks practically glow under the ceiling light and her words slip out in a near whisper. "You're welcome."

The urge to kiss her is almost unbearable. I felt awful when she asked if I was avoiding her because if I'm going to be truthful with myself, that's what I was doing. I didn't lie to her. I was caught up in my art, but I let it happen because it's so hard to resist the chemistry between us. As soon as she stood in front of me, I was lost to her again. To the connection that only grows stronger the more I fight it.

Her lips twitch and she starts to giggle. "I'm sorry, but…"

Alright, I may have forgotten that I look like a giraffe. "Giraffe, right. I'm going to go wash this off."

"There are some cloths under the bathroom sink that you don't have to worry about staining."

It takes some scrubbing, but the colors used were light and that makes it easier. Even on the patches of vitiligo, it comes off. Calli hands me a plate when I return to the living room to sit between her and Lacey.

"Silver, I have bad news and good news," I announce, scooping a bite of cake into my mouth. It's fucking delicious. Calli is looking for new hobbies, but she mastered baking in my opinion. Pies, cobbler, muffins, cake, bread. I've had them all from her and all have been phenomenal. "The bad news is the dark paint doesn't come completely off no matter how hard you scrub."

Silver looks up at me, alarmed. Poor shark. "What's the good news?"

Shrugging, I take another bite before answering. "Only the tip of my nose was dark."

Laughter runs around the room, and Silver narrows her eyes at me. "I went to jail for kicking a man in the balls, smartass. You might want to keep that in mind."

"Threatened by a shark. That's a new one."

Calli tries to help her clean the paint off after we finish eating, but nothing removes all that blue. "You look like you're running out of oxygen," Calli teases.

"My makeup remover at home will take care of it," Silver says, shrugging it off.

I lean down, dropping my voice to ask Calli, "Bonfire?"

A brilliant smile leaps to her face. "Sure."

Everyone is happy to move our party to my firepit but when we reach the entrance of the graveyard, Silver hesitates. "This feels like one of those horror movie moments where I'd be screaming at the women onscreen for being stupid."

"Just don't twist your ankle when you run," Lee says, and she glares at him.

"I'll push you down first."

"You should see it on a cloudy night when it's also full of fog. Can't see your hand in front of your face," Calli tells her, moving to walk with her through the gravestones. "I was thinking we could host a big game of hide and seek, maybe on Halloween."

"You need psychological help."

Despite her reservations, Silver can't take her eyes off the sky full of stars once we crest the hill. Lee and I carried up the cooler of drinks and Calli brought a wireless speaker. She connects it to her phone and turns on some music while I get the fire going.

The second half of the gummy hits her much harder but not in a bad way. Her cheeks are going to be sore from the constant smile on her face.

Lee has walked with Lacey down to my place to use the bathroom when Calli moves from sitting on the log to lying on the grass. Okay, it's probably time to intervene.

"You're going to be bug food," I warn. Not to mention the ground is cold and damp this late in October.

"Look at the stars though," she breathes, remaining on her back. Her gaze moves from the sky to me when I walk over to her. "You are so tall. Like a big gorgeous tree."

She's high as hell.

Silver chokes back a laugh. "Girl, you have to shut up."

"A tree? I thought I was a sexy beekeeper."

She grabs my ankle, staring up at me. "You are. A big sexy tree-keeper bee. Beekeepering tree."

"Okay, come on." She doesn't resist when I pull her to her feet as Lee and Lacey return. "Log or chair, pick a seat."

She glances toward the dark forest. "Let's go to the creek!" She looks over at Silver, who shakes her head adamantly. "It'll be fun!" she adds, undeterred, excitement ruling her voice. She gets about two steps in

127

that direction before I grab her from behind and hold her a few inches in the air. Going into the woods fucked up at night is not a bright idea. I'm not trashed but I have a great buzz and Lacey is the only sober one.

"Put me down!" Calli giggles, kicking her feet.

"Did you just put her in air jail?" Lacey snorts.

The laughter from everyone has her laughing too until I murmur in her ear. "Are you going to sit down, or do I have to carry you back to your cabin?" The fire in her eyes when she turns her head to look at me isn't anger. It's far more dangerous. Her gaze stays on mine as I gently set her on her feet. "The edible is at its peak. Let me keep you safe."

Nodding, she takes a few steps and sits in one of the Adirondack chairs beside Lacey. They start talking about the song that's playing while I try to hide the hard-on that popped up at the way she looked at me.

The effects of the edible slowly wane, and she comes down. The next few hours are filled with music, laughter, and conversation. It's the best birthday I can remember, and I can't stop looking at the amazing woman who put it together.

Everyone is at my house and getting ready to leave when I find Calli in my kitchen, perusing the refrigerator. She doesn't hear me come in, and I watch as she takes a cherry from the container before choosing a bottle of water.

Her body jolts when she turns to see me standing right behind her. "Jesus, Arlow, you scared the hell out of me!"

Chuckling, I pluck the cherry from her hand and wave it in front of her. "Still haven't changed your fruit bandit tendencies."

"You knew what you were getting yourself into." She reaches for the cherry, and I hold it up above her head. Her smirk is adorable. I want to kiss it off her face. "Do you seriously think I'm going to jump for that?"

Before I reply, she jumps and tries to snatch it, cursing under her breath when I raise it just in time. "Not even close."

She turns her back to me, reaching for the fridge handle, and I loop my arm around her middle, pulling her back to me as she laughs. "You're supposed to share with your friends."

Her back lands against my ribs as my hand splays over her stomach, holding her there. "Only if they say please." The words come out huskier than I intend, and I feel her take a deep breath. The mood between us shifts from playful to something more in half a second.

Her body relaxes, and she tilts her head back a bit, resting it against my chest. "Please."

Fuck, what that one word does to me. I want to hear her moan it with my face buried between her legs. The thought alone has my cock hardening, and she presses her ass against it as I bring the cherry to her mouth an inch at a time. My self-control flees as I watch it disappear between soft lips.

The slight shiver she exhibits when my mouth hovers under her ear is as satisfying as the way she tilts her head, giving me access to trace my lips down her graceful neck with light, brushing kisses.

Her eyes fall closed. Still firmly in my arms, she reaches up behind her to graze her fingers across my nape. "Arlow." My name floats out on a breathy whisper. "What are you doing?"

Excellent fucking question.

With a sigh, I lean my head against hers. "Fuck if I know."

Turning around, she gazes up at me while I bring my hands to her hips. She reaches to run her fingertips through my scruff, and my eyes briefly close at her soft touch. "You're drunk."

Ignoring my instinct to deny it, I nod, looking into her beautiful eyes that shine under the kitchen lights. Everything about her shines.

"I think it's time to call it a night." Raising onto her tiptoes, she drops a quick peck on my lips. "Happy Birthday, Arlow."

"Good night, Peach."

It takes me a few minutes to convince myself not to go after her. Fuck. *Fuck. Let her go.* Lee pauses when he walks in the kitchen. "You alright?"

"Yeah, I'm good."

Wordlessly, he holds out a hundred dollar bill to me, continuing our tradition, and I accept it with a nod, tucking it into my pocket. The sight of faint blue smears on his chin makes me grin. "That's one way to remove makeup."

"Fuck off. We're heading out. Happy Birthday."

Silence settles thick over the house after everyone has left. It's late, well past three a.m. when I climb into bed, but I can't sleep. Every time I close my eyes, I think of how Calli softened under my touch, the hoarseness of her voice when she asked me what I was doing. Thank fuck she had the strength to walk away. I'm the one who told her we can't be anything more than friends and here I am, losing control and leading her on when that hasn't changed.

My last thought as I finally doze off is that I'll apologize to her tomorrow because drunk or not, that wasn't fair to her.

CHAPTER 14

CALLIOPE

*O*H NO. *H*OW DID *I* GET BACK HERE?

The pink roofed house looms in front of me as the taillights of my father's car fade into the dark. My feet aren't under my control as they carry me inside.

Time jumps forward and she's right in front of me, my ears ringing from her screams. "Stop fucking crying! You like him so much? Huh? What the fuck does he do for you?" The back of her hand glances off my cheek, soundless and dulled. "He's not the one paying the bills you ungrateful piece of shit."

An overstretched clownish smile builds my terror. "You don't want him to leave? Better get used to it. He's doing drugs and he'll be dead soon. Hope you said goodbye."

Her laughter is deafening and covering my ears does nothing to block it out. It echoes, swirling around, filling me in some deep corners that can't be swept out.

My eyes leap open to find sunlight and safety. Damn it. It's a dream I still have at least a few times a year. Her joyous laugh at the thought of his death, and the way I crumble to the floor. Not only a dream but a memory, words screamed in my seven year old face.

He outlived that bitch, though, didn't he? Anger and spite drive me out of bed. So often those type of dreams ruin half my day, but I'm not letting that happen today. She doesn't get that power. The urn seems to glare back at me from the mantel as I pass through the living room to my kitchen. It's time to dump her ashes over the cliff out back and be done with her for good.

There's still been no word from the private investigator about Dad and I'm tempted to call, but after holding my phone in my palm for a minute, I set it back down. I'm not in the headspace right now to talk about him. Not if I want to shake that dream from my mind.

Coffee helps. So does replaying the events of last night in my head. I was stoned as a gravel driveway, but I remember everything. Arlow behind me, touching me, his breath on my ear, the warmth of his lips and tickle of his scruff on my neck. If I'd let him continue, we would've ended up in the bedroom, but I couldn't. He was drunk, and surprising him on his birthday wasn't a ploy to seduce him when that isn't what he wants. Still, it's confusing. He's so full of mixed signals.

After coffee and toast, I grab a small backpack and chuck the urn inside it. A faint buzzy lightheadedness still sticks with me from last night's edible as I head out my door. Those things have a ridiculous half life. My plan for the day is clear. Dump the bitch over the cliff, come back and pack for my road trip. My friends will be picking me up tomorrow morning.

My phone rings with a call from Silver when I get to my porch. It slipped my mind that she left her car here last night and had Lacey drop her off at home. "Hey, did I wake you?" she asks.

"Nope, I was headed out for a walk. Do you need me to come get you?"

"No thanks. Nina is giving me a ride to work. I just called to let you know I'll pick my car up later." A familiar voice rumbles in the background. Lee spent the night at her place.

"Uh-huh, and does Lee have a ride?" I tease.

"I rode him plenty already."

Chuckling, I sit on my top step. "Are you feeling okay about that?" It hasn't been long since her breakup and I know she had her eye on Lee for a little fun, but that next day remorse can be a bitch.

"I feel fantastic. I'd forgotten what great sex was like."

"Are you going to see him again?"

"No, men are trash and I'm all set for a while now."

"Okay then. I'm going to need you to set aside your man hatred for a moment for a question."

Her reply is instant. "Did you sleep with Arlow?"

"No! I told you we're just friends."

"He barely takes his eyes off you, Calli. I'm serious. Sometimes he looks at you like he worships you and then a few seconds later, like he could eat you for dinner. Neither look screams friendship."

"I…really?" Maybe it's because I spend too much time trying not to obviously ogle him, but other than a loaded glance here and there, I haven't noticed him doing the same.

My chest swells with a deep breath. The phone call I overheard was too personal to him for me to share but I need her opinion. "I think he's still getting over an ex. Even if he's tempted, I don't want to be a rebound, you know? But…would it be completely delusional to think I could make him forget her?"

"Maybe, but I'm here for it. You really have it bad, don't you?"

My groan frightens away a nearby robin. "Ugh, it's ridiculous. I need to get it through my head that we're only friends."

"Maybe you need to get laid too. Find a sexy rocker guy in the crowd, take him back to your hotel, and then you never have to see him again."

"It's not the worst idea you've ever had," I laugh, though I know it wouldn't solve anything. I'm not hungry for sex. I'm starving for him.

"Nina's here. I have to go."

Once we hang up, I adjust my backpack and head into the woods to throw the cremated remains away. It's well past time to rid myself of her completely. Her worthless long term boyfriend, Carl, couldn't even be bothered to claim her ashes. It's too bad she doesn't get to know that the man she put before all others couldn't give one shit about her once she was gone. He's probably moved onto some other nightmare of a person. It's amazing how they seem to find each other.

Despite the reason I'm out here, my mood lightens considerably during the hike. The light breeze clears the cobwebs of the dream away while I breathe in the damp scent of decaying leaves and admire the array of colors dancing around me. The fall foliage is at its peak, spraying the ground with brilliant red, amber, ochre, and golden orange. In a few weeks all this will be bare, then later, maybe coated in snow. I'm excited to experience the forest in all its seasons.

My thoughts drift to the next few days. It's been too long since I've seen my concert friends. Usually, being in a crowd would make me anxious, but this is always different. Whether it's the music, the people, or just the atmosphere itself, standing shoulder to shoulder in a crowd of voices singing our hearts out is the definition of happiness. It feels otherworldly, magic.

It occurs to me that life is pretty good right now. I've pulled myself out of a lot over the past months. Moved, made new friends, found new hobbies. Not long ago, I was hiding inside, barely leaving the house to get necessities, tied to the mundanity of watching TV and scrolling social media. Before that, it was nonstop shitty jobs to try to keep a roof over my head. If you'd told me then I'd be hiking through the forest, infatuated with a kind, gorgeous man, and looking forward to a road trip to see some of my favorite bands, I never would've believed it.

My plan was to take the trail to the bridge, cross the creek then cut back through the orchard to the cliff, but a sudden flash of color between the trees brings me to a halt.

Was that a deer? Keeping still, I watch the area. Was it only my imagination? One of those *corner of your eye* hallucinations? It's not unlikely, especially considering the edible is still influencing my thoughts. Straining my ears, I don't hear anything unusual. There aren't any wild animals to concern myself with here. Nothing big at least. There's more worry over stepping on a venomous snake than seeing a rare black bear or mountain lion that may wander in from western Tennessee.

I've decided to keep going when he steps out from between the trees, the worst animal you can find yourself alone with in the woods. Fear races down my spine, freezing me in place. A dark balaclava obscures his face, but he's looking right at me. A hundred scenarios try to reassure me. Maybe he's a hunter who got lost, a visitor that Arlow didn't tell me about, a random teenager out here trespassing, but none of it lowers the hair on the back of my neck or the goosebumps lining my skin.

Not only because of the mask, but his reaction. He doesn't run, not toward me or away. He doesn't wave or call out an explanation. Instead, he stands stock still, staring at me. I'm too far away to make out what he's wearing, other than a large jacket that ignites the panic smoldering inside me.

No. It's not him. There's no way it could be him. Lots of people wear denim jackets.

Suspended in time, we stand there regarding each other until he takes a step in my direction. My instincts kick in, and I turn on my heel, sliding on the wet leaves underfoot. For one blindingly terrifying second, I'm sure I'm going to fall, but I catch my balance and run. A glance back shows him a little closer to me, but not much. Is he running? I'm not looking back long enough to judge.

I fumble to pull my phone out of my pocket and want to cry at the absence of bars showing no signal. It's always spotty out here. Racing back down the path, my fear builds to pure panic while I wait for a hand to clamp onto my shoulder or arms to grab me from behind. I can't take the awful dread of it. I'm not fast and staying on the trail is probably stupid. Instead, I veer off the path and tear through the woods.

The underbrush may be dying but it's thick and clogged with leaves. It's difficult to run through, as if the ground is on his side, grabbing at my feet so he can catch up with me. My breath bursts in and out of my lungs while branches and twigs reach out to scrape at my skin. I'm not sure how far I've gone when I realize I don't know where I am. Am I even heading in the right direction?

A frantic look around reveals nothing but the overcast forest. I'm lost. My awful sense of direction is going to get me killed.

North. The word filters through my panic. The cabin, Arlow's place, the graveyard, the road, all are north of the forest. No matter where I come out, that's the right direction to go. Thank goodness I have the compass on my phone. It doesn't require service like the GPS.

I'm terrified to stop but I duck behind a tree to quickly pull it up on my screen. Right now, I'm headed east which would only run me into the fence dividing this property from the next. Keeping the compass open on the screen, I take off, running north. The bars on my phone show a signal again, and I tap Arlow's contact without slowing down.

Please let him be home.

CHAPTER 15

ARLOW

MY SLEEP WAS RESTLESS AND I'M ON MY SECOND CUP OF COFFEE WHEN Lee texts me.

> **LEE**
>
> Wake up. I need a ride from Silver's place.

Lee doesn't date or do relationships but unlike me, he isn't a stranger to random one night stands. Lacey must've dropped them both off at Silver's. I'm not surprised, but I'm not going to miss the opportunity to fuck with him.

> **ME**
>
> Wrong number.

> **LEE**
>
> Arlow I swear to fuck.

> **ME**
>
> How bad were you if she won't give you a ride home?

LEE

Her car is at Calli's. Someone picked her up
for work. Just get your ass over here.

ME

On my way.

It's quiet over at Calli's cabin when I leave. She's likely still asleep. I'll catch up with her later to apologize for last night and say goodbye before she leaves for the next few days.

Lee stalks down the steps the second I pull into Silver's driveway. "She put me out on the porch like a damn cat!"

The indignance in his voice is hilarious. "It's probably a little early in the relationship to give you a key. Don't worry, you'll get there."

He pulls open the driver's side door as I slide over into the passenger seat. "Frustrating ass woman!"

My phone buzzes as we back out of the driveway, and I'm surprised to see Calli's number. She always texts. As soon as I accept the call and before I can say a word, her panicked voice is in my ear.

"Arlow! There's a man in the woods. He's following me."

Her shout was loud enough for Lee to overhear, and he jerks his head to look at me, then makes a quick turn toward my place.

"Where are you?"

"I don't know." Her words are filled with despair and interrupted by her heavy breathing. "I got lost. I'm heading north and I think I'm behind my cabin but I'm not sure!"

"Keep running. Keep going. We're right around the corner, do you hear me? I'll be right there. Can you see him?"

"No, I might have lost him. I don't know." Her voice cuts in and out as the signal falters. "Please hurry." The terror in her pleading tone tears a strip from my heart.

"Stay on the phone with me." Lee already has the pedal to the floor, but it doesn't stop me from shouting at him. "Hurry the fuck up!"

Her next words are chopped into unintelligible pieces before the call disconnects completely. "Goddamn it!" I dial her back and get sent straight to voicemail three times.

Lee makes the turn onto my road and floors it again while I curse myself for not having my gun in the glovebox. After our vehicles were broken into before, it didn't seem like a good idea to keep it there. "Do you have your pistol?"

"Yes, do you have any idea who might be out there?"

"I told you Chris Handleman is free. I don't think—I didn't think he would, but..." My fingers scrape through my hair. "I don't know. If he touches her, if anyone touches her, I'll fucking bury them." I'm nothing but turmoil, ready to burst out of my skin. She's out there alone and terrified, being pursued through the woods like prey. If she's hurt, I'll plant whoever is responsible in my graveyard before the night is through. "Just get to her."

Lee slows a little when we near my place and I bark at him, "What the fuck are you doing?"

"If she's lost and running north, I don't want to hit her if she pops out of the woods onto the road."

It's a good point, but the last quarter mile seems to take forever before he turns into our shared driveway while I keep trying to get a call to go through. It finally rings through as we park in front of the cabin. "There she is!" Lee exclaims, pointing to our left.

Calli emerges from the trees on the east side of her cabin, and I run toward her. She barrels into my chest, throwing her arms around me. Her heart hammers between us as she gasps out her words between heavy breaths. "I don't know...where he is."

I hug her tight then hold her out at arms length, so I can look her over. A thin rivulet of blood runs down the side of her neck and there's a tear in the sleeve of her sweatshirt. "Are you hurt? Did he touch you?"

The shake of her head is a relief. "He never caught up with me. I saw him start toward me and I took off."

Her slight injuries are from running full speed through the unforgiving forest.

Lee has his gun in his hand, glancing around us, and paying special attention to the area where Calli exited the woods. "Did you see what he looked like?"

"He's wearing a ski mask."

He looks over at me, his assessment clear in his expression. No one up to any good is going to be out in the woods in a mask.

"I need to grab my gun and we'll search the woods," I tell him, still holding onto Calli's arms. Before he can respond, a motor bursts to life near my barn. We all spin around to look while I shove Calli behind me.

My ATV charges across my backyard, briefly disappears into the thin line of trees then emerges on the road. "Keep her safe," I order Lee, darting for my truck. Calli calls my name, but I'm focused on catching up to this guy. I need to know who it is. Especially if it's Handleman.

By the time I get into my truck and out on the road, the motor is no longer audible. There's no sign of him and it's impossible to know where he may have turned off into the woods or onto someone else's property. Damn it. After driving the length of road twice, I stop and slap the steering wheel in frustration.

Adrenaline courses through me at the fear I felt for Calli mixed with the outright rage that someone would dare come after her. If it's because of me, I'll never forgive myself.

Calli and Lee wait beside her car when I return. "I couldn't find him."

"You only saw one person?" Lee clarifies.

Calli nods. "That was the same guy. With the mask and denim jacket. I guess he must not have been chasing me, but I swear, he stared at me and started in my direction, so I ran."

"He's not doubting you," I reassure her.

Lee shakes his head. "Not at all, but we need to have a look around and make sure there's no one else. Just because he didn't pursue you after you ran doesn't mean he isn't dangerous."

"First, get the cops out here."

Lee frowns, looking over at me. "For trespassing? They aren't going to do anything."

"I know, but that was my ATV. They can at least take a report in case it shows up for sale or at the pawn shops. It might help us figure out who it was."

"Oh shit. Alright. Let's go check if anything else is missing first."

Lee's right. Calling the police is largely a waste of time. The same cop who showed up when our cars were vandalized, Officer Fulton, arrives and takes Calli's statement. The flippant way he talks to her is infuriating, like she's a hysterical woman who got frightened in the woods.

"So, he wasn't following you then?" he says, writing in his note-book. Keeping his head down, he raises his eyes to look at her.

"I guess he wasn't since he couldn't have made it over to the barn without us seeing him."

"Mm Hmm. And when you believed you were being chased, why did you call your neighbor instead of nine-one-one?" A hint of accu-sation resides in his tone.

"My phone couldn't keep a signal and when I saw it had service again, I just…I don't know," she confesses. "He was the first person I thought of."

Those words wrap around me, squeezing tight. In her blinding fear and panic, she wanted *me*.

"We got here a hell of a lot faster than you would have," I point out. "Why wouldn't she call her neighbor?"

"Just trying to ascertain what took place." He flips his notebook shut. When Calli excuses herself and walks toward her cabin, Officer Fulton regards me. "Do you think she might've had a part in this?"

The question stuns me, and he stares at me while I blink at him. "What? She was standing right in front of me when the guy rode off with my ATV."

His expression says I might be the dumbest person in existence. "I'm sure she has friends. It wouldn't be hard to make up a damsel in distress story to distract you while her buddy does his thing. Seen it a million times."

It's so ridiculous. "I wasn't home. Why would she call for me to return then? He could've just taken it and I wouldn't have known."

"I couldn't tell you, but I know I've been out here twice since she moved in, and you never had any trouble before." He starts back toward his squad car, calling back over his shoulder. "You can pick up the police report in two days if you need it for insurance purposes. You know the routine."

Lee glances over at me and shakes his head.

"What?" I ask through gritted teeth.

"Don't say it or do it. Whatever you're thinking."

"Fucking prick," I mumble. "I need to get some cameras and trail cams. I don't know if this was Handleman but twice doesn't feel random."

"Get your gun and let's have a look around."

Calli insists on going with us back into the forest. It's fine by me. I don't want to let her out of my sight. She leads us back to where she saw him and a few footprints are visible in the soft earth, but it's impossible to tell which way he came from or headed. A further search of the woods and fields turns up nothing.

As we're crossing my front yard, an unfamiliar truck turns into the driveway and Calli wraps her hand around my arm, stopping in her tracks as it veers off to park in front of her house. Before any of us can say anything, Silver gets out of the passenger side. The driver gives a wave and drives away.

With a relieved sigh, Calli lets go of me and jogs down the driveway to meet her friend. Judging by the flying hand gestures and Silver's reactions, she's filling her in on everything that just happened.

Lee glances over at me as we take our time catching up to them. I'm sure he didn't expect to see Silver again so soon. "You can wipe that smirk off."

If he thinks I'm not having fun with this, he doesn't know me at all. "This is my normal face."

Silver turns and crosses her arms, leaning against the bumper of her truck. "Imagine seeing you here."

"I found him abandoned on a doorstep. *In the Arms of an Angel* was playing on his phone. It was pitiful," I tell her before Lee can speak.

Calli turns her head, but not quickly enough to hide her laugh.

Lee ignores me and steps closer to her. "I thought you had to work."

"I got off early. You know how that is." Silver's lips twitch up.

"The hell I do."

"Okay," Calli says, grabbing my wrist and pulling me toward her cabin. "We'll give you two a minute."

"Hey, things were just getting good!"

"Let them work through that day after awkwardness." She picks up the bag that she discarded on her porch while we were waiting on the cops, and I follow her inside.

I'm surprised to see her pull the cardboard urn of ashes from the bag and return it to her mantel. That's what she was doing in the woods today? I hate that she was interrupted doing something that must've already been hard for her. "You were going to scatter your mother's ashes?" I ask softly.

Her only response is an absent nod before she ducks into the kitchen. She returns with two bottles of water, handing me one.

"I'll go with you if you want, to spread the ashes."

"Thanks, but I'll wait." Her tone is firm and it's clear she doesn't want to talk about it. "I'm sorry about your ATV."

"It's alright. I'll get another one if it isn't found. I'm just glad you're okay. That scared the shit out of me."

"It was terrifying, but I made it worse thinking he was after me and then getting lost. I am clearly not good in an emergency. At least I didn't twist my ankle or fall. I'd hate to be a cliché."

"Hey." I pull her into a hug, unable to get close enough to her after the scare. "You did exactly what you should've done. But how would you feel about getting a gun?"

"I will when I get back from my trip."

"Good. I'm going to get some trail cams set up. We should put some cameras at our front and back doors if thieves are going to become a problem for us. I can look into which ones work well and order them while you're gone."

"That's a good idea. You can let me know what I owe you for mine." She peeks out the window at our friends and chuckles. "I think it's safe to go out."

Silver waves when we get out to the porch and calls to Calli. "I'm going to take Lee home. I'll text you later."

"Look, she did the chivalrous thing after all," I tease him.

"I don't know. She might put me out on the side of the road."

"Only if you keep talking shit." They start toward Silver's truck, the argument continuing when Lee announces, "I'm driving."

"You are not driving my truck!"

Calli and I look at each other, and she grins. "Your friend has met his match."

"I could say the same thing." I nod toward the truck, where Silver has handed over her keys and opened the passenger door. "I want you to stay with me tonight."

She blinks at me. "I doubt the thief is going to come right back."

"I know." Her anxiety shows in the way she keeps fingering a lock of her hair and pacing around. She's not okay, only pretending to be. "But you leave for a few days in the morning anyway, and I'll sleep better tonight knowing you're down the hall just in case."

Her lips curl up a little as she averts her gaze. "Alright, but you have to let me pick up dinner."

"Deal. Now, I need to go check the hives and harvest the last of the honey for this year. You're recruited to help."

All I want to do is wipe away that tense look on her face and it's a good way to distract her, maybe help her forget the day she's had, but it isn't only for her benefit. The terror in her eyes when she ran to me earlier won't get out of my head. I need to keep her close to me.

———

Calli watches as I load the necessary tools into the steel wagon and wheel it out of the shed. "Can I pull it?"

"Sure, but it might be too heavy when we get to the hill."

"Psh, you underestimate me." Her eyes twinkle with amusement as she takes the handle, and we start toward the graveyard. "After this, I need to get packed for tomorrow."

"Are you excited?"

A brilliant smile raises her cheeks. "So excited. I love festivals, and I haven't seen my concert friends for a long time."

"Tell me about your friends." We wind our way through the gravestones, the wagon rolling easily, until we get to the base of the hill. It takes about three steps for her to realize the wagon is heavier than it looks, but she doesn't complain.

"There are twelve of us that keep in touch online, but we don't all go to every event, of course. Freya, Leo, and Calvin are going to this one with me. They're kind of my little group within the group, I guess. We hit more of the concerts in this part of the country. They're a lot of fun. Sometimes Freya's aunt Helen joins us—she's in her sixties and has seen about every band you can think of live. She's supposed to be there on the third night."

The jealousy that strikes at the sound of the men's names is sudden and sharp. Does she share a room with them? A bed? It's none of my business, but I have to bite my tongue not to ask. She's slowing down, struggling with the wagon. "You alright?"

"Fine."

"Stubborn ass," I chuckle, grabbing the handle.

She flashes a grin at me and moves her hand a little so mine can fit tucked alongside hers. We crest the top of the hill and continue down the other side through the field of clover, stopping when the hives come into view.

"Okay, time to suit up."

She dresses in the suit then picks up the gloves. "Will you help with these?"

The memory of how she melted against me when I touched her last night won't stop running through my head, how she shivered when I kissed her neck. My mouth dries out when she looks up at me expectantly until I take the gloves. "I've got you." Zipping her hood closed first is a self-preservation to keep me from kissing those lips.

She hasn't mentioned anything about the moment we had, probably dismissing it as a drunken mistake. Mistake, yes, but my attraction to her has nothing to do with alcohol.

Once we're both suited up, we continue to the hives. "Okay, these are for you," I tell her, handing her the smoker and the bee brush. Picking up the hive tool, I move the wagon a little closer and open the storage container for the filled frames.

"Go ahead and start smoking them while I take the lid off. We want to keep them nice and calm."

She stays right at my side, bathing them in smoke. "Are those stuck?"

"That's what this is for. You have to go slow and easy." She watches as I use the hive tool to pry a frame free and pull it out.

"Oh wow, that's full." The awe in her voice is almost as cute as her expression. She loves this.

"Yep, they've been busy. Okay, take the brush and sweep the bees off the cells. Gently. They'll take off when the bristles touch them."

Her face crumples into a look of concentration, her tongue peeking through her lips as she follows my directions. "Perfect. Now give them some more smoke."

As she does that, I place the frame in the storage box. We continue through the rest of the frames the same way. "Will they survive the winter?" she asks.

"Sure. They have plenty of nectar and honey stored. We'll check on them and if they do run low, I can feed them some nectar patties to help, especially if spring comes late." She watches me secure the lid on the storage container. "We have to cover this because they will come after their honey."

"You can't blame them." She holds the smoker up like a gun. "We're robbing them at smoke point."

"Do you think they're up here plotting their revenge?"

"There's a thought. What if they covered the house in honeycomb and trapped us inside?"

Chuckling, I put the lid on and grab the handle of the wagon, pulling it behind us as we put some distance between us and the hives. "I'm insulted that you think I couldn't fight my way out of honeycomb."

"They'd swarm over us and build a giant hive around the house. It's a horror movie in the making." Once we're out of the danger zone, she spins around. "Are there any on me?"

"No. You're good."

We both strip out of the suits and deposit them in the wagon. Before we can get moving again, a honeybee appears and lands on her forearm. Most people's instinct is to swat at them, but she doesn't react that way or flinch. Instead, she watches as it crawls lazily down to her wrist, then grins at me. "I don't think I've ever gotten a good look at a bee up close. Hey there, Bee-nadict. Don't sting me, okay?"

"Bee-nadict?"

"Bee-nadict Honeybatch. Look how cute he is."

"You're cute." The words spill out without forethought, and she gives me a shy glance. The bee flies off back toward the hives. "Okay, let's get this to the shed before the rest of them get wind of it."

She wraps her hand around the wagon handle beside mine again on the walk back. The shed has warmed up considerably in the hour since I turned the little space heater on. "Cold honey takes forever to spin, but fresh out of the hives like this and in a warm environment, it'll require a lot less effort."

"Put me to work," she says, watching as I pull the top off the tangential extractor. I love how excited she is and I'm eager to teach her.

A single bee emerges from the storage box, flying straight at me. This one isn't happy. As soon as it touches my neck, it stings me, getting caught in my skin for a second before I brush it off.

"Did it get you?" Calli asks, stepping up close to me.

"Yeah, it's okay."

Her breath wafts over my neck as she looks closer. "Do you want me to get the stinger out?"

"You can try scraping your fingernail over it and see if that works. If not, I'll get it later."

She presses her hand on my head to tilt my neck and runs her finger tenderly over the swelling skin. Christ, her touch. So light and heavy at the same time. Her thumbnail scrapes over the sting and my eyes fall closed. *Don't get hard, for fuck's sake.*

"Am I hurting you?"

Such concern in her sweet voice. "No, Peach." I'd cover myself in stingers to feel her hands on me.

Steadily, she runs her nail over the same spot until the stinger comes free. "Got it." The tiny barb sits on her thumb as she holds it up to show me, then brushes it off. "You had them crawling all over your hands when you were pulling the frames but only got stung by a rogue stowaway." I want to kiss the impish grin from her lips as she adds, "It made a beeline for you."

"It was definitely a premeditated attack." The air is thick with more than the heat as she looks up at me, and I know I'm not the only one who feels it. It takes me a few seconds to break away and step back to reach into the storage box again. "Alright, let me show you how to uncap them. Will you grab that black bucket?"

Propping the frame over the bucket, I take the large, flat knife and show her how to drag it across the surface to remove the beeswax. After flipping it over, I hand her the knife and she takes over, uncapping the other side and scraping the wax into the bucket. "A few of them aren't covered in wax," she observes.

"There are always some like that but as long as about eighty percent of the cells are capped, then it's ready. If we take them too early with too many of them uncapped, it'll be more nectar than honey, and that can ferment. So, you have to let it ripen to this point first."

"Does it matter which way it goes in the extractor?"

"No, you spin one side then the other. Just slide it into the slot."

With a wide grin, she grabs the next one, moves it over to the bucket and starts uncapping it. Once we get the extractor loaded with frames, I grab the honey bucket, set the strainer on top of it, and place it under the spout.

"Now turn the crank to spin the honey out. It'll drip down and gather at the bottom." I flip a five gallon bucket over and pat it. "You can sit here. I'll take over when you get tired or bored of it."

She turns the crank slowly, glancing at me.

"Faster, there you go. Just like that." Her tongue makes an appearance again, tucked between her lips, and I don't manage to cover my smile fast enough.

"What?" Continuing to crank, she regards me with a curious look. "What did I do?"

"Nothing. You're doing great."

She rolls her eyes, then narrows them at me. "You were laughing at me about something."

"I wasn't laughing. You stick your tongue out when you concentrate. It's endearing."

She laughs, shaking her head. "My teachers used to tease me about that when I was in school. It's a habit I've never broken. Kind of like the way you dip your eyebrows and rub your collarbone when you're trying to figure something out."

"Touché."

We take turns spinning all the frames while the honey slowly begins to ooze into the filter. "Okay. It'll take a couple of hours for it to strain so we're finished for now."

"Then what's the next step?" she asks, getting to her feet and stretching.

"That's it. It goes from the honey bucket into jars."

"This was fun. Maybe I'll learn how to keep hives too. If I'm still here next summer, you could teach me how to get started." Her last statement is more of a question accompanied by raised eyebrows as she waits for my response.

"If you're still here?" Does she plan on leaving?

"I signed a year lease. I'll have to decide then whether to stay, assuming Silver's mom still wants a tenant."

The overwhelming alarm I feel at the thought of her leaving is a huge flashing warning that I need to keep some distance between us. A warning I'm going to ignore. "I'd love to teach you."

CHAPTER 16
CALLIOPE

THIS MORNING WAS TERRIFYING. I DON'T THINK I OVERREACTED necessarily—being confronted with a masked man in the woods would make any woman run like hell—but it wasn't him. Of course, my mind jumped to a person I fear in that situation. It was a thief, likely the same one who robbed our vehicles before.

Arlow's plan to put cameras up is a good one, and I'll make sure to shop for a gun when I get back from my trip. It won't be the first time I've owned one but when I moved, I hoped I wouldn't need one again. It was naïve, I suppose. A woman alone is always at risk.

I'm not alone tonight. Arlow hasn't left my side all day. After we finished with the honey, he accompanied me back to my cabin to pack before we returned to his place to eat dinner. We've spent the evening together, playing Scrabble and watching TV. I wouldn't have thought I'd be so relaxed after the day I had but he turned things around. He always does. I wish I could bottle whatever it is about him that calms me. It's like magic.

I'm not sure where I stand with him from one minute to the next and my habit of overthinking everything doesn't help. He said he couldn't be with anyone romantically, and if he's changed his mind, he hasn't voiced it. Silver swears he can't take his eyes off me. That feeling is mutual. I've never been so attracted to anyone, so desperate to feel his hands on me. We claim to be friends, but I know friends don't look at each other the way we do. They don't touch each other the way we do or cuddle together on the couch to watch TV like we're doing right now.

My head rests on his shoulder, and he reaches for my hand. His fingers curl to interlace with mine and the intimacy in such a small thing feels overwhelming. Somehow comforting and thrilling at the same time. We stay like that until the credits roll on the movie we're watching.

"It's late. I should get to bed."

"Mm," he hums, not releasing my hand. "What time are you leaving tomorrow?"

"Around ten. They'll text when they're almost here. Are you going to miss me?" My tone is light and teasing.

He lets go of my hand and brushes my hair back from my face as I look up at him. The ever burning spark between us flares again but this time there's no doubt in my mind that he feels it too. "Calliope." He murmurs my name like a plea or a prayer.

His eyes close briefly when I run my fingers through his scruff. He leans in inch by tortuously slow inch until his lips hover over mine, his breath tickling them. Unlike last night, he's sober. I'm not walking away.

The anticipation is killing me as he hesitates, and my heart deflates a little when he touches his forehead to mine. "This isn't why I asked you to stay."

Space. I need to put space between us. I scramble to stand up and escape across the room. "I know. I'm sorry. I know this isn't what you want."

He's on his feet immediately, pacing to the window and back. "What I *want*," he scoffs. Frustration drives his hand through his hair. His strides eat up the floor, closing the distance between us. Surprised, I retreat a step until my back hits the wall. He pinches my chin, his eyes burning into mine. "I want to kiss you until neither of us can breathe." He leans in, sliding the tip of his nose along my jaw. "I want to peel off your clothes, taste your skin, explore every trace of you with my tongue. It's all I can think about. I want to hear you moan for me and see your face when I make you come." He leans to warm my ear with his heated words. "What I want is to throw you in my bed and fuck you and fuck you and fuck you."

There's no breath left in my lungs. His confession hangs in the thick air as he pulls his head back to look me in the eye. Hearing it in his deep voice, I've never been so turned on and desperate for someone in my life. Despite his words, I can feel the restraint in his tensed body and measured breaths. I don't know if he's hoping I'll be the one to stop this or praying I don't. If he's counting on me to step away, he has the wrong woman.

Instead of replying or kissing him, I kneel in front of him and watch his eyes widen as I slowly pull the drawstring of his sweatpants, giving him every opportunity to stop me. "Do you want this?"

His cock hardens under my palm through the soft material. "Oh fuck," he breathes. I may be the one with my back to the wall, but he's the one who's cornered. Caught by desire that neither of us is willing to fight tonight.

I slip my fingers beneath the waistband of his underwear and pants on each side, waiting until he nods. He plants one hand against the wall as I pull them down. With a man his height, I wasn't sure what to expect. There are so many myths surrounding dick size, but he's perfect. A little on the longer, larger side, but not enough to be uncomfortable or painful. It's a rideable cock if I've ever seen one.

His tongue slips out to wet his lips, and he closes his eyes for a moment as I stroke him. The smooth warm skin is almost as enticing as the tiny sound that escapes him. His body jerks at the first brush of my tongue.

If there's one part of my life where I don't suffer with self-doubt, it's sex. I'm confident in my abilities. There's nothing I want more in this second than to shatter this man standing over me, to make him come apart at my touch.

He pulls in a sharp breath when I slip my lips over the head. I take my time, licking and sucking him. When I move back too far, bringing my head into light contact with the wall, he slides his fingers into my hair, protecting me from bumping it again. The noises he makes as I increase the pressure, curl my tongue around his cock and pull it to the back of my throat spurs me on.

He presses more firmly on the back of my head then restrains himself, moving his hand to my shoulder, but I grasp it, return it to its place, and use his palm to push my head forward, giving him permission to guide himself in and out of my throat. I cup his balls with one hand, rolling them firmly in my fingers while my other hand explores, caressing his ass, his thighs.

"That's so good…so fucking good." The ecstasy and desperation in that deep voice is the sexiest thing I've ever heard. I could do this to him forever. His breaths grow heavy, a rumble slipping into his moans.

"I'm going to come," he warns, urgency flooding his tone as he fights the urge to move his hips, his thigh muscles tensing and releasing under my palms.

"Mm," I hum, acknowledging his words and sucking him deeper. His hands land on the wall and something unintelligible trips out of his mouth when he realizes I'm not going to stop him from finishing right where he is.

He's a sight when I peek up at him. Arms outstretched, he braces himself against the wall, his eyes closed and an expression of pure ecstasy on his parted lips. A second later, he lets out a long groan, spilling into my throat as I swallow.

I sit back and we stay like that for a moment, me on my knees looking up at him, the sound of his breathing loud in the silent room. He reaches down, takes my hand and pulls me to my feet. The look of awe and lustful admiration on his face is only visible for a second before his lips are on mine.

My skin is on fire as he pins me to the wall. His large hands grace both sides of my head, tilting it while his tongue meets mine. The way he kisses me, deep and slow, has my head spinning. As amazing as our first kiss was, this one puts it to shame.

I run my hands under his shirt, unable to get enough of his warm skin, melting as he places a sucking kiss on my neck. As soon as his fingertips brush over my nipple, I pull my shirt off.

"So fucking gorgeous," he says, before kissing me again. He caresses each breast, smiling against my mouth when I moan at the feel of his fingers catching my nipple. I need more of him and tug at his shirt. He pulls it off, giving me a brief glance at the extensive tattoo of a dark, leafless tree that covers his chest and abdomen, only taking his mouth from mine for a quick second, as if he can't bear to stop.

"Bedroom?" he murmurs, nipping at my earlobe.

We head for the stairs, shedding the rest of our clothes along the way. Our hands and mouths keep finding their way back to each other as I walk up the stairs backwards and trip over one of his feet at the top of the staircase. He grabs me before I can hit the ground and grins.

Held aloft a few inches from the floor, giggles burst out of me. "You ran me over with those long legs."

Instead of pulling me the rest of the way up, he lowers me until my bare ass lands on the cool hardwood of the top step and kneels over me. Pleased mischief reflects on his face as he pushes me down until I'm lying back in the hallway. "Are you laughing at me?"

"I'd never."

"I think you are." He dips his head and sucks my nipple into his mouth, ending any argument from me. My hands are in his hair instantly. He bathes both of my nipples with attention and trails his fingertips down my stomach, then looks me in the eye, waiting. It only takes a split second for me to respond.

"God, yes, Arlow. Touch me. Fuck me. I'm going out of my mind."

He leans over to kiss me again as his hand travels downward. "Oh darling, I'm going to make you come until you forget your name and can't stop screaming mine."

I'm going to come as soon as he touches me if he keeps talking like that. My eyes close at the feel of his fingertip on my clit. He circles it gently a few times, then drags his finger farther down, letting his thumb replace it.

"So wet, Calliope. Where are those giggles now, hmm?" he teases, sliding a finger inside of me. My hips flex off the floor. It's the most exquisite torture. He adds another finger and finds my spot, rubbing it while his thumb continues to stroke over my clit.

"Oh." The gasped word is all I can manage. A long, deep kiss sets me on fire while his fingers drive me closer and closer. "Fuck, Arlow."

"Does that feel good?" he murmurs, his mouth hovering over mine.

My hands leap to his sides as the pressure builds, overtaking my ability to think or feel anything except the pleasure he's giving me. "Please don't stop."

"I've got you. Look at me."

It's so difficult to open my eyes as reality hides under pure sensation, but the second my gaze connects with his, an orgasm rocks through me, pulling his name from my throat. He slows his movements, drawing out the enjoyment, and kissing me once more before moving. He kneels a few stairs down and runs his hands up my inner thighs, spreading them.

My entire body jerks at his hot breath between my legs. "Arlow, I don't think I can—"

The words end in a cry as he licks my clit, and my legs try to slam closed of their own accord. I'm too sensitive. It's too much, but oh god, I don't want him to stop. He isn't deterred and pauses only long enough to scoop each of my legs up and drape them over his shoulders. He takes his time exploring me with his tongue and lips before licking back up to circle my clit again.

Sweat coats my skin as I grasp one of the railing slats with one hand and thread my other into his hair. His tongue feels amazing. "Oh god, oh. More pressure, please," I beg. He acquiesces, and his hands stroke along my outer thighs. "Yes, just like that," I groan.

He keeps me right at the edge for what feels like forever, lightening up when the tiniest spasms begin then driving me closer with firmer licks until I'm writhing beneath him. A sharp tug at his hair elicits a throaty moan, and he plants his mouth over my clit, sucking steadily.

His arms clamp around my thighs, holding me in place as I lose my mind and cry out at the overwhelming onslaught of spasms that shoot skin numbing pleasure to every inch of me.

The touch of his tongue is suddenly torture. "Stop! I'm done! Oh god."

He pulls away and softly kisses his way up my stomach before standing up and pulling me to my feet. A satisfied smile tilts his lips when he has to steady me. "Are you okay?"

"Yeah, my legs are just a little shaky."

Without warning, he scoops me up and carries me down the hall to his room. It's dim, with only the bathroom light bleeding in. I'm deposited onto his bed, and he crawls over me. The weight of his body on top of mine feels so right. Perfect. His cock is hard again, and I reach down between us to stroke it.

His breathing speeds up as I rub the head between my lips, coating it with the wetness he's caused. With his arms propped on either side of my head, he gazes down at me, his cock prodding at my entrance.

It feels like the most intimate thing in the world, the way he watches me as he pushes inside, going a little deeper with each flex of his hips. He leans to kiss me, letting his lips linger a moment as his long, unhurried strokes light me up from the inside out. No words are spoken between us. None are necessary as we move together, reveling in the feel of each other. There's no urgency or desperation, only the pure euphoria we're creating, sharing between us.

The little moans he lets out makes me want to hear so much more, and he doesn't argue when I roll us over. Instead, he lies back and watches me, grabbing my hips as I straddle him.

He moans when I sink down on him, taking every hard inch. "I love that sound," I tell him, and his cheeks redden a little, his lips curling up. Christ, he's so sexy and I'm not sure he even knows.

I lean over to suck his neck and kiss down his chest, nuzzling his soft hair. His deep breath when I suck and lick his nipple is something I'm going to remember. He really likes that. When I sit back up and start to move, he grips my hips tightly.

"Fuck yes, ride me," he groans, and I do just that. He reaches between my legs to rub my clit and I'm surprised to feel the need roar back. I'm going to come again. Three times in a night isn't usual for me, but a slow, pulsing pleasure rolls through me, making me shiver and moan.

As soon as I'm finished, Arlow lifts me off him. "Lie on your side." He enters me from behind the moment I do, pulling me back against him. Bending one of my legs up, he proceeds to thrust into me, and I can feel him trying to hold back.

"Harder," I cry, and he gives me what I ask for. He pauses long enough to pull me up onto my hands and knees, then buries himself again.

"That what you want?" he asks, driving into me. It almost sounds like a challenge, but yes, it is exactly what I want, for him to let go. "A good hard fucking?"

"Yes!" My hands clasp the sheets as he shows me what he's capable of. I take everything he has to give until his strokes become stuttered and he stops on a deep thrust, coming inside me with a loud gravelly moan. It's a sound I'll never stop thinking about.

He falls onto the bed next to me, coated in sweat, his hair damp, his face flushed and eyes bright. "You're so damn sexy," I blurt, and his eyebrows leap up.

"That's my line, gorgeous. Come here." I lay my head on his chest with no hesitation. He catches my hand as I trace the tree branches inked onto his chest, brings it to his mouth and kisses it.

I'm not sure what to say, if anything, and he seems to feel the same. Finally, I sit up. "I'm going to shower and get to sleep. Tomorrow is going to be a long day."

He rubs his hand up and down my back. "Use the guest shower and I'll use mine. If I get you in there with me, neither of us is going to get any sleep."

"Good night, Arlow."

"Good night, Peach."

I'm not going to overthink what just happened or what it might mean, at least not right now. It was the best night I've had in years and I'm not going to let my brain spoil it. Instead, I take a quick shower and crawl into the guest bed. Not more than five minutes later, I'm surprised to feel Arlow climb in with me and pull me into his arms.

This man was born to be the big spoon. Satisfied and content in a way I wasn't sure I could feel again, I drift off to sleep.

———

The scent surrounding me is as comforting as the arm tucked around my middle. *Arlow.* His warm figure pressed against my back doesn't budge as my phone alarm continues its insistent serenade. Bleary-eyed, I manage to reach it on the side table and shut it off. He rolls over onto his back but doesn't wake.

It's no wonder since we've barely been asleep for three hours. My entire body aches in the best way, and the memories of last night are fresh in my head. I knew it would be good with him, but that was beyond any expectation. The way he took me, the passion in every touch and kiss and lick. The feral near growl in his voice when he said my name. This sweet, beekeeping, nature loving, unbearably gentle man fucked the absolute hell out of me.

My friends will be here soon to get me, but I can't resist lingering a moment to look at him in the dim light. God, he's so gorgeous. His white lashes rest against his cheek, looking so soft in contrast to the dark locks lying in a tumbled mess on the pillow.

I study his broad shoulders and the planes of his chest. The dark tree tattoo stands out against his lightly tanned skin, and my fingers itch to touch him again, to trace the branches through the scattered curly hair.

My phone beeps with a text from Leo.

LEO

Be there in thirty minutes.

I have to get moving.

ME

I'll be ready.

As much as I hate to leave after last night, we could probably both use a few days to think. Caught up in the moment, we let ourselves give in to the attraction, the lust for each other. I hope he has no regrets. I don't, even if it does turn out to be only one night. He initiated it, but does that mean he's moving on from the ex and ready for more or did our chemistry overcome him?

Sitting here overthinking things isn't going to do me any good. We'll talk and figure things out later. Right now, I have a festival to get ready for. I'm glad the night ended with a shower because there's no time. Arlow doesn't stir when I get out of bed and slip quietly down the hall to the bathroom.

My small suitcase is packed and waiting in the trunk of my car. After I brush my teeth, get dressed, and tame my hair into a half decent ponytail, I sling my overnight bag over my shoulder and peek into the guest room. He's still out cold. I'm not going to wake him. I'll leave him a little note downstairs.

I borrow one of his travel coffee mugs and fill it with cold brew from his fridge, munching on a bagel as I look around for some paper and a pen. I'm not sure what to say. *Had a great time riding the hell out of you. See you in a few days?*

A giggle slips out as I locate a pen on the table and a notebook on one of his bookshelves. Happiness has me almost bubbling over. Last night really was amazing and now I'm heading off to do my favorite thing in the world. Life is good.

Flipping open the tablet, I realize my mistake. It isn't writing paper, it's a sketchbook. The first page contains a rough but skillful sketch of a fallen log. He's so damned talented. Curiosity gets the best of me, and I flip to the next page.

Maybe it's the initial shock or just pure denial at the sight of the incredibly detailed picture of me, but for a moment, I can only stand there, staring like it might change.

He drew me. Under any other circumstance, it'd be flattering. Touching. Except I recognize the moment he's captured.

The only time I've been topless in the woods.

That was right after I'd arrived. We hadn't even met yet, not for another two weeks at least. He had to have seen me to draw this so perfectly, down to the water bottle on the bank of the creek. He was there.

My chest aches, reminding me to breathe. Not knowing what I expect or hope to find, I turn the page to see another drawing of me. This time I'm sitting on the bridge, dangling my feet over. My attention focuses in on one detail, the band-aid on my ankle. I'd scraped it on the edge of a box that morning, only a few days after the day I'd swam topless in the creek.

Tingles run down my spine as I flip through more drawings, all documenting days I thought I was alone in the woods. There's even one where I'm picking his peaches. Finding me in his orchard wasn't an accident. Those times that I felt like I was being watched, when I'd dismissed it as anxiety, he was following me.

Watching me.

My heart leaps into my throat at the sound of my name.

CHAPTER 17

ARLOW

"Calliope." She jerks violently, spinning around to face me, eyes wide with shock. "What's wr—" The sight of the sketchbook in her hand causes any further words to falter.

"What is this?" she asks in a horrified whisper, holding up the page of her topless drawing.

My blood rushes through my veins, heating my face. There's no avenue here but the truth. "I can explain." The quick step back from me when I approach her is a knife in my chest.

"You were following me in the woods. It was you. I thought…" Her chest rises and falls faster. "I wasn't imagining it."

"I'm sorry. When I saw you—"

My explanation is cut short as she rushes out my front door. She's made it down my steps into the yard when I get to the porch. "Calli! Wait."

Pausing, she spins around and shakes her head. "Don't come near me!"

The fear in her voice is tearing me to scraps. "I won't." Holding up my palms, I stay on my bottom step. "Please, don't be afraid of me. I'd never hurt you. Just let me explain."

Fear battles with rage on her face. "Who was the man yesterday?" she demands. "You sent someone to follow me."

"No. Listen, please. That had nothing to do with it. I don't know who that was."

"You were stalking me!" she shouts, throwing the sketchbook at me. "Why?"

The words spill out without thought. "You shine."

It's the truth but not a good explanation. Her frown deepens and she takes another step back. If I don't tell her everything, I'm going to lose her. She's going to think I'm some kind of monster who was stalking her through the woods all this time. "I wanted to draw you. I was out in the woods to do some sketches and I stumbled onto you at the creek. Once I saw you, nothing else was worth touching my pencil. You were so happy and all I could think about was capturing that moment. It was wrong. I should've left or told you I was there. I'm sorry."

"You were there more than once."

"I was. You inspired me." I drag my hand through my hair, desperate to find the right words. "Fuck, inspired isn't a strong enough word. Before you came, I hadn't drawn anything of worth in months. Then I saw you and...you gave me my ability back."

"So, you followed me to keep drawing me?"

"A few times, yes. I swear, it was never threatening or sexual. You triggered something that freed me from a creative block."

"You think that's a justifiable reason to stalk someone? Because you wanted to draw them?"

I'm glad to see her fear fading even as rage replaces it. I deserve her anger. She doesn't deserve to be afraid because of me. "No, nothing justifies it." It sounds crazy and I can't blame her for not understanding. She needs to know what she really did for me. "I need to show you something in the barn. It doesn't excuse my behavior but...please."

She blinks at me, indecision written on her face. "My friends will be here any minute to get me."

I'm not sure if that's a comment on the time restraint or a warning because she's afraid to be alone with me now. "It'll only take a second."

Finally, she nods, and gestures for me to lead the way. What I'm about to reveal to her, only my family knows about, but the risk is worth it to wipe that terrified look of betrayal from her face.

CHAPTER 18

CALLIOPE

THIS IS CRAZY. I MUST BE INSANE TO FOLLOW HIM INTO THE BARN AFTER what I just found, but the truth is I desperately want an explanation that will let me believe him. The way he makes me feel isn't something I want to let go of, especially after how wonderful last night was.

The barn is cool and smells faintly of hay and horses, despite the fact it contains neither and clearly hasn't for a long time. It's been renovated into a large open space in front and smaller rooms on the back end.

He enters one of the smaller rooms, and I hesitate at the doorway, looking around. A camera is rigged up on the ceiling, pointed at an easel that contains a sheet draped canvas. He removes the sheet to display a drawing of cupped hands filled with water hovering over a creek. Stunned, I stare at the amazing detail. The river rocks look like you could pluck them off the canvas, and the water somehow seems to flow on the page. There's something familiar about it. Something I can't put my finger on, but it feels like I've seen it before.

My muscles tense and my stomach falls into my feet when Arlow turns his back and pulls a light gray hooded mask over his head.

Confusion and fear battle inside me, sending me back a few steps. Why is he covering his face? I'm a half second away from running like hell when he turns, and comprehension strikes me.

The hooded mask that fits like a second skin and the round glasses are instantly recognizable. "You're Nameless."

This is why he doesn't allow anyone in his barn. He said he likes to keep his art projects private, but that wasn't strictly true. He shares them anonymously. I gape at him, trying to wrap my head around what he's just revealed as he removes the glasses and mask.

Arlow is Nameless, one of the most well-known artists in the world, due to his unmatched talent at photorealist and hyperrealist drawings, his social media channels that allow the audience to watch him create the masterpieces, and the mystery that surrounds his identity.

His posture is rigid, and he brings his hand to the back of his neck. "Nobody knows except my family and a broker that helps me sell at auction and to galleries."

The real depth of the power he's given me sinks in—the trust he's placing in me not to give away his secret. "Why are you telling me this?"

"I know it doesn't excuse me following you like that, but I want you to see and understand. I explained before how random things stand out or scream at me to be drawn sometimes. It's never happened with a person before, and I didn't stop to think or consider what I was doing. Or how alarming and terrifying it would be for you to discover."

"We didn't meet by chance in the orchard. You followed me."

His throat contracts on a hard swallow before he nods. "That was the last time I did. The decision to talk to you was impulsive, and I went about it in the worst possible way, approaching you in such an isolated place. When you took off, I felt terrible about how badly I scared you."

My mind churns trying to grasp these new discoveries. Yes, I was being stalked through the woods but not for nefarious reasons. My neighbor turned friend who not six hours ago had his face buried between my legs is actually a famous artist that I've followed for years online. All those nights I wondered what he was up to in this barn, he was live streaming and drawing.

I don't work a conventional job. I guess not since I recently saw one of his works go for over a million at auction.

Through the swirl of emotions that I'm trying to wrangle, a mirthless chuckle escapes me when I realize why the cupped hands drawing in front of me looks familiar. "I watched you start on this. The first week I moved in."

It's his turn to be surprised. "You follow me?"

"Well, not through the fucking woods like you did me, but online, yeah," I scoff.

Relief starts to leak into his pinched face. "There's another project I want you to see." He leads the way out of the room and into the next one that has an identical setup. It's apparent he has multiple projects in different stages of completion that he films or streams live from different rooms.

He rubs his fingers over his lips. "I want you to know that I haven't shown this publicly and won't without your permission. I recorded the process but didn't livestream and nothing has been posted."

The sheet is pulled away from a canvas half my size and my breath catches in my throat. In painstaking detail is a drawing of me lying on the log beside the bonfire. I'm looking up at the stars, one side of my face glowing in firelight, my hair flowing to nearly touch the ground. Thin gray smoke almost appears to be moving in the wind. It's the same way the water felt in his creek drawing. I'm stunned beyond words at how he's portrayed me.

The silence must be more than he can bear because my name comes out in a whisper. "Calliope. Say something."

"You've made me so...beautiful."

"I didn't make you anything, I only showed it. Only a fraction of who you are could ever be embodied in any work. You're my muse."

My heart leaps in my chest, swelling with hope. Maybe I'm reading too much into that statement because my feelings are getting too strong to be ignored. The only reason he's given for wanting to know me is that I inspire him to draw, but the soft way he treats me, the passionate night we had, it must be more than that, right?

"That's why you want to be around me?" I clarify, fighting to keep my voice even. "Because it helps you draw?"

He walks toward me with an adamant shake of his head. "No, I want to be around you because you're amazing. You're sweet and smart and fun. I love talking to you. The way we can spend an entire night talking about everything and nothing, I've never had that sort of connection with anyone before. You don't just shine, Calliope, you blind me with it."

His words steal my breath and nearly bring tears to my eyes.

It's unfortunate how often men ruin things by continuing to talk. "Please say you forgive me. I'm sorry. I'm sorry for following you in the beginning. I'm sorry for scaring you. I'm sorry for letting last night happen—as fucking perfect as it was."

It feels like my entire body deflates, and I have to swallow before speaking. "You regret last night?"

"I regret letting things go too far between us when I can't be with you. I don't want to hurt you."

My phone buzzes in my pocket and I'm grateful for the excuse not to answer him, to look away. "My friends are here."

"Calli…"

Looking into his eyes, I find a matching pain there. "I have to go. We have a long drive." When I turn to rush out of the barn, he follows, locking it behind us.

I'm surprised to see Leo's RV sitting in Arlow's driveway instead of mine. He, Freya, and Calvin all climb out, excited to see me. It's been too long since our last concert together.

"I told you it was this place, not that creepy ass cabin!" Leo announces as Freya hugs me. "She swore I had the wrong house."

"You do, actually. I was just talking to my neighbor. I do indeed live in the creepy ass cabin," I inform him, hugging him as everyone laughs.

Calvin points at me and we both shout, "Cal!" before he charges at me, lifting me off my feet with a hug. It's a silly joke on our names that always makes the others roll their eyes but never gets old. God, it's good to see them.

"How are you?" he asks, placing me back on my feet.

My brain is pure chaos and I'm losing my shit in a stunning number of ways. "I'm great. I can't wait to get going. Who's riding with me?"

There's room enough for all four of us in Leo's RV but they'll be heading off to another festival after this one, and if I drive separately, they won't have to bring me home.

"I am," Cal announces, pulling a bag out of Leo's passenger seat and slinging it over his back. "I made a killer playlist with every band that we're going to see this week."

Leo looks past me and nods. "How's it going?"

I didn't realize Arlow was standing behind us until Leo addressed him.

Arlow gives him a nod back, then regards me. Words form and die on his lips multiple times before he mumbles, "Have a safe trip." He doesn't look back as he returns to his house.

"What was that about?" Cal asks before we even make it out of the driveway. "Your neighbor looked like he wanted to bury me in that graveyard. Are you seeing him or something?"

"No. We're...friends." Are we? I'm not sure about anything anymore. "He's just not very social." I nod toward the screen on my dash. "Connect your phone and let's hear that killer playlist."

"Hell yeah."

This is what I need to clear my head. Music and time away. It may not give me any answers, but for a while, I just want to forget. Forget being followed through the woods. Forget busted windows and stolen ATVs and ashes that still need to be dumped. Forget the confusing man who goes from wanting me to wanting me at arms length. For a few days, I want to let it all go and have fun with friends I likely won't see again until spring.

———

The rock and blues festival is the biggest of its genre in the country and the one I look forward to the most every year. It's four straight days of some of my favorite bands along with a lot of newer and smaller artists. Alcohol flows constantly. There are too many delicious food choices to choose from. Just the energy of all the people together, hyped to see our favorites, is such an uplifting experience.

My mind is a mess on the drive but once I get into the crowd with music filling my ears and the drums rattling my chest, everything fades away. This is exactly what I need. We stay in a nearby hotel and exhaustion has me passing out the second my head hits the pillow every night.

It isn't until the third evening that thoughts of Arlow drill their way through the wall of avoidance I constructed. The last band plays, and the soulful sound of the singer's voice brings tears to my eyes. Stars shine overhead and all I can think is that Arlow would love this.

I make my way out of the crowd and wind through the blankets and chairs scattered over the back lawn section until I find a quiet spot. Tomorrow is our last day and then it's time to return to reality.

The reality is that I'm falling for a man who simply doesn't feel the same way about me. I know he enjoys spending time with me, and our chemistry is undeniable, but he doesn't want anything more. Whether it's the ex, a fear of commitment in general, or that I'm just not the one for him, his reasons don't matter. The outcome is the same. So is the decision I need to make.

The truth is I'm not sure I can be his friend. Not right now. It's not that he followed me in the woods or that I don't trust him. I feel too much. His regret over kissing me stung. His regret over our passionate night of mind-blowing sex is devastating. The morning after, I tried to tell myself that even if it was a one time thing, I'd be okay with it, but now I don't know if I can be.

"Hey girl." Freya's aunt Helen sits down beside me in the grass. "Are you okay?"

"I'm fine. Just needed a break."

"You look like you're going to burst into tears. What happened? Did somebody mess with you?"

"No, nothing happened."

Helen is one of the most interesting people I know. She was a psychiatrist for over twenty-five years. A self-described hippie, she has always made time for concerts and festivals. After retiring in her fifties, she decided she was going to do the thing she loved most, watching her favorite bands. She's laidback and such an easy person to talk to that when she tilts her head to look at me, the words spill out. "I'm falling in love with someone who doesn't feel the same way."

Her face softens and she nods, pulling a tissue out of her bag to hand to me when a tear leaks out. "I'm sorry."

"Happens all the time, right?" I ask, trying to keep my voice light as if that might change things. "So why does it feel like the world is ending?"

"Because love is a world all its own and the end of any world is tragic. Do you want to tell me about him?"

For the next ten minutes, I let it all pour out. Meeting Arlow, spending all our nights together, how I fell in love with nature along with him. I tell her he's an artist, and even about the drawings he did of me, how he followed me, but not about his identity. Helen is a smart empathetic woman who counseled people and couples for most of her life. If I want her genuine opinion or input, she needs to know as much as I can tell her.

"An artist," she says with a nostalgic smile. "No wonder he has you in knots. The creative types are always a challenge. They worship love like no other, but they live in their heads and it's not always a good place to be."

"I've never met anyone like him. Kind and gentle but with this rugged masculinity that's irresistible. There's this silent stillness in him that's so calming." My mind flashes back to him thrusting into me, his hands biting into my hips. "And it's the best sex I've ever had, oh my god," I exclaim, letting my head fall back with a laugh. Just getting it all off my chest has made me feel better.

Helen chuckles and pulls her jacket around her tighter. "In my experience, the calm kind-hearted guys are wild in the bedroom and savagely protective if you're in danger. Quiet hearts are soaked in love, and the passion that comes from them can be addictive."

"You sound like you had your own artist."

A fond smile accompanies her nod. "The first man I loved was a painter. The last was a musician. None of the men between could even come close."

"I'm not sure what to do. He's been honest with me from the first time I kissed him that he doesn't want to be with me, but then we can't seem to keep our hands off each other. Is it even possible to be friends at this point? I want to think that I can set stricter boundaries and not lose him completely, but I don't know. Tonight, I miss the fuck out of him."

Helen rubs my shoulder. "I can't tell you what to do, but if you want my advice, I think you need some space. It's only been a couple of days. Do you have to go home tomorrow? Are there responsibilities you need to get back to?"

"I suppose not."

"Don't go back because you miss him. Give yourself a little time and get some perspective. We're going to be traveling for the next couple of weeks, hitting the last of the festivals and a few concerts. Stick with us."

There's no job I need to return to and no reason not to go with them. No reason other than how badly I want to see Arlow. But then what? Try not to want him the way I do?

"Do you think a platonic friendship is possible when one person feels more?"

Helen considers it. "Feels more? Maybe. Love is a different monster."

We stand up as our friends approach us. "Thanks for the talk. I'd love to hear about your artist and musician sometime."

"Stick with us and I might even give you the details." She grins at me. "And they are scorching. My musician was a master with his instrument."

"What are you two laughing about?" Leo asks.

"Musician dick," Helen says, and both of us crack up.

It's late when we get back to the hotel but I'm not tired enough to sleep. Instead, I go online to look at the concerts on the itinerary Helen gave me in case I decide to keep traveling with them. A couple are sold out but there are resale tickets available that aren't ridiculously priced. The last concert is eighteen days away.

Eighteen days of laughing and hanging out with friends, of trying different restaurants along the way, of camping in their RV some nights and staying in hotels on others. Eighteen days to try to get over this feeling that my heart is being slowly peeled like an onion.

Decision made. Once I order my tickets and snuggle down in bed, I'm finally able to sleep.

We wake up to torrential rain and a sharp drop in temperature on the final day of the festival.

"They're delaying for two hours as of now," Leo says. The four of us sit around a table in a coffee shop. It's right across the street from the venue and filled with other concertgoers trying to decide whether to wait it out or not.

Freya holds up her phone with her weather app open. "The forecast isn't looking good. I don't think the rain is going anywhere. We could go ahead to Florida and have a couple of days on the beach before the Rock on the Water Festival." The rest of the festivals and outdoor concerts on our list are in the far south where it's still warm.

"What do you all think?" Helen asks.

"Sounds like a plan to me," Leo says, and the others agree.

I nod and sip my coffee. "Let's do it. I need to stop along the way to shop for some clothes and a swimsuit. I didn't think I'd be gone this long."

"I'm so excited you decided to come!" Freya exclaims. "I'm riding with you today."

"Me too," Helen adds.

Freya beams at me. "Girl's day!"

After finding a hotel online and making a reservation, we agree to meet there tonight, then split up for the drive that takes nearly seven hours. The guys beat us there since we stop at a few stores along the way, but I'm all set to travel with them now.

It feels so amazing to wake up to the sight of sunlight twinkling on the ocean from my hotel balcony.

After breakfast, we all hit the beach, and I send Silver a picture of my view with a text.

Me: Change of plan. I won't be back for a couple of weeks.

My phone rings seconds later and she exclaims, "What the hell? Where are you?"

"Florida today, but I'm going to travel with my friends for a bit and go to a few more concerts before I come back."

"You lucky bitch! It looks amazing. It's freezing here." She pauses for a few seconds. "Are you staying away because of that guy in the woods?"

No, because of a completely different guy in the woods.

"No, I need some space from Arlow."

"Did something happen?"

So much has happened, and it sucks I can't tell her everything. "I may have fucked the hell out of him the night before I left."

Her laughter makes me smile. "And now you want to avoid him, yeah, I get that."

"I take it you haven't had a second round with Lee?"

"No way. The last thing I need is another man right now. What happened with Arlow? Was it…not good?"

"It was so damn good," I sigh.

"And…"

"And then he told me he regretted it and now my head is all messed up."

"Ugh! Why are they all like this?"

Digging my feet into the sand, I tilt my head back, letting the sun warm my cheeks. "I don't know, but I'm not stressing over it for now. I'm going to get nice and tan, drink too many margaritas, and have fun."

"Girl yes! Live your best life and send me pictures. Don't play his damn games. You deserve better." She mumbles something to someone in the background before returning to the conversation. "Mom says hi and to ask if you'll bring her a magnet from Florida. She collects each state."

"Absolutely. How are things there? Everything work out with having Charlotte back?"

"It's like she never left. We're good. Don't worry about anything here. Go have fun. Get some selfies with a hot beach guy and I'll accidentally send it to Arlow."

Laughter spills out of me. She really is the best. "You're crazy."

I haven't heard from Arlow since I left but minutes after talking to Silver, I get a text.

ARLOW

I know you're pissed at me. Can we talk tonight once you're back?

As much as I miss him right now, I'm doing the right thing. Sparing my heart. Because just seeing his name on the screen makes my chest ache.

CHAPTER 19

ARLOW

I'VE RESISTED CONTACTING CALLI, DESPITE THE URGE TO APOLOGIZE again or try to get her to talk to me. She's upset with me and has every right to be, but I hate how we left things between us, especially after the night we had together. Mistake or not, it was the best night of my life. She let herself be so vulnerable with me only to find out hours later what I'd done before we met. I'm not sure if she's angry or hurt or both. I just want to fix it. The last thing I ever want to do is hurt her.

After not hearing from her the last few days, I finally texted her this morning since she's due back any time. She left me on read.

Ten hours later, she hasn't responded. I'm not going to be able to concentrate until I see her get home safely tonight, even if she doesn't want to hear from me. Instead of working in the barn as I have been almost nonstop, I sit on my porch. I'm usually an extremely patient person but every minute that I don't see headlights coming down our road feels like an eternity.

To try to distract myself, I open the app to the new trail cameras I installed in the woods a few days ago. Only two of them receive a strong enough signal for me to get real time notifications and see the

179

pictures on the cloud. The others will require me to pull the memory cards manually.

Two videos wait for me. In one, a deer wanders past, pausing near the bridge to drink from the stream. In another, a rabbit hops by. No men in masks or other trespassers. I've installed some security cameras around my barn and house as well. A package holding cameras for Calli's place waits for her on my kitchen table. I'm not sure if Handleman is who I'm dealing with but I'm not taking any chances.

Minutes tick into an hour and then another. It's getting late, our time of night, and I won't be surprised if it's the middle of the night before she turns into the driveway. My phone buzzes on the table beside me and my heart leaps at the sight of her name. Until I read her reply.

> **CALLI**
>
> I'm not angry. Added some concerts to my trip so I'm not coming back for a couple of weeks.

What? Without giving it a thought, I call her. It goes to voicemail, and after struggling with what to say, I hang up without leaving a message. As soon as I do, another text comes through.

> **CALLI**
>
> I need some space. Your secret is safe. We can talk when I get back.

Goddamn it. I shouldn't have touched her. I fucked everything up. She doesn't even want to hear from me. My instinct is to apologize again and ask her to talk to me for a minute but what's that going to solve? She's told me what she needs. Space. The ache that swells inside me at the desire to hear her voice and know that we're going to be okay after this is excruciating but it doesn't override that fact.

My fingers hover over my phone, hesitating. What is she doing right now? Driving on a dark highway to another concert? Partying at a bar or hotel? Camping out for the night in that RV? It shouldn't matter. She isn't mine. Didn't I just tell her that I couldn't be with her? I have no right to be jealous that she's with that stupid manbun hipster fuck who couldn't wait to hug her before climbing into her car.

Finally, I type out a reply.

ME

I understand.

What else can I say? She reads it immediately and doesn't respond.

The silence closes in around me as I set my phone down. Two more weeks. It feels like an unbearable amount of time to have this uncertainty between us hanging above my head.

Fuck. I get to my feet and head for the barn. There's no need for the mask or glasses. No livestreaming is going to happen. Instead, I uncover the canvas of Calliope and begin to work on drawing the light in her eyes that I always see in her.

It's dawn before I stumble bleary eyed back to my house to fall into my bed, but my sleep is restless and short. It's fine. The earlier I get to Paducah the better. Before I go, I stop by Calli's cabin to fill her bird feeders and note that her bird bath needs to be cleaned out soon. I'll do it tomorrow when I finish getting the last of our firewood stacked.

It doesn't take me long to find the address I'm looking for. Chris Handleman is supposed to be living with his mother, Grace, while he's on parole. An easy internet search gave me her address. Maybe it's a good thing that Calli is gone for a little while longer. It gives me time to figure out if Handleman is the thief that terrified her in the woods.

My plan is simple. Park and watch the house to see if he's living there, then follow him. See where he goes, if he's coming anywhere near my house, and maybe locate my ATV, though that's low on the list.

Fortunately, his mother lives on a busy road lined with houses and duplexes. With the constant flow of traffic and people, a man sitting in his truck all day won't be suspicious. Nobody comes or goes from the small house with the crooked front porch for three hours. I'm about to take a break and find somewhere to get a coffee when the door opens.

It takes me a moment to recognize her when she steps out. With her shoulders slumped and her head down, she doesn't look up once as she trudges to a small white car and gets inside. Grace Handleman is a husk of the woman who once stood over me and told me to rot in hell. Of course she is. Look how much she's lost, what I took from her.

After she drives away, I stay well past dark, but there's no sign of anyone else, and the lights only go on inside the house when Grace returns. If Chris is living here, he isn't around today.

That's how I spend the next week, watching the Handleman house at different times of day and night, trying to catch a glimpse of him. The only people who come and go are Grace and a few other older women.

It doesn't tell me much, other than he's probably not staying where he's supposed to be while on parole. Maybe plans changed and he's nowhere near here. Who knows? Nothing else has happened at my place, and I've kept a close eye on Calli's cabin as well. Nothing has shown up on the trail cameras. I'm not sure what to think anymore.

It'd be much easier to watch Calli's place if I put her cameras up, but I'd need to get inside. After shopping for a new ATV that will be delivered tomorrow, I stop by Lucky's Diner just before closing time to talk to Silver.

The place is empty. Silver sits behind the counter, grinning at something on her phone and does a double take when she sees me walk in. "Do you have a pick-up order? I didn't get anything."

"No, I was hoping to talk to you for a second."

Her eyebrows raise a bit, but she nods and lays her phone down. "Did something happen?"

"No, but you know about the thefts we had and everything?"

"Of course."

"I put some trail cameras up and security cameras around my place. I have some for Calli too, but I need to get inside her cabin to connect them to her internet. Mine won't reach."

"So call her."

"Uh, yeah," I sigh, running my hand over my chin. "She doesn't really want to hear from me right now. I thought if you could let me in long enough to—"

Silver holds her palm up. "Let me stop you right there. You want me to let you put up cameras monitoring the home of my friend who won't talk to you."

"Calli knows I ordered them, and she wants them installed. I'll hand over the access to them when she returns, and she can reset the passwords."

"Absolutely not. First of all, I assume that's illegal. My mother might own the house, but we aren't living in it. That permission needs to come straight from her." She bats down my next suggestion before I can say it. "And I'm not interrupting her fun to ask her for you. Wait until she gets back. Let her have some time without worrying about that shit."

She's probably right about that. I know Calli wouldn't have minded the cameras being put up, but she asked for space. "You're right. It can wait." The next question out of my mouth can't be stopped. "Have you heard from her lately? Is she...doing okay?"

"She's having the time of her life. Lots of pictures at the beach and backstage at a concert."

"Good. Okay. I'm going to go."

"Hang on a second," she says as I start toward the exit. She disappears behind the kitchen door then emerges with a bag in her hand

and holds it out to me, her lips twitching into a restrained grin. "Had some extras."

Two big apple fritters sit inside. "Thank you."

———

It's been eighteen days since Calli left and I haven't heard a word from her. She said a couple of weeks, but what if she's decided not to come back at all? I'm afraid I'll see a mover's truck pull in instead of her car.

The discussion over whether to install cameras at her cabin became moot a few days ago with a notice from our internet provider. The good news is that we'll be getting much better high-speed internet on our entire street. The bad news is it will be down for two weeks while they work on it and install new cables or some shit. The cameras won't work. It also means I can't livestream.

I posted an announcement that there would be no live videos for a while, then spent the last couple of days getting videos scheduled to post during the interim. I've spent my time watching Handleman's house, helping Lee with a few repairs, stocking firewood at Calli's place and mine, getting the hives ready for the cold months, and drawing all night—staying as busy as possible so I don't think about her.

I haven't had the heart to sit by the fire like I used to, but tonight I make my way through the graveyard and up the hill. We're having a spurt of warm weather, the last gasp of fall before winter sets in. No reason to waste it.

The night is cloudy, and I'm almost glad for that. The stars aren't the same without her. The name Calliope suits her, but Persephone would fit as well. When she leaves, she takes all the beauty of the world with her.

The air is still and so silent, filled only with the crackle of the fire and my heavy sigh. She may not come back, or she may only come back to get her stuff. How could anyone blame her? She came here for a peaceful getaway and instead got her car window smashed, ran into a thief in the woods, then found out I followed her.

After all this time, I thought I understood loneliness, the creeping hell of it, but that's something I'd become accustomed to. Now, the thought that she may not want to see me again, that I'll return to a solitary life is horrible.

All I want to do is go back to my porch. It's a struggle not to spend every second there watching for her to pull into the driveway. That's another reason I need to keep things platonic between us. Love and obsession walk a thin line inside me. When I love something, I'll let it take over my life. I found that out when I picked up a pencil to sketch. This is just the first time that feeling has been directed toward a person.

I can't let another minute go by without reaching out to her. Terrified she won't reply, I send a text.

ME

I miss you. I hope you're having a great time.

I can see that she reads it instantly, but no little dots appear to show she's going to acknowledge it. Sitting back, I tilt my head to watch the stars appear a handful at a time from behind the moving clouds.

How can the night feel so empty and heavy at the same time?

CHAPTER 20

CALLIOPE

I've picked up my phone to text Arlow back three different times and set it back down without doing it. He misses me. Part of me was sure he wouldn't be giving me a second thought by now. That he would've moved on to something else that caught his eye and inspired him. Artists are fickle and unpredictable, that's what Helen warned me.

He respected my need for space and hasn't contacted me until today. I want to reply but my head is spinning with so much I want to say and probably shouldn't.

Helen's advice to get away was sound, and as the days have passed, I haven't missed him any less, but I've had time to think and be real with myself. Distance has given me perspective. Maybe I am falling for him, or maybe two years of isolation and loneliness led me to get close to someone too quickly. The same could be true for him and his reclusive lifestyle. He may be attracted to me and enjoy being around me, but he doesn't want anything more. He's important to me and I don't want to lose him, but something needs to change.

My plan when I moved was to get out more and meet people, find new hobbies. And I did. But once we met, a lot of that took a backseat to being with him. It's time to focus on myself again. I need to spend less time with him. He can be an important part of my life, a close friend, without being the center of it. It's funny, I've never been the type to latch onto a man before. I value my independence too much. There's just something about him.

We're going to have a talk about the stalking because I won't forgive that twice.

"Earth to Calli."

My head jerks up to see everyone's eyes on me. The sounds and smells of the roadside diner thrust their way back into my awareness. "Sorry, what?"

Freya tilts her head, scrutinizing me. "Are you sure you're up to driving tonight? You look like you're zoning out pretty hard."

We're all exhausted after weeks on the road but I'm not sleepy, just distracted by a certain beekeeper. "I'm fine. What did I miss?" We're only about five hours from my house so the plan is for everyone to crash with me tonight since it'll be past two a.m. by the time we get there, then we all have to say goodbye tomorrow.

"Nothing, but there's a snowstorm hitting northern Michigan so we're going to have to stop somewhere for another night after we leave your place anyway. If you want to wait and drive back tomorrow, we can grab a room here."

"I'm not sleepy. I was reading a text." An idea strikes me. "Why don't you spend tomorrow night at my place too? We can all sleep in my cabin if you don't mind some pallets on the floor, and it won't be too cold if you decide to sleep in the RV."

"Are you sure?" Leo asks.

"Of course. We can have one more night to hang out. Build a fire, grill out, it'll be fun." We've had such a great time and as eager as I am to get home, I hate to see them all go.

"Sounds great," Cal exclaims, and the others agree. While everyone grabs a coffee for the road, I pick my phone back up and reply to Arlow.

It's been a great time. Be home by tomorrow.
See you soon.

Cal volunteers to drive for a few hours so I hand over my keys and happily settle into the passenger seat while Helen rides in the back. Once we pull out onto the road to follow the RV, I call Silver.

"You'd better not say you still aren't coming home, bitch," she answers, without a hello.

"We're on our way now, but it'll be the middle of the night before we get there. My friends are going to stay tomorrow night too. Do you want to come over and meet them? We're going to cook out, have some drinks and a bonfire."

"Hell yeah. Have you talked to Arlow?"

"I texted him that I'm on my way back, but I haven't talked to him. Is everything okay?"

"Yep. He came in to the diner last week and wanted me to let him in your cabin to connect some security cameras."

I totally forgot about those. "Has something else happened?"

"No, he said everything was quiet."

That's a relief. We've had enough trouble. "Did you let him in?"

"Did I give a man permission to surveille your property? Fuck no. I gave him some apple fritters and sent him on his way."

The familiar sound of the proofing cabinet timer chimes in the background and I have a sudden desire to be in that kitchen, surrounded by delicious smells and laughing with her. "Okay," I chuckle. "I have magnets for your mom from six different states."

"She's going to adopt you. What can I bring tomorrow? Gary made a huge pan of potato salad."

"That sounds great." My phone begins to cut in and out as we enter a rural area. "I have to go. See you tomorrow."

This should be fun, introducing my concert friends to my new friends. I intend to invite Arlow too, but I won't be surprised if he declines, considering it's a bunch of people he doesn't know.

The decision to stay away this long was difficult but I'm glad I did, despite missing Arlow so much. It was such a good time and really helped me get my head straight. Now I'm headed back to my new life to reunite with friends and part with others. I peek up at the stars as we hurtle through the night, my car eating up the miles.

Everything is going to be alright.

CHAPTER 21

ARLOW

THE WORLD SEEMS TO LIGHTEN AROUND ME AS I READ CALLI'S TEXT FOR the third time in ten minutes. *See you soon.* After being afraid she wouldn't come back or wouldn't want to see me if she did, those words bring such relief. I don't expect her to instantly forgive me for following her, but at least I'll have the opportunity to talk to her about it again, to try to smooth things over. It was hard to tell how she felt when she left.

The relief also comes with exhaustion, and I realize how tensed up I've been. Instead of letting the fire burn down, I douse it and go home to get some sleep. I can't remember the last time I went to bed before midnight, but I'm out cold in minutes.

It's midsummer and the golden light tangles in Calliope's hair as she looks back at me, her grin holding the power of endless suns. "Come on, you're the one with the long legs," she taunts, running through the field of clover. "Catch me."

My strides are long but bring me no closer to her. It feels like I'm running in sand, my ankles weighed down. My calls for her only speed her steps. "Wait, please."

She laughs and continues running toward the field of overgrown wild-

flowers. At the edge of the field, she pauses and her smile falls. "Watch out for the shards. They're everywhere. You can't avoid them. They cut so bad." Her hands plunge into her pockets and emerge holding broken pieces of an orange juice bottle. Blood runs through her fingers as she holds them up to show me, then shoves them back into her pockets.

"Calliope!" I scream with all my strength, but it comes out as a hoarse whisper.

She turns and runs again, disappearing into the wildflowers. I don't know what's going on. All I know is I need to get to her. It feels like I've been running for an eternity before my feet land in the flowers, trampling them, shoving them aside. I'm desperate to find her.

My heart leaps into my throat when a different woman blocks my path. "Melody," I whisper.

She flips her blond hair back in a gesture I've seen her do a million times. Her growing smile is scathing. "Do you love her? You never loved me."

"I'm sorry. I'm so sorry." My attempt to run past her is fruitless, my feet glued to the earth.

"You will be." The voice that responds doesn't belong to Melody, but to Chris. He stands beside her, glaring at me. He brings a bright peach to his lips and takes a bite, chewing viciously as the juice runs out through his growing malevolent smile. "Don't worry. I'll find her."

I can't move. I can't reach for him or give chase when he tosses the peach aside and charges into the flowers.

My body jerks as if I've been shoved over a cliff, shocking me into consciousness. My heart races, and I lay a hand on my chest, over the scar, willing it to slow down. Deep breaths. It was only a nightmare. Calli's fine.

The sound of faint laughter and a car door slamming confirms that fact. She's fine.

She's home.

I stumble over my blanket that's been kicked to the floor getting to my bedroom window to look. Calli's car is parked beside the RV, and I watch as she leads a guy up her steps. A peek at the clock shows me it's half past three in the morning. I'm not going to charge over there like a psycho this time of night. She'll probably go to bed as soon as they leave. I'll see her tomorrow.

There's no way I'm going to fall right back to sleep after that nightmare. The sight of her holding out the bloody shards of the broken bottle haunts me, and I deal with it the only effective way I've found, by grabbing my sketchbook.

As I work, I keep an eye on the window, waiting to see the others leave. Instead, Calli comes out with the guy, grabs some stuff from the RV, and they go back inside. Minutes later, all the lights go out.

Jealousy is a snarling monster inside me, eating away. Is it only the two of them? I didn't see anyone else. Were they already inside? Are her friends catching a nap before they continue traveling, or did she bring a man home with her? The thought that she may be in his arms is unbearable.

Do you love her? You never loved me.

I do, I love her.

I can't let her love me.

————

It's dawn before I manage to get back to sleep and my first waking thought is Calli. The RV is still in the driveway but I'm happy to see a woman sitting on Calli's steps. It wasn't only the two of them last night. My jealousy is unfair, but that doesn't make it any less fierce.

After getting dressed, I take my coffee out to my porch and sit in the sunlight. It's unseasonably warm and supposed to stay that way for another day before a sharp temperature drop.

I'm debating whether to text Calli when she comes out of her house, stops to talk to the woman on her porch for a moment, then walks up the driveway.

"Welcome back. Did you have a good trip?" I ask, moving to sit on my top step as she approaches. Christ, she looks more beautiful than I remember. Just looking at her hurts.

"It was amazing. I have lots of pictures to show you. I even got backstage at the Sudden Outburst concert and had them sign a shirt for me."

"Got backstage as in you hopped another fence or got passes?" It wouldn't be the first time she's sneaked backstage from what she told me.

A grin grows on her sun kissed cheeks. "Passes. They have pretty competent security." She takes a seat next to me on the step. "Is your internet out? I can't get mine to work at all."

"Ah, yeah. We aren't going to have service for about two weeks. They're upgrading the whole area. We'll have a much better high-speed connection once it's done but for now, we're screwed."

"Well shit."

I don't want to put off the inevitable with small talk. The knot growing in my stomach is too tight. "Calli, I'm sorry."

She nods, fidgeting with her hands. "I know. You already apologized for following me, and you don't need to apologize for anything else that happened."

My heart lives in my throat when I ask, "Are we alright?"

The seconds of hesitation last a year. Have I lost her? Serious eyes meet mine. "Never follow me like that again. I understand why you did and that you didn't mean any harm, but I have enough issues with anxiety without wondering if I'm being watched. I need you to swear you'll never do that again because I promise our friendship won't survive it a second time. Do you understand?"

"Never again. I swear."

She nods and continues, pulling her gaze from mine. "As for the night we spent together, I didn't do anything that I didn't want to do. We both wanted it at that moment. I can leave it at that and let it go if you can." Before I can respond, she quickly changes the subject. "My friends are leaving tomorrow. We're going to party tonight, have a bonfire behind my cabin, grill out some steaks and stuff. Do you want to join us? Silver is coming too."

There's nothing she could ask me to do right now that I wouldn't jump on to spend some time with her. "Absolutely. What can I bring?"

"Actually, I was going to see if I could borrow your body parts cooler." Her little smirk is so adorable.

"I suppose I could find another place to store the limbs temporarily."

I'd give anything to know what's going on behind those eyes as she gives me a long look before wrapping her arms around me. The unexpected hug is soothing in a way I can't begin to explain. Her warm, soft body close to mine, I breathe in the scent of her hair as she buries her face in my neck. Her words make everything right.

"I missed you too." After we let go, she gets to her feet. "I'll see you tonight."

The day inches by while I keep myself busy. A trip across the state line to the dispensary helps fill the time. Along with my edibles, I get some flower for Calli, since she prefers it. The only thing she asked me to bring was my cooler, but I swing by the liquor store for some beer as well.

A call from my dad surprises me, but he gets straight to the point after hellos are exchanged. "Your mom said you aren't coming for the holidays again."

"She said you were going to Aunt Gina's."

"She also said you're invited, and we'll be there for six weeks. You can't clear a few days to spend at a beach house?" he retorts, having none of my bullshit.

"I'm...pretty busy...working on some projects."

His sigh makes me feel terrible. "We miss you, Arlow. Your mom needs to see you. We'll be passing through your area to pick up one of your mom's friends in Tennessee this weekend. We'd love to visit if you can set aside a night for us."

I miss them too. It's been too long. "Of course, Dad. I'd love to see you. Come and stay the weekend."

His tone lightens considerably as we talk for a few minutes about their new kittens and how things are going. There's no reason to tell him about the trouble we've had here since nothing has happened the past few weeks and there's nothing they can do except worry. They've had enough worry in their lives over me.

By the time we hang up, it's time to go to Calli's. Unlike Calli, I'm not anxious in social situations. I just don't have much desire to be around people. I'm happier alone. At least, I thought I was. Calli grabbed the cooler earlier, so I tuck the weed in my pocket, pick up the beer, and head across the driveway.

They've set up the portable campfire pit behind her cabin and dragged the picnic table over near it. Lawn chairs also circle the fire. The grill sits nearby, being watched over by one of the guys. Calli introduces me to everyone, and I join them at the fire.

Everybody is clearly buzzed and happy. "We were just comparing stories of the most piece of shit cars we've ever driven," Calli says, nodding toward Silver to continue after my appearance interrupted them.

"My first one was a real beater I bought used. I drove that thing into the ground. It was more rust and dents than car. Had to keep oil in the trunk because it ate it up like crazy. It drove okay for a few months then it stopped wanting to get into first gear. So, I'd be stuck at every light while it whined and revved until it would jump into gear and try to give me whiplash. I couldn't afford to get it fixed so I drove it that way for another two months until the transmission failed completely. My friends thought it was hilarious and they'd do that thing where they rock back and forth like that might get the car moving, but I'm sure the drivers behind me were seriously disgruntled."

The light laughter is interrupted by Freya. "Did you guys know gruntled is a word? It means happy. Why do we say disgruntled but never gruntled? I'm going to start using that."

"You do that," Calli laughs. "My dad had a car with no reverse gear. My brother was a teenager then and living with him and it became his job to ride with him and push the car out of every parking spot or any situation where he had to back up. Watching my brother try to get him in and out when he had to parallel park in front of my place used to make me almost pee myself laughing. I wish I'd taken a video of it."

Watching Calli laugh and talk with her friends, seeing her happiness, wipes away all the dark clouds the last few weeks have gathered. Everyone is cool, and after we eat, I pass out the edibles I brought.

Calli refuses and she also hasn't been drinking anything stronger than tea tonight. She looks over at me when I sit in the chair next to hers and hold out a joint. "I thought you might want something that won't put you on the ground."

She beams at me as she accepts it. "Thanks, I've had enough alcohol over the last couple of weeks and we both know edibles aren't always my friend."

An hour later, everyone is stuffed full of delicious food, stoned, and scattered around the fire. Freya lays on the picnic table, looking up at the sky, and Calvin calls over to her.

"Are you okay over there, Miss I Can Handle Two Gummies?"

Freya turns to face us, and everyone laughs at the size of her cheesy grin. "I am *gruntled.*"

Calli's friends are fun, but I'll be glad to get her to myself again.

CHAPTER 22

CALLIOPE

ARLOW IS A LITTLE QUIET AT FIRST, BUT HE LOOSENS UP AND FITS RIGHT IN with my friends. He and Leo end up in a long conversation about a series of fantasy books that I haven't read. Silver also seems to be having a good time. You never know what introducing two friend groups will be like and I couldn't be happier with how it went.

It's late and Silver is lying on the picnic table beside Freya, in the middle of a drunken rant against love that's turned into a debate over whether love is bullshit. "All I'm saying is that we automatically see love as this wonderful thing but what if it isn't? What if it's just another thing used to control the masses? More propaganda we're fed to guilt us into toeing the line. Join the military and sacrifice yourself for the love of your country. Love your husband enough to destroy your body to give him kids. Love your kids enough to sacrifice your dreams to raise them."

Helen leans over to me and whispers, "Is she okay?"

With a nod, I whisper back. "Bad recent breakup."

"Nobody forces us to do any of that," Freya points out.

Silver props herself up on her elbow to look at her. "That's true, but we're taught from the very beginning that love is the most important thing. If you don't love, you're a psychopath or sociopath. You're not a good person."

I can't resist chiming in. If there's one thing I've overthought into oblivion it's being a good person. "I don't think loving necessarily makes you a good person. I'm sure most horrible people still love their family."

"I can vouch for that!" Cal announces, sitting up. "I'm a shit human being but I love my family."

Giggles run around the group as I reach over to fist bump Calvin. "Hey! Bad people club unite."

"You aren't a bad person," Arlow says, like the idea offends him. It's the first time he's spoken up in a while.

He has no idea who I am underneath years of training myself not to be like my mother. My first thoughts were always negative and judgmental. It wasn't until my late teens that I realized I was going to become the person I hated if I didn't take a good look at my own behavior. I don't want to be hateful or bitter. "Okay, but what if I said that I judge people that have *only god can judge me* tattoos just to prove them wrong?"

Laughter fills the night and lightens the tone back up as Arlow smiles at me. "I stand corrected. You're an awful person."

Helen regards Silver. "You're not wrong about love being used to control women and get us to sacrifice for everyone else."

"Here comes the feminist stuff," Leo groans. He looks over at Arlow. "We need another man to weigh in. Arlow, is love a positive or negative?"

Arlow goes quiet for a moment, and I'll admit, I'm curious about his response. Has his last heartbreak soured him to love like it has Silver? Instead of giving a quick answer, he rubs his hand across his cheek. "Years ago, I was driving through a town in Illinois on my way back home when I ran into some storms. They kept getting worse and I couldn't see to drive so I pulled into a little convenience store parking lot.

"Tornado sirens were blaring, and my ears started popping. The rain stopped and suddenly, there it was, not far away. It's the only time I've ever seen a tornado up close, and it was a big one, surrounded by flying debris.

"The convenience store probably wasn't a great place to shelter but it was better than my truck. People were pulling in one after the other, abandoning their cars and running for cover. There was this young guy, not more than twenty years old, who parked near me, and we ran inside together. It was a close call, close enough to shatter the windows and damage the vehicles but nobody got hurt.

It was terrifying, of course, but more than the roar, the sirens, the screams and broken glass...better than my fear in that instant, I remember that guy. The panic in his voice as he announced, 'I love you all. I love everyone.' He came in alone. Didn't know a soul in that place, but in that moment when he thought it might be the last, that was how he felt. So strongly that he kept repeating it. 'I love everyone.'"

Our eyes meet across the fire as he finishes, "I think love is what we are at our core before the world puts its hands on us. I don't know if it's negative or positive or somewhere in-between, but it's human. It's what we do, what we're best at."

Everyone has fallen silent listening to his story, and he seems to realize it, giving a sheepish shrug. "Anyway."

Helen smiles over at him. "I'll take an artist's view of love any day."

Arlow is the first to leave, after giving me a hug and telling me how happy he is that I'm back. The party breaks up not long after and everyone finds a place to sleep—Freya and Leo in the RV, Silver and Calvin in my living room while I share my bed with Helen.

Despite our late night, everyone is up early since they're eager to get on the road to go home. There are lots of hugs all around, and Helen pulls me aside for a last piece of advice. "Arlow seems like a good man. I understand why he has you tied up in knots. Just keep something in mind. The sweet, artistic, deep thinking types aren't always as soft as they appear. They love hard and that can make a person do almost anything."

"He doesn't love me."

Her smile brushes aside my argument. "Just a bit of advice. See you next year."

Over the next two days, I put my new plan to get a life in motion. If there's one thing I've learned over the past months, it's how much I enjoy nature and the peace it brings me. I'm taking that into account with my search for hobbies. Some videos on homesteading have also piqued my interest. With the WIFI out temporarily and questionable service on my cell when I'm home, videos and online research aren't possible, but that's okay. I've been meaning to visit the local library and they have plenty of books on gardening. On a whim, I pick up another on keeping chickens. I wonder how Arlow would feel about having chickens for neighbors? Or maybe a few goats.

If I start learning now, I should be ready to try my hand at growing some vegetables this spring. The kind librarian informs me that they have classes on gardening and canning at the community center starting in March which sounds like a great option. Before I leave, I also sign up to attend a bi-weekly poetry appreciation club. It'll be fun to study poems along with others who love them.

My last stop is a gym where I become a member and take a dance fitness class that is so much fun. I can't wait to go back. I'm on my way to my car to meet Silver for a movie when she calls me.

"Hey, uh…raincheck. I'm at the hospital with Mom."

"What? Is she okay?"

"Better than Gary is going to be when I get my hands on him!" Mona shouts in the background.

"She tripped over a stepstool at work this morning and fell. Broke her knee and her arm. Her knee is going to require surgery." I can hear the stress and exhaustion in her voice.

"Oh, I'm so sorry. Have you been at the hospital all day?"

"Since about six this morning. They've casted her arm and leg, and we're waiting for insurance to approve a wheelchair."

"What can I do to help? Do you need me to bring you anything? Help at the diner?"

"Thanks, but I've got that covered."

"Let me bring you two some food at least."

"I won't argue with that," Silver sighs. After some discussion, I hang up and swing by a restaurant to pick up some BBQ.

Mona looks awful when I locate her hospital room. Gary stands nearby, holding flowers and a box of chocolates. "Oh no, your dominant arm too," I remark, as Silver gets her food ready for her.

"I can punch just fine with my left," she says, glowering at Gary. Considering how many times she told him to keep that stool under the counter and not inside the kitchen door, I can't blame her. It's hard not to laugh at the look on his face. He's out of his element, standing there like he's just shown up for a date.

Silver pulls me out into the hall to give the two of them a minute. "Is she going to be okay?"

We take a seat in the chairs outside Mona's room, and she digs into the BBQ sandwich like she hasn't eaten in a week. "Mmm, you're a lifesaver. It's going to be a lengthy recovery with her knee especially, but she'll be alright. She's going to have to stay with me for a while. The hardest part is going to be getting her to take it easy. She's already said she's perfectly capable of working from her wheelchair."

"That sounds like her."

We talk for a few minutes, and she promises to call me if there's anything I can do to help. On my way home, I make a mental note to put together a care package and some reheatable dinners for them. Silver is going to be busy trying to keep up with her Mom's care and the diner.

I'm lost in my thoughts and plans for the next few days as I park in my driveway and walk up the steps. It isn't until my keys have been retrieved from my pocket that I freeze. The cabin door stands ajar.

Not again.

Did I leave it unlocked? Damn it, why didn't I get that stupid latch fixed?

Swallowing, I survey my dark surroundings. Arlow's truck is gone. I'm not calling that smarmy cop out here again, and there's no way I'm bothering Silver right now.

It's fine. The wind blew it open again, that's all. Despite trying to reassure myself, I take the time to grab my new knife from the glove box, berating myself for not getting a gun. It's just moved to the top of my to-do list.

The door swings open easily with a slight push. All the lights are off, and that first step inside has my heart thumping against my ribs. My fingers fumble across the wall to flip the switch, and my stomach falls into my feet.

My living room is demolished.

CHAPTER 23

ARLOW

THE WEATHER HAS SUDDENLY REMEMBERED IT'S SUPPOSED TO BE COLD this time of year and seems to be trying to make up for it. Even with the heat on, my truck doesn't get warm until I've pulled onto my road. Calli's pie container sits beside me on the seat. Earl has been waiting for her to get back to return it to her. I'm happy to have an excuse to stop at her place.

Her doorway is a bright rectangle in the darkness when I turn into our driveway. I expect to see her coming in or out, maybe bringing in firewood. When she doesn't appear by the time I've parked alongside her car, my concern spikes. Something is wrong.

The pie container is forgotten on the seat as I hurry to her door. The living room is a disaster. Her couch is flipped, the cushions missing. The coffee table lays on its side, cracked down the middle. Papers, her vinyl albums, books, everything is scattered from hell to breakfast.

"Calli!" I shout, running inside. All the air returns to my lungs when I see her standing in her bedroom, a suitcase open on her dresser.

Her eyes are wide, pupils eating up her irises. "You scared the fuck out of me!"

"What happened? Are you okay?" Stupid question considering the tremble in her hands.

"I don't know. I just got home and…" She gestures around her bedroom at the destruction. Her mattress hangs off the bed, slashed in multiple places, all her drawers have been pulled out and dumped. "I can't stay here. I shouldn't have come back." Her movements are frantic as she goes back to slamming clothes into a suitcase.

"Hey." Dodging the mess on the floor, I rush over to her. Her chest rises and falls with quick breaths, but she pauses when I take hold of her shoulders. "Wait. Slow down."

"I can't! Look around! This isn't just a burglary. Someone broke the lock on my door to come in and tear everything up! Why? What the hell is going on? Why can't I be safe *anywhere*?"

The raging despair in her voice shreds my heart, and I pull her into my arms. She holds onto me so tightly, burying her face in my chest. "I was happy here," she mumbles.

"You don't need to go anywhere. You're safe with me." Pulling her back, I look into watery eyes. "Do you hear me? We're going to figure this out."

Doubt lives in her face, but she wraps her arms around me again. "Can you just hold me a second? I'm trying not to have a panic attack."

I'm going to kill Handleman with my bare fucking hands for doing this to her. She's right, this isn't a burglary, it's personal. With our shared driveway, it wouldn't be hard for him to think the cabin was mine too. I assumed it was part of the property when I first looked at it.

"I've got you." Her body trembles against mine while I hold her, rubbing her back. "I'll never let anything happen to you, Calliope. You're safe." Deep deliberate breaths slowly turn into more even ones, and she steps back, more composed.

"You should go check your place. Your barn. Your art."

"I will, but that's not my concern right now."

"I'm alright. I'm going to pack some stuff, find a hotel for a few days until I figure out what I want to do."

If she leaves, I doubt I'll ever see her again. Whatever I've cost Handleman in the past, he isn't taking her from me. "Have you called the police yet?"

"Because they're so much help," she scoffs.

"I know, but this isn't just a broken window or stolen ATV, Peach. They can at least look for fingerprints or something. I'll call them if you want." I understand her reticence considering how that cop dismissed her last time, and she isn't even aware that he tried to shift the blame to her when he was talking to me. But if this is Handleman, finding his prints would be enough to violate his parole and get him locked back up if they can catch him.

Her gaze sweeps around the room as she considers it. "Okay. Let's go check your place first. I'm coming with you." No arguments here. I'm not letting her out of my sight. She pauses on her porch to look at the glider. "At least they didn't damage that."

"Let's move it to my porch for now," I suggest, and she agrees. We load it into my truck, then park in front of my house with the head-lights on to illuminate the porch and barn.

This time, I'm better prepared. Calli shivers as I pull my gun from the glovebox, and I realize she isn't wearing a jacket. Removing my hoodie, I stop her once we're out of the truck so I can pull it over her head. She looks like she might burst into tears as she stares up at me. My mind is a churning nightmare of thoughts right now so I can only imagine the range of emotions she's going through. I just want to get this over with and get her to a place where she can feel safe again. "Are you okay?"

"Yeah, let's go." We start at my house, which is still locked up. Nothing inside has been touched. The barn is also secured without any signs that anyone tampered with the locks or disturbed anything.

After I call the police, we unload the glider then drive back down to her place to wait for them. She's silent as we sit in my truck. My hoodie is comically large on her. She has her hands hidden in the sleeves, her knees pulled up and her arms tucked around them.

"I'm sorry this is happening." She nods when I squeeze her arm.

"I'm not going to tell Silver anything right now. I can get the lock replaced. Her mom is in the hospital after a bad fall. She has enough to deal with." That explains why she's planning to go to a hotel instead of staying with her friend.

"Calli." She tilts her head to look at me. "Stay with me. At least until we get our internet service back and our cameras working. You've been in hotels for weeks."

Her tongue peeks out from between her lips as she considers it. The flashing lights of two squad cars light up her cabin and race across the dark forest, interrupting us.

I'm glad to see it's a different set of officers, a man and a woman. Both listen and take the time to look around her cabin, inside and out. They dust some areas that the intruder would have likely touched for prints.

After Calli tells them this is the third incident on our properties, they ask if we have any enemies, anyone we think might be targeting us. Calli shakes her head, but I'm torn on my response. I have zero evidence that this is Handleman. Only the suspicion because he was recently released from prison. I destroyed this man's life. The last thing I want to do is sic cops on him and do more damage if it isn't him. Then who would be terrorizing who? Let them run the prints first.

One of the officers informs us, "We recently discovered a meth lab set up in the woods about two miles down the road. They had a tent back there and the homeowner had no idea. It's cleaned up, but we haven't located the perpetrators. You never know what they'll do when they're strung out. They trash things, take stuff with no value. It may have been the same people. We'll have patrol keep a closer eye on your road." She hands Calli a business card. "If you think of anything else or have any further trouble, call us back."

Once they leave, Calli leads the way back into her cabin, takes another look at the mess and rubs her forehead with a weary sigh. When she starts to clean things up, I catch her wrist. "You're exhausted. Come and get some rest and I'll help you clean up tomorrow. We'll get the lock fixed and everything, okay? You'll be able to think clearer and decide what to do."

Her hesitation is brief. "Alright, yeah. Let me grab a few things for tonight."

We secure her front door as best as possible from the inside and leave through the back. "Locking the barn door after the horse is gone," she mumbles.

"You don't want to lose anything else. Most of your records and things are okay. Although, it does look like a horse stomped through there."

She glances up at me, snorting out a laugh. "A horse would've been preferable."

"I don't know. Horse shit isn't exactly an air freshener."

I'm glad to see her faint smile as we climb back into my truck and head to my house. "I need to use your shower first thing. After the gym and visiting the hospital, I'm not exactly smelling like a scented candle myself."

She heads upstairs with her bag to get cleaned up while I put the beef stew I made yesterday on the stove to reheat for dinner. While I'm waiting for it to cook, I consider what needs to be done.

I didn't tell the cops it may be Handleman, but if they get nothing on the prints, my next move is finding him. Staking out his mother's house was fruitless. He isn't there. Internet and social media searches turned up nothing. I suppose being a felon on parole isn't something you post about.

While I'm considering what to do next, Calli bursts into the kitchen with an obvious answer. Her eyes are filled with joy—not something I expected to see in them tonight—as she announces, "I got an email from the private investigator about my dad!"

"Did he locate him?"

"Not yet, not exactly, but we know for sure the name he was using so it won't be long. It's just a matter of finding the hotel or short term rental he's arranged under the alias. He was using his brother's name. One of the night clerks at the hotel was kind enough to go back through footage of when he checked in and the investigator sent me a screenshot. It's from two years ago, but it's him!"

She holds up her phone to show me a black and white picture of a much older version of the man in the photo that sits on her mantel. I'm sure it doesn't totally alleviate her fear about him. Since the picture is old, it doesn't prove he's still alive now, but it's good to see the hope glowing on her face as she continues.

"He didn't disappear off the face of the planet. He started using another name because the hotels banned him. He doesn't have my phone number. He usually calls me, but this time, I'm going to find him."

"That's fantastic. I'm so happy you got some good news." The timing was great too. It seems an obvious solution to finding Handleman—hiring a private investigator. A way to find him that isn't sending cops to his door to accuse him if he's innocent, but will determine where he is and if he's our problem.

"I definitely needed it," she agrees, peeking over my shoulder. "What are you cooking? It smells amazing in here."

"Beef stew, and there's bread in the oven."

Her eyebrows raise. "You baked?"

"If this is baking." She laughs when I hold up the tube the refrigerated dough came in.

We have dinner at the kitchen table, and she talks about her dad a little when I ask about him.

"He isn't a terrible person like you're probably thinking."

"I wasn't thinking that at all."

"I'd understand if you did. Most addicts have screwed over everyone in their lives. I've seen how they steal, rob people, or turn violent. He was never like that. At least when I was young and around him enough to know.

"Don't get me wrong, he's hardly a role model. He'd spend his last dollar on a pill, but he worked to fund his habit. Other than the child support that the court took from his check, he didn't do anything to take care of us growing up, but we spent every weekend with him until I was thirteen or so. Even when the drugs really had ahold of him, he was...kind. Compassionate toward other people.

"I never could understand why he wanted to live that way, especially as he got older. This constant cycle of staying high until the money ran out, suffering through withdrawal, then right back at it when he got paid again. Even once he retired, his monthly check would go to whatever hotel had the cheapest rate, and drugs. At some point I had to accept there was nothing I could do. The man is in his late fifties and still..." She rolls her hand.

"Is it heroin?" I ask softly, passing her another slice of bread.

"No, mostly it's speed and pills. He did some crazy stuff with us when we were kids. We were too young to realize how dangerous or illegal some of it was at the time, especially since he must've been high out of his mind. The time he took us out in the middle of the night to spray paint our names all over town is still one of my best memories though," she says with a laugh.

She's lived such a different life than me. Harsher in a lot of ways. "You were a little vandalizing graffiti artist?" I tease. "How old were you?"

"Just that once." A fond smile grows on her face. "I was seven. My brother was eight. I'm surprised Dad didn't get arrested or anything because it was the stupidest crime ever. But I was popular on the school bus when I got to point out my name on a bridge and the dam." She glances up at me. "He did regular dad stuff with us too. Taught us to play baseball, took us to the children's museum and the zoo. That's the stuff I like to remember. He drowned himself in drugs, but he still wanted us, enjoyed spending time with us, you know?"

I reach across the table to squeeze her hand. "Of course he did. He loves you. I'm sure he'll be thrilled when you find him again."

The conversation switches to lighter topics until we move to the living room after dinner. Comfortable silence settles between us as we sit on opposite sides of the couch. Both of us are largely ignoring the movie and staring at our phones. I've found a couple of possible options for private investigators in the area when I glance over to see her looking at hotels in nearby towns.

"You don't need to leave. Stay here. Give the cops time to run the prints. Once the internet is back, we can put cameras up, install burglar alarms, whatever we have to do."

"I appreciate the offer. I really do, but I don't think that's a good idea."

"Please, Calli, let me help. This could be my fault and—"

Her eyes snap from her phone to look at me. "Your fault? Why? Do you know who's doing this?"

"I don't *know*. I have an idea." Her scrutinizing gaze is long and silent, making me shift in my seat as I struggle to find the words to explain.

"You hesitated before you told the cop you had no enemies. I thought maybe I was imagining it," she mutters, more to herself than to me. It's followed by a firm demand. "Tell me, Arlow. Who is it? Do you have a jealous ex-girlfriend or something?" Nothing prepares me for the next question right on the heels of the last. "Is this because of Melody?"

My stomach is on the floor along with my jaw. "How do you know...what do you know about Melody?"

Guilt flickers on her face. "I'm sorry. I should've told you before, but I didn't want to make you uncomfortable. I overheard you on the phone to her once. Just for a few seconds. I wasn't trying to eavesdrop or anything. It was an accident. Is it her? Do you think she's targeting me because of you?"

Christ, what did she overhear? My face burns with the likelihood it was a sobbing apology, especially if I was drinking. "No, it's not her, but her brother is a possibility."

"Why would her brother have anything against me?"

"He wouldn't. It isn't about you."

"I beg to fucking differ considering the state of my cabin, Arlow. Tell me what the hell is going on." Anger swells in her tone.

"Your cabin looks like it could be part of my property. I think it's collateral damage because he wants revenge against me. But I don't know for sure. I'm going to find out. I swear that to you. I'm sorry you got caught in this."

"Why would her brother want revenge on you? What did you do?" The pause I take trying to find the words doesn't exactly set her at ease. "Did you cheat on her?" Her voice falls to a hush as she adds, "Hit her?"

This moment was always going to come, and I've dreaded the hell out of it. I don't want her to know about my condition. She'll see me differently, view me with pity, or as a weaker man. The way she looks at me sometimes makes me see myself through her eyes, as someone good and strong. I don't want to lose that. I don't want her to know I've taken a life and destroyed two others. Now my past is screwing up her life. She deserves to know the truth.

The words stumble out. "I killed her."

CHAPTER 24

CALLIOPE

M<small>Y BODY IS TIGHT AS A FIST, ALL THE MUSCLES LOCKING UP AS THE HAIR</small> stands on my arms and nape. Dizziness washes over me and the only word I can manage while I try to blink it away is whispered. "What?"

"I killed her. I was driving her home and passed out at the wheel. I hit a ditch, rolled the truck, and she didn't survive."

It takes a few seconds for his confession to sink in and relief to loosen the grip of terror that's binding me. "A car accident? I don't understand. I heard you on the phone with her."

He nods, hanging his head as he continues. "You heard me talking to her voicemail. It's the only way I can apologize. Her death destroyed their family. Her father died of a stroke weeks later from the stress of it. Her brother buried himself in drugs and ended up doing years in prison. Her mother…" His voice cracks. "Is a shell of herself."

His guilt is palpable, thickening the air around us. "Were you drunk? High? Driving recklessly?"

"No."

"I don't understand." I understand he'd feel responsible but not why Melody's brother would want revenge if it was an accident. "If it wasn't your fault—"

"It was," he interrupts, getting to his feet. "I need a drink. Then I'll tell you everything."

My mind is spinning while he retrieves a bottle of whiskey and a glass. I thought his quiet, sometimes sad demeanor was from heart-break, from pining for an ex. Not this.

He pours his whiskey and takes a swallow, keeping his gaze on his glass as he begins. "I met Melody at a bar in Chicago. She was visiting with a few friends and so was I. We all went bar hopping and she ended up back at my hotel. We kept in touch afterward when she returned to Paducah. I'd drive down to see her and vice versa over the next six months. We had a lot of fun and she suggested I move near her so we could be together. My art career was going well, but I was at loose ends, looking for a change, and on a whim, I decided to go.

"We became a couple and things were good for a while, but the feelings just…didn't grow. I liked her, cared about her, but I wasn't in love. It wasn't the same for her. She loved me, and I hated to break her heart. I kept putting it off, hoping my feelings would change but they didn't. I broke up with her at a little coffee shop we both liked. She wanted to take a taxi back to her place, but she was so upset, and I didn't want her to leave like that. I convinced her to let me take her home."

He drains his glass and refills it. About a hundred questions beat in my head, but I bite my tongue to keep quiet and let him finish.

"I don't remember the crash. One second I was driving, the next I was on the ground with an EMT staring down at me. When I couldn't tell them anything, they took me to the hospital and scanned my head, though I hadn't hit it. I wasn't even hurt, really, just a few bruises and scrapes from the broken glass. They took my blood and urine to see if I was drinking or doing drugs. The urine came back clean—I didn't even smoke weed at that time—but the blood test would take longer."

Tears fill his eyes, and he shakes his head, averting his gaze again. "It wasn't until hours later when the cop came to arrest me in the emergency room that I found out Melody had died."

The knot in my throat is instant. I close the distance between us to sit beside him on the couch, taking his hand. "I'm so sorry." He presses his lips together and squeezes my hand. "How could they arrest you if you weren't impaired?"

"The officer was convinced I must've taken something or was drinking. The prosecutor agreed and charged me with vehicular manslaughter. He was sure it'd show up when the tests came back, which could take a few weeks. I had no other explanation for what had happened. I had no record of seizures or anything and had never fainted before. I spent two days in jail and Dad came to bail me out. One of the conditions of that release was house arrest since my money made me a flight risk."

He pauses to sip the whiskey and lets me take it when I reach for his glass. I don't care for whiskey, but if there was ever a day that called for it, this is it. It burns down my throat, blooming warm in my stomach. "Did you stand trial?"

"No. I found a good lawyer, who insisted on a battery of medical tests. It was the only time I was allowed to leave my apartment. The blood tests from the night of the crash came back negative and while the prosecutor was searching for some other reason, trying to show I must've been speeding or looking at my phone, a cardiologist found the true explanation. I had fainted. The prosecutor had to drop all charges, and I had heart surgery to repair my mitral valve."

"Arlow," I breathe, unable to resist embracing him any longer. "I'm so fucking sorry you went through all that."

He wraps his arms around me and cups the back of my head. "Don't. Don't be upset for me. That's not why I'm telling you this. You deserve to know why your life is being disrupted. Melody's brother spent a year doing the same sort of thing we're dealing with now. Vandalizing my truck and apartment, following me, threatening me. He went downhill fast with addiction, and it didn't stop until he went to prison on drug charges. I don't know for sure that he's the one doing this, but he was released only a few months ago and he still has every reason to despise me."

Sitting back, I look him in the eye. "It wasn't your fault. You can't blame yourself for a heart condition."

"No, but if I'd broken up with her earlier when I knew things weren't going to work out, or waited even one more day, or let her take the damn taxi, she wouldn't have been with me. I wouldn't have broken her heart and then killed her minutes later." The shuddery breath he takes makes my tears overflow again. "Nobody knows that. I've never told a soul. I was too ashamed. I let everyone believe I lost my girlfriend that day, not an ex. I couldn't bear to admit I hurt her and then destroyed her."

God, he's blaming himself for so much that was out of his control. My voice is firm as I take his hand again. "I want you to listen to me." When he looks down, I slide my hand under his jaw and lift his gaze to mine. "What happened to Melody is tragic and what you went through was horrible, but you didn't do anything wrong. You can't force yourself to love someone. You were honest with her. You were doing the right thing in letting her go, and trying to make sure she got home safe when you knew she was upset. You didn't know what was going to happen. No one could have. None of that was your fault."

His expression reflects so many emotions before he lays his hand over mine. "You see the good in people no matter how deeply you have to look."

He has no idea how wrong he is about that, but that's a conversation for another day. "You're the kindest man I've ever met, and I didn't have to look deep for that."

We sit together for a while in silence, occasionally passing the glass of whiskey back and forth for a sip. "Will you tell me what you're thinking?" Arlow murmurs, the alcohol making itself known in his soft rumbly voice.

A small smile appears at the sound of my chuckle. "I was thinking that this has been the longest day. It feels like a week has gone by since I was at the library this morning or the gym this afternoon. Then the hospital with Silver and everything with the cabin. Time is funny, how it stretches."

"You should go get some rest. Tomorrow may not be much shorter if we're going to get your cabin cleaned up and secured."

"And I'm going to the gun shop." I should go to bed but first I return his question. "Will you tell me what you're thinking?"

He sighs, places the empty glass on the table, then sits back, his shoulder resting against mine. "I was thinking that I'm being selfish asking you to stay here when you may be safer at a hotel, but I hate how the nights feel without you."

There's such a raw vulnerability in that confession. He isn't asking me to stay only for my benefit. This situation is hard for him. He needs me now too. "I don't want to go to a hotel. I feel safer with you." My plan to spend less time with him is not off to a great start. I lay my head on his shoulder, and he tilts his to lean against mine. I don't want to take the conversation back to an upsetting place, but there's something I need to know. "Is your heart okay, now? Was it a congenital thing?"

He seems reluctant to answer but does anyway. "Congenital yes, but it's not limited to my heart. It was a symptom of a condition called Marfan Syndrome. It causes a range of problems and characteristics that differ by case. Some are mild and some are more severe. Excessive height, long limbs and fingers. A lot of people with it are built very slim. Gangly. I was until I hit my twenties and started putting on more bulk. It can affect sight, blood vessels, cause deformities in the breastbone, and in more serious cases, damage your heart. There's no cure, and it can remain undiagnosed for a long time, like it was with me."

"But the surgery fixed your heart, the most serious issue?" I ask, desperate for clarification that will tell me he isn't still in danger.

"It doesn't work that way. That's why I don't date or have relationships. It's better for me to keep some distance so others don't get hurt."

Fear strikes me and I sit up to look at him. "Are you dying, Arlow?"

His smile is full of reluctance, which isn't reassuring. "Not in the degenerative sense. Some people live a normal lifespan with Marfan Syndrome, even when the heart is affected. I take a pill to keep my blood pressure down and I know my limits when it comes to exercise but there's no foolproof preventative. Twice a year, I have tests to monitor my heart, and right now it's okay. But at any time, those tests may pick up on an abnormality and I could die in surgery or of a heart attack. It's always going to be hanging over my head, waiting. It's not good for people to get too close to me when my life could be short-lived."

When I shake my head and open my mouth to protest, he cuts me off. "I don't want to talk about it anymore tonight, okay? Like you said, it's been a long day."

It's hard not to argue and try to change his mind because that's the saddest thing I've ever heard, but I nod, letting it go for now. He's upset, and I hate to leave things this way. "Okay, I just have one more question before I go to bed." He can't disguise his resigned sigh as he regards me. "Has anyone ever made a *Do you know the Marfan Man* joke? Because I'm not going to be able to resist."

Maybe half a second passes before he throws his head back with a laugh and pulls me into a warm hug. "No, only you, Peach."

———

I'm not surprised that both Arlow and I sleep in after our late night, not to mention the alcohol. I heard him go to his room about an hour after me, while I was still reading about Marfan Syndrome on my phone.

Everything I'd assumed about him was wrong. He wasn't pining over an ex but dealing with the memory of a traumatic event—one that may have come back to torment him if his ex's brother is responsible for everything that's happened.

My heart breaks for him. For what he went through and the ways it's still affecting him. There was so much I wanted to say last night. How we're all temporary, medical condition or not. That his guilt and fear of hurting others shouldn't sentence him to a solitary life.

It's terrifying to know that he has a higher chance of another damaged valve, along with other possible issues that would put his life at risk, so I can only imagine how he feels living with that. But if he thinks it'll push me away, he doesn't know me well enough yet. As friends or lovers, I'm going to be here for him regardless.

Since I'm the first one awake, I start cooking breakfast, and call the private investigator to tell him the picture he sent me is indeed my father. He promises to let me know the second they find that name currently checked in or renting a place in Indy. Before I let him go, I add a request that I've been debating over.

"There's another person I need to locate, but under no circumstances do I want him to know or be contacted if you find him. His name is Carl Becker. I'll email you the information I have on him."

"Is this another family member?"

"No, he's a man who has given me trouble in the past. I want to know if he's anywhere near me. My house has been robbed and vandalized along with my car recently. It's highly unlikely that it has anything to do with him. He has no idea where I am and no reason to care, honestly, but I'll feel better knowing he's far away."

He agrees to look into it for me, and I second guess myself the moment we hang up. I'm probably overthinking things. After all, I've changed my name and moved twice. Besides, Carl has no legitimate reason to bother me anymore. His only link to me is dead.

Arlow grins at me from the kitchen doorway. He looks so good, dressed in jeans and a dark blue button up shirt. "I can't remember the last time I woke up to the smell of bacon."

"I figured that would get you out of bed. The coffee is hot, and I'm making omelets. Do you want one?"

"I'd love one."

We avoid any talk of our conversations from last night, and instead focus on our plans for today. I need to go to the hardware store for new locks, the gun shop, and I want to put together a gift basket for Mona. Since Arlow wants to go with me for the locks, he suggests we run our errands together.

"I have an appointment at the barber at two, but you could drop me off and shop for the gift basket stuff then," he says. "If you don't mind driving."

"Sounds good to me." It suddenly occurs to me that he's always asked me to drive if we go somewhere together. The day he and Lee rushed back to help me when the man was in the woods, I noticed Lee was driving Arlow's truck. At the time, I had bigger things to think about and assumed he'd probably had an edible or something. "Do you dislike driving?"

His eyes land on mine for a second. "I don't drive with a passenger. I haven't since the accident."

He's afraid it could happen again, and it may not be an unreasonable fear. "No problem. I like to drive."

After breakfast, we head out to start checking things off our list. The hardware store is a quick stop where Arlow convinces me to get the strongest deadbolt locks, along with new doorknobs. The pistol I purchase at the gun shop is just like one I used to have; one I know I'm comfortable with shooting.

"Are you going to come out with a mohawk?" I tease, as we pull up at the barber shop.

Arlow grins and runs a hand through his shaggy mop that now covers his ears and neck. "I was thinking about spikes, maybe with frosted tips, you know, the whole nineties vibe."

His phone rattles, and he curses under his breath as he reads a text.

"What's wrong?" We sure don't need another problem to deal with right now.

His grin is sheepish. "Nothing, but I completely forgot my parents are visiting this weekend. They'll be here tonight."

"Oh, it's okay. I can go ahead and get a hotel room for a few days."

"No, that's not necessary. We'll give them the guest room. You take my room and I'll sleep on the couch."

"You're longer than your couch," I point out. "And I don't want to intrude on your visit."

"You won't be intruding. Mom is bringing the stuff to make an early Thanksgiving dinner since they're leaving for the holidays. I'd love it if you stayed."

I don't want to leave him right now. I'm trying not to stress over the threat hovering above my head and being near him is the best cure for anxiety I've ever found. I would've been a mess after yesterday if it wasn't for him. "Are you sure?"

"Absolutely. I don't want them to know what's going on right now, though. There's no need to worry them."

"How are you going to explain why I'm staying with you?"

He ponders it for a moment. "We'll tell them you're staying a couple of days while you get your furnace fixed."

He stares at me expectantly until I nod. "Alright, but I'm sleeping on the couch."

By the time I've stopped in the superstore to fill a basket with snacks, a few romance books that I know Mona enjoys, and a couple of gift cards for local restaurants, Arlow texts me that he's ready. I'm surprised to see him standing outside the flower shop that shares the parking lot with the barber, holding a bunch of flowers.

"You clean up well," I remark, unable to resist running my hand over his freshly shaved nape as he climbs into the passenger seat. He's still sporting a slight bedhead look with longer messy locks on top. "Did you get flowers for your mom?" An embarrassed little grin appears along with his nod. He's really going to have to stop being so cute before I kiss it off his face.

"I did. She loves tulips." The tulips are placed in my backseat, but he holds out a small, gorgeous bouquet to me. "These are for you."

For a few seconds, I only stare at him, my mind frozen. "For me? Why?"

"Because you've had a hard couple of days, and I know you love wildflowers." No man has ever given me flowers. Not once. He tilts his head, his smile growing. "Calli, are you blushing? Aw, that's so sweet."

"No, shut up." His chuckle is low as I take the flowers from him. "Thank you. They're beautiful."

Somebody has to help me because I am in deep.

CHAPTER 25

ARLOW

CALLI DESERVED TO KNOW THE TRUTH ABOUT HANDLEMAN BUT confessing the worst of it—how I broke Melody's heart right before she died—wasn't something I've ever admitted or planned to share. She's easy to talk to. I'd kept it to myself for so long, festering under my skin, that it spilled out.

I was afraid revealing my condition might change how she looked at me, or make her keep her distance, and maybe I even hoped for that because as selfish as it is, I can't seem to stay away from her. I'm terrified she'll care too much.

What am I doing? I know better. In five years, I've never struggled to stick to my decision to be alone. What am I even hoping for here? That I'll find a way to keep spending time with her, to love her, without her feeling the same? I'm confused, torn between my feelings and what I know is the right thing to do.

All I know right now is that I need to keep her safe and that means keeping her close. Once all of this with Handleman is over, I'll worry about what comes next.

It's hard to see her upset as we clean up her cabin, though she tries to hide it by joking around. Lee stops by and offers to haul the ruined mattress and couch to the dump since my parents will be showing up soon and that saves us some time.

"Do you want me to go with you to shop for new furniture on Monday?" I ask.

Calli shakes her head. "I'm not sure what I'm going to do yet. May as well wait and see what's going to happen. I don't want to have to move it again."

"Move it again?"

She shrugs, gathering more of her stuff to take to my place. "I'm sure Mona would let me out of my lease if I asked. If the guy isn't caught soon."

Of course, she could pick up and go. That's what she did when she came here. It might be what's best for her but I have to turn away so my expression doesn't reveal the instant anguish caused by her remark. I've never been good at hiding emotions. My sister once told me that my face has subtitles.

Once the cabin is back in order and the locks changed, we go back to my place. Calli moves her stuff from the guest room to my room for the time being, then leaves to take the gift basket to Mona while I wait for my parents to arrive. She texts me as they're pulling in the driveway to tell me not to wait for her or expect her back for dinner because she's going to help Silver for a few hours. I suspect she's trying to give me some time alone with my family before she returns.

Mom grabs me in a hug the second she sees me. "Look at you! You look fantastic. I love the beard." While I was getting my hair cut, I had them line up my short beard and trim it evenly. "So distinguished."

Dad hugs me as well and we spend the next few hours catching up. We've moved to my living room after dinner when I let them know about Calli. "I have a friend who's staying with me the next few days while she waits on her furnace to be repaired." I don't like lying to them but there's no way I'm telling them the truth. Mom would be spreading the word online in seconds and demanding to know where Handleman is. "She should be here soon."

"Oh, I'd love to meet one of your friends," Mom replies. "Tell me about her."

"Her name is Calli. She lives in the cabin next door and she's really sweet. I'm sure you'll like her."

"That's great. The more the merrier. And we'll have four for board games!"

Poor Calli may not realize what she's gotten herself into. My parents are good people, and can be a lot of fun, but Mom is the queen of gossip and will probably ask her a thousand questions before the weekend is over. Before she shows up, I warn Mom not to ask her about her family because it's a sore subject.

Calli arrives as we're getting the Monopoly game out, and after she's introduced to my parents, Mom gestures to the table. "You're just in time to join us!"

"You don't have to play if you'd rather not," I assure her.

Calli smiles and pulls up a chair. "Are you kidding? I'm going to wipe the board with you."

It's a nice night, gathered around my table, laughing and talking with my parents and Calli. Sometimes you don't realize how much you've missed people until you get to spend time with them again.

Calli does indeed beat me, knocking me out of the game first, and then Mom next. She groans when she lands on Dad's property for the second time in a row. "I am mortgaged to the teeth, here. Have some mercy," she says.

"I will accept your forfeit and spare you the indignancy of bank-ruptcy," Dad offers.

"Too late for that. I'm broke. You win."

"That's what you get for targeting me first," I tease her.

"It's not my fault you kept trespassing on my property."

"Payback, little peach bandit."

Both my parents are grinning at us and the look on Mom's face says everything she's thinking. I definitely inherited my transparent expressions from her.

"Can I help you cook tomorrow?" Calli asks her. "I'd be happy to make a pie for dessert if you don't already have something planned."

"Of course! Arie has gone on so much about how wonderful your baking is."

"Is that right, Arie?" Calli peeks up at me, her lips twitching as she uses Mom's nickname for me.

"I may have mentioned you once or twice."

Once Mom and Dad have retired to the guest room, I grab some pillows and a blanket for the couch. "I have my own pillows," Calli argues.

"I put them on my bed."

Her face folds into a cute frown. "I'm sleeping on the couch."

"The hell you are. I put fresh sheets on my bed for you." She dives onto the couch, lies down and stares up at me, crossing her arms over her chest. "Have it your way."

"Arlow!" she laughs, when I scoop her up and carry her toward the stairs. "Put me down!"

"I intend to. On my bed. Where you're sleeping."

"You're too tall for your couch. Stop being stubborn!" She sits up when I toss her onto the mattress.

"I'll fold myself in half." She isn't amused, judging by her glare. "You aren't sleeping on my couch. Do you want to share the bed? I promise not to seduce you."

"Is that what you think happened before?" she taunts with a smirk.

She's so fun to tease. I never get tired of it. "Look, it's nothing to be ashamed about. I'm very irresistible."

"Get in the bed, dumbass."

I'm not going to let anything happen between us again but having her beside me in bed all night isn't something I'm going to pass up either. "Fine, but no hogging the covers."

Calli changes into a pair of pajama shorts and a thin shirt. With her hair down around her shoulders, she's too beautiful to look at. We settle into my bed, and she looks over at me, yawning.

"Your dad is hilarious. And your mom is so sweet."

"They're the best. I've really missed them."

She was surprised earlier when Mom mentioned that they hadn't seen me in person for almost two years, so the next question isn't unexpected. "They don't live that far away. Why don't you visit them more often or invite them here?"

"I told you. It's better if people don't get too close to me."

She leans up on her elbow, and her incredulous look makes me instantly self-conscious. "Even your family?"

I reach over to click off the lamp and lie down beside her. Some things are easier to discuss in the dark. "Have you ever lost someone you loved?" I know her mother passed but it doesn't sound like they were close at all. "Not a breakup, but a death? Where you know you'll never see them again."

"No."

"You don't understand. I didn't either. I thought I did when Melody died until I attended a grief support group. What I felt was guilt not grief, and it was nothing compared to what the others were going through. The ones who lost wives, husbands, children. It was brutal. Lee...Lee lost his wife and there are still times I worry he won't survive it."

Her voice is soft, and I hate the pity that permeates it when she asks, "You don't want anyone to love you?"

"It wouldn't be right. I may not be...lasting."

She's quiet for a moment before she sits up and looks down at me, her face mostly hidden in the shadows. "You love so many things that aren't lasting. Your bees and animals and the forest. Everything has an end. That doesn't mean it shouldn't be loved."

"I don't want anyone to grieve me."

Her next question catches me off guard and I'm not sure how I feel about it. "Have you ever been to therapy?"

"No, the grief group was my first attempt at anything like that and I only went twice."

She slides her hand into mine, interlacing our fingers. "I'm not judging you or trying to hurt you by saying this, but I think you need to talk to someone. They can help you put things into perspective and look at them in a different way. Making your family miss you now so they may not miss you as much later if they outlive you…that's not a healthy reaction to the trauma you went through. I know you're afraid of hurting others after Melody. That kindness and compassion is such a wonderful part of who you are, but you're letting fear make you a martyr. That's not going to spare your family or anyone else who cares about you. I can't stand to see you hurting yourself like this. You don't deserve it, Arlow."

Therapy isn't going to change what I saw in that room. The total devastation, all the faces filled with nothing but torment, the desolate look in Lee's eyes when we met. "I'm not trying to punish myself."

Her hand remains in mine as she lays her head on the pillow. "Are you sure about that? Because I've been there, with the whole self-loathing thing. I didn't want to talk to anyone either, but it was the best thing I've ever done. Therapy helped me a lot."

How could she ever hate herself? I roll over to face her and brush the hair off her forehead. "Will you tell me what you needed help with?"

"I was struggling with anxiety and that's what sent me to a thera-pist. My hope was to learn how to deal with it. You may not know this, but I'm actually a bunch of coping mechanisms disguised as a person," she jokes, flashing a quick smile.

She averts her gaze and absently plays with my hand as she talks. "But I had a lot more going on than I realized. My mother was abusive. Some of it was physical, but mostly it was mental, emotional. She hated me and my brother and she didn't do it quietly. All because she despised my dad, and we didn't. Our last name became an insult to throw at us.

"For as long as I can remember, she used suicide threats to control us. Anytime we crossed her, we never knew whether it'd be the belt, her threatening to eat a bottle of pills, a rant about how we were pieces of shit just like our dad, or all three. The suicide threats didn't work once I turned twelve or so. Eventually I understood she didn't mean it but sometimes I hoped she did. I got away as early as I could, but it messed me up more than I realized. She was such an awful person and I inherited some of that."

"No." The word spills out of my mouth as I pull her into my arms, but she cuts off my argument.

"Yes, I did. Since I was a teenager, I've focused on trying to be a better person. To be the opposite of her. But she's in me, like a virus with no cure. My gut reaction is not kindness or compassion or love. I'm not naturally good-hearted the way you are. I'm still learning to be a good person. Therapy really helped me get a grip on who I was and who I want to be." She wraps her arm around me, cuddling me close. "Just think about going, okay? Not because I hope for anything between us or even for your parents' sake. For yourself."

"I'll think about it." Her eyes close when I drop a kiss on her forehead. "A bad person wouldn't have tried so hard to fix the way they think. You're beautiful, Calliope. Inside and out. And I'm completely capable of being a dick. You'll see."

Her giggles lighten the mood and we both fall silent, lost in our own thoughts. Minutes later, her breathing slows to a steady pace as she drifts off.

What I feel for her is terrifying. It's been so long since I've let myself feel anything other than pain and guilt. A notion slips into my head. I'm not sure where it comes from, but it settles into my brain as if it belongs there.

Whatever shines in her may light my way back to myself. To who I was before.

———

My bed is empty when I wake and a wonderful smell wafts over me as I descend the stairs. The sound of Calli's laughter is followed by my mother's. They stand side by side, leaning against the counter while Mom shows Calli something on her phone.

"Oh my god. Look how adorable he was. How old was he?"

"This was sixth grade graduation so about twelve."

"And already towering over everyone," Calli replies, her grin growing when she looks up to see me watching them.

"He was always the tallest in his class," Mom says.

"Ahem." I draw Mom's attention to where I stand in the doorway, my arms crossed over my chest. "Baby pictures, really?"

There's not a scrap of regret on her face when she smiles at me. "We started with baby. Now we're up to middle school."

"Do you have a high school one?" Calli asks.

"Absolutely not," I laugh, pulling her away. "Where's Dad?"

Mom turns back to the stove as she replies. "He wanted to take a walk and see your beehives. Calli gave him one of the beekeeper suits." She glances at the time. "He's been gone for a while."

Calli looks up at me to see if I'm okay with that, and I give her a quick nod. I knew Dad would be out wandering around. He loves nature as much as I do. If it weren't for my sister living next door to them, he probably would've talked Mom into moving somewhere rural by now. "I'll go check on him."

It's freezing cold outside, but I don't have to go far. Dad walks out of the graveyard, carrying the bee suit. "Well, look who woke up," he teases. Dad may be an artist like me, but my night owl tendencies didn't come from him. "I was checking on your bees."

"How are they doing?" I ask, falling in step beside him.

"All holed up in the hive, vibrating like a son of a bitch."

"I'm not surprised. It's cold enough to snow."

Dad pauses by my barn. "Will you show me what you've been working on? I've seen some of it online."

"Sure." I unlock the barn and take the bee suit from him, tucking it away inside.

"Calli seems like a nice young lady."

"She is. We've become good friends since she moved in next door."

"I'm glad to hear that. Your Mom and I were concerned you were spending all your time alone." He rubs his hand over the graying scruff on his chin as we walk toward the camera rooms.

They had me pretty young, in their early twenties, but the signs of aging are beginning to show on them. It strikes me how the time has passed so quickly, how much I'm missing. "You don't need to worry about me. I have friends. And my art. I'm not unhappy, Dad."

His expression reveals he doesn't quite believe me and that's fair. After Melody, I withdrew completely. Moved away, kept to myself. They've never understood why, that it was for their sake as much as my own.

"I'm glad to hear it. Good luck getting your mom not to worry, though. You know how she is. She heard through her gossip grapevine that Chris Handleman has jumped parole and ran. I told her he's probably in Mexico by now, not concerned with you."

I'm grateful he looks away as he says it because I'm sure my expression would've said too much. He ran. That's why he isn't at his mother's house. He could be anywhere. Including here, terrorizing us.

"Good lord, your skill only improves," he exclaims when I uncover the drawing of the fallen log in the woods. It's the same one I came across the first day I saw Calliope, when the creative block floated away and let me see again. "What did you use for the misty look around the moss?"

We talk for a few minutes while I show him the tools I've been using and some of the techniques I'm trying out. Dad's style is far different than mine. He worked as an illustrator for children's books and graphic novels for his entire career. Now that he's retired, he sometimes paints murals for doctors' offices, hospitals, or schools when they want some bright, friendly welcoming characters. The lens I view the world through has always been darker than his, but he's never failed to encourage me to use that in my work. Although, I think I worried them once when I was twelve and drew the smashed raccoon lying in our road.

We move from room to room, taking our time while we're both in our element, discussing art. The last drawing is the one of Calliope, draped over the log, staring up at the stars.

A full minute ticks by as he stares at it in silence before he turns to look at me, his eyes shining. "You're in love," he says softly.

The remark catches me completely off guard. "What?"

His gaze returns to the drawing. "You're in love with her. Christ, Arlow, this is a masterpiece. Don't sell it." His response makes me think of Calli's reaction when she saw it. She said I'd made her beautiful, but what I see in the drawing is simply her.

"It's not like that."

"Bullshit someone else. I know love when I see it." He tilts his head to look at me. "Does she know?"

A knot forms in my throat. I've never struggled with accepting my fate. I'm fine on my own and always have been, but with her, the pain of it is nearly unbearable. It's so unfair that someone like that— as beautiful and special as her—could want me, maybe even love me when I can't accept it. Insult to injury a thousand times over.

If I can't admit how I feel to her, I can at least admit it to myself and the person who has always understood me the best. "No, she doesn't."

Both of us stare at the drawing as he asks, "Is she with someone else?"

"No, it's just...complicated."

"Usually is." He nods. "But love doesn't come along every day. I've never met anyone who makes me feel like your mother does. If you find that, do whatever is necessary to keep it. It's worth it, son. It's worth everything you have." His dark eyes look into mine. "Do you understand?"

CHAPTER 26

CALLIOPE

ARLOW'S PARENTS ARE SUCH SWEET PEOPLE, IT'S EASY TO SEE WHERE HE gets his kindness from. It's heartbreaking that he avoids any loving connections and I hope the day comes when he realizes that's not the answer. He deserves so much more than he's let himself have.

His mother questioned me about our relationship and didn't seem to quite believe we were only friends, but she didn't press the subject. I'm not surprised. It seemed like every time I looked at him today, his eyes were on me. Every time he passed by me, his hand would land on my back or my side. It isn't the behavior you'd see between platonic friends. I'm sure she also noticed I slept in his room.

They're leaving in the morning, so I excuse myself and head to bed early to give Arlow more time with them without my intrusion. After a long hot shower, I crawl into his bed and lose myself in a romance book. It's nice to read about love that always somehow finds a way. It's too bad real life isn't like that.

I'm so wrapped up in the book, I barely notice when Arlow heads to his bathroom to shower and get ready for bed. The sex scenes are off the chart hot. Arlow walks out just as I've finished a particularly scorching scene. My mouth dries up at the sight of him and my words fall out without a moment's thought. "Oh, you're doing that on purpose."

His brows dip in confusion and he freezes in place, looking down at me. "What?"

"Gray sweatpants and bare chest? Have some mercy. Your parents are right down the hall."

His grin is equal parts pleased and embarrassed. It only turns me on more. That the same man who said he wanted to fuck me and fuck me, who had no problem dirty talking while making me come until my ears rang can look so flustered at a compliment is the most adorable thing ever.

On the night we slept together, the dark helped obscure the scar on his chest that's well hidden in the branches of his tree tattoo. It's no wonder I didn't notice it before.

He shakes his head, grabs a shirt from his closet and pulls it on. "I hooked up my old DVD player if you want to watch a movie."

It's too early for either of us to sleep. Before the trouble started, we would've been out at the firepit, or he would've been working in his barn this time of night.

"Sure. Do you want to sneak out and smoke first?"

"I'll just crack the window a little."

A few minutes later, we're lounging in his bed, high and watching a goofy comedy. Arlow wraps his arm around me, and I cuddle close to him like it's the most natural thing in the world.

As my high fades and the movie nears its end, my fingers play on his collarbone. Relaxed and content, I'm starting to zone out when his husky voice surprises me.

"Calliope, if you keep touching my neck, I'm going to fuck you."

My breath catches in my throat as my hand stills. Do I want this to happen again? It broke my heart that he regretted it last time, but I know now this isn't going to lead to anything more. Soon I'll be back in my cabin, without the temptation of having him right beside me, or I'll be moving again. If he wants this, I'm not going to pass up another chance to feel him inside me.

I slowly run my fingertips up his neck to caress his jaw. He turns toward me, cupping my ass to pull my body against his, and I slip my tongue through his lips with a little moan of satisfaction.

Our kisses are long and slow and blistering hot as we strip off our clothes, our mouths unable to part for more than a second or two. God, why is it like this with him? So intense and all consuming. His touch is all I can think about.

His thoughts seem to be similar when we break the kiss, and he catches my earlobe between his lips. "I've never struggled so hard to keep my hands off someone."

"I love your hands on me. Your fingers…"

"Yeah, is that what you want?" he murmurs, his hand slowly descending. "My fingers?"

Heat bursts across my skin, my only response a small shuddery breath.

"I'm going to need an answer, Calliope," he teases, running his fingertips over my inner thigh. "Do you want to come on my fingers?"

"Yes," I breathe, closing my eyes in preparation.

One gentle sweep of his finger reveals how he's affected me. "You're so wet already."

"Don't let it go to your head."

His chuckle is low before he orders, "Look at me." The firm edge to his voice is so fucking hot. The way he watches my face as he slides two fingers deep inside me has my cheeks set on fire. It makes me feel so vulnerable. The involuntary groan I let out brings a wicked smile to his lips.

"They'll hear us," I whisper, remembering his parents are right down the hall.

"You'll have to be quieter then." He strokes his fingers in and out, finding that perfect spot that has my head falling back, my eyes closing.

It's hard to stay quiet, especially when his thumb joins in, stroking over my clit. His lips close over my nipple and the pleasure of it all has me writhing under his touch. As the feeling grows overwhelming, I fold into him with a whimper, "Arlow."

His deep voice croons softly in my ear. "I know, darling."

The sharp orgasm hits me so suddenly that I press my mouth to his shoulder, trying desperately not to cry out. His rumbling curse seems to reach my ear from the far end of a tunnel.

It isn't until I recover some of my senses that I realize why he made that sound. The little indentions on his skin send heat straight to my cheeks. I can't believe I bit him.

"Oh shit, I'm sorry. I didn't mean to—"

"Don't you fucking *dare* apologize," he growls. In a matter of seconds, he rolls me onto my back, wraps one of my legs around him and thrusts his cock in deep. My hands grasp at his back from the sudden invasion and the firm strokes that quickly follow, while his kiss captures my euphoric moans.

He's wild, unleashed. His mouth travels from mine to my neck and back again, devouring me. His large hand grips my ass tightly, lifting me off the bed to pull me toward him as he fucks me. He's everywhere. All hands and tongue and driving cock. I'm drowning in him with no desire to save myself.

It doesn't take long for the pressure to build again, and he fists my hair, tilting my head back to look at him without missing a stroke. "You're getting ready to come. It feels so fucking good."

"Yes," I gasp, my body inching toward the edge that I know is going to be a steep fall. "Oh, harder."

His eyes blaze, and he grabs my hands and pins them above my head. I wrap both of my legs around him, holding on to him the only way I can as he drives into me.

His lips land on mine just in time. The pleasure takes over, shoving me out of my head and into a blissful fog, the spasms going on for what feels like forever. By the time I've regained control, he's lost his.

He releases my hands and grabs my hips, roughly pulling me onto his cock hard and fast. His ravenous expression reaches into my chest and squeezes the air from my lungs. The intense look in his eyes, fervent and primal as he pounds into me, stuns me into silence while I watch him lose control.

Nothing better than this can exist in the world. His thrusts become erratic, vulnerability seeping into his eyes as he's overtaken. He buries his cock deep, coming inside me with a low gravelly moan.

After a moment, he lowers his body on top of mine without pulling out and plants a kiss on my neck. He keeps his face hidden there as I run my hands over his damp back while we catch our breath.

Fucking hell, I'll chomp on him like a zombie next time.

———

The man fucked me into a coma, apparently, because it's nearly noon when I wake. The bed is empty, and the house is stone silent. My body aches as I get dressed, reminding me of the incredible night we had. Sex has never been like that with anyone else. I love the way he can go from sweet and softly passionate to rough and untamed.

The guest room door is open, and the bed stripped. New sheets sit folded on top, waiting to be put on. I wander downstairs to see what everyone is doing. Arlow sits on the couch, wearing jeans and a soft looking sweater, his bare feet propped on the ottoman. He grins up at me over the sketch pad in his lap. "Good morning, sleepy."

"Good morning. Did your parents leave?"

"Early this morning. Dad always wants to beat the traffic."

"You should've woken me up to say goodbye."

The tiny smirk on his lips doesn't sneak past me. "You were pretty worn out and dead to the world. They said to tell you how much they loved meeting you and they hope to see you again."

"I liked meeting them too." I rub my hand over my face, still trying to wake up. "I'm going to grab some coffee and a shower. Don't let me interrupt your drawing." He hasn't been doing much of it lately with everything we've had going on.

"There are cinnamon rolls on the stove for you, and towels are in the dryer if there aren't any in the bathroom," he advises, going back to his work.

Something about that moment feels so...domestic. From the time he said good morning, to making coffee and unwrapping the foil around the cinnamon rolls, to pulling a warm towel from his dryer. This is what our mornings would always be like if he loved me.

It settles over my heart and puts an ache in my chest. He's such an easy person to love, no one could fault me for falling so fast. That doesn't mean anything has changed between us. We may have trouble keeping our hands off each other, especially trying to share a bed, but he's been clear that he doesn't want feelings involved.

As if that ever stopped anyone from drowning in them.

After a shower, I make up the bed in the guest room and move my stuff back into it, then text Silver to see how she and Mona are doing. Instead of texting back, she calls.

"Hey, were you busy?" she asks.

"Nope. Not at all. How's your mom?"

"About to get that bell her friend gave her to ring for me shoved up her ass if I hear one more ding, but otherwise, she's good."

It feels good to laugh with her again. We talk for a few minutes about how things are going with Mona and the diner. "Actually, that's what I needed to talk to you about. Mom has decided to retire a little early and I'll be managing Lucky's."

I'm not sure whether to congratulate her or if she sees this as bad news. "How do you feel about that?"

"It's great. I'm excited. Mom seems to be too. She said she wants to travel a little to see some stuff, and I quote, 'Before that idiot Gary kills me.'"

"Congratulations, I'm happy for both of you." I can't imagine why she wants to talk to me about it unless she's trying to get me to come back to work.

"The only thing is, for her to have the retirement funds, she's going to sell the cabin." Silver quickly adds, "Not until your lease is up, of course. We aren't trying to throw you out or anything."

"Of course, I understand."

"If you're interested in buying it, you can have first dibs. If not, Arlow will likely want it since he tried to get that piece of land before. Anyway, you have plenty of time to think about it, but I wanted to let you know as soon as possible."

"I appreciate it, and yeah, let me give it some thought."

For a while after we hang up, I consider it. If we figure out who's giving us all this trouble, would I want to stay? When it means living next to the man that I'm struggling not to fall too hard for? I love the cabin and the woods. It's a perfect place to start trying the new gardening and homesteading type hobbies next year, not to mention learning beekeeping from Arlow.

One thing at a time. Right now, I'm just trying to keep it together while we wait to hear back from the cops and for the internet to get restored so we can get my cameras working.

When I return downstairs, Arlow asks me to go with him to swap out the memory cards in two of his trail cameras and to check on the bees. I don't think to bring my gun until we're already outside, but Arlow has his, and I feel safe with him as we start into the woods, the beekeeper suits tucked into his backpack.

"Look at this new app I've been playing with," I tell him, showing him my phone. "It's called Merlin. You record the birds singing and it tells you which species they are." I hit play on my last recording. "See, last time I heard a cardinal and a chickadee."

"That's great. It'll teach you to recognize them pretty quickly."

"Yeah, it's fun to try to tell them apart."

"Turn it on, let's see what it picks up," he says, as we head down the trail. It catches a few songbirds and a mourning dove. After a minute, Arlow leans over and starts tweeting and chirping into my phone.

"You can't trick it," I giggle, stopping the recording. "Oh wait, it says you're a dodo."

241

For a split second, I see his eyes dart toward the screen before he realizes I'm kidding. "Very funny."

Another bird I already recognize starts to sing. "That's a grackle," I tell him. "Grackles are easy to recognize. They sound like a rusted gate squeaking."

We pause to listen, then he grins down at me. "That's a perfect description of it."

"I'm going head-on into becoming a bird nerd. This is your only warning."

"Just please don't send your crow army after me."

"We'll see."

One of the trail cameras is right in front of us. Arlow pops off a cover and switches the memory card inside, then starts leading me toward the next one.

"The app will be a lot of fun in the spring, when I can catch them migrating. There aren't very many species this time of year," I point out.

"It'll be interesting to see what passes through," he agrees. "But if you want more species, I know how to do some bird calls."

What? "You know how to do bird calls? To attract birds?" Doubt fills my voice. This is one of those times I can't tell if he's joking or not.

His face is serious and his voice sincere. "Sure, get your app ready."

We keep walking as I open the app again, then look over at him. He nods, pauses his steps and pulls in a deep breath. "Hereeee birrrrdy. Birdy birdy birdy! Psspsspss."

He cracks up when I shove him back. "I can't believe I fell for that. Asshole." His laughter echoes through the forest. "Psspsspss. You idiot," I scoff, laughing along with him.

We stop at the second trail camera, then head over to the beehives, pausing to put on our bee suits. "Is that insulation?" I ask, gesturing to the thick material he's wrapped around the hives in strips.

"Yes, to help them keep warm. The winters here are unpredictable. We could have weeks of ice and snow, months of frigid temperatures, or it could barely dip below freezing once or twice. I've seen it be seventy degrees on Christmas one year and below zero the next."

"It's already freezing," I point out, and he nods.

"True, which probably means we're in for a colder winter, but that's okay. They're ready."

"Do you need to open the hive?"

"No, we don't want to do that and let the heat they've generated out. Look." He points out a couple of entrances where a few dead bees lie.

"Oh no."

"That's actually a good sign. They're active, removing their dead like they should. Come here, I want to show you something."

When I approach, he takes my hands and presses them on either side of the hive, keeping his hands over mine. A faint vibration tickles my fingers and I'm shocked how warm the box feels under my palms. He beams down at me when I look up at him. "They're clustered together, vibrating their wing muscles to keep the colony warm."

"That's so cool," I whisper, trying to picture them inside. It's wild to think about the whole tiny world that exists for them.

"Isn't it?" The genuine joy on his face is beautiful. I adore that he finds happiness in things like this, how much he loves it.

We check on the other hive, then tuck our suits into his backpack to walk back. At the top of our hill, a spike of panic spears through me, and I grab his hand, pointing toward our houses. "Arlow! I see smoke!"

CHAPTER 27

ARLOW

THICK SMOKE CURLS UP INTO THE AIR FROM THE DIRECTION OF OUR homes, and a brick falls into my stomach. It's too close to be a neighbor down the road doing a controlled burn. Plus, we've had rain for days. Everything is wet. Did I leave the heater on in the honey shed? No, I'm sure I didn't. I was in there the other day and would've noticed.

Whatever it is, it's intentional.

Calli looks at me with wide eyes as I take her hand to run. "Oh god, I hope it's not your house, your studio," she gasps as we tear down the hill and into the graveyard.

From this view, I can see it isn't the barn, and the back of my house looks okay, but the smoke is right in front. It could be the porch, or one of our vehicles.

"What are you doing?" Calli exclaims when I slow my steps, then pause to pull my gun out of my pocket. "Mine is in the house," she adds with a curse.

"It's okay. Just keep aware of our surroundings. If someone is here…"

Nodding, she stays by my side while we make our way between

the barn and the house. Relief pours into me to see the house and cabin are fine. A large fire burns in the driveway, the hulking shape consumed by flames and unrecognizable at first.

"No!" Calli cries. The dismay in her voice is terrible.

The wooden glider that she restored, and I painted for her is fully engulfed. The faint smell of gasoline hangs in the air. One of my gas cans that I left in the back of my truck lies on its side about ten feet away.

"The hose!" Calli shouts, and I grab her arm as she starts toward the side of the house.

"It's been put away for winter. It's too late, anyway."

"Fuck!"

"I know, Peach, but we need to look around and make sure they aren't still here." I doubt it. That fire has been burning for a while. Whoever it was probably watched us leave before dragging the glider from my porch and setting it on fire. For what? What could be the purpose of this shit other than revenge? This is Handleman.

I keep my gun out while we check around the barn. There's no sign anyone has tried to break the locks or get in. The honey shed is never locked but there's no one hiding inside. My back door is still secure. We return to the front where the fire is burning down.

"Arlow!" Calli shouts. She runs up the steps onto my porch.

I'm right behind her, and we both stare at the knife jutting from the wood of my front door, a sheet of paper pinned in place by the sharp blade.

In handwriting so messy that it's almost illegible, is a message.

Send one million dollars to the account below or I'll make your life a living hell. No cops. Don't fucking try me. You have one week.

Under that is a string of numbers, separated by spaces that make it clear it's a bank routing number and account number.

Out of instinct, Calli reaches toward it, but I catch her hand before she can touch it. She looks up at me, her voice hushed as if someone may be listening. "This can't be real. Nobody could be this stupid."

"Don't touch it."

Calli nods and pulls her phone out. "I still have the officer's number from last time."

From last time, not even a week ago. This shit has to stop. While she makes the call, I unlock the front door and we have a quick look around inside before stepping back out to the porch to await the officer's arrival.

Calli sits on my top step, her shoulders slumped, watching the glider turn to ashes. "It was like they knew what I valued most. They didn't burn the fucking lawn chairs or tables or anything else. They chose the nicest gift I've ever been given." She blinks away tears, glancing over at me. "Your art. I'm so sorry."

I sit beside her, rubbing my hand up and down her back. "I'm sorry, sweetheart. Once this is over, we'll scour the flea markets and yard sales for another one. Maybe add in some birds or bees this time."

Her small smile is diplomatic, and her hands tremble as she tucks them between her knees. It's not the cold. She's trying hard to be okay, but who the hell would be? As much as I hate it, she had the right idea before. "You were right. You should go to a hotel. I can help you with money if that's an issue. Or I'll go with you. We can get a room together until this gets sorted out." We've never talked about her finances. It's never seemed like an issue for her. When she quit the diner, I assumed she had savings or a plan.

Her reply is quick and overflowing with furious indignation. "And leave your home and studio unprotected? No. Fuck that. They don't get to do this to either of us. I'm staying. We're going to catch these assholes."

Her courage and determination are impressive, but I don't want her putting herself at risk over my issue. "This is my fault. My problem to solve."

247

"You don't know that." She sighs and shakes her head. "I know it's likely the guy you told me about, but there's someone who harassed me before. I honestly don't think he could find me now if he wanted to and I doubt he'd want to. But it isn't impossible. I need to give his name to the officers too, just in case."

"Who is he?" All this time, she hasn't mentioned anyone, not even when the cops asked about enemies. "An ex-boyfriend?"

"Not my ex. My mom's boyfriend. Or he was until she died." The squad cars pull into our driveway, and she looks over at me. "It's a long story, but I'll tell you everything later. I wasn't trying to hide anything from you. He bailed so fast that he didn't even claim her remains. I thought he was gone, and it just didn't seem relevant, but now that they're asking for money…"

My mind spins with questions, but I only manage one as the officers approach us. "Do you have that kind of money?"

She sucks her bottom lip in and gives a reluctant nod.

The police take this much more seriously than they did the vandalism and burglary. Maybe because the threat is a more serious crime or maybe because they find out that I have the money to pay such a demand if I chose. Like it or not, money commands a respect from authorities that isn't given to the general population.

They call in a crime scene investigator to take pictures. They look for fingerprints on the note, the knife, and the gas can. There's no sign of tire tracks or anything that shows how they arrived or left or how many people it may have been. Both Calli and I are interviewed together and separately. This time I give them all the information I know on Chris Handleman, including that he's on the run from parole.

In the meantime, there isn't much they can do. They suggest security cameras—which I already have if we could get our damn internet access back—and advise us to install motion lights. They promise to keep us updated.

"I can't imagine it'll take long," Calli remarks after they've left, while we're in her car on our way to the hardware store. "Bank accounts aren't anonymous. Surely, they'll be able to see whose account that is."

"We're definitely not dealing with a criminal mastermind," I agree as she parks. "But that doesn't make them less dangerous. I want you right by my side every second until they're caught." When she doesn't respond, I look at her and add, "Do you hear me, Calliope?"

She blinks at me a couple of times. "I'll keep close for the next couple of days but if this drags out, I'm not going to live like a prisoner. I'll stay with you, but I'm not locking myself away."

"I need you to be safe."

"I know. I need the same for you."

We pick up the security lights and hardware we need. There's just enough daylight left for us to get them installed around my house and her cabin. They're motion triggered, and I adjust the sensitivity where they'll hopefully pick up a person but not every squirrel.

"Okay, I'm blind," Calli giggles when we test them out. They illuminate the place like a football field. Nobody is sneaking up here at night without us knowing.

An icy wind cuts through my clothes, tossing around a few wispy snow flurries. "Let's get inside and warm up."

After dinner, I build a fire in the living room fireplace. I waited for us to get the necessary things finished today, but once Calli curls up on the opposite end of the couch, I ask her about her mother's boyfriend and her suspicions.

"I told you that my mom was a horrible person. Her boyfriend is no different. It's amazing really, how those type of people seem to find each other."

I'm already on alert, my muscles tensed, afraid she's getting ready to reveal abuse by the asshole boyfriend as well.

"Anyway, like I said before, I left them as soon as I could. It wasn't easy, and there were times I was close to homeless, sleeping on a friend's couch before finding another place. With only a high school education, my choices were limited, and minimum wage doesn't pay rent. Mom and her boyfriend, Carl, left me alone mostly.

They'd turn up every few months—and sometimes even a year or two would go by between—just to harass me, remind me that I was a piece of shit."

"What did they want from you?"

"Nothing. It was what Mom liked to do when she was bored. I watched her do the same to other people most of my life. She would start shit because it excited her. She said once it was the only time she felt alive."

"She sounds crazy," I remark, not really meaning to say the words aloud, but Calli nods.

"I used to think she was. Or that she had some sort of mental illness, you know? Until I met people who dealt with mental illnesses that affected their behavior. I noticed a big difference. Afterward, when they were stable again, they regretted the things they'd done when they couldn't help themselves. She was proud of it.

She had so many stories about things she'd done, like how she trashed a grocery store because the worker asked her to avoid the wet floor, or how she'd poisoned her neighbor's cat when it wouldn't stay off her porch. One of the worst examples she used to brag about was bullying a woman who lived in the apartment under ours, someone who actually had a mental illness. I'm not sure if she was bipolar or schizophrenic or what, but she was delicate. I remember when I was around twelve years old Mom being so thrilled because she had dumped bleach in all the plants on her balcony and it was the last straw after months of such behavior. It led to the woman trying to kill herself and ending up institutionalized." Calli shakes her head. "Mom kept giggling and saying, "Bet she won't give me another dirty look.'"

"Jesus."

"She wasn't crazy. She was mean, hateful. I have a hundred examples like that, but I'm getting off subject. I just want you to understand this wasn't a typical mother daughter disagreement or me not liking her boyfriend. I couldn't give a shit about him."

"I get it."

"Over the years, I'd have to deal with them showing up to park outside my house and yell insults or threats, but they never did anything violent. Or if she found out where I worked, she'd show up there starting trouble hoping to get me fired. I don't know if she found someone new to torture or just got bored of me, but it eventually stopped. Life was still a struggle. I was working multiple jobs trying to keep a roof over my head, but I'd made some friends and things were getting better. At least I thought so.

"I ended up in a similar situation as Silver did. I was dating Zach, one of the guys that was in my friend group, and when he cheated on me with another of our friends, the group sided with them. I kicked Zach out and cut all ties to them. After I threw all his stuff out, I walked to the liquor store across the street to get something to help me forget. On a whim, I bought a lottery ticket while I was there."

She looks over at me, tucking her legs beneath her. "The next day I woke up with a massive hangover and nine million dollars richer."

Holy shit. "You hit the lottery?"

"I did. A little over fourteen million, but I got about nine after taxes. I almost had a heart attack when I found out. The downside was that you can't claim the winnings anonymously in Indiana. It was on the news and part of the public record. Before I even had the money deposited, Mom and Carl were stalking my house, demanding a cut. It got ugly and the cops removed them a couple of times, though they were never arrested.

"I moved to the other side of Indianapolis without any forwarding address, into a little rental house. I wasn't sure what I wanted to do yet and my worst fear was squandering the money. I've heard how often that happens to poor people who suddenly come into money. Nine million is way more than enough to live very comfortably my whole life but it's also not so much that it couldn't be blown through. Anyway, my plan was to stay there while I figured out what I wanted to do."

She sighs, shaking her head. "It took them less than a month to find me and start in again. I'd always been able to count on them to eventually get bored and give up, but not this time. They were there every day. The police wouldn't do anything because parking on a public street and screaming threats apparently isn't against the law. I knew I'd have to move again, and I hired a lawyer to help me really disappear, starting by changing my last name. I found a luxury apartment located in Cincinnati that had a doorman and good security. On my last night in Indianapolis…" She pauses with a bitter smile and mumbles, "I swear it was like they knew it was their last chance."

"To scream at you?"

"To kill me."

My throat tightens and my fists clench as she continues.

"They shot up my house that night while I was home. It was pure luck that I was sleeping on the floor, because I'd already gotten rid of most of the furniture. A bullet missed me by inches."

My mother's face flashes in front of me. I can't imagine how it must feel to have your own mother try to take your life. Over money. "Calliope." It's all I can manage to say as I move to sit beside her and wrap my arms around her middle.

"I'm okay. It feels good to finally tell someone."

"Did they get arrested?"

"No, I couldn't prove it was them. Nobody had any cameras. Drive-by shootings in the city aren't unheard of and it was written off as probable gang violence. I should've seen it coming, really. I knew she was capable of more if the stakes were high enough, and with me having no other family except for a father they probably wouldn't be able to locate and a brother in prison, Mom would've inherited my money if I'd died.

"So, I left and made it to Cincinnati. New name, no way for them or anyone from my past to find me. I changed my phone number and deleted all social media. The only thing I kept was an old email address that I'd occasionally check because Dad would often use it if he couldn't remember my number. Mom and Carl weren't internet savvy, they wouldn't have the first clue you could track an email or

IP address, but I still made sure to check it from public WIFI spots. They weren't dumb enough to threaten me in writing.

"I was safe, but my mind didn't quite believe it. Anxiety has always been a part of me, but it got drastically worse, until I rarely left my apartment. It pissed me off. Here I finally had some freedom from them and from having to work all the time, but I was trapping *myself*."

"The anxiety was trapping you," I interrupt softly. "And no fucking wonder, sweetheart. You were nearly killed."

"I found a therapist online that worked with agoraphobia and anxiety disorders. We started with virtual visits, but she started insisting I come in more and more. For nearly two years, I worked on getting my anxiety under control. I didn't leave very often. A few festivals with my concert friends are the highlight of those years. Until an email showed up in my box with a copy of my mother's obituary and a request from her church for me to accept her remains. Apparently, they'd paid for her cremation, and Carl had run off without the ashes."

She looks up at me. "I was so relieved. So thrilled she was dead. My anxiety improved overnight." Her tone bleeds shame and guilt. "Of course, I didn't have to take her ashes, but I wanted them. I wanted to look at them and know I was free from her forever. That's why I haven't been able to scatter them. I like to look at them and be reminded that she's finally dead." Bitterness lives in the tiny tilt of her lips. "Because I inherited some of her hateful nature, no matter how much I try to fight it."

"No. Some people deserve that level of hatred and she more than qualifies. You aren't anything like her."

Calli doesn't argue, just leans her head on my shoulder and continues. "I had them mail the remains to a PO Box. It wasn't long after that when I found the ad for the cabin and decided to get out of the city and see if I liked living in nature. Somewhere peaceful." She tilts her head with a small smile. "Where I met a graveyard creeper and stole his peaches."

All I can do for a moment is hold her. Not a bit of me could've imagined everything she'd been through right before coming here. "I'm sorry that's what brought you, but I'm glad you're here."

"You may want to rethink that, if it's Carl that left the threat. I still highly doubt it for a few reasons. He was never the leader when they were harassing me. It was more like he was following her orders which was par for the course. He was always the driver, always the one to wait in the car while she went psycho. Without Mom, he really has no link to me. Cops would be more likely to take him harassing me seriously. And he has to know I wasn't going to give him any money if I wouldn't give it to her.

"Also, I've moved twice now and changed my name. Even if he wanted to try, I don't think he could find me." She hesitates with a sigh. "But there's one thing that bothers me and maybe it's overthinking, but the man who took your ATV was wearing a dark denim jacket. Carl always wore one too."

My question comes out softly. "What's your name?"

"Hmm?" She peeks up at me.

"You said you changed your name."

"I've always been Calliope, but my last name was Raines, same as my dad's. I changed it to Barnes, and started using my nickname Calli, on anything official. Calli Barnes."

I run my hand through her hair. "Calliope Raines. Beautiful."

CHAPTER 28

CALLIOPE

MY BODY IS A LIVE WIRE, BLEEDING ELECTRICITY INTO THE BED SHEETS while my mind races and my stomach churns. So much has happened in such a short time. My cabin has been robbed and ransacked. I've learned that being the anonymous artist called Nameless was far from Arlow's only secret, and I've revealed my true, flawed self and past to him. Someone is trying to extort us, and we may both be in danger. My brain is chaos, filled with warring possibilities, all of them dire.

I don't know what to do. If I thought this was Carl's doing, I'd leave, if only to keep Arlow out of it, but it doesn't seem likely to me. The note said we have a week. Does that mean they'll leave us alone until then? Will things escalate after that deadline?

Am I ever going to be safe anywhere?

That last thought brings tears to my eyes, and I turn over with a harsh frustrated sigh. I'm never going to fall asleep.

"Calli." Arlow's voice is soft, but my body jerks, shaking the bed. "Jesus, you scared me."

"Sorry." He lays his gun on the nightstand and crawls into bed with me. "I can't sleep. You're too far away from me."

Says the man who keeps everyone at a distance. That's another reason I'm not leaving. Arlow is finally letting me in. He may not love me, but he needs me, and I need him.

"I can't sleep either." His scent comforts me as I move closer to him. "Will you hold me for a minute?" Strong arms pull me against his warm body without hesitation, and I lay my head on his chest.

"You're shaking." There's no hiding the tremble of my fingers on his abdomen. His large hand swallows mine and he holds me tighter. "And all tensed up. What can I do to help you settle?"

"You're doing it. I'll be alright." Already my muscles are beginning to soften, my jaw unclenching. "You always manage to stop my brain from chewing on itself. You might be magic. I wish I could bottle you for every anxiety attack."

He strokes my hair, and I close my eyes, wrapping myself in the comfort of his presence. "Not sure how long I'd last in a bottle. It probably wouldn't smell good."

"Shut up," I scoff, lightly pinching his side.

"Have you thought about a pet? I've heard that can help anxiety too."

"Actually, I was going to ask you how you'd feel about chickens, or maybe a goat."

His chest rattles with a chuckle. "I was thinking more like a dog or cat. Something cuddly. Maybe a rabbit."

"Have you ever seen a baby goat? They're the most cuddly thing ever." My heartbeat has returned to a normal rate and the buzzing of my skin is fading.

"And the chickens?"

"Are you judging my emotional support chickens?"

"I'd never dare." The continued brush of his fingers over my scalp soothes me toward sleep. "Everything's going to be alright. I'm not letting you out of my sight until this is over. We'll get through this week together." As the welcoming dark pulls me under, I feel his lips on my forehead. They feel like love.

The next few days are blissfully quiet. Arlow and I fall easily into a daily routine. Whoever wakes first makes coffee and breakfast, then we get anything that needs to be done around the place taken care of. The charred remnants of the glider are cleaned up from the driveway. Arlow spends time drawing while I read and make another attempt at crocheting. We watch movies together, listen to music, and play cards or a game when we're bored. Arlow has an older gaming system that doesn't need to be online, and we spend a fun evening trying to beat one another on games I haven't played since I was a kid.

Arlow slips into bed with me each night without a word, but it's not for sex. As much as we're trying to pretend everything is okay, an undercurrent of tension runs through everything. The suspense is hard to handle, but being wrapped in his arms every night makes it bearable.

We only leave the property briefly to run a few errands or shop for groceries. Neither of us say it, but we're both afraid of what we might come back to if we're gone too long. I call our internet service provider hoping we might get it back earlier than expected but get told the exact opposite. It could be a total of three weeks. They apologize, rattle off some reasons for the delay, and offer discounts when service resumes but that doesn't help us get our cameras online now.

On Thursday, Arlow sticks his head into the living room where I'm reading about the PH of different soils and how it affects which vegetables to plant. "Do you want to go with me to have dinner with Earl? I can call and tell him we won't be there if you don't feel like it."

His reluctance reflects in his tone, but we can't stay home every second forever. "I'd like to go. It'll be good to get out of the house a little. I'll take him some blueberry muffins."

His jaw drops in mock outrage. "You made those for me."

"I made those for *us*, and I'll make you more. Don't be stingy."

"Will you put streusel on top?" His lips tilt into a playful smile that never fails to make me grin too. How can someone so ruggedly handsome also be so damn cute?

"I'll think about it."

I'm happy to visit Earl again. I've only been back once since that first time, and he was thrilled to see me. We played cards again and I'm determined to beat him at Rummy eventually. We pick up dinner at Hatty's Seafood Shack as usual—he's a creature of habit for sure. Arlow said he long ago stopped asking because he always wants the same thing.

It gets dark early this time of year, and I take my time down the winding country road. As we approach Earl's place, red and blue lights flash through the trees. "Arlow," I murmur.

"Something's wrong," he says, and I speed up, pulling into the driveway.

An ambulance sits near a squad car, and an old pickup I've never seen blocks them both in. Harvey runs up to bark at us as usual. "That's Earl's brother, Larry, on the porch," Arlow says.

The words have barely cleared his lips before he's out of my car, his strides eating up the dirt. Harvey gets between my legs, desperate for attention, and it slows me down. Before I even catch up to them, I know Earl is gone by the expression on Arlow's face. He stands with his shoulders slumped, nodding as Larry speaks to him. I slow my steps, hanging back a little to allow them a moment to talk.

Arlow looks back to see me and holds out his hand. "Earl passed away. A stroke they think."

"I'm so sorry for your loss," I tell his brother, squeezing Arlow's hand.

"Thank you. He was a stubborn old bastard. Had two strokes before but he wouldn't give up his beer or fried food. At seventy-five, you can't blame him much, I reckon." His brother looks to be in his seventies at least. He looks up at Arlow and rubs his rheumy eyes. "He was really fond of you. Looked forward to your dinners every week."

Arlow nods, his eyes welling up too. "He was a hell of a guy. I'll miss him." Harvey runs up, nosing his way between us. "Do you need someone to take Harvey?"

"No." He slaps his leg and Harvey trots over to him. "We'll get along okay, I reckon."

Arlow lays a hand on my shoulder. "Can you give us a minute, please?"

"Of course." I swallow the lump in my throat and regard Larry. "If there's anything you need or anything we can do, please don't hesitate to let us know."

"That's very kind of you."

I return to the warmth of the car while Arlow takes a seat on the porch beside Larry. They talk for a few minutes before Arlow shakes his hand and walks back to me. I shift the food we brought to my backseat. It looks sad now. Earl won't get his beloved hushpuppies.

I lean over and hug Arlow as soon as he gets into the car. "I'm so sorry."

He hugs me back. "Thanks. It wasn't unexpected, you know, with his age and health but still."

"I know. Is there anything we can do?"

"That's what I was talking to Larry about. He said they weren't holding a funeral, and I wanted to make sure it wasn't because of financial constraints. It turns out Earl was adamant about that. He told his brother that funerals are morbid and stupid, and people should spend their time focusing on life not crying over worm food." His lips twitch. "That's a direct quote."

"That sounds like him."

"Come on. Let's go home."

Arlow is quiet the rest of the evening. He doesn't want to talk and retreats to the corner chair with his drawing pad, but I stay nearby, a silent presence to make sure he doesn't feel alone. It isn't until we go to bed that he's ready to talk.

We lie facing one another and he rests his forehead on my shoulder. "The coroner said he'd probably been dead for a week before Larry found him. I may have been the last one to see him when I visited last Thursday. I should've checked on him more often."

"Hey." I cup his chin and lift his head. The sight of his reddened eyes raises tears in mine. "You were a good friend to him. This isn't your fault." He nods, and I wrap my arms around him. We hold each other as I run my hand up and down his back.

"I don't want that to be me." Torment permeates the words of his confession. "The thought of being alone for all those years. So alone that no one even fucking knows I'm dead for a week." He pulls in a deep breath, fighting to keep his composure.

Of course he would see similarities between them. Earl may not have chosen a solitary life. For all I know, he simply outlived most of his family and friends, but it comes to the same in the end.

I cradle Arlow's face in my hands and look him in the eye. "That's not going to happen. Listen to me. You're loved. No matter how much you've isolated yourself from your family, they love you. Distance doesn't change that. I know you want to protect them…and me, but that's not how it works."

"I don't want to do that to anyone, leave them to hurt for me."

"I know." He's tearing my heart out. His anguish is palpable. To feel such guilt over letting people love him is terrible. "But that's the price we all pay to love each other. Love and grief are braided together. We don't get to choose between them or opt out of either. That's life. You'll hurt for your friend now, but that doesn't mean he shouldn't have let you in." I brush my thumb over his cheek. "You're afraid to be loved, but that doesn't mean you don't deserve it or that you can avoid it. You aren't alone. There are people who love you whether you like it or not."

The words that want to follow are held tight behind my lips. He doesn't want to hear that I love him, and this isn't the time. He falls asleep in my arms, and I hope I've managed to give him even a fraction of the comfort he brings me.

CHAPTER 29

ARLOW

TODAY IS THE DAY WE'VE BEEN WAITING FOR AND DREADING. IT'S BEEN A week and the deadline scrawled onto the note has come. Despite being on edge, the time has passed without any further trouble. More than anything, I want to think they've given up. That they saw we ignored their instructions and called the police, but that feels too good to be true.

Calli has stayed right by my side the way I asked her to, but I'm already afraid of the day when our internet is restored, and she returns to her cabin. I'll never trust she's safe. What's the alternative? That she moves? I'm sure she's considering it though she hasn't mentioned it to me again.

My head is all over the place, especially since Earl's death. He warned me not to end up like him, but I didn't realize how alone he really was until now. It has me seriously rethinking everything. I'm torn between what's right and what my heart desperately wants—the beautiful, caring woman asleep upstairs.

A sharp knock at the door drives me to my feet, and I touch my gun, reminding myself it's in its holster before looking out the peep-hole to see two officers.

"Mr. Shaw." Officer Anderson nods at me. "We have some follow up questions for you and Ms. Barnes." I'm disappointed to see that Officer Fulton accompanies him. The same one who wouldn't listen to Calli before.

"Come on in." They follow me back to my kitchen where I gesture for them to have a seat at the table, then sit across from them. "Calli isn't available at the moment, but what can I do for you? Have you traced the account number to a name?"

"No, but we've had a hit on some fingerprints," Officer Anderson informs me.

"From the cabin?"

Officer Fulton replies before he can say any more. "When we collected the evidence from your front door, you assured us that neither you nor Ms. Barnes had touched it, correct?"

"That's right."

"Not the knife or the paper?" he presses.

"No, all I did was take a picture in case it fell or blew away before you arrived. No one touched it."

Officer Fulton glances over at his partner with a satisfied smirk. "Two clear fingerprints were found on the handle of the knife. Both belong to Calli Barnes."

He seems to think he's dropped some huge bombshell and stares at me while I search my memory of that night again. She didn't touch that knife. She reached for it, but I caught her hand. "That doesn't make any sense."

"How long have you known Ms. Barnes?" Officer Anderson asks.

His tone is diplomatic—unlike Fulton's—but I don't like where this is going. "Since June. What the hell does that have to do with anything?"

"Wise up, Mr. Shaw," Officer Fulton blurts. "Your little neighbor girlfriend is playing you. I'd bet every dollar I have that we'll find her name, or someone associated with her on that account. She found out you had money and is playing the damsel in distress while you protect her. Has she suggested you just send the money yet?"

I'm sure they judge my silence as shock, but it's rage that I'm trying to suppress. "Calli had nothing to do with this. Have you even looked into Chris Handleman or Carl Becker? Called to see if his parole officer ever heard from him? Figured out what cars they might be driving or if they're in our area? You haven't tracked the account number. Have you done anything that even comes close to helping us or are you only here to accuse her?"

Fulton is on his feet, his fat cheeks growing pink. "You don't get to tell us how to do our jobs. We're asking the questions."

"Not anymore. We're done. You're clearly not interested in figuring out who is targeting us, only in trying to pass the blame to an easy target. I will not be answering any more questions without a lawyer and I can assure you Calli won't either." She's going to be devastated to find out nothing is being done. We're on our own.

Officer Anderson intervenes, also rising to stand. "We aren't here to make accusations. Your fingerprints and Ms. Barnes were collected to differentiate your prints from any that couldn't be explained. You claim she didn't touch the knife, but her prints say otherwise. Can you offer an explanation for that?"

"No, but considering her net worth is higher than mine, I sure as fuck don't believe she's after my money."

That revelation seems to catch them both off guard. Of course, Calli doesn't present herself like she has money. Her car is new, but it's a mid-range sedan. Nothing fancy. She rents a cabin instead of owning a home and doesn't dress in designer clothes or flaunt any kind of expensive jewelry or belongings.

Fulton narrows his eyes at me, doubt permeating his statement. "You're a multi-millionaire."

Officer Anderson interrupts again. "Do you have a reason to believe she has comparable wealth?"

"Yes. She told me."

Fulton laughs and shakes his head as Calli appears in the doorway behind him. Her hair is mussed and she's still wearing the pajama pants and camisole she slept in.

"What's going on?"

I hold up my hand before the officers can speak. "Don't answer any questions. You need a lawyer."

Her brow furrows. "What? Why?"

"You claimed that you never touched that knife in the door, correct, Calli?" Officer Fulton demands, facing her and crossing his arms.

Her puzzled gaze bounces from me to the officer a couple of times, and I can see anger bloom in her eyes. "Yes, that's correct, *Chester*."

"It's Officer Fulton," he replies through gritted teeth.

"And I'm Ms. Barnes." Calli stands firm and returns his glare, refusing to be intimidated.

"Your fingerprints were found on the knife," Officer Anderson tells her. It seems like the tension is getting to him. He looks like he'd rather be anywhere else.

"That's impossible." Calli blinks multiple times, looking at the floor while she ponders what she's just been told.

"Do you have an explanation of how your prints got on the knife if you didn't put it in the door nor touch it afterward?"

She shakes her head, then looks up. "Wait. Do you have a picture of the knife?"

"Not on hand, but it has been photographed as evidence."

"I do," I volunteer, scrolling through my phone. "I took it as she called you."

Calli accepts the phone and zooms in. "It's hard to tell from that angle and it's kind of dark, but I think that's the same knife that was stolen from my car during the break-in. I used to keep it in my glove box." She looks up at Officer Anderson. "I reported the theft when my window was broken."

"That's convenient," Officer Fulton says.

Calli doesn't rise to the bait, choosing instead to address Officer Anderson. "I didn't put the knife in the door. If my prints were on it, they must be from before it was stolen. Do you have any other news for us or is that it?"

"Mr. Shaw has told us you would have no need for money. Would you be willing to share your financial information to corroborate that? We can clear up this misunderstanding and move on with the investigation."

Calli doesn't hesitate. "No, clearly Officer Fulton has some issue with me, and I won't be laying my personal information out for him to peruse. Get a warrant. We're done here. If you have more questions, I'll come in with a lawyer."

"That's fine," Officer Fulton says, tossing a smart assed grin our direction. "I wouldn't be surprised if the trouble stops now."

Calli waits in the kitchen as I escort them out.

When I return, she's sipping on a coffee and pulling a small dish of honey from the microwave. "Do you want some honey on toast?" she asks, putting two slices of bread into the toaster.

"No thanks." I hook my arm around her, pulling her back to hug her from behind. "Are you alright?"

"I'm fine." She pats my arm and lets me hold her a second until the toast pops up.

Releasing her, I lean against the counter. "I think we should get a lawyer on retainer in case they come at you again. And we'll hire our own investigator to help us figure out who's doing this to us."

"Do you think someone could've figured out that you're Nameless? A crazy fan or something?"

"I don't think so, but I suppose it isn't impossible." I hate how stressed out she looks. "Let's go out this afternoon. Let me take you to a movie or shopping. Whatever you want."

"Are you sure? It's been a week. If shit is going to start again, it'll be soon."

"I know. We'll get back before dark."

Her smile is worth any amount of risk. "I'd like that. First, I want to show you something."

She leans on the counter beside me, showing me her phone. "This isn't everything, but it shows some of my investment accounts."

"Hey." I avert my eyes and look into hers. "I don't need to see that. Do you think I don't believe you?"

"No, but...I need you to see it. I won't stop overthinking it if I don't show you that I don't need anyone's money."

"I could kick that cop in the fucking nuts," I grumble and let her scroll to show me her substantial accounts.

She chuckles, setting her phone down to retrieve the honey and a spoon. "I was tempted."

As she drizzles the honey onto her toast, a bit drips onto the back of her other hand. Without a thought, I pull her hand up to my mouth and suck it from her skin. She freezes for a moment. The way her lips part and her cheeks redden has me hard in seconds. Nothing sexual has happened between us in the last week but there's only so long I can fight it. We've both been under so much stress and pressure. We need a release.

She agrees, judging by her next move. With a little grin, she dips her finger in the dish of warm honey and holds it out to me. Before I can move, she pulls it back and lets a few drops fall on her neck. It runs in a rivulet down to her collarbone as she sucks the rest of it from her finger.

She gasps when I grab her hips and lift her onto the table, my tongue catching the honey and following it back up to her neck. She tilts her head as I lick away every trace from her skin. I pull her shirt off and press on her shoulder. "Lie back."

"Here?" she chuckles, when I slide her pajama bottoms off as well, leaving her lying bare on my kitchen table.

I pick up the bowl of honey, testing the temperature with a fingertip. Hot but not too hot. Perfect. "You started it. Now you're just going to have to wait for me to finish eating."

"You're the one who...mmm." Her argument disintegrates as a drop of honey hits her nipple.

"Does that feel good?" I let another few drops fall, then move to cover the other nipple in the sweet warmth before dripping it down her stomach. She looks up at me, her chest rising and falling faster when I push her legs apart to trail honey on the inside of each thigh.

It suddenly strikes her that she's the only one naked. "Take your clothes off."

"You aren't in any position to be giving orders here, darling. Come for me, and then we'll see."

It feels amazing to have her like this, open and vulnerable to me. Leaning over, I kiss her, tasting the honey on both our lips. She closes her eyes when I take her nipple into my mouth, lapping and sucking away the thick sweetness.

I take my time, moving from one breast to the other and back again, loving every little moan and breath from her. Her stomach jumps as I trail my tongue down it, making me grin. She's ticklish.

"Arlow," she breathes, when I move to her inner thigh.

"Patience," I murmur. Damn, I love teasing her. I want to tie her to my bed and keep her squirming under me for hours. Her skin is soft and warm under my tongue. I could do this forever. When I get to her other thigh, I can't resist sucking just hard enough to leave a mark.

The way she melts for me is so satisfying. She has no idea what's in store for her as I slowly get her to relax then cover her clit with my mouth. Her hips jerk upward, but I lock my arms around her thighs as she cries out.

Without mercy, I lick and suck at her. Curses spill from her lips. She pulls my hair, wriggling and groaning. It drives me fucking crazy. In no time, she's gripping the edges of the table and calling my name while her pussy pulses under my tongue.

"Oh, stop!" she demands as the spasms turn to sensitivity.

Standing up, I wipe my mouth and take a second to look at her. Her red cheeks and glassy eyes. It's the sexiest thing I've ever seen. I strip my clothes off, intending to take her where she lies, but she hops off the table and pushes me back down to sit in the kitchen chair.

Without a word, she straddles me, sinks down on my cock and

proceeds to fuck the hell out of me. Her hands are in my hair, her tongue diving between my lips as she rides me. I'm desperately trying to hold off so she can get a second one but I'm losing the battle. She feels so fucking good.

She tugs my hair, pulling my head to the side and her hot breath is in my ear. "Are you going to come for me now, Arlow?" she asks and bites my neck.

My own shout fills my ears as I lose myself completely, spilling inside of her. She stays on my lap as our hearts and breaths begin to slow, our arms wrapped around one another.

When she sits back a little, our sticky bodies pull apart. She chuckles, looking down at my chest. "I don't think honey can be completely removed by licking."

"I'll try harder next time." We share a soft kiss.

She grins up at me, running a finger down my chest. "What will your bees think?"

Nobody can make me laugh like she can. No one else can make me feel like she does. Not another person in this world could take me from such stress to heartfelt ecstasy to soul healing laughter in a matter of minutes. I have to bite back the words fighting to escape. *I love you. Christ, I just love you so fucking much.*

Her giggles light up the room as she climbs off my lap. "I definitely need a shower before we go out."

As happy as I'd be to drag her up to my bed and take her again, if we want to get back by dark, we need to get going. "Me too." I drop one more kiss on her sticky lips. "Let's go."

————

Calli grabs a handful of popcorn from the container on my lap. A silent giggle stays trapped behind her smile when she accidentally drops some on my shirt for the second time.

"Are you trying to cover me in butter instead of honey?" I whisper in her ear.

"Not all of us have giant hands."

"Don't be jealous."

It's been years since I've been to the movies. I've been more than happy to stream them at home. But sitting with my arm around her in the dark theater, her head resting on my shoulder, stealing an occasional popcorn buttery kiss like two dating teenagers makes me feel something inexplicable. Like I'm a real person in the real world, a world I walked away from for too long.

Calli seems to enjoy herself as well, and the peaceful smile on her face when we leave is exactly what I was hoping to see today.

"Where do you want to eat?" I ask, as we get into the car.

"Do you want to go to Lucky's Diner? Silver's working today, and I'd like to see how she's doing. Plus, I've been craving their country fried steak."

"Sounds good to me."

The diner isn't busy when we show up, since it's between lunch and dinner time. One thing Calli and I always share is an unconventional schedule. I don't think either of us has ever gone to bed, woken up, or eaten meals at the normal time. It's a freedom few get—due to their jobs—and I'm grateful for it. How much different would people be without clock hands urging them to go or stay, sleep or eat?

Silver points at me when we enter and calls out, "I don't have any apple fritters so don't you start with me, Arlow!"

"You'd better get back there and get to work then!" I retort, and she flips me off. I think I won her over at some point.

She comes out to talk to us in our corner booth after the waitress has taken our order. "How's your mom?" Calli asks.

"Sitting in her wheelchair in the office right now. She was getting cabin fever, and it was either bring her to work with me or push her into the road."

Calli nearly chokes on her drink as they laugh together. "I'll go back to say hi before we go."

"I'm sure she'll sniff you out before then."

She isn't wrong. About halfway through our meal, Mona rolls out

269

of the kitchen and down to join us. With one leg and one arm in a cast, she looks pitiful, but there's not an ounce of weakness in her voice.

"Silver said you were out here. How dare you not come back to the office to visit me!" she says to Calli.

"Sorry, I was going to after we eat," I reply instead, beating Calli to it and making her laugh.

Mona looks me up and down. "Where were you when we needed something off the high shelf? I wouldn't have tripped *over that step-stool*!" She raises her voice on the last words as a man wipes one of the tables near us.

"For hell's sake, Mona, I said I was sorry. What do you want? Blood?" he grumbles.

"It'd be a start," she replies, then turns back to Calli. "Silver told you about the cabin?"

Calli's gaze flits to mine for a split second before she regards Mona again. "She did. I need some time to consider what I'm going to do."

"Of course. I know we sprung it on you."

"I appreciate you giving me first dibs though. It's a beautiful place."

Calli told me that she wasn't going to inform Silver of the burglary, and clearly she hasn't told her about anything that's happened since, but it sounds like they plan to sell the property.

They talk for a while. I wait until Mona returns to the kitchen and we've finished eating before asking, "Are you buying the cabin?"

Her tongue peeks out between her lips as she hesitates. "How would you feel about it if I did?"

Is she serious? "I'd love that. Are you seriously considering it?"

"I don't know. It depends on how things turn out, I guess. It doesn't seem like the wisest choice right now."

Of course it doesn't. I have to put an end to this bullshit or she's going to leave. I'm going to lose her. "Do you have to give them a decision soon?"

"They aren't pushing me for one. I have some time to think and see what happens over the next few weeks, at least. My lease isn't up until summer but I'm sure both of us are willing to break it at this point."

Silver appears with a box full of donuts and sets it on our table. "On the house," she announces, then adds, "Donuts, not dinner."

Chuckling, I pull my card out and lay it on the check for the waitress, shaking my head at Calli when she tries to do the same. "I've got it."

Silver interrupts her when she opens her mouth. "Let him be a gentleman about it, girl. Besides, he got his apple fritters."

I pop open the box to find that's true and look up at her. "They're warm. You made them just for me."

"I told Charlotte to make some because we were out. Don't be so conceited."

"I don't know. I think I'm growing on you."

"Like a fungus, maybe," she scoffs, leaning to give Calli a hug. "I have to get back to work, but don't be a stranger. I'll call you when I have a night free to hang out soon."

"Call me if you need anything too," Calli replies.

"Your friend likes me," I tease once she walks off and the waitress brings our receipt.

"Well, there's no accounting for taste," Calli says with a grin, grabbing my hand as we leave.

We make a quick stop at the grocery store because she wants to make a pot of chili for dinner tomorrow. After we've gathered all the ingredients, I pause at the baking aisle. "Do you like cornbread or crackers with it?"

"Cinnamon rolls."

"Excuse me?"

She looks up at me and repeats what I thought I misheard. "I like it with cinnamon rolls. What do you eat with chili?"

"Cornbread is my favorite but back up a second. Are you screwing with me?"

271

Giggles rain out of her. "No! You've never had a cinnamon roll alongside chili? You're from the Midwest!"

"I also don't put ice cream on my spaghetti."

"Shut up. I'll make cornbread too."

Our good natured argument continues in the car until we get close to our driveway. Calli sees it at the same time I do and hits her brakes.

"Arlow," she whispers.

"I see it." Dark smoke trails across the sky behind the graveyard. I take a moment to try to decide what to do. I don't want to put her in danger but I'm not letting her out of my sight either. "Do you have your gun with you?"

Her eyes widen, and she nods. "In the glovebox."

"I have mine too. We can go investigate or call the fire department first." We've already decided the cops aren't going to be an option.

"It doesn't look like a lot of smoke. Could it be a fire on someone else's property?"

"Possibly." I doubt it. It looks like it's coming from the clover field.

"Let's go," she says, and continues down to the dirt road on the opposite side of the church ruins. This road is barely wide enough to accommodate her car and she takes her time, careful not to get us stuck while I watch our surroundings.

It could be a grassfire or even a forest fire, but things haven't been nearly dry enough for that to be likely. As it becomes clear where the smoke is coming from, my stomach sinks.

"Oh, Arlow, no," Calli breathes, parking at the side of the road.

We both stare at my beehives, or what remains of them.

There isn't a soul in sight as we walk across the field, our feet crushing the winter browned patches of clover. A sickly sweet scent hangs in the air, the last whiff of scorched nectar and honey. It's combined with the familiar smell of gasoline.

The hives are far beyond saving, the colonies long dead. Burned alive. Rage makes my heartbeat pound in my ears.

I've had enough.

————

Calli is upstairs when I step out onto the porch to call Lee. He listens as I catch him up on everything before I get to the point of my call. "I need to find a private investigator, but I want someone who isn't afraid to break the law to find Handleman and won't question what I plan to do with the information afterward. Do you know someone I can trust?"

"I can make a call. Have you considered some security in the meantime? A guy to watch over shit while you keep your girl safe. It's fucking difficult to do both alone." He doesn't give me a chance to answer before he says, "Give me a few minutes, I'll call you back."

I knew Lee would be willing to help me when I called him, but I didn't expect to see him pull into my driveway just after dark.

He holds up a bottle of whiskey. "I'm crashing here tonight."

"Okay, but I like to cuddle."

He snorts as he follows me inside. Neither of us remarks on it, but I know he's here in case things escalate tonight. I had no intention of sleeping anyway.

"Do you know there's a storm coming tomorrow night?" he asks.

"Snow?"

"Ice, maybe snow. They're talking it up pretty good. Calling it a shutdown storm."

"Do you need help getting any of your properties ready?"

"No, they're good. I'll get my wood in and generators out tomorrow. We probably won't get anything. You know they always get that shit wrong."

Calli joins us in the living room for most of the evening, but we avoid any discussion of the situation at hand. It isn't until later, once she goes to my bedroom for the night to read, that I revisit the conversation with Lee.

"Do you have someone in mind?" I ask, keeping my voice low as I pull back the curtains. The thin blinds block anyone's view inside, but if any of the motion lights around my house or barn are triggered, we'll see it immediately.

Lee props his foot up on his knee, leaning back. "I do. He won't be cheap, but he'll find out who you're dealing with and won't involve any authorities or worry about what you intend to do with that information."

"I don't care about the cost. I appreciate this. I know it probably means reaching out to people you'd rather not talk to again."

He brushes off my concern. "It's not an issue. You're pretty confident this is Handleman?"

"It makes the most sense. If it is, it wouldn't be hard to get him sent back to prison. The cops here may not care, but I bet one call to report his new address to his parole officer would do the trick."

"Likely," he agrees, then stares at me over the top of his glass. "But if it doesn't, or it isn't him, do you know what you intend to do?"

It'll depend on who is targeting us and how much proof I can get. There's only one thing I know for sure. "Whatever it takes to keep her safe."

He nods his approval.

We sit in silence, letting the night deepen around us, each lost in thoughts. Mine keep coming back to the woman now curled up under my covers. I'm not being fair to her. She hasn't asked me for anything, or for any clarification of how things might be between us but telling her I don't want anyone to get attached to me, then spending every day with her in my arms, in my bed. What am I doing?

The answer seemed so clear to me before. I could lessen the pain of my family and never inflict that grief on anyone else. I could live out my life with nature and art and let that be enough. Except eventually it wasn't. I hadn't even realized I was lonely until she showed up.

Being away from my parents didn't diminish the love I have for them, and it wouldn't mitigate my grief if one of them were lost. Why would that be true the other way around? Have I been wrong all this time?

Calliope thinks it's fear. A fear of being loved in a way I've never felt for another person...until now. Is that the truth of it? Am I giving up relationships and meaningful connections because it's better for everyone else? Or because I'm afraid?

The therapy suggestion may be a good one. It feels like too much to sort out.

Lee lives the same way, essentially alone except for his sister, but not because he's afraid or trying to spare anyone. He told me once that no one could ever replace his wife, and he has no desire to try. If there's anyone to answer one question for me, it's him.

"I want to ask you something." He looks over at me, waiting. "About Isla."

For a moment, he doesn't respond, only pours himself a second glass of whiskey, then sits back and gives a silent nod.

"After everything you went through, if you could go back and change things so you never fell in love, would you? Would you spare yourself the suffering?"

"Fuck no."

His reply is immediate. Not one second of thought was required. After watching him teeter on the brink of suicide multiple times because of his grief, I'm stunned.

He looks me in the eye as he adds, "I'd go through it all again, every day for the rest of my life, for one more minute with her. I wouldn't change a fucking thing."

I nod, unsure how else to respond. The window to our right is suddenly illuminated by one of the outdoor lights, and both of us are on our feet to look. A deer raises its head to look at us for a second before bounding off.

"I'm going to have a look around the house," I tell him, picking up my gun.

"Scream like a little girl if you see anything," he replies, breaking the tension.

The night is frosty and clear. The crisp air feels invigorating. I've been indoors too much lately. As soon as this is over and we're safe, I'm going to show Calli how wonderful a bonfire feels on cold nights. A walk around my house and barn reveals nothing. Everything is quiet.

I'm glad to have Lee here as some back up for tonight, another set of eyes and ears. The predicted shutdown storm will be a welcome thing as well if it materializes. It doesn't take much to make our road impassable and it's unlikely anyone is going to be out here fucking around in an ice storm. It buys us a few days to get ahold of Lee's connection and put some security in place.

When I return to the house, Lee has hooked up my old gaming system and turned on some music. "All clear?" he asks, without looking away from the screen.

"All clear."

"Grab a few hours of sleep. I'll keep an eye on things and wake you when I'm ready to crash. I slept half the day anyway."

"Alright. Thanks." I'm not sure whether I'll be able to sleep, but crawling into bed with Calli sounds too inviting.

He puts the cap on the bottle of whiskey and holds it out to me to put away. When I grasp the bottle, he holds onto it, looking me in the eye. "You haven't lost your chance. Don't fuck it up."

CHAPTER 30

CALLIOPE

DESPITE THE STRESS OF YESTERDAY, I SLEPT WELL. ARLOW'S BODY wrapped around mine always seems to have that effect. "Hey," I call, joining him on the couch. "Is Lee gone?"

"He left this morning."

"Any new chaos I should know about?" I ask, stealing a sip of his coffee.

"How about some good news for once? Our internet is back on."

"Really?" I grab my phone to see the WIFI is connected again. "About time."

"I want to talk to you about the next few weeks. I'm going to hire private security. Lee knows some reliable people."

"Bodyguards?" His concern is warranted but I'm not going to have a guy following me around.

"No, just someone to keep an eye on things, especially while we sleep or if we aren't at home. We can't watch every second, even with cameras."

"Okay. Is that happening today?"

He shakes his head and gestures to the television. "The predictions for the storm keep getting worse. It's going to shift between ice, snow, and a mix of the two. Our road will likely end up impassable for a day or two at least." The look he gives me says I'm not going to like what he has to say next. "I reserved us a hotel room for the next few days. Just until we can get some security in place. I'm not going to take the chance of him showing up while we're trapped."

Sighing, I sit back. "Riding out a winter storm with a possible madman lurking around does sound like stupid horror movie behavior, I guess. But we can't leave your place unguarded. He burnt your hives. What if he burns the house or the barn?"

"I can keep an eye through the cameras if the power stays on."

"And if it doesn't?"

"I'll risk it. I won't risk you getting hurt if we stay."

"Us."

"What?" He cocks his head to look at me.

"We won't risk *us* getting hurt if we stay." His eyes soften as I run my hand through his hair. "I need you to be safe too. What time do you want to leave?"

"Right before dark. The storm isn't coming until near dawn, and I want to install cameras at your cabin and make sure the trail cams are back online. Plus get the generator out in case we return to a power outage."

"Okay, I can help. Just tell me what to do."

A grin grows on his face. "You could make that chili and cornbread we didn't get yesterday."

"And cinnamon rolls."

"If you insist on that abomination."

His smile doesn't fool me. He's pretending he's okay because he wants me to be alright, but I saw his face yesterday when we found his hives destroyed. He was devastated. All I can think about is how happy he was when he first took me to meet the bees. The joy in his voice when he placed my hands on the hive to feel the warm vibration. He loved those bees. Of course, the hives can be replaced, but the thought of someone burning them as they huddled inside for warmth is such an awful thing.

He's convinced that Handleman is the culprit, but if it's Carl, or anyone trying to get at my money, I'll never forgive myself for that look on his face as he watched the smoke pour from the hives. He's had such a terrible week, losing his friend on top of everything else. Whatever he needs or wants from me today, he's got it.

While he gets the cameras installed over at my cabin, I do a load of laundry for both of us and pack a bag for the hotel. He's in and out most of the day, working between my cabin, the barn, and the house.

"Are you finished?" I ask, looking up from the pot of chili on the stove to see him smiling at me.

"Almost. I need to run to the gas station to fill the cans but I'm not leaving you here."

The oven timer dings, and a pan of cornbread joins the plate of cinnamon rolls sitting nearby. "Do you want to eat first? Everything is done."

"Absolutely, I'm starving."

We get settled at the table with our food and he exclaims over how good the chili is. The expression on his face when I chase a bite of chili with a bite of cinnamon roll makes me giggle. "I feel judged."

"Your feelings are valid."

"Okay, smartass, now I'm going to have to insist you try it. How can you call yourself a Midwesterner? I'm embarrassed for you." I pinch off a bite of cinnamon roll and hold it out to him. "Take a bite of chili first."

"It's kind of hot when you boss me around like that," he teases, plucking the roll from my hand. He takes a bite of chili, then pops it into his mouth afterward. His face is inscrutable as he chews and swallows, then takes a sip of iced tea.

"Well?" Without a word, he puts a cinnamon roll on his plate beside the cornbread. A smile threatens to break through his impassive expression when my laughter rings out. "It's okay. You don't have to say I was right."

"I wasn't planning on it." He shovels in another bite.

"It's enough that *I* know I was right, and you were wrong. And clearly, *you* know I was right, and you were wrong, so there's no need for you to make such a big deal out of it."

"Are you about finished?" Amusement shines in his eyes and it's the first genuine smile I've seen all day. Mission accomplished.

"Sure. Wait until I introduce you to peanut butter and syrup sandwiches."

"Well, now you're just making shit up."

We're both in a more upbeat mood after dinner. We make a quick run down to the gas station to fill the cans and store them in the shed.

Arlow packs his bag and calls down the stairs to me. "I'm going to take a quick shower, then we can go."

"I'll be ready!" I shout back. Am I ready? I take a quick walk around the house trying to see if I've forgotten anything. Wait? Where's my phone?

It isn't on the kitchen table or coffee table. Not on the charger or beside the bed. I stop and try to think back. I don't remember taking it out of my pocket when I got back from the gas station, and if I did, I would've laid it down near my keys. I'll bet it fell out of my pocket in the car.

It's not full dark yet, but the motion light blinks on, shining the way to my car when I dash out, hoping to see my phone waiting on my console. No such luck. Did it fall between the seats?

The enormity of my stupidity sets in at the sound of a familiar voice. "You stingy bitch." A sharp pain shoots across the back of my head as I'm jerked out of my car by my hair. My ass hits the ground, and I look up into the barrel of a gun.

The black ski mask covering his face is completely pointless since I know his voice. "Get up." He holds up my phone. "Looking for this?"

Rage charges through me and I scramble to my feet. "You motherfucker."

"Technically I was," Carl chuckles as if he's having the time of his life. "But she's gone, and I'm broke. So, you have a choice." He throws my phone at my feet. "Transfer the money now or die right here."

My panicked gaze leaps to Arlow's front door. He doesn't even know I'm out here. My gun sits on the table in the living room. How fucking dumb can I be?

Carl glances at the house then back at me. "Stall until your boyfriend shows up and I'll shoot him first. Transfer the fucking money now."

My mind is working at a breakneck speed, trying to figure out what to do. I can't let this turn into a shootout between them if Arlow comes outside. Part of me wants to call his bluff, put my phone on speaker and dial nine-one-one. Take the chance that he'll run. The problem is I'm not sure that he's bluffing. If he's stupid enough to do this, to think that a million dollars could be sent to another person through a payment app just like that, as if you were paying a friend back for lunch, then he could be crazy enough to do anything.

He was never bright. His stupidity is what I have going for me in this situation.

"I can't. It isn't in a bank!" It isn't hard to let my fear show in my voice but restraining my anger is tough. "I buried it."

"Quit fucking with me." He raises the gun to point at my head.

"I'm not! Please! The news said the banks could fail so I had it all converted to gold and silver coins. I only keep a couple thousand in the bank to pay bills. I can't transfer anything," I babble, throwing in a sob for good measure. His eyes brighten when I add, "I can take you to it. Just don't hurt me or him."

He stares at me for a moment. "Where is it?"

The rest of the plan forms in my head. I need to get him to follow me quickly. Arlow's porch camera will have alerted, and he'll see it as soon as he's out of the shower. There's a way to keep him out of this, keep him safe and end this threat permanently. "In the back field between two trees. I'll take you there now."

After another minute of consideration, he waves the gun at me.

"Go. Lead the way. If you're lying to me, bitch, I'll leave your body in the woods for him to find before I kill him too."

"I'm not lying. It's there."

My steps are hurried and the hair on my nape stands up as the gun is pointed at my back while he follows me to the rear of my cabin. "Stop!" he orders. "Where the fuck are you going?"

"I need a shovel. It's buried deep," I explain, gesturing to the shovel that's on my back porch.

He nods his permission, and I grab it. I've complained about how heavy this shovel is and planned to get something easier to use, but I'm happy for the heft of it now. Better to knock his fucking head off his shoulders.

We start into the woods, the shadows wrapping around us as the weak winter sun rapidly descends below the horizon. He stays well behind me as if he's afraid that I'll suddenly turn and lunge for the gun. My heart races and adrenaline puts a metallic taste on my tongue.

Absolutely not, Calli. Hold it together. You can have a panic attack once you hear his skull crack at the bottom of that ravine. You can do this.

After worrying my whole life over what kind of person I am, one thing is clear. I'm capable of worse than I imagined. What's the alternative? Let him continue to stalk me? Hope that I can get him arrested and then what? At best, he does a year or two and is right back at it. As long as he's alive, I'm the one imprisoned.

The creek is low, the water icy as it penetrates my socks and shoes. For the first time since entering the woods, I look back. Carl splashes through and raises the gun at me again. The shovel is a comfortable weight in my hand. Dad taught me how to swing a baseball bat and I'm going to put that knowledge to use at the right moment.

A faint blue light flashes on the trail camera hidden in the bushes on the far bank of the creek. If Carl notices he doesn't say anything, but I know that sent a notification to Arlow's phone as well as mine.

This should look like an accident, an unfortunate fall from a trespasser if the body is ever found, but Arlow will know the truth. How will he see me once I'm a killer?

A light appears behind me as we exit the forest into the dark back field, chilling me to the bone with the fear that Arlow has found us.

"Turn around and fucking walk!" Carl barks when I look back to see he's turned on a flashlight. "How much farther?"

Slowly, I raise my arm, letting my hand tremble. It's not hard. I'm shaking like a leaf despite my determination to do this. "In that strip of forest. We're almost there."

The thick dead grass isn't the easiest to trudge through, but I keep my speed, ignoring the burn in my legs and my breath heating in my throat.

We finally reach the last little strip of trees. A memory flashes through my mind of Silver warning me not to come out here at night because it's hard to see the drop off. Standing in the midsummer heat, the sun beating down on us, I was so eager to get a fresh start here. Was that only five months ago? It feels like I've lived another lifetime.

I take him as close to the edge as I dare. I don't want him to see it or me to end up going over it. The first thing is to get that damn gun away from him. "Here," I announce, stopping between two random trees.

"Well, what the fuck are you waiting for? Dig."

"Will you point your light at the ground? I can't see anything."

He complies, keeping the gun aimed at me with one hand and the phone pointed at the ground with the other. I stab the ground with the shovel and begin to dig. His stare is centered on the dirt, his eyes wide behind the mask. With every shovelful I shift, he inches a little closer. All of his attention is focused on the shallow hole as he waits for the treasure to be revealed.

The shovel dings off a rock, making a loud noise. "There it is," I announce. "I felt it."

He takes another step closer to me, dropping his arm enough so the gun isn't pointed directly at me and cranes his neck to peer into the hole.

Knock the gun from his hand. Shove him over the cliff. Now, Calli. You can do this.

With a sudden step back, I bring the shovel up and swing as hard as I can. A loud clang echoes through the trees and the gun goes flying, disappearing into the shadows. He screams something indecipherable as his phone falls from his other hand, taking our only light with it.

It only takes me half a second to raise the shovel again, this time aiming for his head, but he tackles me before I can swing. "You stupid bitch!"

Pain shoots up my back when I hit the ground, and his heavy body lands on top of me, driving the breath from my lungs. His fist glances off my eye, but in my rage, I barely feel it. He's not going to win. I can't let it happen like this.

He's strong, but I'm furious. I raise my knee with as much power as possible, squashing his nuts. The satisfying squeal he lets out will stick with me for the rest of my life. It gives me enough time to shove him and roll out from under him. Scooting away like a crab, I manage to put some space between us. My stomach suddenly drops at the feel of the crumbling edge of the cliff, and I reverse my direction, scrambling to get to my feet.

His curses rain around us while I draw in a whooping breath. He's near the edge, and I pull back my foot to kick him in the side, hoping to move him in the right direction, but he catches my leg and twists it, sending me back to the ground.

One of my punches connects as I fight to get free of him. His nose crunches, but it doesn't keep him from getting me pinned. Straddling me, he rips his mask off and stares down at me with a bloody grin. "I want to be the last thing you see, you worthless bitch."

His hands wrap around my throat, cutting off my air. Panic is a wild animal in my chest as I buck under him, trying my best to get him off me, but it's useless. My fingers claw at his hands. They only tighten, making my head feel like it might explode.

I'm not sure how much time passes. It feels like forever and none at all. My eyes shift away from him to look at the sky behind his head. Clouds draw away, their jagged edge revealing a spattering of stars. The moon slips out from behind them, brightening the night in seconds.

It's beautiful. At least the last thing I'll see in this world is beauty. Arlow will have to look at the stars without me. I should've told him I loved him. Tears leak from my eyes, but a peaceful feeling begins to take over. I'm dying. This is what dying is like. I'll be reabsorbed by the universe. Maybe in some distant future, our atoms will clash, and I'll find him again.

My artist. My Arlow.

The world tunnels, closing around me to a pinpoint, all the noise fading to the murmur of my slowing heartbeat.

"Calliope! Come on, baby, look at me." My eyes leap open to see Arlow's terrified face. My burning throat despises every ragged breath but it's still the best feeling in the universe. "Yes! Oh thank fuck!" he cries.

A wave of dizziness shifts the ground beneath me as I sit up and try to piece together what's going on. Arlow kneels beside me, a gun in his outstretched hand. In his line of fire, Carl sits on the ground with a large split on one side of his forehead and his face covered in blood.

"I'm okay," I croak. "I'm okay. Don't take your eye off him."

"He's not going anywhere." To hear his usually kind, soft voice filled with threatening hostility makes the whole night feel even more surreal.

My mind clears and I bite back the pain of my body to stand up beside the man who just saved my life. "I'll be okay," I repeat, hoping to convince both of us.

"Don't fucking move!" Arlow roars when Carl starts to get up.

His eyes wide, he freezes in place. What to do now? Shove him over the cliff while Arlow watches? I can't involve him in a murder. Damn it.

"I just wanted the money!" Carl shouts. "All she had to do was give me the fucking money!"

Ignoring him, I pull my phone from my back pocket, then look up at Arlow. "I don't have a signal to call the police."

Arlow keeps the gun on Carl as he looks into my eyes. "We don't need the police yet. Go back to the house. I'll be right behind you."

The cold resignation in his voice sends a shiver down my spine. I'm not the only one who comprehends his intention.

Carl's demands and shouts take a sharp turn. He gets up on his knees. "No! Please, don't. I'm sorry. I'll go. I won't ever bother either of you again," he begs, frantic.

His words fall on deaf ears as Arlow gazes at me.

He loves me. The realization strikes me and shouldn't hold such power in this moment, but it does. There's no doubt in my mind. After suffering so much from causing a death, he's ready to have another on his conscience. He's willing to risk being arrested and charged again. For me.

I can't let him do that. Tears slip down my face. "No, give me the gun. I can do it." The shake of his head is firm as Carl continues to plead for his life. Blocking him out, I look Arlow in the eye. "Listen to me. That's why I led him out here, to push him over the cliff. I can do it. I want to do it. You can't kill him for me. It isn't your burden to carry. It isn't your responsibility."

"No, it's my privilege," he replies, his deep voice back to a soft rumble.

"Don't. Just give it to me."

Carl is a blubbering mess on his knees in front of him. I'd be lying if I said it wasn't the most satisfying thing I've ever seen. I hope he's as terrified as he and my mother made me over the years. Part of me wishes she was on her knees here beside him.

Arlow's lips press together. He lowers the gun a few inches and barks at Carl. "Stand up."

The relief in Carl's face is instant. "Thank you! I swear you'll never hear from me again."

Arlow glares at him. "It won't look like self-defense if you die on your knees." The last word has scarcely left his lips when a sharp crack echoes through the night.

Everything slows and sharpens into focus. The following seconds feel like they hold a lifetime as a dark hole materializes between Carl's brows. I watch, rapt, as blood hesitates, taking its time before oozing out to drip between vacant eyes. His muscles suddenly realize he's dead and his body slumps heavily to the ground.

Arlow lowers the gun, walks over to him, and bends down to make sure he's really gone.

"Is he?" I breathe, nausea twisting my stomach.

Straightening his back, he nods. "He's dead. Now we can call the police."

Sobs pour out of me as I rush at him and throw my arms around his middle. He embraces me carefully, mindful of my injuries while I cling to him. "I'm sorry! I went out to the car without telling you or grabbing my gun. It was so stupid."

"It's okay." His large hand cups the back of my head, brushing over my hair. "It's going to be okay. It's over."

"No." Stepping back, I scrub my hands over my face. "Now you have another death on your conscience because of me."

"Calliope." His firm voice demands my full attention. "He hurt you. I won't lose a wink of sleep over this. Do you hear me? I'd do it again."

This can't happen. He can't ruin his life for me. A stalker killed on his property and in self-defense, I would hope that he'd be okay, but it's not worth the risk. You never know how things are going to go when you involve authorities.

"We aren't calling the cops. We need to bury him." Arlow blinks and his lips part, his brows rising, but he remains quiet as I continue.

"We didn't ask for this and we don't deserve what they're going to put us through. The whole town will know. Even if neither of us are charged, things will never be the same. We have a whole graveyard and forest to hide him."

Finally, after a long silence, he nods.

CHAPTER 31

ARLOW

WILLING MY HEART TO SLOW INTO A SAFER TEMPO, I PUT THE SAFETY ON my gun and tuck it in my waistband. I have to keep reassuring myself that Calli is okay. I made it here in time. When I clicked on the notification for the trail cam, all I expected to see was another deer or raccoon. My heart must be okay, because the sight of Calli marching past with a gun held to her back should have been enough to stop it. I've never felt such terror and panic. I couldn't tell you anything I did or thought between grabbing my gun and running to the woods.

I knew one thing. If I found him, he wasn't leaving the forest alive. No one is taking her from me. If he was arrested, his jail sentence would end eventually. She'd have to leave and run again.

It never occurred to me that she led him out here to kill him.

She steps up and cups my face, looking into my eyes. "Are you okay?"

Look at her, standing here bruised and scraped with blood splattered on her. Asking if *I'm* okay. "Now that I know you're safe, I'm fine. How do you feel? Your breathing…"

"I can breathe fine. I'm just sore."

I take her hand and lead her back toward the field. "Come on. We need some stuff to move him."

At least we have over twelve hours of darkness to get him underground. There's little chance anyone will see us. I can't remember the last time someone set foot in the graveyard unless they were with me. That's the best place to put him. The forest will be hard to dig, too full of roots. Plus, I already have a long strip cleared that I planned to plant bushes in this spring.

The motion lights blink on when we get back to the driveway and I pull up the app that controls them, shutting them all off, along with the security and trail cameras. I'll have to go back and delete everything they picked up so far.

Calli closes her car door that's still standing open, then asks, "Are we taking the ATV?"

"You need to ice your neck, drink some water, and rest. I've got this."

"Absolutely not. I'm helping put that motherfucker in the ground. Don't waste your breath arguing."

I didn't expect her to agree but I had to try. It's hard to see her so banged up. "Alright. We'll take the ATV and the log hauler. It'll fit through the forest easier than the trailer. Where's your metal detector? We need to find his phone and gun."

"At my cabin. I'll get it."

"Do you want me to—"

She flaps her hand back at me, already on her way. "He's dead. The threat is gone. I'm not afraid."

She isn't afraid but she's running on pure adrenaline. I can hear it in her voice. How long will this terrifying night haunt her?

That's a problem for later. Right now, I need to move. While she retrieves the metal detector, I run in my house and take one of my pills that keeps my heart rate and blood pressure lower. Shoveling for hours isn't exactly an approved exercise but it needs to be done.

Calli meets me beside the barn as I'm connecting the log hauler to the new ATV. I hand her a couple of pain pills and a bottle of water. "Take these, sweetheart."

She swallows them with a slight grimace. "Where do you want to bury him? Behind the cabin?"

"No, at the perimeter of the graveyard. I'll show you." After we get the supplies we need loaded onto the ATV, she climbs on behind me. Her arms wrap around my middle, and I take a moment to squeeze her hand. It feels like I'm functioning on auto pilot mode as we make our way back through the forest and field.

It's all happened so fast. We're heading out to pick up a dead body—a man I killed—and bury him on my property. Surreal isn't a strong enough word. Not one ounce of me regrets it.

"Will you look for the gun and phone while I get him chained to the hauler?" Calli nods and turns on her metal detector. The faint beeps play as I wrap the chains and straps around the body, strapping it to the hauler like I've done so many logs.

My stomach flips at the way his head hangs, dangling to look at me with open blank eyes. Before Calli can see, I toss a tarp over his top half.

"Got them," she says, returning with the gun and phone.

"Good. Let's go."

The trip back through the forest is uneventful. The creek is low, and I make sure to cross at a spot that the hauler had no problem handling before. The last thing we need is to get stuck. A bitterly cold wind strikes us as we pull into the clearing of the graveyard, and I feel Calli press her face into the back of my coat.

We'll be warm soon enough. Digging is hard work.

I park the log hauler in the trees at the edge of the graveyard. It isn't hidden. I'm not worried that we'll be interrupted but this is going to take a while and we don't need to look at him.

"Right beside the other bushes? Is that what you're thinking?" Calli asks.

"Yes, it won't look like the ground has been disturbed in a strange spot if the police end up investigating us. We'll plant more bushes over him. In spring, he'll be covered by foliage."

She nods and tosses me a pair of gloves, then puts hers on. "We should burn him like he did your poor bees." I'm glad she's angry. It's as good a way to get through this night as any. "We only need to put him about three feet down. That's deep enough to keep animals from digging him up." She shrugs when I look at her with my eyebrows raised. "I watch a lot of crime shows."

"Good to know."

We start digging and it goes a little quicker than I anticipated. "We're lucky only the top crust is frozen," I remark, stepping on the blade of the shovel to drive it deeper. "Another month and the ground would've been too solid."

Calli nods, wiping sweat from her forehead and leaving a streak of dirt behind. We're both covered in grime. I'm surprised to see her lips tilt into a grin. "Remember the day I brought you the cobbler?"

Of course I do. I remember the fear on her face at the sight of the burlap bundles and shovel, and how we laughed after I explained what was going on. "You said burying people is more of a winter activity."

She gestures to the snow flurries with a chuckle. "I was right. This would be awful in the heat."

Maybe she will be okay after this. Maybe we both will.

The moon rises as we work, casting a blue hue over everything. It makes me think of the first night I brought Calli to the firepit. She was afraid to walk through the graveyard alone. Now she's burying someone here without any qualms. Life is so twisted sometimes.

"I think that's good enough, don't you?" Calli says, flopping down to sit alongside the grave and blowing out a harsh breath.

Assuming he hasn't gone into rigor, and we can bend him a little to stuff him in, it should work. "I think so."

She guzzles her water then holds it out to me for a drink. A sudden realization strikes her. "Arlow, your heart. Are you supposed to…this is too much, isn't it?"

"The list from the cardiologist didn't specifically say no murder or body disposal." She gives me an exasperated look. "I'm fine, Peach. And we're almost done. Filling it in will be easier and we have all night. I'm not in danger."

After a moment of thought, she seems to realize there isn't any other choice and nods. She waits by the grave while I move the log hauler over. There's no good way to release the body and it plops to the ground once the chains are undone.

"Wait," Calli says, when I start to roll him into the grave. Her face crumples in disgust as she searches his pockets and pulls out a wallet. "We don't want to leave identification on him."

"Good thinking."

She kneels beside me to help roll him, but before he budges, her hand clamps onto my arm. My name slips out in a cracked voice, filled with despair and terror. "Arlow." Her wide eyes are locked on the graveyard where a man makes his way toward us. "Someone's coming."

I'm not proud of the thought that hits me in the first few seconds, before I recognize who it is. *We'll have to dig a deeper hole.* That I could even entertain killing a stranger because we were caught is terrifying and my only excuse is that I love her. I won't let anything happen to her, no matter who stands in my way.

"It's okay." I lay my hand over her fingers that are digging into my bicep. "Calli, it's Lee. I'll talk to him. It'll be alright. I promise."

The tears that slip out of her eyes say she doesn't believe me. She doesn't know Lee's background, or the things he's done. Though he's moved on from his former life working for a vigilante group, this isn't anything he hasn't seen or participated in before.

And he's my best friend.

He stops a few feet away, his gaze skipping between Calli, the body, and me. "I was going to say you better have a damn good reason for ignoring my calls, but this is a hell of an excuse."

"He came after her. I didn't have a choice."

Lee nods, and though I doubt he needs any convincing, I pull out my phone and load up the video of Calli being marched through the woods at gunpoint.

He looks up from the screen to Calli. "He choked her."

"I got there just in time. She was losing consciousness."

"Do you think he had any partners?"

"There's no reason to think so. He's the one she saw in the forest before. If he had help, they would've stepped in once I showed up."

He drops his voice so she can't overhear. "Is this a secret you think she can keep? Can she live with it?"

It's a fair question, but not one that worries me. "She led him to the woods to push him over the cliff herself."

His lips twitch up. "Good for her."

Calli looks up at him with fearful eyes when he approaches her. She doesn't resist when he lifts her head to look at the angry bruises on her neck. "You won. Whenever this night comes back to haunt you, remember that. You won." Her stiffened posture relaxes as he continues. "Did you check him for ID?"

She nods and holds it up. "And his phone and gun."

"Good." He picks up her shovel and runs his hand along the blade of it, then picks up mine and does the same. "Look away," he tells her, holding the blade of the shovel over Carl's fingers.

Calli jerks her head away and closes her eyes while he chops off the tips of the fingers, driving the shovel down with his foot. It takes a few tries on each hand, but he manages. Calli hands over the ID when he reaches for it. He walks a few feet away, then drops the fingertips and ID in a pile. He pulls a lighter out of his pocket, cracks open the bottom of it and douses them in lighter fluid. The last of the fluid is used to strike the lighter and set the pile aflame.

The ID melts and blackens almost instantly and the smell of the fingers makes me never want barbecue pork again. Leaving it to burn, he approaches the body and nods at me. "Let's get this done. I want to get home before the storm."

With Lee's help, it doesn't take long to fill in the hole and even out the ground. The whole area is dirt and will be muddy soon with a storm coming. It won't look like we've been digging here. Calli sits at the edge of the grave to rest while Lee collects the gun, phone, and charred remains of the ID and fingers.

"I won't take the SIM card out until I get to the lakes," he says. "This looks like a burner—no contacts or anything in it—but if anyone ever tries to trace it, it'll end at the lakes, not here. It'll be on the bottom of the lake with the gun." He sweeps his eyes over us. "You two need to clean everything the body touched with bleach and burn the clothes you're wearing."

Calli doesn't ask how he seems to know what to do, but I can see her curiosity as she nods. "Lee," she calls as he starts to leave. He pauses to look back. "Thank you."

"Thank me by keeping this between the three of us. No one else. Ever."

"I swear."

After he leaves, I hold out my hand to help her to her feet. We still have a few things to do before the night is over, but all that falls away when she cradles my face in her hands, stopping me in place.

Her thumb brushes over my jaw as she looks me in the eye. "I love you."

It's the last thing I expect to hear and my heart races every bit as fast as it did on my run through the woods. My tongue sticks to the roof of my mouth, and the shake of my head is an involuntary denial. "Calliope." Her name slips out on a whispered prayer to the heedless universe.

"No." Her voice is unwavering, resolute. "You don't get to kill for me and then say I can't love you." She kisses me softly, then rests her forehead on my chest. "All I could think about as I was losing consciousness was that I should've told you before it was too late. I'm not asking you to feel the same or say it back, but I need you to know."

Her words crush me. I'm overcome by so much emotion. The intensity of my love battles with guilt for letting it happen and allowing her to think for even a moment that it's one-sided. I can't let her go another second believing she's the only one.

"Look at me, sweetheart." She gazes up at me, and I cup the back of her head gently. "I love you to the edges of my sanity. If I felt any more, there'd be nothing of me left, only you filling the space."

The tears that slip from her eyes break my heart. After everything she's been through tonight, that she would cry for this. For being loved.

We're both exhausted. I wipe the tears from her cheeks. "Come on. Let's get the clean-up finished so we can go home."

It's after three in the morning by the time we have the log hauler and all the tools we used cleaned and put away. Both covered in dirt, blood, and dried sweat, we strip down in my bathroom to share a shower.

"I liked those jeans, damn it," she mumbles, throwing her clothes into the paper bag along with mine to be burned in the fireplace.

I'm too busy running my eyes over her to respond. In the harsh overhead light, the finger shaped bruises on her neck are more noticeable, along with the swollen lump under her eye. Dusky purple splashes across her ribs on both sides. He must've been squeezing her with his knees as he straddled her. When she turns to step into the shower, an array of bruises and marks are visible on her back as well.

My frozen stare draws her attention as she steps into the spray. "What's wrong?"

It takes me a minute to swallow the rage and let the knot in my stomach loosen before stepping in to join her. She looks up at me as I run my fingertips gently over her bruised ribs. "He hurt you so badly. I wish he was standing in front of me right now so I could kill him slower."

She swallows hard. "He's dead. That's what matters. It's over. We won." Her words are strong, but exhaustion washes out her face.

"Let me take care of you." There's no argument when I take the soft washcloth from her hands and gently run it over her shoulders. She tilts her head, letting me continue to her sensitive neck. I wash her from head to toe, wishing I could erase all the painful marks as tears slip down her cheeks.

She looks up to let me shampoo her hair and winces when my fingers brush over a small lump on the back of her head. "Sorry," I murmur, being more careful rinsing out the soap. "Did you hit your head too?"

"He slammed it into the ground. Good thing it was mud." Her quick, forced smile isn't reassuring.

"I think you should go get checked out at the hospital. You could have a concussion, broken bones. We can think of something to tell them. A random attack...attempted carjacking." It's not the most realistic idea but what if she's seriously injured?

"No. It's been over eight hours and I'm not dizzy or anything. I don't even have a headache. I'm just sore and tired. I'll be fine." She traces the scar on my chest and looks up at me. "Are you okay?"

It feels like so much is contained in that question. Am I okay after killing a man? Is my heart okay after a strenuous night? Am I okay with her loving me? "I'm with you, darling. I couldn't be better."

Her lips lift into a cautious smile. She hooks her arms around my neck, folding her hands over my nape. "Are you? *With* me?"

I am. Selfish or not, I'm done spending my time alone, desperately struggling to rearrange the pieces of my life to hide the gap love has left. She loves me and I've never loved anyone like this. She's mine. "If you're sure that's what you want. For what it's worth, you've got me."

Her smile widens and her wet lips brush mine. "It's worth everything. Every risk and worry running through your head right now. You're worth it. So let that go and just tell me you love me."

Our warm wet bodies press together when I pull her close. "I love you, Calliope."

CHAPTER 32

CALLIOPE

A GROAN SLIPS OUT OF ME BEFORE I'M FULLY AWAKE, DRIVEN BY THE DEEP ache that's devouring my body. The bed next to me dips, and Arlow's concerned face comes into focus as I blink away the grittiness.

"Hey, how do you feel?" His soft voice wraps around me.

"Like I was strangled in the woods."

"You aren't funny." He brushes my hair back, gazing down at me.

"Sorry. I'm sore, but I'm okay." It's a bit of an understatement. I'm sure nothing is broken but I'm so stiff and full of pain. On top of the injuries from the attack, I'm not used to hours of shoveling heavy dirt.

Arlow lays a large hand on my back, supporting me as I sit up with a wince. I reach up to touch my cheek under my eye where Carl's fist landed. It's tender but not terribly painful. A spot on the back of my head is sore, but there's no bump like last night.

"What time is it?" I ask. The dim light coming through the windows makes it look like it's late in the evening, but surely I haven't slept all day.

"Just past three." A sudden wind howls, whipping ice against the

299

house with a thousand little ticks, and the lights flicker for a moment. "It's been storming for a while."

Damn, I slept almost eleven hours straight. Not even alcohol and weed knock me out like that. Trying not to die then burying a body is tiring. The reality of what we did last night slams into me. "Is everything okay? Did Lee…you know…has anyone been here…our clothes, we have to—"

Arlow stops my panicked words by palming my face. "Everything is fine. I burned the clothes. No one has been here, and no one will be able to come for days with the storm. I talked to Lee. He did what he promised. There's nothing to worry about."

"Are you sure we can trust him? How did he know what to do so quickly?" I'm not giving him a chance to answer one question before I fire off another but it's terrifying that there's someone who knows what we've done.

"Yes, we can trust him. His past isn't mine to share or discuss, but I promise you he's a safe person. He understands that sometimes you have to do things yourself." Amusement seeps into his tone. "I think he was as proud as I was at your plan to shove him off the cliff."

The heavy feeling on my chest lifts for the first time since I found my cabin ransacked. "We're safe."

He nods and plants a gentle kiss on my lips. "We're safe."

"Did you get any sleep?"

"A good eight hours that went by in a blink."

I link my arms around his neck. "How are you doing with… everything?"

A small smile accompanies his response. "I'm good."

For a long moment, I only look into those soft brown eyes, trying to find the right words. What do you say when the sweetest, most peaceful, kindhearted man in the world kills for you?

A man who once captured a bug in the bathroom to set it free instead of squashing it, who was broken hearted at the death of his bees, who has never shown an ounce of aggression in any situation, just shot a man while he begged for his life. Then buried the body on his property. All to protect me.

The sobs well up from so deep inside that my entire body shakes as I choke out the words. "Thank you."

"Oh sweetheart," he rasps, pulling me gently into his arms. "Don't. You don't have anything to thank me for, or to feel bad about. He was fucking with both of us and he was never going to stop. I did what I had to do." He pulls back and wipes the tears from my face. "*We* did what we had to do. I have no regrets, understand?"

My emotions are all over the place, but I nod. "I'm glad he's dead. It's over."

He holds me for another minute until we both compose ourselves, then asks, "Are you hungry?"

The question makes me chuckle because how can life just go on normally after such an eventful night? "Starving."

"Good. Let's go eat. We'll watch the storm updates and see how long you're going to be trapped with me," he teases.

"Forever wouldn't be long enough."

The genuine smile that rises on his lips assures me everything is going to be okay. Not only with what we've done, but between us. He meant what he said last night in the heat of such an emotional moment. *For what it's worth, you've got me.*

He's ready to let me love him.

The next week passes in a blur. The sky dumps ice and snow on us—living up to the shutdown storm prediction. We lose power for a couple of days, but it doesn't matter. Curling up together in front of the fire is all either of us wants to do. My aches and pains slowly improve. Arlow fusses over me constantly, trying to make me comfortable, making sure I eat, drink, and rest. We don't talk a lot, and not at all about everything we've just been through.

We've always been comfortable with silence between us. Our actions speak for us while we sort through our own thoughts and come to terms with what we've done. His hand always finds its way into mine. I scratch at his scalp the way he likes, and he runs his fingers lightly up and down my arm. We can't pass one another without some kind of reassuring caress or touch. If we're sitting in the living room or lying in his bed, we're wrapped around one another. The constant affection is healing in a way I can't begin to explain.

There's no more need for a security guard or anything like that. I let my private investigator know that he doesn't need to look for Carl after all. He doesn't ask why, and I don't elaborate.

After the first week, my face is completely healed—good thing it was only a glancing blow—and the marks on my neck have faded considerably. A little makeup will cover them easily now when we're ready to venture out again. We still have over a foot of snow on the ground, and plenty of ice under it, but the roads have been cleared. My plan to ask Arlow if he'd like to go with me to trade in my library books and pick up some snacks is stopped short when I spot him on the couch.

He's absorbed in the book he's reading, giving me an opportunity to drink him in without his notice. Dressed in jeans and a dark gray sweater, he sits with his long legs outstretched, his feet propped on the edge of the coffee table. The sunlight from the nearby window illuminates his white lashes and emphasizes the pale patch of skin on that side of his face. He's so handsome.

He raises his eyebrow when he catches me. "What's that look for?"

"What look?"

His book is set aside as I walk toward him. "You're staring."

I straddle his lap, and his hands land on my hips. "You're gorgeous. I can't help it."

That sweet flustered smile never gets less adorable. I love catching him off guard with praise or a compliment just to see it surface. He presses a soft kiss on my jaw, keeping his lips there as he murmurs, "Are you trying to start something with me, beautiful?"

"That obvious, huh?" I run my hands over his chest. "Blame the sweater. It does something to me."

His lips crease in amusement as he pulls back to look at me. "The sweater?"

"Mm hmm. It makes you look so soft."

His hands travel around, cupping my ass. "And here I thought you liked me better hard."

"I like every part of you."

He leans to feather his lips over my neck. "You aren't healed. I don't want to hurt you."

"You won't," I assure him, running my hand under his sweater to feel his warm skin. "I feel fine." I flex my hips, shamelessly rubbing against the growing crotch of his jeans. "Except for this ache for you. I need you inside me again."

"Jesus, Calliope," he growls. Sitting up, he suddenly tosses the throw pillows from the couch down to the rug in front of the fireplace. I pull his sweater off, and he removes my shirt. His hand gently kneads my breast as he kisses me, and I unbutton his jeans.

When I scoot back to kneel on the floor with the intention of blowing him, he shakes his head. "Not this time." He grabs my hand and rises to lead me over to the pile of pillows in front of the low burning fire then slides my leggings and panties off. "Lie back."

No arguments here. The rug is plush under my bare body and my mouth dries as I look up at him. Shirtless, his jeans unfastened to show the waistband of his boxer briefs, he slowly drags his gaze over me, up and down, making a blush warm my cheeks. He doesn't say anything until he's stripped off the rest of his clothes and crawled over me.

His lips brush my skin just below my navel. "Calliope." God, how his deep smooth voice caresses my name. I never want to hear anyone else speak it again. Only him. He drops hot kisses up my stomach, over my breasts to my neck as he continues, "My gorgeous muse."

When his tongue slips between my lips, my hum of pleasure is involuntary. My hands wander through his hair, over his back, everywhere I can reach. He takes his time, caressing and kissing my body until I'm desperate for him. My head falls back when he slides one finger inside me to stroke over the spot that sends fire crawling over my skin.

"Oh, please." I turn toward him, and he rolls onto his side so we're facing one another. I hook my leg over his and he looks me in the eye as he eases his cock in deep. His large hand rests on my ass, gently urging me toward him as we move together. This time is different. It feels so intimate and emotional. There's no dirty talk between us. No frantic movements.

Every stroke is deliberate, drawn out, unhurried. The world fades as I succumb to him, to the warmth and comfort our bodies create together. His gentle touches, the way he keeps coming back to search my face. He isn't fucking me, he's loving me.

His slow, deep thrusts and passionate kisses overwhelm me. "Arlow," I whimper.

"I've got you," he murmurs. His words fade into the distance as the slow, pulsing pleasure rolls through me, the intensity growing until I feel like I could happily die from it.

Both sated, we cuddle together in front of the fire, trading an occasional soft touch or kiss. I run my finger over his brow, through the white stripe of hair.

"Is your vitiligo because of the Marfan Syndrome? Does it come with it?"

He shakes his head. "No, it's not related. I lost the DNA lottery twice."

"No. I love it." He closes his eyes as I brush my fingertip over the ivory lashes. "They're beautiful. Like delicate feathers. Fairy lashes." I get a flash of his sheepish smile before he forces a frown and shakes his head. "Sorry, I meant big, tough masculine lashes." His chest rattles with a chuckle that I can feel as I press my lips to the scar. "You're perfect."

His Adam's apple bobs on a hard swallow, and he looks down at me, running his hand through my hair. "Do you have any idea how much I love you?"

My answer is caught in my throat as I gaze at him. What a tragedy it would've been for him to never allow himself to be loved again when he loves so much. His friends, nature, art. And me. He hemorrhages love. "I don't know," I tease. "I might need to hear more about it."

He rolls toward me and scoots down until we're face to face. "You're so sweet and funny and beautiful, but it's more than that. I've always been a solitary person. People don't come easy to me. They never have. But you…" He brushes his fingers down my cheek. "Loving you came as easy as nightfall."

A lump grows in my throat. "Okay, stop, you're going to make me cry." His soft lips land on mine for a brief moment, and we cuddle close again. After another minute or two, I break the silence with a silly question. "Would you love me if I was a worm, though?"

His instant answer makes me giggle. "Absolutely. I'd get you a nice big flowerpot full of nutrient rich soil."

"That's true unconditional love. I'm touched."

"What about you? Would you love me if I…" He pauses, giving it a moment of thought. "Turned into a vampire?"

"I'd put out the sun for you and thrive in darkness by your side."

"Good, that's all I'm asking for, really."

"If vampires drink human blood, aren't they just cannibals with extra steps?"

His laughter rolls over me. "Says the girl who bites."

"Yeah, I should probably stop that."

"You'd better fucking never."

CHAPTER 33

ARLOW

Two weeks after that terrifying night that changed everything, the snow and ice have finally disappeared, giving us a good view of the graveyard. As I'd hoped, the top of the grave looks no different than the many other bare patches this time of winter.

Calli points her finger toward it, drawing a line through the air. "You plan to plant the bushes down this way?"

"Yes, I should be able to get them planted in late March or early April, depending on the weather."

Her phone buzzes, and she checks it as we walk back toward my house. "It's Silver. I'm supposed to meet the realtor with her and Mona. Her eyebrows raise as she peeks up at me. "Are you sure you want me for a neighbor permanently before I do this?"

"I want you in my house permanently, but I'll settle for next door."

Her grin dismisses my statement as a joke. Because of course I wouldn't be asking her to move in with me after a whole two weeks of officially being together. That'd be crazy despite it being exactly what I want.

"Okay, I'm going to go. Don't wait on me for dinner. I'm going to shop for new furniture with Silver and then go to the gym. You'll probably be in the barn when I get back. You're livestreaming tonight, right?"

It's on the tip of my tongue to tell her screw the livestream, that I'll skip it to shop with her or make us a late dinner, but I restrain myself and drop a kiss on her lips. "Yep. Back to work. Be careful and have fun."

If she had any idea how obsessed I am with her, she'd probably want to rethink this relationship. She waited for me to be ready and I'm not going to ruin things by smothering her, as hard as it might be not to. We need our own lives too.

Before she can get into her car, a squad car pulls into the driveway. She turns to me, wide eyed, and I slip my hand into hers, giving it a quick squeeze. "It's okay. Deep breath. They don't know anything. We don't have to answer any questions we don't want to."

Nodding, she releases my hand.

I'm glad to see it's officer Anderson at least, not the asshole. He nods at us. "Mr. Shaw, Ms. Barnes. Have you had any more trouble?"

"No," Calli replies, her voice calm and even. "So far so good."

"Do you have any updates for us?" I ask. There's a lawyer on retainer for both of us now. One wrong word, and I'll end this conversation quick to call him.

The officer pulls out a notebook. "Do you recognize the name Mariah Kenneth?"

"No, it doesn't sound familiar," Calli says as I shake my head.

Officer Anderson nods. "The account number you were given traces back to the name Mariah Kenneth. She's deceased but the account was never closed. She has no next of kin as far as we can tell." He looks from me to Calli and back again. "Do you have any idea who might have access to her bank information?"

"No, I've never heard of her."

"Also, the man you informed us about." He looks at his notebook again. "Christopher Handleman was arrested on violation of parole eight days ago in Eastern Tennessee. Neighbors say he's been staying there for more than a month."

"It wasn't him then," Calli replies. "That's good to know."

"We haven't been able to locate the other man you mentioned, Carl Becker. The last address we have for him is in Indianapolis, but he no longer resides there. There's no car registered to him or forwarding address. If he's the one who has access to the bank account, there's no record of it. We'll continue monitoring the account for any new activity."

They'll be wasting their time. The man responsible is currently feeding the worms and beetles not far away.

"Alright." He tucks his notebook back in his pocket. "If you have any more issues or think of anything else, please report it. There's not much else to be done at this juncture."

"I understand," I tell him. "Hopefully they've given up since it didn't work for them."

"If they're smart," he agrees. "You all have a good day."

Calli lets out a long breath after the squad car pulls out of the driveway. "The Kenneth's were an elderly couple who lived next door to Mom and Carl years ago. They probably stole her bank information when she died."

I take her hand in mine, feeling the slight tremble in her fingers. "There won't be any more demands, or further activity on that account. There's nothing else for them to investigate. We're good." She looks up at me when I squeeze her hand. "Are you alright?"

"Yeah, I think so. I just want to move on and put all this behind us." She gives me a quick hug. "I'm going to go meet Silver."

As I watch her drive away, it hits me again how extraordinary she is. So resilient and determined to get her life back when I know she's constantly battling an undercurrent of anxiety and fear to do it.

And she does. Over the next few weeks, we return to our lives. Calli gets her cabin refurnished and inhabitable again. She joins a poetry club at the library and enjoys her walks in the woods like she used to, cutting them a little short due to the cold. I work around the property, spend a couple of days with Lee, fishing and helping him paint a vacant lake house, and return to drawing at night. Calli and I trade house keys, and each night finds her in my bed or me in hers. We spend Christmas high on my couch, eating cookies and watching movies—when we can pull our naked bodies apart for long enough.

The sound of a door closing upstairs makes me smile. It feels like I've awakened to dawn after years of night. This is what love sounds like. It's the tap of her footsteps, the way she hums when she's baking, her voice singing in the shower, the little snort she makes when something funny catches her off guard.

My guilt for risking her heart because of mine hasn't disappeared, but I've had an appointment with a therapist to try to overcome it. We'll be meeting a few times per month. Calli was right. It helps having an outside perspective, another person to reassure me that I'm not doing the wrong thing.

"Good morning, sleepy. Do you—" My words die when I turn to see Calli's tearful face. She makes a beeline into my arms, burying her face in my chest. I cup the back of her head, holding her tight. "Hey, what's wrong? What happened?"

She sniffs, keeping her forehead against my shirt. "The private investigator called. My dad passed away."

Fuck. She had such high hopes of finding him, the only family she had any desire to see again. "Oh darling. I'm so sorry."

She nods, still keeping her face buried. "Over two years ago. He was using another name so there was no way for authorities to reach me. They didn't even know who he was." Her voice cracks. "He died in some cheap motel alone where no one knew who he was."

All I can do is hold her tighter as she cries and murmur reassuring words that probably hold little comfort. After a couple of minutes, she looks up at me. "Will you go to Indianapolis with me? The hotel manager said she held onto some of his things, in case anyone ever came looking."

"Of course I will."

The next few days are hard for Calli after getting such shocking news, but she seems to be feeling a little better once we're settled into a nice hotel on the north side of Indianapolis.

"I think I kind of expected it, you know? After all this time, he would've found a way to get in touch. He wouldn't have cut contact with my brother either."

"Are you going to let him know?"

She nods with a frown and pulls out an envelope. "I wrote him a letter to tell him. With no return address. I'll mail it while we're here, so the postmark won't tell him my state—not that I expect him to try to contact me anyway."

"At least he won't be left wondering."

"Yeah." She checks the time on her phone. "We can go anytime. The hotel manager should be in. We might have come for nothing. His remains were disposed of by the city a long time ago and his personal effects are likely just a few old clothes."

"No, sweetheart." I reach out to take her hand. "We came so you can say goodbye."

She nods, giving me a small smile. I'm surprised to see her pull the container with her mother's ashes out of her bag. "I'm dumping these today. They aren't coming home with me again."

"Okay, we can go wherever you like after the hotel."

As hard as this is, the trip will probably be good for her in the end. Maybe she'll get some closure and be able to leave them both behind.

The hotel is everything she told me it would be. Small, rundown, and dirty, in a dangerous part of town. A man sits on the ground at the edge of the parking lot, his belongings piled around him.

Calli leaves the urn in the car when we enter the small office. It stinks of years of cigarette smoke and mildew. A bored looking guy looks up from the desk. "You need a room?"

Calli steps up closer. "No, I need to speak to Jill Tolin, please."

"Jill!" he shouts toward the doorway behind him. "Someone's here for you!"

A moment later, a woman who looks near my mother's age pokes her head through the door. "Are you Calli?" She doesn't give her a chance to answer before answering herself. "Of course you are. Look at your smile. Just like Harry's."

"You knew him?" Calli asks.

"I did. He stayed here for, oh, at least six months, I want to say. Sweet guy. I liked him. I'm sorry for your loss."

"Thank you. You said he left some stuff?"

She nods, digging under the counter. "I don't usually hang onto stuff that gets left here for this long, but I didn't want to throw out pictures. And the cops came back hoping he'd listed some emergency contact or something since his ID turned out to be fake. I figured when they tracked down his family, I could give them back." The words are spoken matter-of-factly, without any judgement or surprise. I imagine it wouldn't be the first time someone has used a fake ID here.

Calli's eyes light up at the mention of photos. "Thank you so much for holding onto them."

"You're welcome." She pushes a small carboard box across the counter. "This is everything. Excuse me."

Two women are screaming at each other in the parking lot. The clerk sighs and accompanies Jill outside to break it up.

"Let's take it to the car, alright?"

She agrees and walks past the scene outside without giving it a glance. The box gets deposited into the trunk. "I'll wait until we get back to the hotel to go through it." Instead of getting in to leave, she grabs the container of her mother's ashes. "I just need to do one more thing."

"Where are you going?" I ask as she heads for the alley that runs alongside the hotel.

"To throw this in the dumpster."

CHAPTER 34

CALLIOPE

"Calli!" Arlow calls, rushing to catch up with me. He captures my wrist. "Are you sure you want to do this? You're upset right now."

My steps slow, but I continue to the metal dumpster that sits flush with the side of the hotel. "I'm sure. He died here. His ashes are in some mass grave. Why should she get a pretty final resting place? I want to be done with it. I need to let them both go."

"Okay." He lays his hand on my back.

"Just keep an eye out because I doubt this is legal." The garbage truck must've recently been by since the dumpster is empty, but it still reeks of old trash.

"There's nobody around."

There are no words that I need to say. She's long gone, I know that, and they would've been wasted on her anyway. Nothing I said ever mattered. I loosen the top of the cardboard urn that was lightly glued on, pull it off, and dump it unceremoniously into the dumpster.

A loud clang rings out and Arlow's gaze leaps to mine. "What was that?"

313

"I don't know. Bone, maybe?"

"It sounded like metal."

"Maybe she had pins from a broken bone or something. Do they leave those in cremated remains?" I step up on a nearby crate to look inside. Arlow leans over to pluck something from the inside wall of the dumpster. "What is that?"

He holds it out where I can see it. "It's a GPS tracker. A magnetic one meant for cars. It stuck to the side when you dumped the ashes."

Both of us stare at each other for a long moment as the pieces fall together. "That son of a bitch," I exclaim. "That's how Carl found me. He put a fucking tracker in my dead mother's ashes to be mailed to me."

The whoop of a siren is accompanied by red lights that chase each other down the side of the building. The police aren't interested in us, only the fight that's going on near the lobby. Still, we need to go.

"Throw it back in there," I order and drop the empty cardboard container, stomping it flat before tossing it into the dumpster as well. "Let's get out of here."

Arlow nods, and I hear the tracker ding against the metal again. We return to the car and head for our hotel.

"Are you alright?" Arlow asks, squeezing my knee.

"Yeah." I shake my head, scoffing. "I worried about him finding out my new name and where I was, so I had the ashes sent to a PO Box. At the time, I thought I was being too paranoid. I guess not."

"Jesus, Calli. He was crazy."

"He was. I'm surprised he thought of it, to be honest. He wasn't that smart." A realization hits me. "If I'd dumped the damn thing in Cincinnati before I moved like I should have, I could've spared both of us all this trouble. Or if I would've ignored the stupid email in the first place and not accepted the urn." Arlow wouldn't have killed a man for me. If only I hadn't toted around the ashes as some kind of reassuring trinket.

Arlow's response is instant. "No, you don't get to blame yourself

314

for anything to do with this insanity. You didn't do anything wrong. This isn't on you."

Arlow carries in the box of my dad's things when we get back to our hotel. As eager as I am to see what pictures are inside, I'm also nervous. It's all I have left of him. All I'll ever have.

The box waits in the middle of the spare bed, and after I spend a couple of minutes staring at it, Arlow sits beside me, sliding his arm around my middle. "Whenever you're ready. There's no hurry. We've got all night."

Nodding, I swallow the knot in my throat as a memory comes back to me. "Did you see the elevators when we came in?"

His head tilts, and he blinks before answering. "Yes, I saw them."

I'm sure it's a strange question to hear out of the blue. "They're made of glass, so you can look down on the lobby when you ride them." A smile grows on my face. "When I was a kid, I thought that was the best thing in the world. My brother did too. There was this big fancy hotel downtown with a huge lobby that felt like a palace, and it had glass elevators. A lot of places have them now, but back then they were the first I'd seen. Dad never had money and always found free stuff to keep us entertained on his visitation days. One of our favorite things was to walk downtown and ride the glass elevators up and down."

Arlow smiles at me and kisses the top of my head as I continue. "I can't remember when we stopped doing that, but it was something I never forgot. Like that day he carried me home in the snowstorm. I dream about it sometimes. Just standing with my hands on the glass, looking down as the people grew smaller or larger."

With a sigh, I open the box. On top are a few items of clothing. Threadbare tee shirts and ragged jeans. A bus pass, a business card for a free clinic, a couple of paperbacks bearing submarines on the front. The sight of them makes me chuckle. "Some things never changed. He was a big Tom Clancy fan. If there wasn't a submarine in the story, he wasn't interested."

Arlow runs his hand up and down my back. "He had good taste.

The Hunt for Red October was one of my favorites when I was in high school."

The small stack of pictures is stored in a baggie in the bottom of the box. The one on top shows dad and my brother when he was around fifteen. They sit on a porch I vaguely remember, with a beer in both their hands. "Him and my brother. I'll send this with the letter," I mumble, setting it aside.

The next shows a group of people I don't recognize. Dad isn't in it, and there's no description or date on the back. It's just a few men and a couple of women sitting around in lawn chairs. Probably at a cookout judging by the grill in the background. "I don't know any of them. Some old friends, I guess."

The next picture shows a smiling blond. "I remember her. They dated when I was ten or so. Damn, I can't remember her name. I don't think it lasted long."

"She must've meant something to him to have kept the picture," Arlow says.

"Yeah, maybe she was the one who got away."

The last picture chokes me up. We stand against a red brick wall, Dad smiling down at me. Arlow silently pulls me into his arms as the picture blurs through my tears. It takes me a minute to compose myself enough to look again. "I remember the day this was taken. I was about eight years old. We're standing outside my elementary school. He was a janitor there for a while. He used to leave me little notes in my desk to say hi until they transferred him to another school. A teacher had brought her camera to school, and she took the picture. I don't think I've ever seen it before."

I lean against Arlow's shoulder with a sigh. "I'm glad I came. Just for this."

"You might not know if he remembered that day in the snow, but he remembered this. He loved you."

"Yeah." I swipe at the tears that drip down my cheeks. "I've never really doubted that. He wasn't a good person, I know that. He didn't take care of us. He was neglectful and probably put our lives in danger more than once. Mom wasn't wrong about that. She was the one who provided, and she resented us because that didn't matter to us."

Arlow nods, his arm around my shoulders. "Kids don't care who buys their food or pays the electric bill. They care about who is kind to them."

"I think I would've respected her position more, understood more once I grew up, if she wasn't so cruel. In her mind, if you feed a dog, it's yours to kick. Our last name—Dad's last name—became an insult to use whenever we pissed her off. We were a piece of shit like the rest of the Raines."

With a sigh, I lean against him, so grateful to have him by my side. "I wish I could tell him I was never ashamed to be a Raines."

"I'm sure he knew that, sweetheart."

"I hate that drugs took priority over us, but a part of me understands. He was born dirt poor and never found a way out. He had a terrible life. Drugs are what he had. They were the only escape or peace he found. Yet, it never made him hateful. He was good to us when he was there. I think it was as simple as that."

Arlow holds me for a long time before I finally pack Dad's things back into the box. The rest of the evening is subdued, and I'm tempted to head back home. It's late, but we could be home by dawn. Before I can suggest it, Arlow sets my shoes in front of me.

"Come on, Peach."

"What? Where are we going?"

His smile is sweet as he holds out a hand to me. "To ride the glass elevators."

———

The trip to Indianapolis did me good. I feel lighter, like I've finally let the past go. In the month since we've returned, Arlow has spent almost every night in his barn, drawing. I love the new project he's been working on, an outstretched hand covered by crawling bees.

About an hour after he disappears into the barn, I'm surprised to see him coming through the front door of my cabin with a canvas in his hand. He holds it facing his body where I can't see.

"I have something for you," he announces. There's no smile on his face. He seems a little nervous, hesitant. As if I won't love anything that this incredibly talented man created for me. I get up from my seat as he rubs a hand over his collarbone. "I thought this would be the next best thing to having a picture."

He turns the canvas around where I can see it. Like all his drawings, the subjects look lifelike enough to be a photograph, but unlike all his other drawings, this one makes me burst into tears.

My dad smiles from the canvas while the little girl version of me clings to his back. Snow swirls around us, coating our hats, coats, and gloves. My arms are wrapped around his neck and his are tucked beneath my legs as he gives me a piggyback ride through the storm. A row of houses peeks out through the curtain of snow in the background.

It's exactly how I described it to him.

"How?" I whisper, barely managing the word and trying not to let tears fall on the artwork. There's no way he completed this in a month.

"Do you remember the night you told me about that memory? The night you asked me to come and catch the cave cricket?" He continues at my tearful nod. "I took a picture of the photo of your dad you kept on the mantel. I thought I'd draw him in the snow for you. I had most of him finished but once you got the photo from the hotel that he carried of you...I thought this was better."

It's hard to look away from the drawing as I keep noting so many small details. The way tiny snowflakes are caught in both our eyelashes, the gap in my teeth that I had until I was ten, the way Dad's glasses sit crooked on his face.

When I finally set it aside, it's to throw myself into his arms. "It's everything. It's exactly how I remember that day. This is the best gift anyone has ever given me. Thank you."

He holds me tight and brushes his hand through my hair with a chuckle. "I didn't mean to make you cry."

I pull him over to sit beside me on the couch where I can continue to admire the drawing. "You started drawing this right after the cave cricket night? But we weren't even…that was a few days after I kissed you and you weren't interested in me then. Was there something about the picture of him that made you want to draw it? Did it shine like your storm drain?" It doesn't make sense that he'd want to do this when he'd just rejected me.

"You shine, Calliope. You light up everything around you and make it stand out. You made it important. I was afraid when you first kissed me, but there was never a time I wasn't interested in you. I loved you from the first moment I saw you eating a peach with your feet in the creek."

"If you want me to stop crying, you're going to have to stop saying such sweet things." He grins at me, tucking me under his arm, and I interlace my fingers with his. "Do you know what my first thought was when I saw you in the forest?"

"Run, he's probably got a cooler full of body parts?"

"The first word in my head when I looked up and saw you standing over me was *gorgeous*. You startled me and scared me, coming out of nowhere, but you were so striking." I reach up to scratch at the white patch in his scruff. "So handsome, but there was something else about you I couldn't put my finger on. I still can't. Some special quality I can't describe."

His adorable flustered smile is firmly in place. "And then you threw peaches at me and ran like hell."

Giggles spill out of me. "You were still a stranger in the woods. Then I learned you were also kind and funny and caring. You calmed me and made me feel safe even with all the chaos we've dealt with since I moved here. I stole that first kiss, and I stole your peaches, but you stole my heart from the very beginning. I never had a chance." Now it's his turn to be emotional as he hugs me, tucking his face into my neck. "You also fuck like a god but that goes without saying."

He stands up with me in his arms and carries me toward the bedroom. "I'm going to need to make you say it again."

We spend the rest of the night in my bed where he proves my statement was true. Sex with him is sometimes tender and sweet, sometimes rough and wild, but always passionate and mind-blowing.

The drawing is hung in the living room of my cabin where I can admire it and be reminded of the two men in my life who have loved me.

A few days later, I wake to Arlow standing over me, biting back a grin, his arms crossed over his chest. "What?" I ask, recognizing that expression. "What did I do?"

"What *did* you do, Calliope?" He waves a sheet of paper in front of me that looks like a delivery invoice. "Would you like to tell me why a truck just delivered two massive boxes onto our lawn?"

"Um...surprise?" Damn it. They weren't supposed to be here until tomorrow.

He dives onto me, pinning my hands to the mattress and looks me in the eye. "You got me new hives?"

"Three of them are for you. One is for me. So, you can teach me. I also have the bees and queens already reserved for when they send them out in the spring." He hasn't made any attempt to replace his hives or even mentioned it. I don't want him to give up on something he clearly loved because of what Carl did.

"You are the best girlfriend ever." He punctuates his last three words with firm kisses. "Let me tell you what's going to happen tonight. I'm going to build a giant bonfire, spread a nice thick blanket beside it, then fuck you so good I'll have to carry you back."

"You might want to bring an extra blanket to put around my shoulders so I don't get a chill when I'm riding you."

He lets out a groan as he rolls me over and swats me on the ass. "Come on. Get up. Let's go unbox the hives."

Seeing Arlow happy and excited is my favorite way to start my day.

CHAPTER 35

ARLOW

SPRING HAS COME EARLY AGAIN THIS YEAR, OR MAYBE WARM temperatures at the end of March are going to be the norm now. Our hives are set up and we're waiting to see which queens will be accepted. Wild violets and clover are sprouting everywhere. Calli is excited to get her garden started and I'm happy to help her. We also have some strategic bushes to plant.

It's been a little over four months since that night. A walk through the graveyard shows no sign of what we did, and we haven't heard a peep from any authorities. Things are good. Better than good. I'm happier than I've ever been and when I mention to my therapist that I think we can discontinue our sessions, he makes a suggestion. One more bit of homework to do first—visit Melody's grave and say goodbye.

Calli offers to go with me, and on a warm sunny day, we head to Paducah. The cemetery where she's buried is large and almost unnaturally green. I've never been able to make myself come here before. It takes us a few minutes to locate the section with her grave and park nearby.

Calli stays by my side as we walk through the manicured grass, searching for her. My attention is so focused on reading the names that I don't notice the lady kneeling down to brush the dirt from one of the headstones until she stands up.

I freeze, nearly dropping the flowers in my hand, and Calli looks up at me, concerned. "Arlow?"

"That's Grace, Melody's mother." We haven't spoken since that awful night at the hospital when she screamed at me to rot in hell, right after Melody's death.

Calli slips her hand into mine. "Do you want to speak to her?"

No. It's the last thing in the world I want, but I should. Especially because she has already spotted me. "I should do it alone. Can you give us a minute?"

She squeezes my hand. "Of course. I'll be nearby."

Grace stands at the edge of the grave as I approach her. "Ms. Handleman." I greet her with a nod. "I wanted to leave some flowers if that's okay."

I'm waiting for her to tell me to fuck off, to scream about how I ruined her life, took her daughter away from her, caused her husband's stroke and son's addiction.

"There's room in the vase."

She doesn't speak again as I kneel to add my flowers to the sunken vase below the headstone. Guilt and sorrow wash over me, pulling me back to the place I've been digging myself out of through therapy. Stepping back, I force myself to look at her. "I'm so sorry. I don't know what else to say."

Without breaking eye contact, she replies, her voice firm. "I have something to say to you."

My body feels like a stretched rubber band ready to snap under the pressure, and I try to steel myself. "I'm listening."

"I forgive you." Her words hit me in the chest, knocking me back a step. Before I can reply, she goes on. "There's nothing you need to be forgiven for, but I know you need to hear it and you can't hear it from her. This was never your fault. It was an accident."

I can't speak around the lump in my throat, only nod while I try to get ahold of myself. It's so far from what I expected to hear.

"You haven't called her phone in a few months. I hope that means you're healing too."

Oh god. "You listened to my messages?"

Her lips nearly disappear as she presses them together. "I did. I'm sorry for what you went through but it helped me to hear how much she was missed. How much you cared for her. You should know I turned her phone off last week. It's time to let her go." She glances over at Calli, who waits beside the car. "It's okay to move on. She loved you and she wouldn't want you to keep blaming yourself."

She gazes down at her daughter's headstone and her voice softens. "This frail thread that connects us to our lives can be cut so easily. You never know how much time you have. Don't waste it."

I call her name as she starts to walk away, and she turns to regard me. "Thank you. I hope you're healing too."

A small smile struggles to rise along with her nod. "Take care of yourself, Arlow."

It feels strange to see Melody's name carved in the stone, and I squat down to trace it with my finger. "I know I've said it a thousand times, but I'm sorry." My mind plays through moments from our relationship. Meeting her at the bar, our first night in my new apartment when I moved to town, the way she always laughed when I bumped my head on the doorway. "I'm sorry I chose the worst possible moment to end things with you. I did care for you very much, and I hope you knew that. Thank you for loving me. I'll never forget you. Goodbye, Melody."

Calli quietly takes my hand when I return to her.

"Her mother forgave me. She doesn't blame me."

She pulls me into a hug. "I hope that helps you stop blaming yourself. Are you okay?"

Resting my chin on the top of her head, I take a deep breath, feeling my body loosen. "I'm good. Let's go home."

———

"All I'm saying is that if we're going to get two goats so they won't be lonely, why not get three?" Calli says, pushing the cart out to her car.

"Why not get ten?" I tease, and she grins up at me.

"Now you're getting it."

"How about you let Lee and I get their shelter built first before you decide to have us knee deep in goats?"

"Fine, we'll revisit this once you've finished." She checks her phone and frowns. "I need to stop and get some batteries. My front door camera is dead."

"I have some spare ones." She pops her trunk, and I start shifting the bags of birdseed. "You have enough seed here to feed a pterodactyl."

"I need all four bags because they attract different types of birds. I'll mix these two together for the new feeders I bought," she explains, slapping the bags.

"And which one is for the squirrels?"

She narrows her eyes. "Fuzzy little bastards will eat anything. I'm devising a plan to keep them off. Greasing the pole only works for so long." Laughing, I close the trunk and Calli points to the horizon. "Look at that sunset. It's beautiful."

"You're beautiful." She beams at me and leans in to give me a quick kiss before I put the cart in the corral, and we head home.

"I can't believe how warm it is!" Calli exclaims as we climb out of her car and start for her cabin. "Do you want to have a bonfire tonight?"

"Do you mean bonfire or *bonfire*?" I tease, bouncing my eyebrows.

She rolls her eyes. "I ride you by the fire one time and you never let it go." Her gaze leaps over to me as a grin appears. "I'm in."

Her laughter joins mine, startling away the birds from her feeder. Spring's early arrival has both of us in a good mood. Winter was such a dark tunnel for us to climb through and we've finally reached the sunlight at the end.

Calli unlocks her door as I remember that her camera isn't working and reach to remove it to change the batteries. What the hell is that? A black plastic bag covers the camera, and I yank it off.

"Calli!" My hand lands on her shoulder a second too late. The door swings open, and she freezes after her first step inside.

A woman sits on her couch. They stare at each other, neither saying a word until finally, the woman sits back, crossing her arms across her thin chest. A twisted smile grows on her face that chills me for reasons I can't put my finger on. It's not only predatory but skirting the edges of sanity.

Calli shakes her head, trying to deny what she's seeing as the woman laughs. "What? You can't say hello to your mother after I came all this way?"

Her mother, Mallory. The mother she ran and hid from. The mother Calli couldn't quite believe was dead without having the ashes nearby to remind her, sits on her couch.

I step in front of Calli, guarding her from whatever the hell is happening. I don't see a weapon but that doesn't mean she doesn't have one. "What the fuck is going on?"

Calli gapes at the disheveled woman. "You're dead. I dumped your ashes." Haunted despair soaks her voice. "You can't be here."

"Dog ashes are pretty easy to get. You just have to mix a couple together."

"Get out. Get out. Get the fuck out!" Calli's voice rises with each word, from a whisper to a scream.

Mallory doesn't budge or look the least bit concerned at her reaction. "Or what? You'll call the police? Go ahead. We'll have a little talk about Carl." She turns her attention to me. "You remember him, the man rotting under the bushes in the graveyard?"

A brick falls into my stomach as I watch our hopeful future fizzle away. She knows, not only that I killed him but where he's buried. This isn't going to end well.

Calli looks up at me and I see the same realization dawning, filling her eyes with anguish.

"This should be an easy choice for you now. Give me my fucking money or your boyfriend gets life in prison for murder, and you can join him as an accomplice."

Every word out of her mouth has me seething through my fear. *Her* money. The callous way she talks about a man she's been with for years. She isn't upset over his death, only using it to get what she wants.

The expression on Calli's face—she's terrified. Panicked. I won't let this woman pull her apart again. "Calli had nothing to do with it. I killed him and buried him." If I end up in prison, so be it.

She rolls her eyes. "You found a real hero here, didn't you? I was there, you stupid motherfucker. I know what happened."

"You faked your death," Calli says, her tone low and stunned. "To find me. The tracker in the ashes."

A proud smile blooms on her mother's face. "Carl didn't think you'd actually fall for it when I had him create the fake church email, but I did a good job on that obituary. I knew you wouldn't leave my remains to be abandoned. Like it or not, I'm your mother. You love me. But I'm done dealing with your selfish ass. I want two million dollars, or you can both spend the rest of your lives in prison."

"Watch her," Calli says to me, and I catch her wrist as she tries to walk away.

"Calliope."

"I need a minute." She shrugs out of my grasp and stalks toward her bedroom.

The monster on the couch gives a shrug and a clownish smile. "Take all night. I have nowhere to be."

The gleeful satisfaction in her voice turns my stomach. I wish she would've shown up when Calli wasn't home. I could've planted her in the graveyard with her dead boyfriend and spared Calli from ever knowing.

When Calli emerges a minute later, her expression is impassive.

Strength and determination show in her posture. Spine straight, shoulders back and her chin held up. She's made a decision.

She lays some cash on the coffee table in front of her mother, who leans over and scoops it up instantly. She looks up with a sneer. "Five hundred dollars?"

"That's all the cash I have on hand, but I'll get more."

"Calli...no." She holds her hand up at my intrusion and looks me in the eye. The coldness there is disturbing, but I let her finish. I'm not sure what her plan is or what we should do, but letting this bitch control us isn't the answer. Hopefully, she's stalling for time or has an idea to relay to me later.

She regards her mother with the same distanced demeanor. "You win, but I don't have the money you think I do. I spent it, vacations... buying this place." Her mother's eyes narrow and she starts to speak but Calli cuts her off. "But I have enough to buy you a house and a car. I can send you five thousand dollars a month, every month."

They stare at each other, neither breaking eye contact for a good minute. The air is stuffed with tension. "Of course you blew most of the money, stupid bitch," her mother says with a chuckle.

Calli doesn't blink an eye. "The choice is yours now. You can call the cops, have us arrested, and my money can keep our commissary accounts full. You can go back to scrounging for food and shelter. Or you can have more than enough money to live on and leave us alone. If you ever show up again to bother me or Arlow or anyone I care about, the deal is off."

After a few tense seconds, Mallory tucks the cash in her pocket. "Don't use the account number Carl left. You can pay me in cash."

"Fine, but that's more than I can withdraw from an ATM. It'll take a couple of days for me to deal with the bank. In the meantime, I'll take you to an ATM and pull out five hundred more for now. You can stay in a hotel until we find you a house."

Mallory gets to her feet. "Let's go."

"There's something I need to know before we leave," Calli says, and suspicion furrows Mallory's brow as she waits.

Calli looks her in the eye. "Did you watch him choke me? In the woods that night, if you were there, you must've seen what he was doing."

For the first time, Mallory seems to falter and weighs her words after a long pause. "He wasn't going to kill you. I wouldn't have let him kill you."

I'm not sure what Calli expected to hear. Her stony expression gives nothing away as she nods and picks up her car keys.

"You aren't leaving here with her," I exclaim, grabbing Calli's arm as they start toward the door.

"Ride with us or follow in your truck, but I'm going." She jerks out of my grasp and opens the front door, stepping outside. Of course I'm going. Once she gives this bitch some money and drops her at a hotel, we're going to have to figure out what to do because this is not the answer. "Lock the door," she orders, thrusting the keys at me.

Mallory is a step or two ahead of her as they exit the porch into the yard. My back is turned for a few seconds to lock the door when a shot rings out.

Time stutters and slows. My heart thumps like a bass drum in my ears. It feels like it takes an eternity for me to turn and look for her.

Calliope.

It's dark, but the motion light has blinked on, illuminating the scene and glinting off the gun still held in a shaking hand. Calliope's hand.

She looks down at the body of her mother slumped a few feet in front of her, then back at me. Wide blue eyes washed to silver under the bright light find mine as she says, "We're going to need more bushes."

CHAPTER 36

ARLOW

EVERYTHING HAPPENED SO FAST THAT IT TAKES ME A SECOND TO CATCH up. Thirty minutes ago, I was teasing her about birdseed. This was all supposed to be behind us. It's been over four months. My brain finally kicks my ass into gear. I have to take care of this. I need to take care of her.

Calli stands over her mother's body, staring at it like she may get up again. Judging by the amount of blood pooling around her head, that's not going to happen. Calli isn't crying, just frozen. In shock.

Her head jerks in my direction when I wrap my hand around the gun. "Let go. I've got it," I say softly.

Some awareness trickles back into her eyes, and she releases it. "I had to. I didn't have a choice. You would've gone to prison. I couldn't let her ruin your life too."

Nothing I've ever heard has affected me as intensely as what she just said. She did this for me. She killed her mother to protect me. "It's going to be okay. Listen to me." I cup her face and look into her eyes. "Everything is going to be okay. I want you to go inside and let me handle it this time."

The shake of her head is instant and adamant. "No, I need to do

329

this. I need to bury her. For good." She takes a deep breath, pulling herself together. "I'm okay."

I'm in awe of her strength and determination. "Alright. Can you go grab the shovels from the shed? I'll get her to the graveyard." We're too exposed standing here under the bright light, visible from the driveway. I'm not going to waste time getting my ATV out or anything. She can't weigh a hundred pounds.

Calli nods, looking down at the body again.

"Go ahead. Don't look back. You don't have to look at her again."

Relief softens her face as she whispers, "Never again."

As soon as she turns away to walk to the shed, I pull Mallory's head out of the puddle of blood, strip my hoodie off, and tie it around the wound so there won't be a trail of blood. I throw the body over my shoulder and rush toward the graveyard. I'm not overly concerned with getting caught. No one shows up here unannounced at night. Lee only came last time because he knew we were dealing with a threat, and I didn't answer my phone. My concern is getting her out of Calli's sight. No matter how much she may have hated her mother, I worry how she's going to feel when what she's done sets in.

I set the body down at the edge of the woods nearby where it isn't visible before I go through her pockets. No phone or ID to worry about this time, only the cash Calli gave her. If I had to guess, she's been living on the street, maybe in the woods.

Calli walks toward me through the graveyard, and I meet her halfway. "Where did you put...?"

"Out of sight for now. Are you sure you want to do this? I can take care of it." When I move to put my arm around her, she steps back, shaking her head.

"I'm sorry. I'm just...I'm holding it together and if you hug me, I might not so...let's just get to work, okay?"

"Alright. This is going to take a while, with it being only the two of us this time. If you need a break—mentally or physically—take it. Do you hear me?"

She nods without replying and silence reigns for the next couple of hours as we dig. I'd give anything to know what's going on in her head but if she needs space to zone out right now and not think about any of this, I can do that.

It isn't until she turns and starts gagging that I toss my shovel down and go to her. She waves me back. "It's the blood on me. It stinks so bad. I need to wash it off."

"Okay, let's take a break, go back to your cabin and—"

"No. Stay. Keep digging or it might be daylight before it's finished. I'll jump in the shower and come back."

I don't like it, but I nod. "Ring my phone if you need me and I'll be right there."

Once she walks away, I activate her porch camera to keep an eye until I see her make it safely inside and turn on the notifications, so I'll know when she leaves. Then I shovel like hell. The faster I can get this done, the quicker I can comfort her and put all this behind us.

Sweat coats my skin, attracting the dirt like a magnet. My back and shoulders scream in protest at the sudden vigorous exercise but they're easily ignored. All I see is Calli's face, her voice confessing that she did this for me. When I shot Carl, no part of me expected her to have to do the same. It wasn't a favor she should have ever had to return, especially by killing her own mother.

It takes nearly an hour to get the grave deep enough. It doesn't need to be as wide as our last, which helps. Plus, the ground is soft but not too wet or heavy. I scoop up the body again and carry it to the hole. My hoodie is soaked in blood when I remove it from her head. It'll need to be burned later. After a moment of consideration, I don't mimic what Lee did, cutting off fingers. If these bodies are found, we're done for regardless. A DNA test would link her to Calli. There's no reason to think anyone will come looking. She certainly didn't have any friends or any help, judging by the state of her.

After I dump the body in and toss a dozen or so shovelfuls of dirt to cover it, I take a break to call Calli. She's been gone too long. She shouldn't be alone. Before I can call, a notification shows up from her camera as she leaves her cabin.

After another couple of minutes, she approaches me, holding out a bottle of water. Her wet hair is pulled up into a bun, and she wears an old sweatshirt and worn leggings. "Take a break before you give yourself a heart attack." She winces and looks up at me, her lips nearly forming a smile. "Sorry, poor choice of words."

"I'm fine. All I need to do is finish filling it in."

Her face is puffy from crying, but she seems more alert, more herself as she starts shoveling in the loose dirt. Between the two of us, we get the hole filled with plenty of time to spare before sunrise.

"I'm not sorry," she announces, tossing her gloves aside and sitting in the grass beside the grave. "I don't care if that makes me a horrible person just like her. She's been a monster in all my closets, peeking out to remind me she's still there and can start screwing with me again at any time. I'm glad she's gone. I'd do it again." She looks up at me. "For both of us."

"You aren't a horrible person. There's only so far any of us can be pushed. You're nothing like her." One thing puzzles me. "She looked like she was homeless. If she's known all this time, why wait all these months to show up?"

Calli's laugh is bitter. "Because that's what she always did. Give you time to feel safe, to remember how good things are without her, before showing back up to ruin everything again. It was part of her game. She got off on it."

"You're safe now."

"Are you going to be able to look at me the same?" she asks, averting her gaze as I sit beside her and pull my gloves off.

That's what she's worried about? "Calliope." She drags her gaze to mine reluctantly. "When I look at you, I see the strongest, bravest, sweetest woman I've ever known. I'm in awe of you and fucking stunned that you love me like you do. What you did tonight—"

She brushes her fingers over my face. "Was no more than you did for me. We protected each other."

"There's nothing I wouldn't do for you." The truth in my statement should be concerning, and her response is unexpected.

She straddles my lap, grips my face and parts my lips with her tongue. My arms wrap around her automatically as she deepens the kiss and slips her hand onto my nape. The effect she has on me is remarkable and something I may never understand but I don't care. I slide my hand under her hair, gripping it close to her scalp and tug her head back until she's looking me in the eye.

The air heats as everything around us fades to nothing. All I see is her. Her chest rising and falling faster, the desire in her gaze bordering on desperation. My cock hardens in seconds, and she flexes her hips, pushing against it. "Calliope." Her name falls out, half question half supplication.

With her eyes burning into mine, she nods, and our mouths collide again. She rips my shirt open, sending the buttons flying, and runs her hands over my chest, grinding on me. I pull her sweatshirt off, tossing it behind her and dip my head to suck her nipple.

Her fingers fumble with the button of my pants. I scoot her off my lap, laying her on the ground above the buried evidence of our devotion. She frantically removes the rest of her clothes while I strip my bottom half.

When I kneel to plant my face between her legs, she shakes her head. "Just fuck me. Hard, please."

Something ignites inside me at her plea. Some buried part of myself that will never again let me doubt humans are animals, despite our civilized performance. Her legs wrap around me as I bury myself to the hilt and catch her sudden shout in my mouth. The way her pussy clenches around my cock has me seeing sparkles in the darkness behind my eyelids.

Fingernails dig into my ass as she urges me on with curses and cries for me to fuck her harder, faster. If that's what she needs, I'm going to give it to her. I pound into her, losing myself completely in the pure primal ecstasy of it. Our voices fill the air, a cacophony tossed into the night for the dead around us to hear. If they crawled out of their graves right now, I couldn't stop. I'm too far gone. We both are. I don't know where I end or she begins, and I never want to.

"Oh fuck, yes," she gasps out a second before her shout encompasses me, forcing me into that moment of devastating, blistering pleasure with her. "Arlow!"

My mind blanks. She's all that exists in that sweet all-consuming darkness. If this is what death is like, let me go, as long as she's there with me.

I open my eyes to see her lying with her head tilted back, her eyes shut as she catches her breath. Lying down beside her, I roll her onto my body, off the cold ground. She tucks her head under my chin. We lie there in silence, covered in soil and grass, moonlight painting our naked bodies in blue.

There are some things neither time nor miles can put behind us, and I know this moment is one that will never be forgotten.

The chill of the air can't be ignored for long, and we rise to get dressed. "Are you okay?" I ask.

She looks over at me, her lips twitching before laughter pushes through. "Silver once asked me if we fucked in the graveyard like a couple of ghouls. She was teasing but imagine what she'd think of this deviance."

"Good thing only the sky was watching," I quip.

She grins, picking up her shovel. "I'm sure the stars have witnessed worse."

I grab my shovel in one hand and take her hand in the other as we walk back across the graveyard toward home. She's quiet but I hope she's feeling what I am. The fulfillment and security that comes from knowing the best and worst of each other. No judgment exists between us, only a powerful, obsessive love.

We put away our tools, and I spray away the puddle of blood left at the edge of the driveway, dumping bleach on it and covering it with more gravel. I'll need to make sure things are cleaned up better tomorrow but for tonight, we're good.

We shower together, crawl into my bed, and sleep.

A sharp pain shoots across my chest and into my shoulder, waking me earlier than usual. Calli is still asleep beside me and doesn't budge when I slip out of bed. The pain comes again, not as sharp, but now it's steady, spreading across my collarbone and down into my ribs.

Fuck. No, please. Just let me get things finished today. I need time to check the graveyard and make sure there's no evidence left in the driveway.

I pull my blood pressure cuff out and try to keep calm while it squeezes my arm, so my fear won't affect the reading. It's normal. So is my heart rate. I run it again. The cuff has a setting to detect an irregular heartbeat as well, and it doesn't trigger.

Okay. I'm okay.

Ignoring the pain, I get moving. After another bucket of bleach water and some rearranging of the rocks, the driveway is done. I pick up the gloves we left near the grave. There's a bare patch but it isn't in an unusual spot, and it'll be fine until I can get more bushes. There's nothing left behind inside Calli's cabin, but I find my stolen ATV parked around the side. I guess we know how she got here now.

The pain only gets worse and more concerning. There's no denying I'm going to have to get checked out. I'm not going to let Calli find me dead of a heart attack after all this.

When I walk back into my living room, she's standing by the coffee table where the blood pressure monitor that I forgot to put away sits. She looks from it to me. "Are you alright?"

"I'm going to be...but I need to go to the hospital." It's a hard thing to tell her when she must already be overwhelmed. "My chest hurts."

She rushes over to me. "Are you dizzy or anything?"

"No, plus my blood pressure and heart rate are normal. I'm probably fine, but it isn't something I can ignore. I need to leave a message for my cardiologist."

She shoves her shoes on and grabs her keys. "Call him from the car. Let's go."

CHAPTER 37

CALLIOPE

I'M DOING MY BEST NOT TO LOOK AS TERRIFIED AS I FEEL. I'M NOT SURE I'm doing a great job at it when he looks over at me while I'm driving. "Don't speed. If I thought it was an emergency, I would've called an ambulance."

"I know. I'm not speeding. I just need to get around this guy out here taking his car for a walk."

His smile makes me feel a little better.

The emergency room is busy but they're expecting him, and we're escorted straight back. I guess when you're dealing with a heart patient, they take no chances. We're tucked into a corner room where they attach electrodes to his chest.

"Looks good," the doctor says after a few minutes. "No sign of a heart attack. Dr. McAllister has ordered some further testing, an echocardiogram and a cardiac MRI. Have you had any symptoms before today?"

"No, I've been fine."

"Any change in your routine? Taking your meds? Increased exercise?"

Arlow glances over at me and his response is reluctant. "I've been overdoing it a little. Some more vigorous exercise lately...farm work."

Oh god, this is from the digging. I asked him before, when we were burying Carl, if it'd be too much and he said not to worry, that he knew his limitations. He accomplished so much during the hour I left to have a private, sobbing breakdown because he overdid it. I do my best to suppress the guilt. This isn't about me. It's about saving him.

The doctor nods, noting it down. "Okay, they'll be in to get you for the tests soon and your cardiologist is being updated as we go."

Once the doctor leaves, I move beside the gurney to grab his hand. "How do you feel?"

"The same. I'm not dizzy or weak or anything. It just hurts."

A nurse comes in to remove the electrodes and instructs him to change into a gown. "Woo, sexy," I tease, helping him by tying the back closed.

If he's afraid, it doesn't show. He grins and climbs back onto the gurney. "These were not made for someone my height."

"I think everyone's ass hangs out of them," I giggle, pulling the thin blanket up over his legs.

The orderly comes to take him to another floor for the tests, and I drop a quick kiss on his lips, squeezing his hand. "I love you."

"Love you, Peach. Be right back."

Tears fill my eyes the second he's out of sight and I let them fall. I'm terrified. Anything could happen. He could need surgery or have a sudden heart attack. After everything we've been through, I can't lose him already. We've fought to be together. We deserve some happiness. I can't imagine my life without him, never hearing his voice or seeing his smile.

The tests take over two hours—the longest of my life—and by the time they roll him back in, I've regained my composure and washed my face. "About time. I thought maybe you got bored and went home," I quip, moving my chair closer to the gurney.

"I tried after they lubed up my chest, but then they locked me in a tube."

"My poor guy." His smile is sweet when I kiss his forehead.

It's another hour before the doctor returns. "All your results look fine, but your cardiologist wants to review them with you before we discharge you."

As if his words conjure him, a gray headed man strides into the room, plants his hands on his hips and shakes his head at Arlow like a disapproving mother. "Just what the hell have you been doing?"

The emergency doctor chuckles and excuses himself.

"Dr. McAllister, hope I didn't interrupt something important," Arlow says, noting the dress clothes his cardiologist is wearing.

"Actually, you got me out of the world's most boring charity event so thanks for that, but that's not the point. Your heart is fine. No changes since your last scans. The pain is from costochondritis. It's an inflammation of the cartilage in your ribs and presents with cardiac symptoms, but it's completely unrelated to your heart."

Relief pours through me. It's not his heart. He's going to be fine.

He notices a blister on Arlow's finger and picks up his hand to look. "The doctor told me you reported some vigorous exercise. What were you doing the last few days?"

"Uh...some yard work around my property."

"Digging," I announce. We can't tell the truth about what we were digging, but I can make sure his doctor has all the information that might be pertinent. "We were digging some ditches for irrigation pipe in our back field."

Doctor McAllister looks at Arlow then me. "Your girlfriend has sense enough to tell on you. I like her."

"Calli," I introduce myself as Arlow sits up.

"It's nice to meet you. Calli."

He turns back to Arlow. "Hot and cold compresses and some rest will take care of the pain. Before I discharge you, I have a question. Do you want me to crack your chest open again? Was it such a wonderful experience that you want to recreate it?"

"Definitely not."

"Then get somebody else to lay the irrigation pipe. No more digging. No shoveling snow. Nothing more than moderate exercise. You know these rules. This time you got lucky but next time you may not. Keep taking your pill and monitoring your blood pressure. People tend to grow lax after a time when things are going well. Keep in mind that following those guidelines is why you aren't having issues. So don't be an idiot."

Arlow's grin has a tinge of embarrassment as the doctor scolds him. "Understood. I'll take it easy."

He's direct. I like him. They talk over his test results for a few minutes, and he informs him that since they've done the routine tests a bit early, he doesn't need to see him again for six months.

A few minutes later, we walk out of the hospital, and Arlow interlaces his fingers with mine. "I'm sorry I scared you."

"Don't apologize. I'm just glad you're okay. Are you hungry?"

"I could demolish a cheeseburger about now."

"Sounds good to me."

It did scare the hell out of me, and the anxiety will always be there when it comes to his health, but he's worth it. Over the next few days, I don't let him do anything but rest. We spend our time curled up together with a heating pad on his chest, and his pain quickly resolves.

He's livestreaming tonight, and once he's cloistered in the barn, I make my way to the top of the hill to build a bonfire. It's funny. Not that long ago, I would've been nervous to walk through the graveyard alone. To be out here by myself at night at all. Now it's only peaceful.

Arlow's trip to the hospital has me concerned but not about his heart or what may happen in the future. His doctor says he's doing well. This is the first time he's had a scare like this since we got together, and I'm worried he'll go back to his old way of thinking. That he'll want to spare me future terrifying situations.

The fear is probably unfounded. He hasn't acted any differently.

Despite how much it's improved, I'm sure it's my anxiety leading the way, but I still need to talk to him about it. I need some reassurance.

Barely an hour after I've started the fire, Arlow sits beside me on the log. "Hey," he says, softly. "Do you want company?"

"I always want your company, but I thought you were livestreaming until midnight?"

"I wasn't feeling it. Couldn't focus."

"Is your chest hurting again?"

"No." He slides his arm around my middle, tucking me against his side. "I feel fine." He presses his lips to my temple. "But something is on your mind."

It's strange to be so easily read by someone, to be known that well. My only response is a nod while I try to find the words to explain. "I was going to talk to you about it tonight."

"I know I scared you. That you got a peek at how…temporary this could be. Are you reconsidering things between us, Calliope?"

"No!" I turn to him, horrified that he'd even think that. The way his expression relaxes with relief breaks my heart, and I run my fingers through his scruff. "I love you. I'm not going anywhere. All we ever have is now, and if now is all I get, I'll take it. You're worth every moment of fear and worry. Don't you understand that?"

He delivers a quick, soft kiss on my lips. "I do understand. If I lost you tomorrow and had to live with half a heart for the rest of my life, I'd have no regrets."

"I was worried the health scare might've changed your mind about us. You were so set on not dating or letting anyone get close to you before," I confess.

"I was wrong. You helped me see that. The therapy you suggested helped me realize it too." He holds me tighter. "Do you remember the drawing of the storm drain we talked about? With all the trash caught in it?"

"Of course I do."

"You did for me what I did for it as a teenager. You cleaned away all that litter and freed me, not only to draw again but to feel again. I love you. I'm yours for as long as you want me."

"Forever sounds about right."

"Forever then." Amusement seeps into his voice. "I do have a request that you might find a tiny bit scandalizing."

I peek up at his grinning face. "I'm intrigued."

"Model for me this summer. Let me draw you naked by the creek where I first saw you. It's a vision that never leaves my mind."

I imagine it, lying on the bank completely nude for hours with his eyes on me.

He pulls in a deep breath as I run my nails over the back of his neck. It never fails to raise goosebumps on his skin. "Only if you fuck me right there afterward."

He nips at my earlobe. "Until you beg for mercy."

We sit there by the fire under the stars the way we did our first night together. He isn't the only one who feels changed. I don't worry as much about what I may have inherited in my blood or what kind of person I am deep down. He's shown me we're all capable of wonderful and horrific things, especially when it comes to love.

He's taught me that soft and sweet doesn't mean weak, that the kindest most respectful man on earth can also be the one who won't hesitate to kill for you then fuck your brains out.

So much can be true at once. Arlow is a sweet, thoughtful man who can't stand to see a bug suffer. I'm a woman trying to overcome my upbringing by choosing to be better and more kind. We both cherish our friends, care for animals and revere nature. We also killed two people and fucked on their graves in the moonlight. Are we good? Evil? I don't know. The truth is I don't care.

Watching the smoke swirl into the air, I think about how we're all fucked up. Just damaged people interacting. How we bounce off each other, our insecurities grating together, our bruises not quite matching. How we hurt each other. How we heal each other.

Love isn't what it's portrayed to be, a soft fragile thing draped in flowers and hearts and sweet words. It's gritty and painful and terrifying. It reveals truths about our nature and shows us we're capable of things we never imagined doing before.

Love exposes us. Like a swelling sun, it illuminates us from the inside out, its light revealing every intimate corner and vulnerability to each other. We shine with it. Nothing remains hidden.

I see him, and he sees me. Good or evil, together we know who we are.

I wouldn't change a thing.

EPILOGUE

ARLOW

TEN YEARS LATER

THE BED SHIFTS, NUDGING ME FROM SLEEP AND I FEEL THE WEIGHT OF HER body on mine before I open my eyes.

Calliope's bright smile greets me. "Are you going to sleep your whole birthday away? I know old men of forty-four need their rest, but we have things to do today."

"I'll show you old man once I get you by that creek."

She giggles as I abruptly roll her over and suck on her neck. "Arlow! You're going to leave a mark and your parents will be here tonight."

"I want to add a little something to this year's drawing," I murmur, sucking the same spot again. Despite her protest, she melts underneath me. She always does and it's still the best feeling. The way she wants me. The way she loves me.

She tugs my hair when I cup her ass. "Stop it, or we're going to end up in bed all day."

"You smell like cinnamon."

"Mm hmm, that's because there are homemade apple fritters waiting for you in the kitchen."

I pull my head back to look down at her. "Well, why didn't you say so?" She lets out a squeak when I pinch her ass and hop out of bed.

"I really should've led with that. It's supposed to rain later so unless you want to postpone—"

"Nope, I'm up. I'm getting dressed. It's warm enough, right?" Judging by the fact she's wearing shorts, I'm confident of the answer.

"Almost eighty degrees."

"Thank you, climate change. Give me ten minutes to eat."

She shakes her head. "You want the same gift from me every year. Don't you get bored of drawing me so many times?"

I grab her from behind by the waist. "Do you get bored of watching the sunset or staring at the stars?" Her hand runs over my arm as she turns her head to give me a blushing smile. "Aw, speechless, I love it."

"Shut up. That was really sweet."

All these years together, and she still looks at me like I'm the most important thing in the world. I'm the luckiest fucking man.

"Do you want my hair up or down?" she asks, and I consider it.

"Up, so I can see my handiwork."

She rolls her eyes and lays a hand over the love bite on her neck, but her pleased expression gives her away. She loves this as much as I do. "Okay, go eat while I get ready."

I'm raring to go when she joins me downstairs about twenty minutes later, her hair piled on top of her head in a messy bun. With my bag of supplies over my shoulder, we head outside. The late morning sun glints off our greenhouse. It didn't take long for Calli to discover she has a green thumb and a love for horticulture. She spends almost as much time at that as I spend drawing.

Our little herd of goats bleat at us as we pass.

"Wait until your mom sees the new baby goats. She's never going to want to leave," Calli says.

"I'm more interested to see Dad fight our chickens again."

Our laughter drifts through the forest. My parents visit often now. They adore Calli and after she moved in with me, we turned the cabin into a guest house for them. My sister also visits in the summer with her kids. Calli is their favorite aunt, especially since she took them to their first music festival.

I wonder sometimes if she realizes how much she changed my life, how different things would be if it weren't for her. My family and I are closer than we've ever been. I've made new friends. We travel, not only to see our favorite bands play, but to art museums and national parks, and anywhere else our hearts desire. Mom and Dad are happy to come and care for the animals when we take a trip. Sometimes Silver or Lee do as well.

Those first months we knew each other may have been full of chaos and trauma, but the peace we've had ever since has made it all worth it. The secrets that lie under the bushes in the graveyard don't haunt us anymore.

The forest closes around us as we follow the path back to the creek. As soon as we reach the spot, I can see her there again in my mind's eye. All the memories of her in this place haven't overwritten that first one and how the sight of her made me feel. I can still see her smiling at the rock she found, biting into a peach, dipping her hair into the creek, the water cascading over her breasts. Glowing as if she were sunlight itself.

Don't you get tired of drawing me?

How could I when she is everything?

"Where do you want me this time?" she asks.

"Wherever you want to be. Pretend I'm not here."

Her grin is mischievous. "Fair enough considering I wasn't aware of your presence the first time." She chooses an area covered in a thick bed of moss near the creek bank.

"Are you ever going to let me live that down?"

"Maybe when we're old and senile." She grabs the hem of her

shirt and pulls it off, baring her breasts. My gaze is locked onto her as she kicks off her shoes then slides her shorts and underwear off.

"The moss is cold," she chuckles, sitting down on it and reclining against a boulder. After getting comfortable, she calls. "How's this?"

"Perfect. You're perfect."

She is, and I can't believe I almost let her go because of my fear. We've had a slight scare or two since that first one, but my heart is still going strong, with no additional damage. There's no reason to believe I won't be bringing her out here in ten more years.

I sit at the base of a tree and pull out my sketchbook, one devoted completely to this, and flip through the other pages of Calliope. All nude drawings in different poses in this same spot, they show the subtle changes in her body over the years that have only made her more beautiful.

She closes her eyes to daydream while I get to work. I could spend days at this, making sure I get every line right, but there's only so long I can ask her to sit naked in the cool forest. Once I have the larger picture, I can add more detail later from memory. She's not easily forgotten.

An hour slips past and I'm just about to ask her if she wants to stop when a rumble of thunder sounds in the distance. I quickly tuck the sketchbook into a plastic bag then back into my backpack and leave it under the tree.

She sits up as I approach her. "We can head back and—"

"Absolutely not. A deal's a deal, sweetheart." This is how we always do it. I draw her, and then we fuck each other with all of nature watching.

A curse leaps out of her when I bury my face between her legs. "Arlow, fuck!" Her hands grip my hair, tugging it as I lick and suck at her clit until she's trembling under me. Her cry of pleasure echoes through the trees, stolen away by the increasing wind.

She grabs the bottom of my shirt and pulls it off as soon as I sit up, then unfastens my jeans. I yank them off along with my underwear, tossing it all aside. Her fingertip brushes over my tattoo, gently tracing the dark, bare tree branches. She leans forward to press a kiss to the one bright peach inked over my heart. It's been there for over nine years now, but her reaction is always the same. That soft, sweet kiss.

Then she shoves me so I'm sitting with my back to the boulder, climbs onto my lap and sinks down onto my cock with a groan. A few sprinkles give a brief warning before the sky opens up and rain douses us as she rides me. October rain isn't the warmest, but she doesn't stop.

Her soaked hair clings to her face as she leans forward to kiss me then puts her lips to my ear. "I'm so close. Come with me."

"Yes, oh fuck." My head falls back, giving me a look at the tree branches swaying against the cloudy gray. The sky, her cries, the warmth of her skin, and the feeling that drags me under until I can comprehend none of it, I'm drowning in the sensation of it all.

We hold each other for a moment, our bodies pressed together as we catch our breath. "Fuck, that was good," I sigh.

Calli sits back and grins at me. "Definitely some of our best work."

The rain hasn't let up and she's starting to shiver. "Come on. Let's go home and get you warmed up."

The walk back is rushed. We keep glancing at each other and laughing at our chattering teeth. The hot shower we share puts an end to that, and we end up on our front porch, sitting on the glider painted with songbirds.

I throw a blanket around us, and she tucks in close to my side. We curl up together, warm and content, watching the storm move away.

THE END

Thank you so much for reading! If you liked Arlow and Calliope's story, you may enjoy this romantic suspense duet.

Get book one here: https://geni.us/AlmostHim

Ella returns to her hometown and reunites with her first love, the bad boy neighbor who used to climb through her window. They're determined to make things work this time, but a tragedy followed by an arrest throws everything into jeopardy.

MORE BY S.M. SHADE

Whether you're in the mood for an emotional romance or looking for a fun book to make you laugh, I've got you covered. I write both spicy romantic comedies and steamy contemporary romances. Check out more of my work below.

THE ALMOST DUET

Emotional, Second Chance, Friends-to-Lovers

1. *Almost Him*
2. *Almost Us*

IN SAFE HANDS SERIES

Alpha Male, Protective

1. *Landon*
2. *Dare*
3. *Justus*
4. *Tucker*
5. *Jeremy*

SLUMMING IT SERIES

Romantic Comedies, Can Be Read as Standalones

1. *Unsupervised*
2. *Overachiever*
3. *Incorrigible*

STANDALONE

ACKNOWLEDGMENTS

I've always wanted to write a morally gray hero who is also soft and kind. It's also been a goal of mine to write something with a bit of a dark gothic vibe set in nature. This was the result, and as always, there are a lot of people who have helped this book come to fruition.

My amazing alpha and beta readers. Nicole Everett, Amanda Gibson, Jami Kehr, Aimee Degagne, and Kelly Tucker. Thanks for catching my mistakes and for all the work you put into helping me polish this story. A special shoutout to Nicole Everett, who read through this almost as many times as I did. You're the best!

The cover was created by Qamber Designs and I absolutely love it. Thanks so much.

Finally, thank you to Wordsmith Publicity for handling this release, and thank you to everyone else who helps me get my books out there. Whether you're an author, booktoker blogger, influencer, page owner, or reader, thank you for sharing and supporting me.

WHERE TO FIND S.M. SHADE

I love to connect with readers! Please find me at the following links:

Website: www.authorsmshade.com

Amazon:

http://www.amazon.com/S.M.-Shade/e/B00HZZP9MM

Facebook Page: https://facebook.com/smshadebooks

Instagram: https://www.instagram.com/authorsmshade

Newsletter: http://bit.ly/1zNe5zu

Email: authorsmshade@gmail.com

I also have a private book group called Shady Ladies where no one outside of the group can see what you post or comment on. It's adults only and is a friendly place to discuss your favorite books and authors. Drama free. I also host an occasional giveaway, and group members get an early peek at covers, teasers, and exclusive excerpts.

You can join Shady Ladies here:

https://www.facebook.com/groups/shadyladiesplace

Made in the USA
Monee, IL
30 October 2024

69018690R00215